D0402047

"What befell you that you would join a convent?"

Jacqueline felt her lips tighten in frustration. "I have a vocation," she insisted.

He shook his head, smiling slightly again. " 'Tis not fitting for one who would become a novitiate to lie so much as you do."

"I do not lie!"

Angus shook his head. "Aye, you do."

She folded her arms across her chest and glared at him. "I tell you no lie. I have a calling to serve Christ, to use my gifts to bring the love of God into the lives of others. I want naught more in this life than to serve the Lord and serve His will I shall. Surely you can understand what 'tis to yearn for something beyond all other desires?"

If she had expected Angus to be contrite, she was due for disappointment. He chuckled and lay back once more, granting her a sidelong glance that made her flesh warm. "I owe you an apology," he murmured. He had that predatory look about him again, and though she did not trust him by any means, still she was curious as to what he might say.

And she was encouraged that he did not seem to take offense when she spoke her thoughts.

"For delaying my devotion?" she asked.

He shook his head, clearly more bemused than angered by her. "Nay. I apologize for stealing a kiss from you. I did not guess 'twould be so horrific that 'twould make you flee."

Dell Books by Claire Delacroix

The Bride Quest series:

The Beauty

Claire Delacroix

A Dell Book

Published by
Dell Publishing
a division of
Random House, Inc.
1540 Broadway
New York, New York 10036

ISBN: 0-440-23637-1

Printed in the United States of America

Published simultaneously in Canada

January 2001

10   9   8   7   6   5   4   3   2   1

OPM

For Dominick Abel,
the voice of reason,
with thanks.

Prologue

DO YOU NOT THINK 'TIS SOMEWHAT HARSH?" DUNCAN watched his wife don her veil. She was garbed in somber indigo from head to toe, her fingers devoid of any jewel beyond the simple silver ring he had put upon her left hand.

Eglantine was grimly determined and had he not been so skeptical of the choice she had made, Duncan would have held his tongue while she was in this mood. They were still in their chamber and, though the assembly waited below, 'twas not too late for Eglantine to change her thinking.

"The girl must learn the price of her folly, and better she does so before 'tis too late to change her course." Eglantine anchored the veil with a heavy circlet, then started to pull the sheer fabric across her face.

Duncan caught her hand in his, stilling her gesture. " 'Tis cruel to make your daughter witness her own funeral."

" 'Tis our way, Duncan. 'Twas always done thus at Crevy-sur-Seine, by my great-grandfather's decree."

"Not *exactly* thus." Though he knew this to be the tradition of his wife's family, 'twas not Duncan's own, and he found it distasteful. All the same, he tried to be respectful.

Eglantine sighed. "If we had been at Crevy and Jacqueline chose to take the vows of a nun, then such a funeral would be held—for a nun departs the land of the living as surely as if she had died. 'Tis not so appalling to give Jacqueline a taste of what will ultimately come of her choice to become a novitiate at Inveresbeinn."

When he said naught, she continued, her eyes glittering. " 'Tis no more easy for me, Duncan, than for you to witness this ceremony, but would you not have Jacqueline understand all that she is destined to lose before 'tis said and done?"

"She might find that the life of a novitiate does not suit her, at any rate, and never take her final vows."

Eglantine frowned, her gaze dropping to their entangled fingers. "She might," she ceded quietly, then met his gaze. "But I cannot rely upon that chance alone, Duncan. I must do *something*! 'Tis my task as her mother to save her from foolish choices."

" 'Tis your task as her mother to love her no matter what choices she makes."

Eglantine sighed with exasperation and turned away. "Duncan, you do not understand. I sacrificed all to grant my daughters the chance to wed for love . . ."

"All?" He endeavored to look indignant, hoping that he might make her smile.

Eglantine did, if fleetingly. "And I gained much, 'tis true, but I so wanted to give them the opportunity to find true love. From Alienor I expected trouble, for she was always willful."

"Marriage seems to suit her well enough."

Now Eglantine smiled in truth. "Not to mention a child more demanding than she herself. She has no opportunity to be selfish these days." A frown creased Eglantine's brow. "And from Esmeraude, of course, I expect a challenge, for she may be even more willful than Alienor."

"A terrifying thought."

"Indeed." Eglantine shook her head. "But Jacqueline has

always been the quiet one who blossomed when given the opportunity. I was certain that 'twas she who would benefit most from the chance to choose love."

"She has chosen."

"This is no choice! I will not permit her to become a bride of Christ so readily as this."

"But, Eglantine, if she has a calling . . ."

She turned away from him, pausing at the portal of their chamber. "Duncan, if she had a calling, I would bless her path, but what Jacqueline has is a fear of men. That demon Reynaud has left a scar upon her that can only be erased by a man wrought of flesh and blood, as well as merit." Eglantine sighed. "She is but twenty years of age, after all."

"Aged for a virgin to remain unwed in any land, Eglantine."

His wife frowned, then appealed to him. "But, Duncan, 'tis the mark of Reynaud! Jacqueline is a beauty, she does not lack for suitors. But, because of Reynaud and his crime six years past, she will not even look upon a man. 'Tis wrong!"

"Eglantine—"

"I have asked her only to wait two years before becoming a novitiate."

Duncan was taken aback, for he did not know this.

"Two years, Duncan! 'Tis naught, but it might well be time enough for her to meet that man of merit who will change her thinking. She is too innocent of the world to make a choice that will govern her life."

"Is that not what marriage is?"

"Duncan! She will not be happy as a cloistered celibate, and 'tis her happiness I would ensure, at any cost."

With that Eglantine swept from the chamber. Duncan followed her, if more slowly. He respected his wife's intent, if not her means. His own child, Mhairi, all of four summers of age and blessed with Eglantine's golden hair, took his hand when he reached the hall, her brow puckered in confusion and dismay.

What could he say? Duncan picked her up and kissed her brow, while murmuring reassurances to her.

'Twas then he spotted his stepdaughter, veiled, solemn, standing aside from the proceedings as if she had indeed ceased to draw breath. When he noted the resolve in Jacqueline's pale features, Duncan feared that Eglantine's way of bidding her daughter adieu would only leave bitterness between mother and daughter.

But then the censers swung, filling the air with heady clouds of scent. Candles were lit and held high, banishing the gloom of an overcast day. The household fell into order, those of rank before those of less rank—first Eglantine, then her sisters Alienor and Esmeraude. They were followed by Alienor's husband and child, then the closest members of Eglantine's household. The vassals filled most of the procession, though 'twould have been otherwise at a great French estate like Crevy. There would have been knights and squires there, visiting nobles and rich relations.

Not so here, and Duncan marveled again at what his wife had left behind in her flight to Scotland. 'Twas indicative of her determination, and his admiration for her blossomed anew.

Eglantine truly desired only happiness for her daughters. The assembly began to chant a mournful dirge. The priest began the procession as the empty coffin was hefted to be carried behind him.

Duncan reluctantly stepped to his wife's side, unable to resist a last glance at Jacqueline. She remained to one side, outside the procession. No one spoke to her, no one so much as looked at her, by Eglantine's dictate—and indeed, by the custom of their own ritual.

She stood with her mother's straightness of spine, her chin

high, her lips set. She was a beautiful young woman, one who usually had roses in her cheeks and stars in her eyes, one whose sweet and giving character was a delight to all in the household. Indeed, in Jacqueline, beauty ran to the core.

She stood there, so determined to be brave, to stand steadfast, that Duncan's heart nigh broke in half. He watched her catch her breath and blink rapidly when she spied her mother's funereal garb. He guessed that she was not so certain of her choice as that.

Aye, Reynaud had terrified Jacqueline. Duncan wished he could make the matter right. He was tempted to lock her up, to convince her not to sacrifice all her choices for the sake of one night's sorry events.

And that urge to sequester Jacqueline showed him that he was not so different from his wife, after all.

"God in heaven," Eglantine muttered through gritted teeth. "I cannot imagine how the girl comes by such a stubborn nature. I do not recall that her father was so obstinate."

Duncan knew better than to suggest the obvious. The procession wound its way past Jacqueline and out of the hall toward the chapel. The skies hung heavy and gray, threatening a greater downpour. It seemed that even the land mourned his stepdaughter's choice.

How Duncan wished that he knew in his heart 'twas the right one.

Chapter One

CEINN-BEITHE WAS BEHIND JACQUELINE, ONLY HER vows ahead. Her mother was wrong—Jacqueline had a calling and she knew the truth of it. She had not been swayed by well-intentioned argument, though she had come close, simply because of the price of her choice. Her mother's point was well made and well taken.

Though it changed naught. Tears pricked at Jacqueline's eyes as she realized how much she would miss her mother's and Duncan's protective love.

She tried not to think overmuch about leaving Ceinn-beithe behind forever as her small party rode toward the hills that sheltered the holding on the east. On the far side of these hills and a little farther on, down a ragged trail from what might be generously called a main road, lay her destination—the convent of Inveresbeinn.

Her parents had selected these four men to accompany her because they trusted them. They were simple men, hardened by the elements rather than by warfare. Ceinn-beithe had been at peace for so long that their military skills—or lack thereof—were of little import. All knew this road held no threat.

All the same, there was not a one among the party with whom she might have shared a friendly word. 'Twas a lesson, just as the funeral had been a lesson. This was a lesson in the limited appeal of solitude and silence.

She had made her choice and would live with the result. She believed 'twas in the cloister her intellect would be appreciated, 'twas there that the gifts granted to her could be given and accepted in kind. Mortal men wished only to possess her because of her appearance, and Jacqueline had no interest in becoming an ornament in a man's life. She knew she had the wits to do more and the compassion to give more, and she would not waste the gifts that God had granted her.

'Twas her calling and her choice, and she would defend it to her last breath.

Aye, and as a novitiate, Jacqueline's world would be one of silence. She knew that and anticipated difficulties with it. Even understanding what her mother did and why did not make the sense of isolation easier to bear. Already the silence pressed against her ears, making her want to shout, to laugh, to scream.

But Jacqueline would persevere, for she had chosen rightly. She straightened in her saddle, reminding herself that 'twould be a long day's ride to the convent, and began to murmur her rosary.

The hills rising before them were shrouded with mist, a fog gathering undoubtedly in the valleys. The sky was darkening to a gray the shade of pewter and the hills seemed clad in myriad greens and blues. 'Twas a tranquil scene, filled with the serenity that would characterize the remainder of her days, and Jacqueline told herself that she was content.

But there was more than silence lurking in the hills ahead.

"There." Angus knelt in the shadow of the stones, his stallion hidden behind an outcropping of rock. Only the beast's ears flicked, as if he too understood the need for concealment. Angus's vantage point overlooked the road that wound toward Ceinn-beithe, home of the man who had betrayed Angus's family.

His loyal companion hunkered down beside him and peered into the mist that had followed the rain. "God's teeth, boy, but Dame Fortune cannot be finally smiling upon you." Rodney's comment was typically skeptical, though there was a glint of humor in his eyes.

"Surely 'tis not so unlikely as that," Angus murmured, "when all has gone awry for so long."

Rodney chuckled. "Do not tell me that you believe in good outweighing bad in the end?"

Angus almost smiled, but he was intent upon studying the small party upon the road below. 'Twas critical that they make no error in this moment, for Fortune would not smile so sweetly again.

A woman shrouded in white rode in the midst of the group yet slightly apart, her position revealing her station. Her guardians were more stocky than fearsome, and Angus guessed that they had not seen battle so recently as he. They were likely to be lax in their defenses.

"Who is she?" Rodney whispered.

"Who else might she be than the daughter of Cormac MacQuarrie?"

Rodney granted him a skeptical glance that he could nigh feel. "She could be any woman at all."

"Nay. Not so guarded as this. This is a precious woman, as only the daughter of a chieftain can be. And she leaves Ceinn-beithe, for there is naught else on this road other than the sea beyond that estate."

"Then why is she abroad at all?"

Angus set his chin upon his gloved fist and considered the matter. "She must go to wed. Mhairi would be aged for such a rite, but then, Cormac was always said to overvalue her merits."

The older man chuckled, his gaze flicking over the situation of the road below. "You said his daughter was the only creature he truly loved."

"Aye. 'Twould not be implausible that he could not find a match to suit afore his daughter was nigh unweddable. Perhaps she weds for the second time."

"But someone weds her now."

Angus felt his lips thin. "Cormac is a formidable ally."

"And an equally formidable adversary," Rodney concluded, quite unnecessarily to Angus's thinking. Then he scoffed. "Look at these louts! They are ill-prepared to defend her. Such is the price of prosperity and peace."

"And you mock the hand of Dame Fortune in this," Angus muttered. " 'Tis the first matter to go aright in years. Let us not lose the chance to make amends."

The two men discussed their plan of attack and pointed out details of the landscape to each other. Rodney slipped into the shadows and mounted his steed.

"Now Cormac will pay dearly for his daughter's safe return!" Rodney murmured gleefully.

"He has only one thing to surrender that I desire." Angus took one last look, saw no complications, then swung into his own saddle and held the reins tightly. Lucifer did not so much as move. The two men waited until the sound of the approaching party echoed on the road just before them, then, at Angus's nod, they erupted from the shadows as one.

✸

With lightning speed, two men on horseback appeared from naught, swinging their swords as they roared. The little party froze as the bandits bore down upon them.

They were still on Ceinn-beithe's land! Jacqueline halted her steed to stare. One of her escorts swore, then slapped the buttocks of her horse, sending it fleeing from the fray.

Jacqueline could not help but look back.

The attacking knight in the lead struck down two of her escorts before those men even had time to draw their blades. A knight? One heard of knights turning to villainy in France, but not here. Fear rippled down her spine—Jacqueline had learned to expect ill of knights from abroad. The third in her party was engaged in battle with the knight's companion.

The fourth had drawn his sword but was no match for the knight's prowess. He fell to the ground and moved no more.

Then the attacker's course was unobstructed.

He rode like an avenging angel, and one determined to smote those who defied him. He was tall and broad of shoulder. His red cloak flared behind him, his tabard was white with a cross of blood red on the shoulder. His mail gleamed, even though the day was overcast. His large ebony stallion was caparisoned in white and red, that extraordinarily fine beast fairly snorting fire.

And when he turned his steed toward her, Jacqueline thought her heart might stop.

In panic, Jacqueline dug her heels into her palfrey's sides. The horse needed little urging to run at full gallop across the peat but was no match for the long strides of the black stallion in pursuit.

The stallion drew closer, until she could see the steam of its breath just over her shoulder. Jacqueline gave a little cry and urged her horse to go yet faster.

But the knight snatched her from her saddle, so quickly that her breath was stolen away. He cast her across his own, so she lay on her belly before him. The sight of the rollicking ground beneath her made her dizzy. He was strong, wrought of muscle and steel. Jacqueline screamed and fought him all the same.

He swore and caught her against him in a tight grip, his

arm locked around her chest and arms. He turned his steed and slowed it to a brisk canter. Jacqueline heard her own palfrey continue to flee into the distance.

She bit his glove and kicked his steed, and he swore with ominous vigor. He pulled her up so that she sat before him now, though she was no less free to move with his arm locking her elbows to her waist. Indeed, she could feel every relentless increment of him, his chain mail digging into her back.

"Let me go!" Jacqueline screamed.

"Nay." He spoke grimly, his French as fluent as her own. "Be still or you will frighten the steed."

"I should think naught would frighten this monster," Jacqueline snapped. A French knight holding her captive was no reassurance at all—she could not help but think of Reynaud, holding her down, heaving himself atop her.

The knight laughed under his breath though 'twas a mirthless sound. He pinned her against him with one arm, so casually that he might be accustomed to capturing innocents, and rode back toward his companion. Jacqueline squirmed, though she made no progress against his strength.

Just as she had made none against Reynaud. The breath left her chest for a moment, leaving her dizzy with fear, but she forced herself to breathe deeply. Somehow she would escape!

The knight doffed his helm and cast it into his open saddlebag. When she heard it land there, Jacqueline could not restrain her curiosity.

She turned and her heart trembled, so certain was she that she looked into the face of a dark angel. Her captor's lips were drawn to a tight line, his gaze narrowed. He would have been a handsome man—had it not been for his ferocious expression and the scar upon his cheek.

And the patch over one of his eyes.

Then he smiled slowly, like a dragon anticipating a hearty meal, and Jacqueline panicked. She punched her attacker's nose, then drove her heel hard into the stallion's belly. The beast shied—'twas too large and vigorous to be more than startled—and Jacqueline jumped from its back.

She turned her ankle on impact but ran all the same.

The knight swore with savagery behind her, but Jacqueline did not waste a moment in looking back. She leapt into a scree of rocks, knowing that the stallion could not follow her, and ran as if the devil himself pursued her.

She was not entirely certain he did not.

The knight did pursue her, though, punctuating his progress with oaths. Jacqueline would not consider how he would hurt her if she was caught. Oh, he was furiously angry and would desire vengeance, just as Reynaud had desired vengeance.

And was likely to claim it in the same way. Jacqueline pushed her fears of that aside and simply ran.

He gained upon her all too quickly, for he was much taller and more agile than she. Jacqueline glanced back when his footfalls grew loud, her own steps faltering at his proximity and his fury. She stumbled, then fell with an anguished cry, and he was immediately upon her.

He was quick with the braided leather he carried, but to her astonishment, he was not harsh. He bound her knees together loosely, though she could not have fled. He tied her wrists behind her back, moving with such speed that Jacqueline had no hope of a second escape.

She writhed on the ground, seeking a weakness in the knots that she did not find. He stood and stared down at her from his considerable height, his expression unfathomable and all the more terrifying for that.

Finally, when she had nigh exhausted herself with her struggles, he drew his blade, then crouched before her. Fearing the worst, Jacqueline flinched.

"You are worth more to me whole," he snapped, then cut a length of cloth from his tabard. She stared at him in confusion.

When he reached for her injured ankle, Jacqueline cried out and squirmed away. She would not suffer him to touch her! She rolled and desperately tried to crawl away from him, though 'twas not easily done with hands and knees bound.

He snatched at her foot and caught her all too easily. He held her captive thus, his fingers exploring her ankle as if he were blinded in both eyes. Jacqueline shivered, then felt the heat of a blush stain her cheeks at his familiarity.

"A fine view, but you cannot imagine you would get far."

"I will not lie meekly while I am raped!"

He laughed then, the sound so surprising that Jacqueline turned to look at him once more. He was crouched behind her, holding her ankle in one hand, his grip resolute but gentle.

He did not acknowledge her gaze, though he must have known she looked. Nay, he frowned in concentration, focused on his task. He removed her shoe and stocking with surprising care. He had doffed his gloves, and his hand was warm against her bare flesh.

"If touching a woman's foot is akin to rape," he said mildly, "then there are far more lawless men in this world than even I imagined."

He glanced up, his smile broadening as he considered her expression. His smile was cold, but there was a heat in his gaze that made her tremble. "Or are you so innocent of men that you do not know the nature of intimacy?"

There was a look about him that warned Jacqueline he had thoughts of contributing to her education.

She decided to feign boldness, for a show of fear would

win her naught. "My innocence is not of issue here," she retorted, and tried to draw her ankle away.

He moved his thumb smoothly across her instep, the deliberate caress making her shiver with something that was not
entirely fear. "I should say 'tis. And the preservation of your
innocence shall be a considerable concern . . . at least for
others."

He flicked Jacqueline a hot glance that made a lump of
dread rise in her throat. He did not wait for an answer, but
checked the way her ankle had already begun to swell, his
fingers moving deftly and gently.

She deliberately kept her expression impassive, hoping
she could hide both her terror and the curious sensations his
touch awakened within her. He finished binding her ankle
with the cloth, his gaze hooded as he gave his attention to the
task.

" 'Tis not broken," he informed her, then sat back on his
heels. He donned his gloves once more and watched her intently. " 'Twill heal quickly enough, Mhairi."

Jacqueline blinked. "Mhairi? I am not Mhairi!"

He shook his head. "You lie."

"Nay. I *never* lie!" Jacqueline bristled. "And I would not
lie about my own name. Mhairi is my younger sister; she is
but four summers of age." 'Twas a golden opportunity to
pretend she did not fear him, and she lifted her chin proudly.
"Most can tell us apart."

This seemed to amuse him, however fleetingly. "The
Mhairi I seek would be of an age with you." He studied her
intently, as if reaffirming his assessment, though Jacqueline
could not guess his conclusion. "More or less."

"Then she is not me." Jacqueline spoke firmly, determined
to save herself with her wits and the truth. Naught else could
aid her here. "So, you had best release me. This is a simple
enough error to amend."

"Indeed?" His gaze flicked over her ample curves. "Then who are you, if you would not be Mhairi?"

Certain her identity would prove his error and win her freedom, she answered honestly, "I am Jacqueline of Ceinn-beithe."

Something flickered across his features, though Jacqueline would not have gone so far as to call it doubt. His words, though, were even more terse. "Who holds Ceinn-beithe in these days?"

"Duncan MacLaren, my stepfather. And my mother, Eglantine. Who are you?"

The knight shook his head, ignoring her question as he stood once again. "I do not know that name. You lie."

"I do not!"

"Then how did this Duncan come to wrest Ceinn-beithe from Cormac MacQuarrie's grip?"

"Duncan is Cormac's chosen heir. He is the chieftain of Clan MacQuarrie."

"Nay, in this you clearly lie." His lips tightened to a harsh line again. "Cormac is the chieftain of Clan MacQuarrie and Iain his blood son. He would never surrender Ceinn-beithe to another."

"Cormac has not been chieftain since he died some ten years past. Duncan was his foster son and is his heir."

The knight regarded her in silence for so long that his tongue might have been stolen. "And what of Cormac's daughter Mhairi?" He eyed her distrustfully.

Understanding swept through Jacqueline. "Oh, you seek *that* Mhairi! She is long dead, for she killed herself upon her father's insistence that she wed a man she did not love. 'Twas her loss that killed Cormac, to hear Duncan tell it."

"That I can well imagine," he said. He glanced back at his companion. To Jacqueline's relief, the men who had accompanied her were not fatally injured, for they were being marshaled toward her. Their hands had been trussed behind their backs, and the other attacker urged them forward at the point of his sword.

"Well?" the knight's comrade called.

"She claims she is not Mhairi, that Mhairi is dead," the knight replied. "She claims to be the stepdaughter of the new chieftain of Clan MacQuarrie."

He then smiled down at Jacqueline. 'Twas not an encouraging smile, and Jacqueline suddenly doubted his intent to free her. He bent and picked her up in his arms, cradling her weight against his chest.

"Either way," he said silkily, "she will do very well."

"You cannot do this!"

That smile broadened, no less disconcerting from such close proximity. "Can I not?"

"But you have not even told me who you are, or what you want. I have told you everything!"

He chuckled then, a low dark sound. "Your mistake, my beauty. Now you have naught with which to bargain." His teeth flashed in a wolfish smile, and he suddenly looked both wicked and dashing. Jacqueline's heart stopped cold. "And I, for once in all my days, hold every advantage."

"Nay!" Jacqueline screamed but made little sound before the knight clamped one gloved hand over her mouth. She struggled but to no avail. The man kept her silent and powerless with disconcerting ease.

She was helpless in a man's grip once more, prey to his every whim, and his intent was naught good. Fear rose to choke Jacqueline with the taste of that leather, her memory of being captive beneath Reynaud too similar to be denied. She fought to stay aware, knowing that if she fainted she could not aid herself.

But the terror of that memory and the similarity of her circumstance was too strong to be denied. Jacqueline's last glimpse was of the resolute lines of the knight's visage, the flicker of desire in his eyes.

God in heaven, but she could not change the truth. She had fallen prey to a demon on her way to the Lord.

Chapter Two

NGUS HAD NOT EXPECTED HER TO BE SO FRIGHTENED.
Fear he had expected, but her terror was uncharac-
teristic of the intrepid Mhairi he vaguely recalled.

But then the reason was so evident that he felt a fool for
forgetting. Aye, one look upon him when he was angered
might make even the bold Mhairi faint. His quest had
changed more than his character—it had destroyed his face.

In contrast, Mhairi was more lovely than he had ever expected she might become. She was a beauty of flaxen hair
and emerald eyes, a daintily wrought woman yet with ful-
some curves. Her flesh was tanned to a golden hue, a shade
that made her hair seem like burnished gold. Her eyes were
startlingly clear, of the particular green hue the sea could
take on a summer's day.

'Twas astonishing to Angus that it troubled him so much
when she fainted. She was no more than a means to an end to
him and one he did not intend to see harmed, but her terror
concerned him.

He was simply not accustomed to the company of women
any longer—nor, indeed, prepared for her recoil from the
sight of him.

His first impression was that she was younger than he had
expected, but then he had learned 'twas impossible for a man
to accurately guess the age of a beauteous woman. They had

secret arts to preserve their youth. If Mhairi had waited so long to wed because her father deemed her a prize, 'twould serve her well to hide the full number of her years.

Just as such women could hide the truth to suit their purposes, he was not surprised that Mhairi claimed to be other than herself in the hope of seeing herself freed. That was deceptiveness of an ilk with her father's.

Aye, he had called it aright. She lied. She was Mhairi, she was his captive, and Cormac would willingly pay his due.

Angus whistled to his steed and instructed him to stand over the woman now laid upon the ground, knowing that Lucifer would hold his place at his master's word. He spoke softly to the horse, steeled his heart against the woman's ploy to soften his resolve, then turned to the small cluster of men who had accompanied the maiden.

The captured man whom Rodney urged forward was the first to speak. "Who are you?" he demanded in Gael. "And by what right do you make such an attack upon the very land of Clan MacQuarrie?"

His outraged manner did not hide either his suspicion or his uncertainty of his own fate. The trio of other men were similarly wary.

They had naught to fear, in truth. Angus had no desire for slaughter—if he ever had, his years in Outremer would have thoroughly sated any such yearning. On this day he had need of naught but a messenger, and these four would suit him well enough.

He had, however, learned to anticipate treachery from every turn. These men would have no chance to pursue him or retrieve Mhairi.

"I am Angus MacGillivray, son of Fergus MacGillivray, once the comrade of Somerled and, as entrusted by the dictate of that King of the Isles, loyal defender of Airdfinnan."

The man's previous doubt was naught compared to the

suspicion that now crossed his features. "You cannot be! Angus MacGillivray is dead, just as all of the family MacGillivray are dead. All know the truth of it." His companions nodded in solemn agreement.

"Yet I stand before you."

The man's eyes narrowed further. "Then you are naught but a rogue, stealing the name and repute of a ghost."

"Nay, I am Angus MacGillivray." Angus drew his sword quickly and touched its tip to the man's throat. The man flinched, expecting the worst, but Angus merely nicked the skin. "Perhaps you recall my father's blade?"

The man's throat worked silently as a single drop of blood trickled from the minute wound. He flicked a glance at the distinctive hilt, embellished with a pattern of Celtic knots, then paled as he clearly recognized it. "Odin's Scythe. Where did you find it?"

"I did not *find* it." The very suggestion that 'twas not rightly his own irked Angus as little else could have done. " 'Twas granted to me, by my father's own hand, as all men of honor come to carry legendary blades."

The man stared back at him, disbelieving the truth.

"And truly, as I am of that ill-fated family MacGillivray, I am a man with naught left to lose."

The man held his gaze, clearly aware of the fate of Airdfinnan. He jerked his head in the direction of the woman. "And what has that to do with our charge?"

"It has little to do with her and much to do with your clan. She is but a pawn in a larger game."

"You cannot make the lady pay for the loss of your family! 'Twould be unjust!"

"Aye? And how is it unjust for the MacQuarrie clan to be asked to repair what they have set awry?"

The man snorted. "If you speak of the assumption of Airdfinnan, that had naught to do with us!"

Angus let his own skepticism show. "Nay?"

"Nay! Your father died without an heir! Your brother was dead and you were well known to have died in Outremer."

Angus leaned closer. The man could not step back as Rodney's blade was still behind him, and the color drained from his face in his fear.

"My father was murdered," Angus said deliberately. "My brother was murdered. 'Tis by the grace of God alone that I survived, and that I did survive means they will be avenged." He stepped back and sheathed his blade. "Tell that to the Cormac MacQuarrie." He turned to Lucifer, that beast bristling with impatience to be gone.

"Cormac is dead," the man retorted.

Angus turned back to find the man watching him, arms akimbo. "Then who is the chieftain of the clan now?" he asked softly, testing the information the maiden had given him and fully expecting to hear Iain's name.

But the man replied as she had done. "Duncan MacLaren was named Cormac's heir by Cormac himself. 'Tis he who rules the clan and he who will demand restitution for the capture of his daughter Jacqueline."

Angus glanced to the woman, marveling that she had not lied. Still, 'twas as he said—she would serve his purpose as well as Mhairi would have done. "Then 'tis to this Duncan you shall give my message."

"But what of Jacqueline?"

Angus granted the man a smile so cold that he visibly shivered. 'Twas important not to reveal too much of his intent too soon. "You shall hear, eventually."

"But you cannot do this! You—" The man fell silent, undoubtedly encouraged to do so by the tip of Rodney's blade.

Angus ignored him. The woman stirred as he approached his steed. Her eyelids fluttered, her eyes opening wide when she saw him so close, and she stiffened.

"I have told you once to be still lest you frighten the steed," he said sternly, for only her panic could disconcert the horse.

Her gaze flew over Lucifer, who stamped his great hooves with excellent timing. She swallowed and closed her eyes as if drawing upon some inner strength but moved no more than that.

At least she did not faint again. And color blossomed again in her cheeks. Perhaps she was wrought of sterner stuff, in truth.

He fetched some cloth from his saddlebag, spoke again to the steed, then returned to Rodney's side. Without further ado, he blindfolded the captured man.

That man sputtered. "You cannot do this. You cannot steal our steeds . . ."

"I have stolen naught. Your skittish steeds have fled, as poorly trained mounts oft will do."

"But what of us? I beg of you not to kill us!"

The other men were blindfolded quickly, though Angus did not waste time with reassurances.

"Turn in place," he commanded, touching his blade to the throat of the man before him when that man hesitated. Rodney did the same, until each man was so encouraged to spin in place.

"You cannot leave us to perish in the wilderness," the leader protested.

"Nay, you cannot!" argued another, all beginning to clamor. Angus was not stirred to sympathy for he knew they only sought to be aware of each other's locations.

Rodney dug his blade a little deeper into that man's flesh. "Hush, or you shall have to be gagged as well."

The man's lips clamped in a tight line.

"Tell your comrades to do the same."

The man gave a terse command, and the four men shuffled

in silence. Rodney and Angus exchanged a nod, then led two of the men in differing directions, leaving the others turning in place.

Ultimately the four men stood spinning silently, hundreds of paces apart from each other. Their footsteps could not be heard at such a distance, though Angus could nigh taste their fear and uncertainty.

Angus lifted his captive before himself and mounted his steed. She held herself stiffly, as if she would make space between them, but he had no patience with such maidenly modesty. He pulled her closer, then touched his spurs to the steed.

He rode toward the man who had said so much, Rodney riding by his side. "I will watch you to the count of five thousand," he whispered, making Lucifer walk around the man in the opposite direction to which the man turned. "Have you sufficient skill with numbers to count so high?"

"Nay!"

"Ah, then count to a hundred, and do so fifty times."

"But I cannot." The man was already becoming dizzy, his steps faltering.

All the better to disorient him. He would not be able to guess in which direction they departed.

Angus leaned down, his words a low threat. The woman held herself so rigidly before him that she might have been carved of wood. "Count as high as you can, then count that high over and over again. If you move too soon, speak too soon, cease to spin too soon, I will ensure you feed the worms as surely as my kin. Do you understand?"

"Aye."

"And if indeed you find your way back to Ceinn-beithe, I would have you tell this Duncan MacLaren that the payment for the sins of Cormac MacQuarrie has come due. I care only for the return of what is rightly my own. And your chieftain's sole desire, I would expect, would be for the survival of his beauteous daughter."

"But how—"

"Have you not heard that when the will is sufficient, the way will be found?"

"But, but—"

Angus had no interest in excuses. "Tell your chieftain to await my terms at Ceinn-beithe. Begin to count immediately. Keep your voice low."

The man did so, punctuating each number with a step in his circling. Angus cast an eye over the foursome, watching as Rodney gave the same instruction to each in turn. The sun was yet high and he knew they would become bold enough to call to each other before long. Aye, they would be safely home at Ceinn-beithe before night fell, even walking as they must.

Satisfied with what he had wrought, Angus turned his steed for the hills, his captive clasped to his chest. He halted at the last turn of the road, and smiled at the sight of the men turning silently on the moors, while Rodney's steed galloped toward them. 'Twas a sight he would not soon forget, though 'twas but the beginning of his vengeance.

"They will perish, and for what reason?" the maiden asked in soft recrimination. "How does this ensure your message will be delivered and this Airdfinnan surrendered to you?"

He realized with a start that she might well reveal their course, if she was ransomed as he fully expected. And the MacQuarries were a vengeful lot—he would not have them know who had sheltered him before Airdfinnan and its high walls were his own.

Although he could not guess whether Edana still drew breath, he meant to seek refuge at the old storyteller's hut. If she lived, she would aid him, and she could tend the woman's ankle far better than he. He intended to return this woman in the fullness of health so that no insult could be taken.

In addition, Edana's abode was deep in the forest and not readily found—even if the *seanchaidh* drew breath no longer, Angus would find shelter there while he allowed Duncan to fret. Indeed, anxiety would bring a quicker resolution once his demands were made.

He wanted naught but to see this injustice resolved.

All the same, Angus would see that none paid a price for aiding him. His captive could not witness where they rode, lest she alert her father of Edana's location once she was ransomed.

"Give me another length of cloth," Angus demanded of Rodney. The woman caught her breath and shrank away from him, but he blindfolded her all the same.

'Twas her hair that slowed his task, for he hesitated to tighten the knot lest it pull at her golden tresses. He shed his gloves and carefully worked each silken strand free of the cloth. Her lips worked in silence, their movement drawing his attention to their ripe softness.

He wondered how sweet she would taste. It had been long since he had lain with a woman, and longer still since he had lain with one who was not a whore. This woman was all soft curves, her fine if simple garb revealing her privileged station. She was indeed a beauty, and unless he had forgotten much of the world, an innocent who had been sheltered from men.

Which would explain her fear of him. Indeed, he knew that he cast a fearsome image, what with the scars he now bore. He wondered where she had been going with this group of guards, what man had won her as his bride.

To his surprise, her lips set as the blindfold was finally knotted, as if she were annoyed with him.

Perhaps she was not so meek as he might have believed.

No doubt she rode to her nuptials on this day. The unwelcome thought came to him that if she was to wed an ally of the MacQuarries, then there was another compensation he might claim. He could steal what another man had bought and thus render injury against his father's traditional foes. Angus let his gaze wander over the woman's ripe curves and was tempted by the possibilities.

Another man might have taken what he could. But Angus was not a man to claim what was not offered, and he heartily doubted this beauty would offer him much beyond her fear and then her scorn.

"You have not answered me," she insisted with unexpected impatience. "How does abandoning these men serve your purpose?"

"I owe you no explanation."

"I should think that you do! These men serve my stepfather loyally and have done naught to earn this fate. How could you abandon them so? 'Tis heartless. 'Tis unfair!"

"Ah, but I have learned that what is fair has naught to do with matters of war," he murmured. "And my heart, if ever I had one, has been lost so long that I scarce miss it."

Her mouth opened and closed, the ruby softness of her lips inviting his touch. She might have argued further, but he bent to brush his lips across hers.

'Twas only to silence her, or so Angus told himself.

Her lips were breathtakingly soft, the taste of her gasp unbearably sweet. Desire raged through him and his hand fell to the indent of her waist. He caught her against him and might have deepened his kiss without another thought.

But she recoiled and her breath caught, her panic nigh tangible. Angus lifted his head as she froze. She trembled like a spring leaf before him, and he instinctively tightened his arm around her, stunned at his unexpected urge to protect her.

Even from himself.

Indeed, the demoiselle's terror gave full credence to her claim that she was not Mhairi. Though it had been more than fifteen years, he could well recall the audacity of Cormac's daughter. A wee lass, she had been confident in her sire's adoration and protection—she had feared naught from the moment she could crawl. No woman could feign such fear as this one showed.

He supposed his scars were worse than he had feared, or appeared worse in this land so little accustomed to the brutality he had witnessed and endured.

"They are men of resource," Angus said gruffly, disliking his need to reassure her. He would not apologize for his touch. "I have no doubt my message will reach listening ears."

And with that, he gave Lucifer his spurs, leaving the counting men of Ceinn-beithe behind him.

❋

To Jacqueline's thinking, hers was not an enviable situation.

A man who might well have been Reynaud had captured her and meant to finish what that French knight had begun. There was no one to aid her, none who even knew what had become of her, and surely he lied about the chances of her guardians surviving. She did not even know herself where she was, much less where she was headed.

Though she had a very good idea what her fate would be once they arrived.

She had to escape. It did not matter what lie she must tell, what deception she must make, what injury she had to inflict. None could aid her this time, so she must keep her chastity intact herself.

Jacqueline was not entirely certain how that might be managed, but she had faith that an opportunity would arise. She would pray, she would be patient, and she would be as observant as she could under the circumstances. And she would hope.

She certainly would not provoke her captor with questions again, nor would she draw his attention to her in any way. Aye, 'twas best that she be nigh invisible, motionless, silent, unworthy of his attention. She tingled from head to toe in the wake of his kiss. The sensations within her were unfamiliar, doubtless a product of her terror.

She refused to think upon that, though her lips burned, as if they would chastise her for the boldness of her curiosity.

The priest of Ceinn-beithe oft said 'twas her cross to bear.

They rode for what seemed an eternity, no sound reaching Jacqueline's ears beyond the steady beat of the horses' hooves and the whisper of the wind. She tried to gauge their direction. Though she failed to discern anything from the wind, she guessed that they must ride to the east.

After all, only Ceinn-beithe and the sea lay to the west, and she knew they did not ride there. She would have tasted its salt in the wind if the knight had taken that unlikely direction.

Beyond that 'twas difficult, for she knew that once they reached the hills, a hundred roads and paths forked in a hundred different directions, then forked again and again. It seemed imperative that she deduce where she was being taken, but she could conclude naught with certainty beyond a general sense of leaving her family behind.

And security with them.

'Twas a different manner of isolation and silence than she had expected to find in this eastward ride, and she was filled with a terror beyond any she had felt before. The lure of the convent brightened during that endless afternoon, for it seemed a haven of security and femininity.

Somehow she would escape her captor, flee to the convent,

and complete her novitiate with all haste. If naught else, her circumstance proved that the world was filled with dangers and threats and uncertainties that she would prefer to avoid.

Jacqueline was relieved when the knight's companion began to grumble, as much for the relief from the turmoil of her thoughts as from interest in what he said.

She had noted already that he was older than the knight and was garbed as a mercenary. He was completely bald, his head a gleaming tanned pate, and he had a pointed, carefully trimmed beard in the Norman fashion.

He spoke Gael with a cadence slightly unfamiliar to Jacqueline, as if he came from another part of these Celtic isles. This was surprising, as she had assumed from his appearance that he was from Sicily or some other Norman province.

"Aye, and a fine lot of trouble you have found yourself with this scheme," he muttered. "How would you be seeing the resolution of this?"

" 'Twill be exactly as we discussed," the knight said stiffly. He held her so tightly against his chest that Jacqueline could feel the rumble of his voice in her own bones.

"Bah!" The other man spat. "A fine plan 'tis, that was what you told me, and a plan that cannot fail!" The other man scoffed. "Cormac will sell his soul to win back his beloved daughter, upon that we can rely, 'twas what you said."

" 'Tis a good plan."

"Aye, perhaps 'twas. But she is not Mhairi, and her father is not Cormac, and both they two are dead."

The knight cleared his throat. "It matters naught—she is the daughter of Ceinn-beithe, one way or the other."

"So you say. But if her father is disinclined to meet your terms, then we may have saddled ourselves with a woman for naught!"

The knight refused to raise his own voice in response. "We know naught less or more than we did afore. All plans are fraught with risk—indeed, the greater the prize, the more considerable is oft the risk."

"Your wits are addled, boy!" the man declared darkly. "You were kicked in the head one too many times by a Saracen, Angus, and that is the truth of it. Though I suspect that you have been stubborn from the first."

The knight chuckled, though 'twas not a merry sound.

Angus. His name was Angus. 'Twas odd for him to have a Celtic name, for Jacqueline had been certain he was a French knight. But if he had had any doings with Saracens, then he had been in Outremer.

That detail was enough to awaken her cursed curiosity.

Suddenly the red cross she had spied upon his tabard made more sense. He was a crusader, which meant he had been gone for years. Her heart warmed slightly in his favor, for crusaders left all the temptations of this world behind to fight for the greater glory of Christ. Had he seen Jerusalem, that fabled city of gold? She wondered how she might ask him of it.

Of course, it took years to travel to Outremer and years more to travel back, which explained why he knew naught of Mhairi and Cormac's deaths. Evidently he had originally come from hereabouts, which was why Gael fell from his tongue with such ease. She wondered how long he had been gone and from whence exactly he had come. And she listened more avidly as his companion ranted.

"What manner of man sends his daughter abroad with such slim protection as that? Not one overly concerned with her safety! Not one inclined to surrender much for her return!"

The knight sounded reasonable in comparison, his words

soothing in their assurance. " 'Tis the mark of a man confident in the safety of his holding, no more than that. You forget what 'tis to not expect deceit at every turn."

"Whereas you would imagine there is naught wicked in this land," the other man grumbled.

"Calm yourself, Rodney. We must learn more before decisions can be made."

"Calm yourself," Rodney echoed disparagingly. "Bah! There is a simple enough solution that could be made immediately—we could be rid of the woman. We could abandon her somewhere where she will be quickly found and leave this deed behind us. I told you all along 'twas an ill-fated plan, and now even you must have seen its weaknesses." He warmed to his theme. "Think, Angus! 'Twould be the most sensible solution—abandon this folly before 'tis too late!"

Jacqueline's heart leapt.

But Angus spoke sharply. "I will not surrender the only advantage I have in this!"

"Surrendering her might well save your sorry hide. To capture a woman and return her shortly, unscathed, may not earn the vengefulness of the menfolk in her clan. But the longer you keep her, the more uncertainty there will be of her chastity—and thus the higher the retribution sought against you."

"I did not seize her for my pleasure," he snapped, but Jacqueline's lips tingled as if to argue the point.

"Who will believe that? And aye, the longer we keep her, the more she knows of you and the more readily she will lead her family to you once she is released."

"You speak nonsense, Rodney. They will have no reason to seek retribution from me."

"I hope they have the wits to see matters in the light you so choose." The other man harumphed and the pair rode in uneasy silence for a long time.

Finally the companion sighed and appealed once more. "Angus, you cannot have been absent from the company of men for so long that you forget that the truth has naught to do with it—the lady herself might claim you had sampled her and none would question her claim. Bloodthirst runs hot in these lands."

"She will have no reason to make such a claim."

The older man snorted. " 'Tis the ways of women that you forget, that much is clear. Do you not think she will be irked with you when all is done? Do you not think she will seek vengeance?"

" 'Twould be a lie."

"And who will be caring whether she lies? They will seize upon any excuse to take your hide, that much is certain."

"Will you seek vengeance?" the knight demanded, tightening his grip slightly on Jacqueline so that she could not doubt she was being addressed.

She opened her mouth, then closed it again when she realized she had yet to reveal that she understood their Gael speech.

But the knight chided her. " 'Tis clear enough you are following every word. I swear you have not taken a breath for fear of missing anything."

Jacqueline lifted her chin. "I would never lie."

"Aye, but would your family care?" Rodney demanded. "If you returned to them a month hence—"

"A month!"

"—in no small state of dishevelment, would they not seek retribution from the man who had captured you? Would your father not demand the head of this knight in compensation for all you had borne?"

Jacqueline hesitated to answer. Though she knew that Duncan would indeed defend her, she was not certain what answer would better ensure her survival.

"Would he?" the knight prompted, giving her another squeeze.

"I cannot guess my stepfather's intent—"

"Bollocks!" Rodney roared. "You know he would do so! There—the evidence is before you. A woman can lie with ease beyond expectation! They are all wrought this way, Angus, and you would be better off without this one in our small party."

The knight was resolute. "We shall keep her until we know our plan to have failed."

Jacqueline itched to ask the details of his plan but did not dare attract his attention and potentially his ire again. It took all within her to hold her tongue.

"And when will that be?" Rodney demanded. "We shall not have an answer soon, upon that you can rely, and until then—bah! We are stuck with a woman, and a fair lot of trouble they are, no less a woman who may have no value to us whatsoever."

"She has made no demands as yet."

"You have but to wait." Rodney raised his voice in an apparent mimicry of a woman's tones. "Her bed will be too hard, her supper will be too coarse, her bonds will be too tight." He growled low in his throat. "And she will have to piss more times than you can imagine. No sooner will she return from pissing than she will have to do so again. There is something awry in the making of women, for they have to piss more than a man could possibly imagine."

The knight seemed to stifle a laugh. "Indeed?"

"Indeed. You know little enough of women, my boy, but upon this fact you can rely. They must piss before dinner and after and during, they must piss before coupling and after and oft enough they excuse themselves during the great act itself for such relief. And 'tis not enough that they must piss, but the place in which they piss is a matter of much deliberation as well. One would think that if one did this deed with such frequency that one would regard it as less of an event, but nay, 'tis never thus with women."

Truth be told, all Rodney's talk was reminding Jacqueline that it had been quite a while since she had relieved herself. To her dismay, she could hear a stream rushing in the distance, its volume growing as the horses drew nearer to it.

That sound only made her discomfort worse.

"And at night," Rodney continued darkly. " 'Tis worse at night, for they cannot bear to go and piss alone. Nay, they must awaken a man, for he must hold the light if they are within a keep, or he must find a suitable place if they are in the wilds. A man cannot even sleep through the night without a woman needing to piss—and no sooner does he finish his duty and return to slumber, then she has need of his services again. Such a load of fuss 'tis over a deed which should be no bother at all!"

The rush and gurgle of the water grew louder, increasing Jacqueline's discomfort with every passing moment. They halted when it echoed loudly, the sound of the horses drinking from the stream carrying to her ears. Jacqueline could imagine the water swirling around the horses' hooves and she fidgeted. The knight tightened his grip upon her, apparently thinking that she was trying to escape him.

She wriggled, her need increasing by the moment, and heard the knight catch his breath. His fingers spread out, his gloved hand spanning her belly as he urged her buttocks back against a part of him that had not been there before.

Jacqueline froze, knowing with sudden clarity what she felt, her earthy urge forgotten. She had not been raised on a farm without seeing what was what. The imprint of his erection told her more than she truly wished to know of his plan for her.

He was indeed like Reynaud. The knight's fingers moved

in a languorous circle, burning a trail of heat through her kirtle. Jacqueline's heart began to pound.

He lied about seizing her to serve his pleasure.

He had already stolen one kiss, after all. Jacqueline could guess what he would demand of her this night. God in heaven, but she had to escape!

"And another thing—" Rodney began, but Jacqueline interrupted him sharply.

"I have to piss!"

Chapter Three

ACQUELINE USED RODNEY'S LANGUAGE, THOUGH IT sounded coarse on her tongue, the knight's touch feeding her urgency. "I have to piss now!"

"You see?" Rodney crowed. "They are all the same. Now, Angus, you who have insisted upon keeping this wench can find her a spot to her liking." He laughed, obviously enjoying that his own prediction was coming true. "And we shall see how long you wish to keep her after that."

"You shall have to wait for a moment or two," the knight said tersely. Jacqueline heard the stallion cross the stream, leaving the garrulous Rodney behind. Angus dismounted and her back was suddenly cold without his strength there. He rummaged through something as she sat alone and she assumed he tethered the great beast.

Mostly she worried about sitting so still and straight that she could not lose her balance and fall. 'Twas difficult to do with the blindfold, and she realized how much she depended on her vision. That only reminded her that she would not be able to flee while she was bound and blindfolded.

Somehow she had to persuade him to set her free.

Jacqueline started when Angus slipped her shoe upon her bound foot, then nearly smiled that he ensured her foot was shod. 'Twould be easier to run through the woods with her shoes.

She jumped when his hands closed around her waist. He could take her now, and there would be naught she could do to defend herself. Who would aid her in this wilderness? Not Rodney.

Indeed, he might take his turn.

Jacqueline clenched her teeth in terror. The knight lifted her down, and she did not know whether 'twas by accident or design that her breasts fairly slid down the length of him.

"I thought you had another urge," he murmured under his breath.

'Twas precisely the wrong comment he might have made. Jacqueline felt her cheeks burn, then knew she paled in fear. "Never!"

That only made him chuckle, and a more ominous sound could not have been. He urged her forward but she could only shuffle, between the restriction of her bound knees and injured ankle. Jacqueline forced them both to a halt.

"This is nonsense," she said with all the indignation she could muster. "I cannot relieve myself this way. How shall I see to keep my garments from being soiled?"

Angus hesitated for a moment, then pushed her blindfold over her head. Jacqueline winced at the brightness of the light, then looked up at the man watching her so carefully. Distrust shone in his gaze, but she did not care. She dared not show her fear.

Indeed, she drew complaints from Rodney's diatribe.

"And my knees? How am I to keep from pissing all over myself with my knees so bound together?"

His eyes narrowed. "You mean only to flee."

"I mean to piss and as soon as possible, if you please!" Jacqueline rolled her eyes as if he made much of little. "I can only hobble with this swollen ankle, so you have naught to fear."

He considered her for a long moment.

"If you please!" She shifted her weight from foot to foot in seeming impatience. Rodney started to laugh. Angus scowled and bent to untie the braided leather rope knotted about her knees. He might have said something but Jacqueline turned her back and pushed her bound wrists toward him.

He hesitated again, but she had expected as much. She cast an arch glance over her shoulder. "I will not suffer either of you to lift my skirts out of the way or ensure I am dry afterward."

He shook his head and untied the last knot. He might have bound her to him—Jacqueline would not have put such a deed past him—but she scampered into the woods.

"You will learn much of women this day!" Rodney cried, laughing good-naturedly as Angus pursued Jacqueline.

First, she must put distance between the two men. She deliberately favored her ankle more than was deserved, to lull the knight into believing her more wounded than was the truth.

The stream was rocky on either side, its flow caught in endless little pools and eddies. The trees met overhead. Though the undergrowth was thin on the banks of the river, it grew more dense the farther one looked into the woods, and the shadows were deep. Jacqueline realized that she would not have to get far to disappear from Angus's view.

She managed to stay ahead of him by darting between the rocks, slipping through spaces that were too small for him or ducking under tree boughs that were too low for him.

He muttered a curse, then snatched at her wrist. "Here! This is a fine place."

Jacqueline considered it, then shook her head. In truth there was naught wrong with it other than its proximity to

Rodney. "There is moss on the rock and I would sit for a moment."

She smiled at him, which seemed to startle him, then spun to march onward.

He found a rock with no moss upon it and she complained of the shade. He selected one in the sunlight and she pointed out a snail upon it, making a great fuss about the shiny residue left in its path. The next spot she declared a certain haven for snakes, the next too close to the woods. The next was, of course, too far from the woods.

If naught else, the man was diligent. She assessed his expiring patience as well as she could and when his features had set, she declared his next suggested rock to be the perfect one. There was naught to be gained in angering him too soon. After all, they were quite some distance from both Rodney and the steeds.

She had a sense that Angus was more concerned with honor and chivalry than he would have preferred she know.

Jacqueline grabbed her skirt in two fistfuls as if intent upon beginning what had to be done, then gave the knight a stern look. There was a deep pool behind the rock that she had chosen, and Angus stood at its lip. Her rock was directly beside him.

She tried to look as indignant and forbidding as her mother could. "Well?"

Angus folded his arms across his chest and planted his feet hard against the ground. "Well?" He stood only two arm's lengths away.

"You have to leave!"

He shook his head. "I thought you had to piss."

Jacqueline did not have to feign her blush, nor the way it deepened with each word she uttered. "I do, but you—but you cannot, you cannot stand there and *watch* me do so!"

"I most certainly can and I most certainly will."

Jacqueline flung down her skirts. "Nay. I cannot do this!" He was as calm as she was frustrated with his refusal to do as she desired. She needed a chance to put distance between them. "I cannot permit it. 'Tis not proper!"

"Proper?"

"Aye, *proper*! 'Twould not be right."

He looked pointedly to the left and the right. "We are hardly constrained by the manners of a court here."

Her cheeks burned. " 'Tis—'tis *indecent* for you to watch me!"

Angus seemed to find this amusing, the hint of a smile softening his features. "If it soothes your pride, I have seen many piss, both men and women."

Jacqueline stared at him for a moment, aghast that he should be so bold, then lifted her chin. "My pride is not at stake. 'Twas you who said I should be returned as I was found. I will not be shamed by a man's glance—or I shall claim that you stole more than that."

She folded her arms across her chest in turn, quite pleased with her own quick thinking. " 'Twould be your word against my own if I claimed you ravished me here. Who do you think my stepfather would believe?"

Any hint of humor faded from his expression. He uncoiled that cursed leather rope from his belt and moved so quickly to knot it about her waist that she had no chance to dart away.

"What is this you do?"

"I ensure that you play no games with me." He flicked her a dark glance, then knotted the rope securely about his own waist. When her mouth dropped open in horror at his proximity—indeed, he stood closer than before, by dint of the rope's length—he smiled that slow, wicked smile. "You need not fear. I will not gaze overmuch upon your maidenly virtues."

Jacqueline's breath was caught in her chest even as he turned to stare at the opposite shore. This was the worst result possible! He stood directly beside her—she would never be able to escape this way.

Her gaze fell upon the length of cloth, still stuffed in his belt.

"You must wear the blindfold so I can be certain," she insisted.

His sidelong glance was wry. "Odd how your need for relief seems to have passed."

"On the contrary, it grows more urgent with every passing moment. But 'tis no small thing to have a man of unknown intent watch this deed!" Jacqueline lifted her chin in challenge. "You must wear the blindfold or I will not be able to relieve myself."

He looked pained. "After all of this trouble?"

"Aye." Jacqueline squared her shoulders. "And we shall have to find another suitable place in no time at all. Such matters cannot be postponed indefinitely."

Angus grimaced, then shook his head. He pulled out the blindfold, evidently confident that she could not go far while tethered to his waist. Jacqueline knotted it securely around his head, her fingers inadvertently touching his hair.

'Twas as black as midnight, thick and wavy and surprisingly soft. It hung to his nape and curled about her fingers as if it had a mind of its own. She shivered, remembering all too well her earlier conviction that he was a devil made flesh. She recalled the illicit tingle his kiss launched within her and did not doubt that he could awaken much wickedness within her.

She had to escape him.

Jacqueline made a fuss arranging her skirts over the rock

and scrambling about to find a comfortable seat. She made sounds of disgust as she apparently found bits of moss on the rock, then brushed them away with more fastidiousness than they deserved. She insisted that Angus turn farther way, claiming that she did not trust the blindfold. To her surprise, he was indeed as chivalrous as she had hoped, for he indulged her whims.

But all the while that she fussed and fidgeted, Jacqueline desperately tried to loosen the knot in the leather around her waist. Angus had tied it with a vengeance, and she feared that she might not be able to loose it at all.

She had to succeed! This might well be her last chance for escape. She kept a tight pressure on the line with one hand as the other picked at the fearsome knot. She broke two fingernails and her heart hammered with terror that she would not accomplish the deed in time.

"For a woman feeling such urgency, you are taking a cursedly long time about this task," Angus complained. "Now or not at all, make your choice."

In the last possible moment, the knot loosened in her hand. Jacqueline was free!

"Now will be my choice!" she cried.

Angus must have heard something in her tone, for he snatched at the blindfold. Jacqueline bounced to her feet, despairing that he perceived her intent. He stepped after her, anger flashing in his eye.

In terror, she pushed him hard.

Angus roared. He snatched at her but missed, losing his balance, and fell into the pool with a splash. Jacqueline was already running in the opposite direction. She ducked low beneath the branches that snagged at her clothes, ignored the brambles that scratched her flesh, and fled as fast as she could into the forest.

She knew her captor would not be far behind.

But the forest was thicker even than Jacqueline had anticipated. She had a hard time making her way through the underbrush, the only consolation being that Angus would have a harder time because of his greater size.

"Zounds, woman!" he bellowed altogether too close behind her. "Are you mad?" Jacqueline heard naught but the anger in his voice and knew she could not let herself be caught.

God only knew what he would do to her.

She leapt through the thicket, oblivious to the thorns and the ache of her ankle. Angus shouted when he spied her, but Jacqueline did not look back. She ran and ran and ran, each step punctuated by a pound of her heart and a stab of pain.

The forest was so dense that she could see no more than five or six steps ahead. The branches of the trees interlaced so tightly that the sunlight only reached the forest floor in intermittent patches of gold. She halted, panting, and strained her ears, but heard naught.

'Twas no consolation. For all she knew, Angus was skilled in silent pursuit. Had he not been to Outremer? Aye, a hardened warrior would better know how to hunt than she knew how to flee. She rounded each tree with her heart in her mouth, half certain he had somehow circled around her and would suddenly appear in her path. Furious, of course.

Aye, 'twas true that he knew something of these woods if he was from these parts originally.

She disliked her disadvantage and hated him for putting her at it. She wished she were safely at Inveresbeinn by now! She wished she were recounting the rosary, safe in the embrace of her sisters pledged to the service of the Lord.

Curse Angus!

Jacqueline heard a sudden crackle, precisely the sound a stout stick might make breaking under a booted foot. She plunged away from the sound in panic. The brambles tore at her hands, gnats flew in her face. She burst through a group of bushes and plunged into a cold stream before she knew what lay ahead of her. Her ankle wrenched hard against the stones on the riverbed, the resulting pain bringing tears to her eyes.

But she dared not linger. She hobbled to the opposing bank, her tears of frustration falling when the mud and the weight of her wet skirts made it nigh impossible to scramble up the bank.

Nay, nay, time was of the essence! She grabbed at roots and struggled to climb the bank, glancing over her shoulder with certainty that Angus was fast behind. 'Twas only when she heard a slight sound overhead and glanced up that her heart stopped cold.

For a grim knight offered her his gloved hand, anger bright in his eye.

※

Angus had circled around the maiden on silent feet. The panicked sound of her flight was impossible to miss for one so accustomed to hunting as he. He gritted his teeth in frustration as he stalked her, for this was his own fault.

He would never have trusted a man as he had trusted his charge. Indeed, he would have had no reason not to stand directly beside a man and watch as that man relieved himself. The respect his mother had engrained within him for women had betrayed him in this—he had thought this maiden too innocent to be capable of such a trick. He had thought her shy, a delicate and fragile flower.

She had made him look like a fool. And truly, a man who granted trust so foolishly, especially after all he had endured, *deserved* to look like a fool.

That did naught to improve his mood. He was tired and

soaked and irked beyond all. The key to his plan had slipped away from him. Worse, 'twas his own fault that she was in such circumstance. If he did not retrieve her, whatever befell her in these woods on this night would be his fault as well.

He would find her, if 'twas the last thing he did.

'Twas then that Angus caught a glimpse of her through the trees. He planned his course, deliberately stepping on a heavy stick so that it snapped. The woman bolted in the opposite direction, precisely as he had hoped. He quickly encircled her and reached the opposing bank while she chose what to do.

He intended to stop her when she crossed the river, though he nigh leapt after her when she clearly injured her ankle anew. He was surprised at her determination, no less by the terror evident in her manner. He had done naught to make her so very fearful.

Had he?

Then she looked up and all the blood drained from her fine features. Angus feared she would faint anew, perhaps slip beneath the water and drown. That would not serve his ends! He snatched at her, guessing instinctively what she would do.

She did indeed try to bolt, but Angus caught her around the waist. She struggled like a wild bird, kicking and thrashing, but she was far smaller than he. Angus cast her over his shoulder with some effort. He was already sodden from his plunge into the pool, so he waded through the river again, ignoring her frenzied struggle.

"Now you know in truth the trouble a woman can bring," Rodney began, but Angus held up one hand to silence him. His companion had said more than enough on the matter already.

"Enough."

Rodney granted him a sly glance and made one last comment beneath his breath. "How much do you wager that she has not yet had her piss?"

The two men shared a smile, even as the lady in question made a sound of frustration. Rodney made to bind her ankles, but Angus halted him.

"Bind her knees again. The ankle is swollen already and she has injured it yet further. The rope will chafe and make matters worse."

"She had no care for her own wound," Rodney retorted, though he did as he was bidden. 'Twas no small feat, given the lady's thrashing. "Why then should we?"

"One fool in a party is more than enough," Angus said mildly, though he was thinking of the vigor of the woman's response. Was she so witless that she did not realize the risks facing her in the forest at night?

Then he knew he wondered too much about her, this woman who was naught more than the key to his plan. He should not be concerned with her, beyond ensuring that she was unharmed.

"She will flee again," his companion predicted skeptically.

"I heartily doubt her ankle will bear the weight of her very far."

Rodney snorted. "Yet still you would have her knees bound." He worked quickly and knotted the leather most securely.

"This lady has a way of confounding expectation."

"Trouble 'tis what she is. At least you learned something of women this day."

When Angus said naught, Rodney marched back to the horses, muttering his usual refrain about Angus having been kicked in the head once too often.

"You cannot do this!" She struggled, sounding as if she were close to tears. She was clearly terrified.

Again he felt the unwelcome urge to reassure her.

"I cannot suffer you to flee." He spoke in a reasonable tone, but she was not consoled.

" 'Tis loathsome to truss a woman like a Christmas goose before raping her."

'Twas the second time she had mentioned rape. That could be no coincidence.

Angus paused and let her slide to the ground before him. She hissed and wriggled like a furious kitten, her fair hair coming loose and falling over her shoulders. She shook within her bounds and her flesh was colder than it should have been, but her eyes snapped with defiance. He had the sense that she refused to faint lest she show herself weak again, and despite himself, he admired her valor.

Angus caught her chin in his hand and stared deliberately into her eyes. She trembled and her breath caught, but she did not look away.

"I have told you once that you are worth most to me whole," he said firmly. " 'Tis no lie." Her lips trembled, their softness tempting his touch, but he refused to yield to desire again.

One fair brow lifted in a bold expression, though her words fell breathlessly. No doubt she was trying to make him think she was less fearful than she was. "And what is 'whole' to a lawless brigand? You have already stolen one kiss, and 'tis said that a man's actions speak louder than his words."

Angus was intrigued by her suspicion. "I am my father's son and I take naught that is not mine to have."

She glared at him so hotly that he barely managed to hide his surprise. "I was not yours to capture this day."

"True enough," he mused, watching her reaction. This agreement troubled her, and when she was troubled, he had already noted, she was silent. In silence, 'twas easier for him to think of her as merely baggage. "Perhaps that does indeed make you mine to have."

She paled, frightened and mute once more.

Angus smiled with slow deliberation, intent upon keeping her disconcerted. His urge to reassure her was doubly confounding—not only did conversation make it more difficult for him to use her for his means, but it led to his granting answers to her. 'Twas imperative that she know as little as possible of him and his plans.

Her fear was a means of ensuring that.

"I thank you," he whispered, "for making the possibilities most clear to me."

She made an agonized sound beneath her breath, though she said naught more.

Angus leaned closer and watched her breath catch, her lips part. He planted his thumb across her lips, noting how she shivered at the caress of the smooth leather. He bent and brushed his lips across her brow, not failing to note how she trembled at such proximity to his scars.

His words fell more harshly than he intended. "We will ride forth in silence from here, my beauty. 'Tis your choice to be silent willingly or to be gagged."

She swallowed beneath his touch, her eyes wide and very green. "Silent," she whispered behind his thumb, her voice husky with terror again. His gaze fell to the flutter of her pulse at her throat and compassion stirred within him.

But she would be ransomed soon enough and he would never see her again. Angus bent and hastily hefted her into his arms. " 'Tis time enough we were upon our way." He cast her over his shoulder, so he would not have to gaze upon her fear, and began to stride through the woods once more. It did not take long to draw near the tethered steeds.

"I would not have thought it a shortcoming of yours to be

ignorant of women, not until you had this fool plan." Rodney did not seem to think his theme exhausted, though Angus did not encourage him with a reply. "Did you not sample every whore in Jaffa?"

Angus lifted the woman to his saddle, knowing full well that she was listening avidly.

"Ah, but I recall the truth of it now." Rodney snapped his fingers in feigned recollection. "You did not linger with a one of them, boy, which is clearly why you know naught of their true, manipulative nature. 'Tis no surprise at all that the lass tricked you. A man who knows better would never trust a woman."

Angus slanted a glance at his smug companion. "Yet you imagine that you can see the intent of women beforehand?"

Rodney had a talent for wisdom that was crystal clear in hindsight, though he imagined that he saw much in advance. 'Twas not usually an annoying trait, though in this moment Angus found it irksome.

"Aye. I would have guessed that she would deceive you. There is no other way for such a beauty as she to have her way, and beauties have black hearts as a result. 'Tis clear enough that you noted her many charms—"

"But you did not trouble yourself to warn me?" He swung into the saddle behind his captive, and she stiffened before him. " 'Tis some fine comrade you make."

Rodney huffed with indignation. "You would not have listened to me, boy! You have listened to naught of my advice from the moment you spied the flag of another fluttering from—"

Angus drew his steed up short, then whirled on his companion. "Enough! The woman is not struck deaf!"

"I merely said—"

"I heard what you said. We shall discuss the matter no further."

Rodney gave him one look, then had the wits to hold his tongue.

Angus blindfolded the woman once again, and she did not so much as murmur in protest. They rode in silence back to the road and Angus forced his temper to cool. He had never told his friend how the welcoming courtesans of Jaffa had *not* welcomed him. Most had averted their faces in horror. He had lain with far fewer of them than any had imagined.

The woman before him seemed to have ceased breathing. Was it because of his anger? He would not apologize for that! If naught else, she remained blessedly silent and still.

'Twas better for all of them this way.

He looked around as he rode, noting the peacefulness of the woods, the darkening sky stretched overhead, the road that had never been stained crimson with the blood of slaughtered men. He shivered in the chill of his wet tabard, knowing he would never look upon the world in the same way as he had all those stolen years ago.

He was not thinking merely of the effect of his lost eye upon his vision. The puckered skin on his chest itched in recollection of what it had endured, his eye patch seemed to burn. He had yet to sleep a full night when he found himself enclosed by walls of stone.

But he had had high hopes of his homecoming. Angus had expected matters to be so different here at home, here where he had known such peaceful days. He had expected to come home to find his family living happily in prosperity, untouched by all the wickedness he had witnessed.

He had found a travesty of his memories. His family were all dead, killed too soon. Now he wondered whether some sickness had infected men all across Christendom, compelling them to seize what was not theirs to take, to shed the blood of others without remorse, to rape and pillage and kill.

Even his hand fell more quickly to the hilt of his sword than it had once.

And women shrank from him in terror, when once they had welcomed his attentions. He felt not only scarred but tired, tired clear to his bones, his earlier certainty that his scheme could not fail suffering as a result.

He spoke aright when he said this woman confounded his expectations.

After long moments, Rodney passed a hand over his brow and sighed. " 'Tis not the ends I question, Angus, but your means. You should have let the woman flee."

"We could not abandon her to the forest, Rodney." Angus spoke firmly. " 'Twould compound my errors if I were to abandon her after my intervention in her fate."

" 'Tis those cursed knightly vows complicating our days and nights again," Rodney grumbled but there was a thread of affection in his tone. "Naught good will come of this course, boy, mark my words."

"Naught good would have come of our abandoning the lady."

" 'Twas her choice to flee."

"A bad one and one made impetuously." Angus did not explain his conviction that 'twas her fear of his damaged features that sent her fleeing, nor his resulting sense of responsibility.

"There are wolves in these woods and few dwellings where she might find shelter," he continued, as much for her own edification as anything else. " 'Twas my fault that she is not protected as her family desired and my error to amend in retrieving her. I care naught for her personally, as you well understand. The lady, after all, is but a pawn in the greater game, and her health should not suffer." He gave her waist a squeeze, in no doubt that she attended his words. "Do you not agree?"

"I would have willingly faced the wolves instead," she muttered with unexpected spirit, and Rodney laughed.

"And now?" that man prompted.

Angus smiled. "I may know little of women, Rodney, but I know much of men. The only way to persuade a man to relinquish what he holds dear is to offer something or someone he holds more dear in exchange." The woman shivered as he pulled her closer and he knew 'twas not just the evening air against her wet clothes. "She will not have the chance to escape me again."

❄

He would never so much as loose her bonds again.

Jacqueline knew the truth of it with every fiber of her being. She was captive and there was naught she could do about the matter. No one knew where she was—even she could not fathom a guess—and certainly none would know where she was going. Angus had a definite purpose, for he did not hesitate and it seemed to her that he rode in a reasonably straight line. He had a destination, though she did not know where 'twas.

And she did not doubt that her situation would be more helpless once they arrived there. She had angered him and he would take his vengeance. Worse, he would take it in a way that would not leave a visible mark, and he would do so in some remote place where none could come to her aid.

There had to be a solution. She had a calling. She had been summoned to serve God and God would not abandon her so callously, so completely, as this. 'Twas a test and one at which she would succeed. She prayed and found strength in her faith.

Then she reviewed her circumstance.

Her shoes were sodden, as were her stockings, the hem of her skirts, and the cloth bandaging her ankle. The wool was cold against her flesh but she refused to shiver, lest Angus consider it an invitation of a kind. Her hair hung loose around her face, the blindfold itched, the braided leather rope was restrictive without hurting her. Her ankle throbbed, for she had been a fool to run so far upon it.

And all for naught. She could smell his flesh, the wetness of steel and leather and horse, masculine scents and doubly troubling for all of that. His embrace spread unwelcome warmth around her waist, heat that she yearned for as the evening fell but not at the price of turning to him. Angus held her so tightly against him that she knew he missed naught that she did—indeed, she feared that he could even read her thoughts.

A frightening prospect indeed. Aye, the curse of her curiosity was awakening, and her desire to know only brought trouble on its heels. She wished she could cease her wondering, but 'twas futile.

Jacqueline longed to know where they were going and what wicked plan Angus had in store for her. She wanted to know whether his scheme would differ if she managed to persuade him that she was not Mhairi.

'Twas tempting truly to find out the truth. She chewed her lip but, mindful of his threat, did not dare to ask him more. To be gagged would make her even more helpless. Jacqueline sat still and straight and silent, and desperately tried to find something good in her situation.

She was not dead or ravaged yet, but beyond that, matters showed little promise. Undoubtedly Angus was merely waiting to take his due until they reached wherever they were going. Jacqueline swallowed and felt goose pimples rise across her flesh.

'Twas all the more reason to ensure she was not gagged. She might well need to scream.

Perhaps, oh perhaps, he insisted upon her silence because

they would pass near a dwelling or a village. Jacqueline's heart leapt and she strained her ears for some faint sound of other people. There was always a slender chance that some-one might hear her cries for aid.

Indeed, 'twas the only chance she had.

Chapter Four

HE OLD WOMAN HAD SMELLED THEIR ARRIVAL IN THE
wind for days. She had seen glimmers of it in the
pool, she had felt a telltale prickling on the back of
her neck. The foresight haunted her; nay, it plagued her. She
had known with dreadful certainty that a knight came, a
knight with a mission, a knight who would be familiar to her
in some way though she could not see his face in her dreams.

Indeed, they were nightmares, not mere dreams. She
awoke in their midst shivering in the chill of the night, a line
of cold sweat sliding down her spine. Naught good came of
knights on proud steeds, that she knew in her very bones.

Her visions left her with the certainty that not only would
she face such a knight soon but that he would request her aid.
And, more terrifyingly, that she was destined to give it. She
thought of leaving the hut, but she had nowhere else to go.

Her fate came, with the rhythm of hoofbeats in the night,
too soon for her taste. She listened, fearing she dreamed with
her eyes opened, but 'twas no dream this time.

Two fine horses rode toward her abode, their trap jingling
in the wind. Her own heart raced at the distinctive sound of
armor and weaponry, of men of war coming ever closer. She
rose to her feet, feeling old and feeble and afraid, yet needing
to do more than sit passively and wait.

She had made that error once, long ago, and would not soon forget its price.

None came here by accident, or in passing. There was but one path to the hut and 'twas hidden to those who did not know its location.

Or those by whom she preferred not to be found. 'Twas galling to realize that she had not succeeded in turning the eye of this knight, whoever he might be, away from her door. She felt suddenly hunted and, worse, cornered in her own home.

The uncertainty tormented her. The dreams had not told her what this knight would demand of her, what he would take, much less what toll his presence would steal from her.

She knew how high the price might be.

Even though she expected naught else, the sharp rap on the door made her jump.

"Edana *Seanchaidh*!" The deep, unfamiliar male voice made her quake, even though he honored her with the title of storyweaver. "Do you still haunt this abode?"

The determination in the man's voice did naught to reassure. The old woman suspected he would break the door if not offered admission, and truly there was no place to hide. The door was old and rotten and would not bear much resistance; the hut was small and spare.

She had never chosen to be a coward and she did not choose so now. She had lived long, longer than most, and she was proud of most she had wrought. She would not die cowering in a corner before an unknown foe. Aye, she would know this one's name before he took his toll of her.

She opened the door, her chin held high. "I am Edana. Who comes to my door in the night?"

At first it seemed she had not opened the door, for a shadow filled the portal as surely as if it had still been latched against the darkness.

'Twas the knight who filled her vision, she realized with a start. Indeed, he stood two hands taller than the door; his shoulders were wider. The night could not slip past him into the hut.

He was young and strong, but when he doffed his helm and shook out his hair, there was something familiar about his stance. He stepped forward and the light of the lantern within the hut caressed the white of his tabard, glinted off his mail, touched the ruby cross embroidered upon his shoulder.

And she knew him.

Against all odds. She stared at him in the flickering light, desperately seeking a hint that she was wrong. She knew no man with a patch over his eye, no knight sworn to the battle of Christ, no man bearing a scar upon his face. Her memory was long, but filled with twists and crooked alleys as a result, places where visions and memories intermingled.

Did she know him in truth?

Or had she merely glimpsed his face in her vision?

And then he smiled and murmured her name again. 'Twas a smile that pulled only one corner of his mouth, a rueful smile that she remembered all too well.

Oh. Her heart faltered, then raced. She knew him, though it had been many years.

Indeed, she had thought him long dead.

His gaze fixed intently upon her, as if he would will her to recall him. She recoiled from his regard, pulling her hood further over her face and lowering her chin.

But she needed no such urging to confirm her memory. The smile had told her all. Aye, she had known a child with such a smile, a smile so much older and sadder than a child's smile ought to be. It belonged to a child who had left these lands as a mere lad, a child long disappeared over the hills, a child she had never thought to see with her old eyes again.

"Angus MacGillivray," she whispered, not daring to believe 'twas the truth.

"Aye, Edana, 'tis I. I am returned."

But the old woman could not always tell the difference betwixt her sightings of this world and the other. And this knight was so clear to her, so sharply defined, that she doubted her failing vision saw him in truth.

It could well be yearning alone that prompted this sighting. Aye, Angus might be newly dead, leagues away, his shade having come to say farewell when he could not. One heard of such visits.

She had to be certain.

Dreading what she would feel, she reached out one shaking hand to touch the man before her. She planted a fingertip cautiously upon the place she perceived his chest to be, half expecting her hand to slide through him.

He might have been wrought of stone. He did indeed stand before her. She began to shake with the force of her relief. She laid the flat of her trembling hand upon the knight and felt her tears rise at the thunder of his pulse beneath her palm.

Her boy was finally home, against all odds and expectations.

He stood silently before her, neither stepping away nor sweeping her into an embrace. Of course Angus had never been an affectionate boy, never one to initiate a touch, though he would not spurn one offered. 'Twas so like him and as compelling evidence of his presence as the heat of him beneath her palm.

"Angus. Home." She shook her head and looked upon his beloved face. She reached for him with her other hand.

He caught her tightly against his chest, just as she had expected, just as she had hoped.

"Aye." His breath was a welcome heat against her ear. She closed her eyes and leaned against his strength, trembling inwardly that this gift should be hers. Overcome by his presence and his embrace, she wept upon him as never she permitted herself to weep, uncaring of anything else. "I am finally home, Edana."

His utterance of that name made her eyes fly open. She pulled back and stared at him, seeking something in his gaze but not finding it there. He smiled slightly at her, a wary man encountering an old woman, one of no blood but as familiar as an aunt. She was not surprised by this, though she was surprised by the weight of her resulting disappointment.

What else had she expected of him?

Indeed, was it not better thus?

Angus shook her shoulders slightly when she did not speak, humor unexpected in his words. "Did you not see me coming? There was a time when you knew all before anyone else could believe 'twould be true."

She pushed away, uncertain what to do with the maelstrom of emotion loosed within her. "Aye, I did, you rogue, but I saw not your face." She straightened and scolded him, for lack of a better choice. "Indeed, I would not have recognized it if I had. What have you done to yourself, lad? What folly has cost you an eye?"

His features set. "Naught of import."

"A lie if ever I heard one," she retorted, though she was content to leave him his privacy for now. He would tell her, if 'twas intended for her to know, in his own time.

Stubborn like his father, that was Angus MacGillivray.

She swatted him, and he winced, though her feeble blow could not have wounded him. "I have learned to expect little good of knights. You have given me a fright, Angus."

He inclined his head slightly, probably not realizing the startling resemblance to his father in that one gesture. "You have my apologies." He stepped back then and she saw that he was not alone. A companion rode with him, that man's horse nudging against the knight's great destrier.

But the stallion's saddle was not empty. A woman sat there, a woman bound and blindfolded and shivering, though whether 'twas with fear or cold was unclear. The old woman spared a glance to Angus, who watched her carefully.

"What is this?" she demanded, fearful suddenly of his intent.

"I seek sanctuary for a few days."

Her mouth went dry. "What have you done, lad? What do you want of me? Who is this woman?"

"She is the key to my vengeance."

"Has she a name?"

"Not to you."

She stared at him, willing the truth to fall from his lips, but if ever she had been able to accomplish that feat, she could no longer. He was no longer the boy she had known, and the realization was most troubling.

She lifted her chin. If Angus meant to keep his secrets, then she would keep her own. But she would not aid him in whatever scheme he had made for this woman.

" 'Twould be rude to deny hospitality to any who come to one's door in the night. Make your bed where you will," she said curtly, and turned back into the hut.

"The woman is injured." Angus spoke as if he did not realize she was annoyed with him. "I had hoped you might tend her."

She turned to meet his gaze. "Is that all you seek of me?"

"Nay." That hint of a smile touched his lips. "I come also for the truth."

The old woman caught her breath, wondering whether he knew what he asked of her. He could not, for he made no effort to offer the truth himself. "If 'tis meant to be known, the

truth will unfurl itself in its own time." Before he could reply, she bent to coax her fire to life. "Send the nameless
woman to the well, if you would have her tended."

"She cannot walk. 'Tis her ankle is injured."

"Then bring her there, for I cannot bear her weight."

Angus said naught more, but turned and left her alone.
She gathered her herbs and her cane, a length of cloth and
the lantern, then made her way toward the spring. Indeed,
she might benefit herself from a visit there this night, for her
own joints ached most painfully.

She hoped those aches were not a portent of whatever
Angus brought to her door.

❉

Jacqueline jumped when Angus removed her blindfold. Here
was the moment she dreaded! He plucked her from the saddle, his expression impassive, then cradled her in his arms.
He said naught but strode down the slope of the land in pursuit of an old woman.

That must be whose voice Jacqueline had heard, whose
words she had not been able to discern. Her heart thundered
with fear of what these two had planned.

'Twas much darker now and clouds were gathering overhead. She tried to guess how long it had been since she had
been captured and knew only that it had been earlier on this
same day. 'Twas perhaps close to the dinner hour now, for
her belly had its complaints to make as well. Aye, and she
was thirsty.

Not that that was of any import.

In the distance a wolf howled mournfully, its call quickly
echoed by more of its kind. Even knowing of the predators'
presence, she wished she had succeeded in her escape. She
would have survived, for Duncan had taught her much of this
land's bounty. She had once known which roots to eat and
thought she could remember the better part of that instruction.

She could have, if necessary, hunted with little more than her belt and her patience, as Duncan had taught her.

Indeed, 'twas reassuring to think of her stepfather, who was never troubled by whatever the world cast into his path. She let the memory of his sensible advice echo through her thoughts and found herself calmed.

'Twas then that she noticed the rags.

Jacqueline stared. The rapidly sinking sun sent golden rays through the leaves of the trees, gilding the tree trunks and illuminating thousands of dangling rags.

For a moment, Jacqueline thought they could not be real, for both Angus and the woman acted as if they did not even see them. She watched as the lengths of cloth rippled in the breeze. They twisted and turned, strange ornaments to the trees.

There were thousands of them, in all colors and all states of disintegration. Some were clean and new, as if just dyed and torn from a length of cloth. Some were woven in a pattern, most were plain. Some were so ancient that they looked as if they would crumble at the merest touch.

Jacqueline could not imagine why they were hung this way. Was this the site of some strange pagan rite? Were these tokens of sacrificed victims? Her imagination ran wild.

There was something odd about the place, perhaps the hue of the sunlight playing amidst rags, perhaps the unexpectedly vivid green of the moss below, perhaps the comparative silence. It seemed that the forest held its breath in this tranquil glade. She heard a trickle of water falling, though she could not see it anywhere.

Jacqueline saw naught, naught but rags and moss and distant shadows. She realized now that the glade dipped like a bowl, albeit one with rippled edges, thus fostering the illusion that the rags hung into the distance.

It seemed that not so much as a bird moved, and the echo of Angus's footfalls seemed unnaturally loud. The old woman's passage was silent. The sunlight twinkled abruptly gold and Jacqueline realized that the sun was on the very horizon. Soon 'twould be dark. What wickedness would befall her here on this night?

The old woman halted on the lip of a hollow, her fingers shaking as she relit the lantern that she carried, which had blown out as they walked. The flame leapt in the oil just as the sunlight died, making the woman look like a gnarled gnome. Jacqueline started, even as Angus set her down on the lip of a dark pool. He undid her bonds and she rubbed her hands together cautiously, restoring the feeling but not wanting to be so lively that he was tempted to truss her anew.

"Remember the wolves," he whispered, then gave her a hard look. Jacqueline blinked at him, fearing that she would be abandoned in the woods defenseless by his choice.

But Angus stepped away, leaving her alone with the woman.

What was this? He strode away, without a backward glance. He had not so much as touched her! Jacqueline frowned, then turned to stare at the woman.

The old woman smiled calmly. Her face was lined and her skin was tanned dark, her back was crooked and the hand braced upon her walking stick was gnarled. A twinkle lit her eye, the sight of it banishing Jacqueline's fear of any malicious intent.

"And how have you injured yourself?" she asked, her voice a thick burr of Gael.

"In fleeing adversity."

There was a sound that might have been a chuckle from Angus. Jacqueline could not guess how far he had retreated, for the happy burble of the spring disguised the sound of his footsteps. She twisted around and caught one last glimpse of his tabard before he disappeared as surely as if he had never been.

She shivered, certain she could yet feel the weight of his gaze upon her. What game did he play?

"So you come to the cloutie well for a cure?" the old woman demanded. "Or do you come to seek the legendary healing powers of Edana herself?"

Understanding dawned. Angus had brought her to one who could tend her ankle. It seemed he did indeed intend to keep her whole.

For whatever his dark plan might be.

"I know naught of cloutie wells or even of Edana, however great her fame," Jacqueline admitted. "And I did not arrive here of my own volition."

That nigh made the woman smile. "No doubt, no doubt," she murmured, then winked conspiratorially before continuing in a louder voice. "My fame is considerable, make no mistake of that. There were times when all came to hear the wisdom of Edana, to press trinkets into her hands that she might peer into the future days at their behest." She frowned, her gaze slipping over the well with evident sadness. "There were days."

The old woman lowered herself carefully to a rock, then sighed, her features looking suddenly careworn. She laid her walking stick aside and crackled her knuckles, the sound echoing loudly.

Jacqueline bit her lip, uncertain whether it would be best to change the subject or respect the old woman's silence. She had the sense that she might make an ally here and did not want to give insult.

Finally, though, her curiosity had the better of her. "What is a cloutie?"

Edana fixed her with a sharp gaze. "These are clouties hanging in the glen, as any child of a Celt should know."

Jacqueline dropped her gaze, instinctively disliking how

quickly her roots were discerned. Still she had to know. "Why?"

"They have been dipped in the healing waters of the well, then wrapped about the wounds of many. When wounds are healed, the once-wounded return to surrender their cloutie and give thanks to the lady of the well."

"And you are the lady of the well?"

The woman laughed, a dry cackle that made her wheeze. She coughed heartily, wiped a tear from one eye, then looked hard at Jacqueline. "You are not from hereabouts, are you, lass?"

"Ceinn-beithe. 'Tis near enough."

The woman watched her intently. "Yet occupied by foreigners 'tis said, a family from abroad who might know little of the tales of these lands."

"I know many of the tales, for Duncan has told me!"

"Ah, but every Celt child knows of the lady of the well, the guardian of the waters and the keeper of great secrets. I am not the lady of the well, lass, for she is greater and wiser and older than any of us mere mortals. I am naught but Edana, a simple healer long in her service." The woman smiled wryly. "But any Celt could tell you as much as that."

"My stepfather says we are all Celts, in some strain or another, for the Celts once held all the lands clear to Rome and left many a round belly in their wake."

Edana chuckled. "So, you are the stepchild of a wise man."

"And he is proudly a Celt."

She laughed then, a hearty ripple that tempted Jacqueline to join her despite her woes. Edana, though, offered naught even when her laughter, and then her smile, faded.

She but watched Jacqueline and waited.

" 'Tis true enough that I was not born here, just as 'tis true that I love this land more than my own. Indeed, I think of it as my own," Jacqueline argued with quiet resolve. "Will you deny me aid by accident of my birth alone?"

The woman watched her, eyes dark, expression unfathomable. "You know little of healers either, lass, for 'tis not our way to deny anyone the aid which they seek."

"Will you tend my ankle? 'Tis true that I have twisted it."

Edana cocked her head. "What will you surrender in exchange?"

Jacqueline opened her mouth then closed it quickly again. In truth, she had not expected to be asked such a question. "You may have my shoes, or my belt."

Edana shook her head. "Of what value are these fripperies to an old woman living alone in the woods?"

"You might simply like to have it."

"I might not."

"I have no jewelry . . ."

"I have no need of worldly gems."

They stared at each other, the lantern flickering between them. Jacqueline felt as if she guessed a riddle, one to which she was given few clues. "I do not know what you desire of me."

The woman leaned forward, her eyes sparkling. "What of a tale?"

"But any Celt will surely know all the best tales already and indeed would not desire to hear them told by a foreigner."

Edana laughed and shook a finger at Jacqueline. "You do know much of Celts, after all!"

"Aye, my stepfather is a great teller of tales. I could not tell a one of them as well as he, but I would try, if 'tis your pleasure."

Edana's expression turned mischievous. "What of *your* tale, lass? 'Tis no Celt tale you can sully, of that I am certain."

" 'Tis not much of a tale." And Jacqueline suspected 'twas likely to have a poor ending.

" 'Tis probably more of a tale than you imagine it to be, and one that only you can truly tell. No matter how trite 'tis, 'twill do, for binding an ankle is not such great labor even for an old woman."

"I thank you."

Edana abruptly looked up at Jacqueline, appearing as pert as a sparrow. "I would not show such haste in thanking me."

"Whyever not?"

"The ankle is not yet repaired. And we have yet to discover whether 'tis truly only aid for that ankle that you desire of me."

Jacqueline blinked that her objectives might be so readily guessed. "I do not know what you mean."

"Do you not, lass? Do you not?" Edana fired a shrewd glance at Jacqueline. "You find yourself in danger, lass, and before this is done, you will seek my aid."

Jacqueline held her tongue, as she was as yet uncertain she could trust this woman so evidently allied with Angus.

"You have a tale to tell, lass, I would wager my soul upon it, and doubtless you have a name as well." Before Jacqueline could reply, Edana cleared her throat and leaned toward the surface of the water. "Come, come. Let us beg the aid of the lady of the well in healing your wound. Of course, a Celt would need no such warning, but I would not suggest you mock either her powers or her presence."

❋

She was naught to him, Angus reminded himself. Naught but a tool to win his objective. It mattered little what she told Edana and what Edana told her, for 'twas not simple to find the old woman's dwelling in the woods and his captive would never be able to retrace their steps.

Still, he halted halfway back to Rodney and listened to the distant music of the maiden's voice. He could not hear her words, and he wondered what she confided in the old woman. She laughed and he glanced back for a fleeting moment before he turned and trudged onward.

Angus had no right to want to hear whatever she told Edana. Her woes were not his own. Nay, he had responsibilities on this night: a tired and wet horse to tend, wet garb of his own to tend, a meal of some kind to prepare.

The woman was no more than a burden to be borne until Airdfinnan was his own again. She did not have so much as a name, as far as he was concerned. He did not care where she had been going or why, whom she was intended to wed or what she thought of that man. He knew he should be relieved to abandon her to Edana, if only to avoid the horror in her eyes each time she looked upon his ravaged face.

Edana would not let her escape. Indeed, 'twas a relief to find one soul he could trust.

But even after reminding himself forcibly of all of these things, Angus was still cursedly curious about his captive.

He obviously had need of sleep.

❄

Edana's twisted fingers worked with surprising grace once she had dipped a length of cloth into the well. The lantern sputtered from its perch on a moss-carpeted rock, and Jacqueline felt the watchful eyes of the forest hovering beyond the halo of yellow light.

She sat on a rock herself, Edana up to her knees in the dark bubbling well that sang softly to itself. She wrapped Jacqueline's ankle firmly but gently in the wet rag, muttering words that the younger woman could not discern.

Were they spells? Jacqueline wondered, nearly recoiling in distaste of pagan witchery. But then she reasoned that they were probably harmless spells and could not hurt one so resolute in her faith as she. Indeed, the cool water felt good against her swollen ankle.

She heaved a sigh of relief, closed her eyes, and her thoughts drifted to Angus. She recalled what he had said—or, more accurately, what his companion had said to him and of him—and made more sense of it now that he was not so close at hand.

Angus was a knight, though 'twas clear his origins were local. And he had been to the Holy Land, he had taken the cross and battled the infidel for Christ. She felt an odd kinship with him for all of that, a unity of faith that was unexpected.

He had been imprisoned by those Saracen infidels, a history that no doubt was responsible for his scars and whatever had happened to his eye. She almost smiled to herself at his companion's accusation that he had been kicked once too many times in the head by a pagan foe.

Though Jacqueline did not find Angus slow of wit. She had deceived him, 'twas true, but she knew that she had only briefly taken advantage of his gallantry. She shivered, uncertain whether he would be so gallant again, now that she had vexed him so thoroughly.

She glanced uncertainly about but caught no glimpse of him in the surrounding shadows. He lingered nearby, of that she had no doubt. She could not see him, though, and wondered whether he was within earshot or not.

Perhaps he had returned to tend the steeds with his companion. She strained her ears but heard naught beyond a distant nicker.

Who was this woman and what bond was between the two? Might Edana aid her once she had heard the truth? The old woman certainly seemed inclined to be friendly.

Her heart began to pound. If Angus lingered nearby, she dared not consider his potential retaliation for her seeking escape again. But if he had returned to the steeds, this might be her sole chance. Jacqueline had no choice but to try to change her fate. She realized belatedly that the old woman was watching her with a hooded gaze.

"You are thinking of a man," Edana accused.

"Aye, I was," Jacqueline admitted.

Edana smiled a secretive smile. "A *handsome* man."

It had not been the precise direction of her thoughts, but Jacqueline did not want to alienate her potential confidante. She decided that despite the patch over his eye and the harshness of his expression, Angus was indeed a handsome man.

"Handsome as the devil himself," she admitted. "How did you guess?"

Edana smiled. "Bonny lasses only notice handsome lads."

"Perhaps that is true of Celts," Jacqueline retorted, well and tired of people assuming they understood her on the basis of her looks alone. "But I prefer to assess a person by his or her character."

"Indeed?"

"Indeed. The man of whom I was thinking would not be called handsome by many. He is scarred from battle, and clearly bitter. It shows in his face that he has seen much ill in his days."

Edana's gaze was considering. She wrung out a rag with care and placed a few leaves upon it. "Yet you call him handsome," the old woman mused. "As the devil, even. Do you not mean that his heart is filled with evil?"

Jacqueline thought of this for a moment, soothed by the ministrations of the older woman and the silence of the night. "I am not certain. He is fierce in anger, of that there can be no doubt," she admitted with a frown. "He has not hurt me, though he had the chance. Indeed, he brought me here to be tended. And he has not forced himself upon me, though I was certain he would."

"Perhaps he but waits his chance."

"Aye, undoubtedly he does." Jacqueline held her breath, doubting she could be more blunt than that.

Edana glanced up with mischief glinting in her eyes. "Or perhaps he did not find you fetching, lass."

Jacqueline smiled, unable to be insulted when the old woman's expression was so impish. Edana was teasing her, as an affectionate aunt might. "Perhaps not."

" 'Twould not be the first time a man's taste changed to women with skin of darker hue, with black eyes and thick lashes, adorned with lush perfumes and adept at amorous games. They are of another breed, those women of the East, and men are oft enchanted by their charms. If your handsome man has been to Outremer, he might well find you naught but a pale and uninteresting virgin."

Though the assessment was a reasonable one, it rankled unexpectedly. Jacqueline reminded herself that 'twas far preferable to have Angus consider her unappealing than for him to feel compelled to sample her. Indeed, it might be a sign that someone watched over her fate, that someone ensured that her chastity was maintained so that her pledges could be made.

But then she remembered the heat of his stolen kiss, the press of his erection against her buttocks. He had been attracted to her, but he had denied his desire.

Because the presence of his companion deterred him?

"I fear him," she whispered.

The old woman stilled at that confession and looked up. The mischief faded from her eyes as their gazes held. "As do I, lass," she admitted softly. "As do I."

Jacqueline's heart sank. They could not both be prey to the knight's whim. "But you know him!"

"I *knew* him." Edana tied the end of the bandage around Jacqueline's ankle with efficiency. " 'Twas a long time ago."

"But how? But when?"

" 'Tis not my tale to tell." Edana pushed to her feet and spoke brusquely. "Come along, lass. 'Tis too chill for an old woman's bones to linger here. I will have your tale by the fire."

Edana, having stood in the healing waters of the spring, moved with unexpected agility, her cane swinging in her grip. More important, the lantern was in her other hand, and the light was fading into the distance with great speed.

Jacqueline leapt to her feet, not wanting to be left alone amid the eerie clouties. She frowned and tested her weight upon her ankle twice, but it seemed more likely to bear her weight than before. She glanced back at the bubbling well and wondered.

But she was not one to credit pagan magic, not she.

No doubt the flesh was numb from the chill of the water. Aye, that was it. Jacqueline considered the forest for a long moment, even as a wolf howled in the distance.

She could flee again.

But Edana halted and glanced back, as if she had heard the younger woman's thoughts. "He will have my head if you do not return with me," she said darkly, and Jacqueline had no doubt 'twas true. She could not repay the woman's kindness with such a selfish gesture.

And perhaps, together, they might escape whatever Angus had planned. At least, they might bar the door against him this night. 'Twas encouraging not to face such adversity alone. She picked up her skirts and darted after Edana.

Chapter Five

DANA FELT A SYMPATHY FOR JACQUELINE'S PLIGHT, for she had no better idea what this changed Angus might do than the lass did. She was more than agreeable to the plea that they bar the door against the men, a deed that seemed to amuse Angus more than it troubled him. The old woman knew that she was not alone in understanding that it could be forced, nor evidently was she alone in thinking it harmless to reassure the maiden.

This she found most interesting.

"We could escape through the back," Jacqueline whispered. "The wood is aged there, and none would know the truth of it in the darkness."

Edana snorted. "You are his prize, lass, and no man lets a prize escape so readily as that. No doubt they check the perimeter moment by moment."

Jacqueline heaved a sigh of frustration. "I imagine you speak aright. The man will be cursedly vigilant now."

Edana chuckled despite herself. "Aye, he was oft known to be strong of will."

"You know his tale, though, and you could share it with me."

"I know but part of his tale, lass, and 'tis not my tale to share."

"He will never tell me of it."

"Perhaps not."

"Will you?"

Edana shrugged.

Impatience lit Jacqueline's features. "What harm is there in sharing a tale? You are the most reticent lot I have ever known!" she declared, and Edana could not help but smile. The maid took her expression as encouragement. "Will you answer me one thing, if naught else?"

"Perhaps one thing," the old woman agreed slowly.

"How has he changed? What was Angus like before?"

Edana dropped her gaze to the pot, stirring in silence. Indeed, she had to sift through her thoughts and impressions to find the kernel of his change.

"In the years since I have seen him, he has come to know wickedness," she finally said, her voice low. "And, as wickedness so often does, it has left its stain upon him."

A shiver slid visibly through the younger woman, and Edana was certain her curiosity was sated.

Jacqueline sat on the floor of the hut, clad in no more than her chemise as her kirtle dried. She watched Edana with bright eyes pick at this herb and another. "What are you doing?"

"Are you always so intent to know what others do not tell you?"

The maiden laughed lightly, the sparkle in her eyes most fetching. "Aye. Curiosity is said to be my curse."

Edana snorted. "I'll make something to fill your belly. Are you not hungered?"

"Aye!"

Edana poured the heated water over the lot, sniffing as the herbs released their potency. She stirred, then added a measure of honey, before handing it to Jacqueline. "Too sweet?"

"Nay, 'tis perfect."

"Good, then drink it down."

Jacqueline sipped, her gaze watchful. The men's voices carried to them intermittently, though no one came to the door. Edana settled onto her stool and braced her hands atop her cane.

"And? What do you know of him?" Jacqueline asked pertly.

"Naught that is yours to hear. At least not afore you share your own tale." Edana shook a finger at the lass. "You have a debt to pay, need I remind you?"

Jacqueline smiled. "Aye, I know it well. This morn, I was en route to a convent . . ."

There was marvel in her tone at the change of her situation. Edana heard much that was said and just as much unsaid, and was as intrigued by the omissions as the facts included. The maiden had not been in her vision, though 'twas clear she played a key role in whatever Angus had begun.

This Jacqueline was young and sweet and innocent of much of the world, yet she saw much more than even she knew she did. She had a sharp tongue on occasion, and her commentary could make an old woman smile—though Edana imagined that those at the convent she was destined to join would not be so amused by such cheek.

'Twas true that she was beauteous, but her gaze was sharp with intellect. Edana came quickly to see the wits first and the beauty second. She wondered how many others did the same.

As she recounted the tale of her abduction, Jacqueline's eyelids drooped. She valiantly forced them open time and again, clearly not one to surrender without a fight. Edana knew 'twould not be long before she guessed the truth.

When her head nodded once more, and she jerked upright

yet again, Jacqueline hefted the cup she had emptied in Edana's direction. " 'Twas a potion, was it not?"

Edana smiled. "Aye."

"You tricked me!"

"Nay. Sleep is the best aid for a wound." She watched the maiden's eyes close once again. Each time they were slower to open, Jacqueline's responses dulling with the power of the brew. "Especially for one devoid of stalwart Celt blood."

Jacqueline's eyes snapped open, though she smiled when she spoke with mock indignation. "The blood of my forebears is stalwart! My mother is wrought of steel and silk, so my stepfather oft says—"

A rap at the door stopped her tirade and she hiccuped sleepily even as her eyes widened. Edana opened the door to find Angus there, waiting expectantly though he could have forced his way within.

"She cannot be trusted," he said simply. "I will sleep within, while Rodney sleeps without."

"She is but a mere maiden," Edana retorted.

"And crafty despite all of that." He fixed a gaze upon Jacqueline, who visibly quaked. Indeed, she tried to rise, as if she would flee him, but her body betrayed her and she slumped against the wall of the hut.

"What have you done to so frighten her?" Edana demanded.

Angus scowled. "She had but to look upon me."

The older woman felt her eyes narrow as she considered him and Jacqueline's statement that he was a handsome man. She suspected that he, not atypical of a man, had named the cause of her distress wrongly and even—yet more typical of a man—might not realize what he had done to so upset Jacqueline.

"She has taken a sleeping draught and will not awaken

again this night. There is no need for you to remain," Edana hissed, but Angus was not persuaded.

"Already she has tricked me once. 'Twill not happen again, not when the stakes are so high." He crossed the room and squatted down beside her. "Come, my beauty, on this night we slumber together."

Jacqueline could not have been more distraught. She cried out, tried to flee, but only crumpled in her fear of him.

And 'twas Edana's own fault that the lass was trapped, for 'twas her potion that took away Jacqueline's ability to flee. The old woman stepped forward to intervene, but the unexpected tenderness in Angus's expression halted her.

Indeed, he lifted the unconscious Jacqueline gently and wrapped her within his cloak, then lay her upon the pallet Edana had offered. He drew his blade and laid it beside the maiden, then sat so that the blade was between them and folded his arms across his chest. He fixed Edana with a challenging stare.

This was the boy she remembered!

"You care for her welfare," she charged softly, much reassured.

"Her welfare is critical to winning my objective," he said crisply. "She means no more to me than that."

She would have wagered that 'twas a lie, but Angus gave her no chance to question him. His eye gleamed as he steadily met the gaze of the older woman. "Make no mistake, Edana. I have learned that a man must hold fast to his goals if he means to succeed."

"What is your goal?"

He did not answer her, but lay down beside Jacqueline, still fully garbed. "I would ask you to remain within the hut this night," he said quietly. "There should be a witness that I have done her no injury."

"She fears you."

"All women fear me." There was bitterness in his words, though she had no chance to ask another question. Angus closed his eye, effectively ending their discourse, and she knew he would ignore any word she uttered.

But Edana watched the pair for a long time, long after the breath fell slowly from them both. Indeed, the maiden might need some understanding of this knight after all. He had changed, but not so much as the old woman had first feared.

✸

Jacqueline awakened slowly, her thoughts uncommonly clouded and her tongue thick. She winced at the pounding behind her temples, then her eyes flew open in sudden recollection of Edana's brew. Had the old woman deceived her, so that Angus might have his will when she was powerless to fight?

Fearful of what she might find, she ran her hands down her body. Her chemise was perfectly dry and perfectly in place. There was naught damp between her thighs.

The roof of the hut was painted with the pearly light of the dawn and echoed with the gentle patter of rain. Jacqueline was warmer than she had expected to be, though that might have been a lingering effect of the herbs.

A man snored, but at a distance, and she guessed that Rodney slept outside with the steeds. Edana snored more softly and at closer range. She turned to seek out the older woman and found her vision completely blocked.

Aye, Jacqueline herself lay against the back wall of the hut, a certain knight lying full length beside her. He was a considerable obstacle, responsible for a good part of the heat she felt.

He had not forced himself upon her. She thought "not yet" again, then wondered whether he even had any intent to take her. What *did* he desire? What kind of man was he? She swallowed and studied him carefully through her lashes, seeking answers in his features.

His patched eye was the one closest to her, so she could not discern whether he was awake or not. He lay on his back, so still that she was not entirely certain that he even breathed. His hair fell back in dark waves from his tanned face, and even in profile, he looked uncompromising and harsh.

Aye, his lips were set in a resolute line even now. He wore his tabard and chausses and boots, the toes of those black leather boots far beyond her own toes. His belt was fastened loosely about his waist. His hands were folded together on his chest, like a man laid out for a funeral. His scabbard lay on the floor beyond him, evidently empty.

She looked for his sword and found it between them, the hilt at his hip, the tip of the weighty blade between their shoulders. The steel gleamed coldly upon cloth, and Jacqueline realized belatedly that she was also warm because the knight had cast his red cloak over her. She could smell his flesh in the wool hood nestled around her neck, the unexpected familiarity making her yet warmer again.

She was tucked within the circle of the cloak, enfolded within it with his weight and his blade securing the ends. 'Twas as if he meant to secure her from assault, even while he slept, and Jacqueline wondered at the import of this.

Did he only mean to save her for himself?

Or did he not mean to rape her at all?

She stared at the blade between them, recalling too well a tale of Duncan's in which a man of honor laid his blade between himself and a chaste maiden to ensure her purity was whole in the morn. In the tale, 'twas a signal of the man's chivalrous intent, and Jacqueline, faced with this sign, could find no other explanation for it.

She did not intend to wait until Angus awakened to ask

him the truth of it. She eased away from him until her back collided with the wall. He made no sign of awareness, though she heartily disliked that she could not see his good eye. Slowly, holding her breath, she began to sit up, certain he would hear the clamor of her heart, and ease out of the cocoon of wool.

He did not move.

Jacqueline sat up all the way, carefully settling the cloak between them so that its weight did not fall upon him and awaken him. 'Twas wrought of good heavy cloth, and, indeed, she shivered slightly at the chill in the morning air when she was without it. Protected by the folds of the cloak, she lifted her chemise and peeked beneath herself.

No blood.

Edana muttered to herself, then snored once more. Still Angus did not move. Jacqueline could see all of his face now, but his other eye was closed. Oddly, he no longer gave her the impression of a cadaver. Nay, Jacqueline had the sense of his being a man very much alive, a dangerous and unpredictable man, a warrior who had learned the merit of feigning what he did not feel. She did not doubt that 'twas useful to be so still as this, particularly when hunted by a bloodthirsty foe.

One who might well claim an eye. She watched him suspiciously for a long time, certain he must move eventually and betray that he was indeed awake.

But he did not and she dared to be encouraged. Aye, the longer she hesitated, the more likely 'twas that he would awaken.

Jacqueline took a steadying breath, then pulled her knees beneath her slowly and silently. She braced a hand upon the floor behind her and coiled to spring over his legs.

"I would not attempt that, in your place," Angus murmured, his words low and surprisingly lazy.

Jacqueline gasped.

Now his gaze was fixed upon her, though still he had not moved. His eye was the deepest hue of brown that ever she had seen. It was so dark as to be wrought of shadows and secrets. She felt pinned in place, forced by his gaze and his will alone to be still.

But Jacqueline would allow no man such easy power over her.

She lifted her chin bravely. "I have to piss."

"Then use the bucket at your feet or wait." He made no move to rise and accompany her, nor indeed to stop her.

But one glance at the dirty bucket was enough. "I will wait."

His lips quirked so briefly that she might have missed his response had she not been watching him so closely. "I suspected as much."

Jacqueline lay back down with a thump, careless of whatever noise she might make now. She pulled his cloak over herself, painfully aware of the minute distance between them. "I am not lying," she said irritably.

He said naught, which implied much.

She turned to look at his profile, irked beyond belief with his certainty that she meant to deceive him and yet more annoyed by the possibility that she was so easily read as that. "You might at least look at me when I am speaking to you."

He rolled to his side, propping himself on one elbow to regard her. The span of his shoulders cast Jacqueline in shadow; the glint in his eye was suddenly far too close. There was naught but the width of that sword between them, and she realized somewhat too late the error of her request.

He smiled at her flush, undoubtedly guessing the reason for it.

"I did not expect you to comply," she snapped.

He arched his brow. " 'Tis the task of every honorable knight to cede to the whim of a lady."

"What if I were naught but a milking maid?"

"You are not."

"You cannot know for certain."

"Milking maids do not ride fine palfreys, much less have an escort of guards."

"Oh." Jacqueline supposed not. She eyed him warily, distrusting how he regarded her.

That smile quirked the corner of his mouth again, making him look unpredictable and wickedly attractive. Jacqueline's heart skipped a beat.

"Nor are milking maids oft so innocent of the men as you would seem to be." His words were low, little more than a rumble in his chest that would not carry far.

It seemed strangely intimate to talk with a man like this, both exciting and frightening. Jacqueline imagined that wedded folk talked abed in such tones, or lovers, and that after they had shared intimacies she had not shared with Angus.

She felt her cheeks heat and cursed herself for such bold speculation. The memory of his kiss rose in her thoughts at this most unwelcome moment, as did the recollection of the tingle that had danced beneath her flesh. She was well aware of Angus's intent gaze upon her and did not doubt that he could read her every wretched thought.

That made her flush deepen, much to her own mortification. She huddled beneath the cloak, took encouragement from the sword's presence, and tried to seem confident of his intent. Edana was but two steps away, and the knowledge that she was not entirely alone with this knight lent boldness to her manner.

She could scream and Edana would aid her.

"Where were you going, Mhairi?"

"Jacqueline. My name is *Jacqueline*. I told you as much already."

"So you did."

"Then why do you not address me as Jacqueline?"

"Because obviously I choose not to do so."

Jacqueline flushed at his implication. "I am not a liar, if that is your import! If you must address me, then at least do me the courtesy of using my own name." She froze then, afraid he would not take well to her criticism.

He studied her silently, then inclined his head slightly in agreement or perhaps merely concession. She did not doubt that his conviction remained unchanged.

He did not repeat his question. The silence pressed upon Jacqueline as surely as his will and she found herself answering, though she had had no intent of doing so.

"I was going to the convent. I *am* going to a convent. To become a novitiate."

"You?" Surprise raised his brow for a heartbeat and Jacqueline felt a fleeting sense of victory before his next words made her angry. "Surely such a woman as you would not become a nun?"

'Twas too familiar a charge for Jacqueline to hold her tongue. "Why? Becuase I am fair of face? What has that to do with the strength of the faith that lights my heart?"

"Naught." His gaze darkened, though she would not have believed it possible just moments past. "Though it might have much to do with the price that could be had for your hand. Not many a father would surrender such a possible reward, even to serve the eternal good of the church."

He said this last phrase with a certain harshness that Jacqueline did not fail to note. She could make no sense of that, and, indeed, she was more interested in defending the integrity of her mother's spouse.

"Duncan is my stepfather. He supported my desire in this."

"Indeed?"

"Indeed. 'Twas my mother who opposed me." Jacqueline closed her mouth hard at this confession, for she had never intended to admit as much. She rolled to her back and stared at the roof.

Angus watched her carefully, and Jacqueline felt that cursed flush flooding her cheeks beneath his scrutiny. "Why?" he asked finally, the word as smooth as velvet.

"It matters naught."

"I think it does."

"I think 'tis not your affair to know."

He chuckled then, a sound so unexpected that she glanced his way. Again, he had a devilish look about him, one that made her heart race. "I thought you feared me."

"I fear naught," Jacqueline declared boldly, though the words caught in her throat.

"Liar." He eased ever so slightly closer and Jacqueline swallowed carefully. She could not look away from him, even as he bent over her, his eye gleaming. "Why did you flee?"

Jacqueline could barely catch her breath. "Any woman of sense would flee a man who captured her against her will."

"Not without regard for her injuries. 'Twas fear of greater injury that made you risk hurting your ankle more."

Jacqueline tried desperately to think of an excuse. "Your companion would surely assert that women have no sense and that you have no knowledge of women."

"Aye, he would." Angus seemed untroubled by this, though his gaze turned suddenly so piercing that Jacqueline wanted to squirm. "But he would be wrong."

"You know naught of me!"

"I know that you had the wits to deceive me." He leaned yet closer. "And I know that you fear me, perhaps more than circumstance demands." Jacqueline felt her breath catch but could not tear her gaze away from him. "Is it the look of me that so terrifies you?"

That question surprised her. She watched him, not wanting to insult him or, worse, anger him, yet unable to shake the sense that he truly wanted to know.

And that he did not underestimate the marring effect of the scar upon his cheek. Indeed, she thought he granted it too much import.

She stared and knew she had not lied when she called him handsome. There was something compelling about him, perhaps the directness of his glance and his determination, that made a woman disregard the patch upon his eye.

"Nay," she admitted, without intending to do so.

"Indeed," he breathed, and reached one fingertip to touch her chin. His fingers were warm and she could not draw a breath.

Jacqueline hastily looked away, cursing her own stupidity. He had nigh granted her the perfect excuse to recoil from him, but she had been too witless to take it.

Indeed, she had *encouraged* him!

She groaned inwardly when he touched her chin with a fingertip, then compelled her to look into his face once more. His touch was tender, his expression fierce.

"What befell you that you would join a convent?"

Jacqueline felt her lips tighten in frustration. "I have a vocation," she insisted.

He shook his head, smiling slightly again. " 'Tis not fitting for one who would become a novitiate to lie so much as you do."

"I do not lie!"

Angus shook his head. "Aye, you do."

She folded her arms across her chest and glared at him. "I tell you no lie. I have a calling to serve Christ, to use my gifts to bring the love of God into the lives of others. I want naught more in this life than to serve the Lord and serve His will I shall. Surely you can understand what 'tis to yearn for something beyond all other desires?"

He was listening to her, much to Jacqueline's astonishment. She was not accustomed to men—other than her step-father—listening to what she said.

"Why would I understand?"

"Because you departed on crusade, because you put your faith before all else."

He seemed to find that amusing, though Jacqueline could not guess why. "Did I?"

He studied her, his gaze flicking over her features, and she feared again that she said too much.

But he only watched her and she dared to continue. "I was en route to Inveresbeinn yesterday and should have been there by this very evening had you not intervened."

There! The accusation was made.

But if she had expected Angus to be contrite, she was due for a disappointment. He chuckled and lay back once more, granting her a sidelong glance that made her flesh warm. "I owe you an apology," he murmured. He had that predatory look about him again, and though she did not trust him by any means, still she was curious as to what he might say.

And she was encouraged that he did not seem to take offense when she spoke her thoughts.

"For delaying my devotion?" she asked.

He shook his head, clearly more bemused than angered by her. "Nay. I apologize for stealing a kiss from you. I did not guess 'twould be so horrific that 'twould make you flee."

Jacqueline swallowed. " 'Twas not so terrible a kiss as that," she muttered, blushing when he smiled slowly.

"Was it not?"

Jacqueline wished the earth might swallow her whole. She

tried to turn away, but his fingertip was still upon her face and he gently coaxed her to look his way.

And once she met his gaze, she was snared anew.

Angus's fingers moved slowly over her chin, making her breath catch as shivers launched over her flesh. 'Twas not an unpleasant sensation, but still she trembled slightly.

"I take naught that is not mine to take," Angus said with all the vigor of a man making a pledge. "Remember this. If you desire that I take something from you, you will have to offer it. And if you desire something of me, you will have to ask for it."

"Then grant me my freedom."

He chuckled then, the edge of his thumb sliding briefly over her lips in a disconcertingly intimate gesture. "Nay, not that, my beauty. Not that. Your freedom will be bought when the ransom I demand is paid."

Jacqueline gritted her teeth and shook her head. "What will you demand?"

His eye narrowed, though there was no censure in his tone. "You are a most curious woman, Mhairi. 'Tis an unlikely trait in a novitiate."

Jacqueline exhaled in exasperation. "Already I have told you that I am not Mhairi! Do not call me by the name of a dead woman. 'Tis a portent of bad fortune."

"While your fortune runs so well in this moment?"

If she had not known better, she might have thought he was teasing her. His expression was serious, though that eye almost twinkled, in much the same fashion as Duncan's did when he teased. She stared at him, trying to discern the truth, and his expression changed as he returned her glance.

Aye, he sobered in truth. A new heat of awareness rose between them. Jacqueline licked her lips, though she did not recall any decision to do so.

Angus's gaze dropped to her mouth and he leaned ever

closer. "Many a man might perceive that as an invitation," he whispered, his voice sending a shiver down her spine.

"Aye." The word fell breathless from her.

Angus paused, his lips not the width of a hand from her own. "Is it?"

She felt the edge of the steel blade forced against her arm by his move, the thickness of the wool keeping its chill and its bite from her flesh. Its presence reminded her that he was a knight. No less, he was a knight who asserted that she was worth more to him whole.

He had not hurt her—all harm had been done by herself in her panic to escape. He had not bound her tightly or bruised her. He had not terrorized her, beyond the terror that his gender and her circumstance awakened in her heart. He had not raped her.

He had chased her through the woods when he might have let her flee, perhaps to escape, perhaps to be beset by wolves. He had brought her to this healer to be tended. Angus's actions confirmed that he intended to keep her unscathed.

Reynaud, in comparison, had insisted only upon taking whatsoever he desired.

Was Angus a knight who placed as much value in his vows as Reynaud had not? 'Twas a tempting, and dangerously romantic, possibility. He certainly had been indulgent of her maidenly modesty, even at the cost of looking foolish himself.

And he had kissed her. Once. Gently. With that, he had awakened an unfamiliar yearning within her. Jacqueline did not doubt he knew how to sate it.

Now he awaited her answer, as watchful as any predator on the hunt. Her mouth went dry. Jacqueline found herself lost in the depths of his gaze, caught by the heat she saw there. He desired that kiss as much as she did. The very idea emboldened her as naught else might have done.

Because he awaited her agreement. She held the power to beckon him closer or turn him away; she, an unarmed maiden, could spurn a man so much larger and stronger than herself, and that with a single word. If she said nay, Angus would roll away.

For the first time since their paths had crossed, she felt powerful and in command of her fate.

'Twas all she needed to make her choice. She wanted to know whether her response to his first kiss had been wrought of no more than surprise or fear.

She was most curious.

"Aye," Jacqueline whispered, her voice oddly hoarse. She had not a moment to reconsider before Angus's lips closed over hers.

Angus meant only to frighten her.

'Twas easier when she was frightened, even when she fainted, for then she was naught but a burden that could win back his prize. 'Twas simpler to think of her as booty he would trade for his true desire.

But when she spoke, when she smiled, he could not deny that this booty had a name, a life, a heart. She was a woman then, a desirable woman even, one whose very manner and expectations reminded him too clearly of the innocent optimism he himself had lost. Sleep had done naught to bolster his resistance to her; indeed, his desire to know more of her had seemed redoubled this morn. And when she confided in him, 'twas enough to make him want to see her free once more, whatever the loss to himself.

'Twas infinitely simpler to have his hostage fearful and silent.

Angus knew he should not touch her. He had no intent to taint her. Airdfinnan was all he desired, though this woman aroused desires long forgotten. And what man would not desire her, with her lush curves and tempting lips, her clear green gaze and quick wit?

With her refusal to fear what he had become.

She was a reminder that he was yet a man, despite his scars. He had been without this particular luxury for far too long. But Angus preferred women well familiar with love's games. Fear killed his ardor, it always had, and he had teased her only to ensure that his desire died.

Frightening her, then, offered two benefits.

Her lips were softer than the fur beneath a hare's chin, she tasted sweeter than the most exotic fruit. Angus was reminded of the honey of the bees his mother had once kept at Airdfinnan, honey of deep golden hue—precisely like this maiden's hair, by curious coincidence—sweet yet complex. That honey was laden with mingled hints of the unexpected hint of lavender and heather and clover, the flowers upon which those bees had fed.

She gasped and opened her mouth, inviting him onward as a flower invites a bee to explore its secrets. Angus deepened his kiss, tasting her more deeply without intending to do any such thing. He found himself easing his weight over her, sheltering her beneath him, savoring her soft heat.

His hand found the perfection of her breast, the merest touch of his fingertips making the nipple bead beneath his hand. His fingers curved around her fullness, seemingly of their own volition. He caressed her, heard her gasp, felt her arch against him.

And his desire raged. Zounds, but he *wanted* her.

Dimly he was aware that the door to the hut opened, for a cool draft touched him, but her tongue touched his tentatively and he forgot all else. Her hand, so small, so fragile, so feminine, fell upon his shoulder, her very uncertainty making him want to shield her from all the ills this world might offer.

'Twas all new to her, he knew it well, and a part of him savored that he not only had the chance to introduce her to pleasure but that he did so to her evident delight.

Indeed, the darkness that rode with Angus every day drew slightly aside. She had inadvertently shared with him a moment of awakening, of innocence, of the discovery of a new wonder. That she should trust him with something both so great and so little as a first kiss let a ray of unexpected sunshine touch his hardened heart.

A memory of his mother's garden appeared suddenly in his mind, that familiar space flooded with sunlight, humming with bees, adorned in the raiment of a thousand different flowers, each bobbing in the summer breeze. He heard the sparkle of his mother's laughter once more, a sound he had thought forgotten for all time.

He wanted more, he wanted all she had to grant. He slanted his mouth across the maiden's lips and hungrily deepened his kiss.

"So this is to be the way of it?" Rodney demanded. "I am to sleep in the rain with the steeds, cold and hungry, while you take your pleasure abed with the wench? Was *that* a part of your scheme? If so, I knew naught of it!"

At the sound of his companion's voice, the darkness returned, as surely as a prison door slamming, the key turning in the lock to abandon him to the terrors of captivity. Angus was immediately reminded of all he had lost, of all that had been stolen from him, of all the dues he had been compelled to pay.

He tore his lips from his captive's, hardened himself against the way her eyes widened in awe. Her lips were ripe and ruddy, bruised from his touch; she looked disheveled and willing.

But she was a madness in his blood, this one. She distracted him from his purpose, and he could suffer naught that might lead to failure. Rodney's persistent tirades against the charms of women echoed through his thoughts, and Angus fortified his will against this one. He had meant to frighten her, after all, though she had readily persuaded him to forget that detail.

In compense for his failure, he acted quickly. He let a cold smile curve his lips and tightened his fingers over her breast.

"Forgive me, Rodney," he said, his gaze fixed upon her, watching as dismay lit those fine eyes. " 'Twould have been rude not to partake of the feast the lady offered."

She gasped in horror, but Angus bent and kissed her hard, sliding his tongue between her lips with an aggression that startled them both.

Then he rolled away and stood, apparently indifferent, though he was not. He told himself that her disgust should please him as he got to his feet, then slid his blade into its scabbard without another glance to his captive. Angus ignored both the weight of the woman's gaze upon him and the censure in Edana's expression.

Yet his gut curled with guilt that he had wrought naught but ill when he sought to right a wrong. This innocent maiden wanted only to pledge herself to the faith, and he was knave enough that he could not be kept from tainting her with his touch. A prolonged captivity surely would keep her from her only goal.

Angus knew, whatever the wrongs committed against him, he had no right to steal his captive's dream. But if he released her, he would be left with naught once again and would become a hunted brigand as well.

Nay, there was but one solution. In that moment, he dismissed his original intent to let the woman's father fret for a week before demanding his due. Rodney would ride out this very day. This matter had to be resolved and soon, lest it not come to success after all. He would have Airdfinnan and be rid of his captive before he was fool enough to err again.

"You have changed much," Edana whispered as he passed her side. Her tight lips revealed her view of that change.

Angus was sufficiently angered with himself to need no criticism from another. He paused, staring down long enough that she might see the fury that burned coldly within him.

Edana flinched and drew back.

But 'twas better if they thought him a cold-hearted knave, if the maiden feared him and stayed from his path. That way there was less chance that he might lose the only advantage he had in this endeavor.

"Aye," Angus murmured with rare heat, "that I have, and woe to any so foolish as to stand in my path."

With that he marched out into the gentle rain of the morning, haunted by the lingering sweetness of the maiden's kiss.

Chapter Six

JACQUELINE WAS MORTIFIED. NOT ONLY HAD SHE IN-vited Angus to kiss her, but she had enjoyed his touch.

At first. That parting kiss, though, had stolen away both her surprise and pleasure. Aye, he revealed then what he thought of her, and she recalled all her mother's admonitions to her half-sister Alienor on the comport of whores.

Her cheeks burned with shame and she could not meet Edana's gaze. She sat up and pushed her hair from her brow, unwilling to remain abed where he had touched her thus.

Edana's stare was too unswerving to grant Jacqueline any faith that her discomfort was truly hidden. Her braid had loosened during the night and she made to unfurl the tangle, hiding her face beneath its golden curtain. Her fingers shook as she unknotted the lace, the task taking longer than ever it did. Even behind her hair, she knew that Edana watched her, unblinking, like her mother's prized peregrine.

A heavy silence pushed at Jacqueline's ears, until she thought she could bear it no longer without screaming. Suddenly Edana shoved to her feet, her cane tapping as she crossed the hut. To Jacqueline's relief, the old woman did not come to her or speak to her.

Not immediately. Once the fire was lit in the small brazier

and a dented pot of water was set to heat, Edana rummaged through a small chest, then offered something. Jacqueline pretended not to see the gesture, an easy deed since she had bent her head so that her tangled hair spilled forward.

" 'Tis a comb, lass. Take it," Edana said impatiently.

'Twould have been rude to spurn a well-intentioned offering. The comb was missing a few teeth but was not an unwelcome aid. Jacqueline tugged the comb through her hair with savage gestures, not caring how it hurt. Indeed, she deserved whatever injury was inflicted as penance for being such a fool.

Edana watched her. "Why did you ask him to kiss you?"

"You were awake!"

The older woman almost smiled at Jacqueline's dismay. "I seldom truly sleep, lass. And indeed, 'tis why he—" She halted and shook her head.

"Why he did what? And who do you mean?"

Edana smiled. "You did ask him to kiss you, did you not?"

"Aye." Jacqueline fairly growled the admission. "Though I know now the magnitude of my error."

"How so?"

"He is no man of honor."

"Because he took what you offered?"

"Because he forced more upon me!"

Edana clicked her tongue and poked at the pot with her walking stick. "Where is it writ, lass, that a kiss between a man and a woman is under the jurisdiction of one or the other? Hmmm? A kiss is wondrous yet magical all the same. It takes from both participants and makes something new of itself. 'Tis not uncommon to hear that a kiss became a force of its own."

"The only force was in that second kiss," Jacqueline insisted. "For 'twas inflicted upon me."

"And so different from the first, was it not?"

Jacqueline looked up, but Edana did not meet her gaze.

"Almost," the old woman mused, her voice so low that Jacqueline had to strain to hear the words, "as if 'twas given by another man. A second man within the skin of the first." She flicked a glance across the space.

Angus had listened to her, and teased her, much as her step-father would have done. But the second kiss was indeed so different that it might have been rendered by a different man.

A man not unlike the many suitors who had courted her. Or like Reynaud.

But the Angus to whom she had granted that kiss willingly had been another matter indeed.

And that made Jacqueline wonder. "You knew him before. You said he had changed."

"Aye." The old woman nodded, as if reluctant to say much further. "And aye again, I must admit."

"How did he change?"

"He would not have me speak of him."

"He need not know you did."

Edana raised her brows.

" 'Tis true!" Jacqueline protested. "I will not tell him of it if you speak to me of him. How has he changed?"

"How has he *not* changed?" Edana finally sighed, and leaned closer. " 'Tis true that I knew Angus once, though not in such garb and not so scarred as this. Indeed, I scarce recognized him when he stood before me last eve."

Jacqueline watched her carefully, anxious to learn more.

But Edana did not indulge her. "Why would you join a convent?" the older woman asked with some irritation. "You must know that you are fair of face. 'Tis the choice of an old woman, one tired of life's pleasures, to retreat to a convent, not that of a young demoiselle who has yet to sip from that fount."

"So all are quick to observe." Edana's gaze was unswerving

and Jacqueline felt compelled to continue. "I have a calling to serve Christ and share my gifts with the church."

"Nonsense." Edana spat into the rushes in the corner. "You flee something, just as you have tried to flee Angus. To flee your captor is a deed I can understand, though in my time Ceinn-beithe was not a place worth fleeing."

"I flee no one."

"Then why? You have a greater reason than the one you give."

Jacqueline sighed and put down the comb. "Because I believe that 'tis within the embrace of the church that I will be appreciated for the full bounty of the gifts I can share, not for how well I might adorn a man's arm, his table, or his bed."

Edana studied her. "You have been pursued for your beauty alone?"

"Aye."

The old woman smiled and cast a handful of herbs into her pot, pausing to stir the concoction. "Then I approve of your choice," she said unexpectedly.

"You do?"

"Aye. A woman is not an ornament and she should not be treated as one."

"Indeed!" 'Twas a delight to Jacqueline to meet someone who did not try to dissuade her from her course.

Edana held up one finger. "But not all men make the mistake of seeking only beauty. There are men who see past a woman's youthful charms, men who know that 'tis the woman herself with whom they may have the grace to grow old."

Jacqueline tied her braid decisively. "Perhaps, but I have not met such a man."

Edana tilted her head to watch her, her eyes bright. "Have you not?"

"I stand corrected. My stepfather is such a man, and perhaps my uncle Guillaume—"

"Let me tell you a tale, my demoiselle," Edana interrupted. The French fell so readily from the older woman's tongue that Jacqueline blinked in surprise. Before she could ask Edana's origins, the woman continued. "I will tell you a tale, for the lady of the well claims she is well pleased with you, and I too find you a charming maiden."

"Will you tell me how you know Angus?"

Edana pursed her lips. "Now there is a tale, and one too long to be readily told."

"You might tell me some of it. You might tell me the truth."

"And what is the truth, lass?"

"The honest tale of what happened, with no embellishment or omission. The truth is simple, the whole truth even more so."

"You speak with the conviction of the young." Edana seemed to find this amusing. "Naught is simple about the truth. There is the truth of what happened and the truth of what I believe happened and the truth of what I still remember to have happened. And that does not embrace the truths perceived and remembered by others, let alone whether any of us witnessed the fullness of the truth in the first place."

"You speak in riddles."

"I speak in truths." Edana grinned then, as if well pleased with herself.

Jacqueline sighed in frustration, not sharing the older woman's delight in their conversation. "Very well. Will you tell one truth that you recall of what you perceived happened when you met Angus?"

Edana sobered and straightened. "You have an audacious tongue, lass, for all the beauty of your face." Jacqueline blushed, but the old woman continued. "When first I saw you, I feared you would be witless or bland or uninteresting in some other way. 'Tis a pleasant surprise to discover fine company."

Jacqueline did not know what to say to that. Edana, her ancient fingers sorting dried leaves into two virtually indistinguishable piles, fetched her stool and seated herself beside Jacqueline. Jacqueline recognized neither the leaf nor the scent.

"Once upon a time, a young beauty, not unlike yourself, was betrothed to a chieftain considerably her senior. She was afraid of the match, for her groom was said to be bloodthirsty and boisterous, but her parents believed it to be a good one. An obedient daughter, she met the chieftain before the doors of the church on the agreed day to take her vows. 'Twas said her heart nigh stopped when she saw the size of the warrior in whose bed she would lie."

"But she wed him?"

"Aye, she was a dutiful daughter, as I have stated." Edana worked for a moment in silence as the rain pattered on the roof. "And their nuptial feast was a merry one, involving days of singing and dancing. But in the midst of the festivities, an emissary came to the door of their abode.

"This man had ridden from the Norman court of a distant cousin of the lady. He brought a gift for the nuptials, a marvel that enchanted all." Edana paused to lick her lips. "What do you think 'twas?"

"Jewels and gold."

"Nay."

"Exotic silks, or dyes, or perfumes."

"Nay again, though you draw close."

"Some marvelous foodstuff. A fruit from the South!"

"Nay. One fruit would not have fed that gathering, and once 'twas gone, 'twould have been gone forever. That would have been a gift that brought disappointment, and thus no token of esteem. Nay, a nuptial gift must endure for as many years as the match it celebrates."

"Then I do not know."

Edana smiled, looking as mischievous as an impish faerie from one of Duncan's tales. She tapped a finger on Jacqueline's knee. "He brought a colony of bees."

Jacqueline was incredulous. She hugged her knees and listened avidly, for she dearly loved tales. "Bees? But how?"

"In a woven skep of clever design, though 'twas no small trouble. 'Twas early in the spring when he arrived, so his charges had been slumbering for most of the journey. Yet in that skep was a queen and all the drones to make a larger colony and a fine supply of honey. They were particularly fine bees and inclined to make much honey, by his telling.

" 'Twas a most generous gift, so generous that the recipients hesitated before accepting it. 'Twas said the lady wondered what her cousin wanted of her."

"Did she accept it?"

Edana smiled at the prompting. "Aye. 'Twas coyly chosen, for in truth she could not have denied it. She had a fondness for a sweet, did the lady, and there is no sweetness to match that of fine honey. And as the emissary was a priest, 'twas felt denying the offering might be a poor choice. The priest insisted that the Norman lord who was the lady's cousin wished only to ensure that this family listened to his news and counsel. The only thing required of them in return was their attention to the priest's news.

"To this they willingly agreed. All of the household was assembled in the hall to hear whatsoever the priest might say. The minstrels were silenced and the peasants gathered with all the chieftain's men. The priest spoke with such charm and character that none found his recounting to be dull—indeed, 'twas the stuff of a wondrous tale he revealed.

"Unbeknownst to all those within this remote household, the Latin kingdom of Jerusalem was being besieged by the infidel. The Saracens had already seized the county of Edessa. There was great fear that all that had been gained in the Holy Land with the blood of courageous crusaders would be stolen away once more. The pope, Eugenius III, had called for a new crusade to right this wrong, to reassert the claim of Christendom to the Holy City where Christ had met his end and risen again."

" 'Twas the crusade endorsed by Bernard of Clairvaux, the founder of the Cistercian order," Jacqueline contributed, re-calling well her lessons from Ceinn-beithe's priest.

"Aye, though 'twas to be led by no lesser men than the Holy Roman Emperor Conrad III and Louis VII, King of France. 'Twas said that a grim Day of Judgment would be visited upon those Christians who did not take up the cross to defend what should have been most holy to them and their faith. The priest, delivering this missive at the behest of the lady's family, called for her husband, the chieftain, to take up arms and lead his men to join this quest."

Edana paused, rising to fetch more of her leaves. It seemed to take her overly long to gather them, and Jacqueline's toe tapped in her impatience to hear more. She barely managed to wait until the older woman was seated again before her question burst forth.

"And? Did they go?"

"There was a difficulty." Edana pursed her lips. "The chief-tain himself had not been raised in the faith of Christians. He had permitted himself to be baptized solely that he might wed his chosen bride, whose family insisted upon as much."

"He was pagan?"

"Nay, 'twas more accurately said that he was indifferent. As a man wholly enthralled with matters of this world, he had little interest in faith of any kind. And he had less inter-est in traveling the breadth of Christendom, to be parted from his new wife for years, to father no sons, and perhaps to die far from hearth and home. He was no longer a young man, and he certainly had no fear of any pending judgment.

"In fact, he immediately declined to go. 'Twas his manner to make choices quickly and cling to them tenaciously. And without his endorsement of the righteousness of this battle, not a single man from his household went."

"The priest must have been disappointed."

"Aye, I expect he was. And truly, there was some concern of repercussions. The lady's cousin, after all, had merely wanted to warn her family of their possible peril. 'Twas a message sent in good faith, no matter what its result. The chieftain insisted upon granting the priest a similarly generous gift to return to the cousin so that relations would not worsen between them.

"The priest, however, would not accept such a gift, though he did not discourage the chieftain from sending it with a different envoy. Indeed, he had seen how thin the veil of faith was in these lands, and he resolved that he would bring all these wayward lambs beneath the shelter of Christ. He vowed to stay and preach."

"It sounds as if his teachings were well needed."

Edana did not reply to that, though she gave Jacqueline a censorious glance. "The chieftain, seeing his opportunity to make something of naught, granted an endowment to found a monastery. The priest graciously accepted this gift and set about preaching the word to all who would listen.

"He showed the lady how to care for the bees, the monastery prospered, many of the people pledged to the chieftain converted to the faith. For a long time the troubles in Outremer were forgotten."

"Until their judgment came."

Edana paused and studied Jacqueline. " 'Tis a remarkable trait among Christians that they take great delight in hearing of others chastised for their transgressions, when I had always understood that one of the great Christian teachings was compassion for one's fellows."

"Nay, 'tis the mark of Celtic tale to see wickedness punished and goodness rewarded."

Edana chuckled to herself at that. "Aye? I suppose 'tis the mark of any good tale, if not of life itself."

"Well? Did any illness befall them?" Jacqueline asked.

"Oh, some said it began from the outset. The bride did not ripen with child as all might have expected. The priest made no associations between one event and the other, though people tend to gossip about such matters. There was no doubt, after all, that the chieftain anxiously sought his wife's bed."

"And she? Did she still fear him?"

"Nay. Although she went to her nuptials with great trepidation, she soon discovered that he was a man of a kind and generous heart, a heart nigh as large as he. He separated all the world into those who were with him and those who were against—the latter he slaughtered without remorse, the former he protected with a passion unmatched. She was at the pinnacle of those he cherished, and, as such, her life could not have been more sweet.

"A gentle soul, she turned a blind eye to the strife that oft surrounded them. War and blood feuds and alliances were those matters she saw as a constantly shifting and confusing realm of violence in which she desired no part.

"A woman with little patience for needlework, she abandoned the shuttle to create a garden. Perhaps she sought to prove that men and women could foster beauty in this world, instead of all the wickedness we usually breed.

" 'Twas originally a garden justified by the needs of the kitchen, filled with herbs for healing and for flavor as well as onions and tubers for the soup pot. But slowly she added flowers for the glory of their color and for the bees.

"Word spread of her strange preoccupation. Courtiers seeking the favor of her indulgent husband brought her gifts from the South that would be unwelcome in any other household—bits of root, and slips of leaves, seeds and pods and fruit. And so her garden grew, a glorious refuge into which she and her husband oft retreated. 'Twas a world outside of the world in many ways, a place out of time.

"And none could match this couple's delight when some six years after their vows were exchanged, the lady bore to the chieftain a fine son. She then bore another, and he vowed she had made him the happiest man in all of Christendom. The wagging tongues fell silent, and it seemed that all was right again in the chieftain's domain."

"Was it?"

"Aye, for a long time it seemed that way."

"But eventually . . ."

"Aye, *eventually* all went awry and did so quite suddenly, as a ball of wool wound tight will unfurl when cast across the floor. Alliances dissolved, battles turned against the chieftain, the winters became cruel, and the crops failed. The hunting was poor and many peasants died. The prosperity that holding had long enjoyed faltered. The chieftain refused to believe that 'twas more than bad fortune, until his eldest son, his heir, fell ill.

"A ripe young man, not eight and ten summers of age, he was nigh at death's door in one short week. The chieftain was beside himself in his anguish, the lady wept, the younger son did all that could be done for his brother.

"But precious little could be done. The priest was called, and he named the handiwork of God in what the family endured. He called this their Judgment Day for failing to answer the call to arms of the pope. And truly, 'twas well known by that point that the crusade he had preached on his arrival had gone poorly. The infidel breached the walls of Christendom with increasing boldness, and 'twas feared that the Holy City itself would be lost.

"But now the chieftain was far into his winter years and 'twas unlikely he could add much more to the battle than a pilgrim or a penitent might."

Edana worked mutely for long moments, then frowned. "Silence filled the chamber after the priest named his remedy. That silence was broken only by the cough of the ill son, until the younger son spoke. He vowed to go to Outremer, to redeem his family's honor, to do battle for Christ against the Saracens. He was six and ten years of age, though tall and finely wrought and deft with a blade.

"And then there was jubilation, for all were certain this would change their fate for the better. The priest affixed the red cross of the crusader to the son's tunic that very day. The son was dispatched with all honors, with a fine steed and a stalwart companion, with a heavy purse and his father's legendary blade. His mother was inconsolable, for she was certain she would never see her youngest again.

"The chieftain was burdened by guilt, for he believed that 'twas his own decision that had brought such misery to his family. He feared too late that his own refusal to depart was naught but selfishness and that 'twould see his lady's heart rent in two.

"Can you guess the departing son's name?" Edana glanced at Jacqueline, and the younger woman's mouth went dry.

"Angus."

"Aye, 'twas."

Jacqueline caught her breath. "When did this happen?"

" 'Twas five and ten years ago."

Angus had been gone fifteen years! "And the elder brother?"

"Died shortly thereafter."

"God bless his soul." Jacqueline crossed herself, but she was unprepared for the flash of anger in Edana's eyes.

"Indeed? And what favoring god would surrender a blessing after compelling his faithful to suffer such pain? How is this good, that the family is divided and their son lost to war across the seas in Outremer?"

Jacqueline had only the answer oft given by Ceinn-beithe's kindly priest. " 'Tis not for us to know the ways of God."

"Nay." Edana spat on the floor. "Only to obey his edicts, like the sheep to whom his priests so oft compare us."

Jacqueline had never met anyone who questioned the teachings of the church, and she knew not what to say. Her own faith burned brightly in her heart, and she felt compelled to argue in its favor.

"There must have been a greater purpose," she insisted. "Perhaps Angus had a critical role to play. Jerusalem has not been lost, after all."

Edana made a noncommittal sound in her throat. She separated her plants with less care than before, her fingers shaking with passion.

"You said you would not tell a tale that was not your own," Jacqueline reminded her, watching those agitated fingers. "Yet you tell this one, and you tell it with the conviction of one close to its occurrence."

Edana turned a look upon her so cold that it nigh froze her marrow. "I knew this chieftain and his bride," she said fiercely. "They were good people, honest and loving people, and did naught to deserve such pain. 'Tis no crime to share the heartbreak of a kindred soul."

"You speak of them as if they draw breath no longer."

Edana looked back to her plants, her lips tight. "They are all dead. All save one." And she flicked her head toward the door, toward the murmur of men's voices and horses' nickering, toward Angus. "Though his heart has been turned to such a stone that he might as well be dead."

"Edana! 'Tis bad fortune to say such a thing."

The older woman swallowed a wry laugh. "The man could hardly have worse fortune than is already his own." She shook a finger at Jacqueline. "And in saying as much, you show yourself more a Celt than you guess, and perhaps more superstitious than is fitting in a novitiate."

Jacqueline ignored the second comment. "What do you mean about Angus's fortunes?"

"You will have to ask him yourself, my curious demoiselle," Edana got to her feet once more, shuffling to an array of dried plants hung from the roof at the other end of the hut. She murmured to herself as she plucked and chose from the leaves, pinched and sniffed, discarded some and gathered others into one fist. She returned and cast them into the pot, with a murmured verse.

"Be warned that I will drink no more of your potions," Jacqueline insisted, though her suspicion seemed to prompt no more than an arch smile.

"Aye? How is your ankle this morn?"

Jacqueline rose and, to her surprise, her ankle was fully able to support her weight. It seemed completely healed, but she unbound the cloth carefully, expecting the bruise to linger.

There was none. Her flesh was as unblemished as it had been the day before, before she tripped and injured herself. She looked up at Edana in amazement, only to find the old woman smiling smugly.

"Perhaps you owe some gratitude after all."

Jacqueline folded her hands before herself and bowed slightly. "I thank you from the bottom of my heart. Your craft is not small, though it be unworldly."

Edana shook her head. "Your thanks are owed to the lady

of the well, not to me. A truly grateful soul would hang that cloutie in the glade and make an offering as a token of esteem."

"A token?" Jacqueline could not hide her horror. "Must I slaughter some innocent in the way of pagans?"

Edana chuckled. "Oh, I am tempted indeed to tell you that you must, if only to see your dismay. But nay, lass, 'tis not that way. Sacrifice something of import to yourself, that is all the lady asks of you."

"What does that mean?"

"A shoe, a trinket, a belt." Edana gave Jacqueline a hard look. "A judgment or preconception, perhaps even a dream. It matters not what you choose, nor even whether you confess the truth to another. The lady will know—and further, she will know whether the gift comes truly from your heart."

"And if it does not?"

Edana smiled and stirred her brew.

Jacqueline donned her shoes, then paused, facing the older woman. Edana said naught. 'Twas as if she had ceased to be, though Jacqueline guessed matters would change as she moved toward the door.

And she would prefer to not be trussed up again. If 'twas an oversight on Angus's part that she was free this morning—and she could not imagine why 'twould be so otherwise—then she did not intend to remind him to redress his error.

"Am I permitted to simply walk to the glade alone?" she asked finally. "Or will it be assumed that I am trying to escape?"

"I do not know Angus's intent. You had best ask him that as well." Edana spoke mildly, then straightened and lifted her head to listen. "He has not gone far."

The old woman said no more, her attention apparently fixed upon her brew.

Mist gathered in the hollows of the land even as the rain eased to a halt, turning the shadows beneath the great trees into mysterious havens. The leaves glistened and silvery drops dripped all around. Jacqueline heard the music of their falling, mingled with the chirping of birds and the distant gurgle of the stream.

And the stamping of horses bred for war. Aye, Rodney swung into his own saddle and the men conferred even as she watched.

Jacqueline was curious whether what Edana had told her was true. She stared at Angus from the doorway, her thoughts spinning with all she had just learned of him.

Indeed, it seemed that Angus lived some old tale that Duncan might recount. A knight of honor departed from his home to set matters right yet returned to find his family dead. She could well understand how he sought to repair his own fate, no less how he could have become so embittered.

Goosebumps rose on Jacqueline's flesh as she thought of it. Aye, she was susceptible to a heroic tale, she knew it well—indeed, the priest of Ceinn-beithe oft despaired of her affection for such tales over those in her testament.

Would Angus confide in her? 'Twas unlikely, but she was oddly reassured by this tale of his origins.

Perhaps he was not the demon she had assumed him to be.

Jacqueline stepped across the threshold, but the old woman did not stir.

"Take the bucket," Edana commanded softly. "And see it filled, if you please."

Jacqueline lifted the bucket, left the hut, and took a cleansing breath of the damp air. She was free once more, though there was no telling how long that might last.

She had best make the opportunity count.

❋

Angus knew that Rodney would have much to say of what he had interrupted this morn. That man stood beside his steed, fairly tapping his toe with impatience to begin a diatribe, even as Angus left the hut.

Despite the turmoil within him, Angus jabbed a finger through the air at his companion. "Are you not departed yet? I thought you were the one in haste to see this matter resolved. If you intend to make Ceinn-beithe by the morrow's eve, you had best hasten yourself."

Rodney blinked. "I am leaving on this day?"

"I cannot imagine why you linger, unless you are as lazy a comrade as I was warned you would be."

Rodney grinned. "That, boy, is the first sense to fall from your lips in a day. Since sleep has made you sensible once more, perhaps we should review the wisdom of your plan."

"You must ride there, Rodney. It seems to me now that haste is of import." Angus did not choose to explain why.

Rodney, typically, assumed they were in agreement. "Aye, but why even trouble with the matter? Let the woman be free. Let us raise an army from your father's allies and capture Airdfinnan by force!"

Angus sighed heavily. "You forget, Rodney, that I was raised within those walls. I know better than any other that Airdfinnan cannot be taken by force."

The older man's eyes narrowed. "I suspect you make much of memories. You might find differently if you looked with the eyes of one who has seen more of war instead of a son fondly recalling his sire."

Angus shook his head. "I did look, Rodney. I looked when we were so briefly within its walls again, and, truly, the keep is more heavily fortified than I recall. My father always said it could be taken only by treachery from within."

"Yet that is how he lost it."

"A cruel irony, is it not?" Angus felt his lips tighten. " 'Twas brilliantly done, if naught else. His enemy spied his weakness and made the most of it."

Angus fell silent, wondering whether his father had perceived the treachery before he died. He hated that a man of such honor had been cheated of his due—and hated more that he had not been present to offer his aid, for whatever it might have been worth.

He had failed his family's expectation on every front.

Rodney laid a hand on Angus's shoulder. "You, at least, will never make such an error. We have seen much of what evil can lurk in a man's heart."

"Much indeed."

Angus did not doubt that his companion was recalling the crimes they had witnessed, both alone and together.

Rodney swung into the saddle, then granted Angus a cocky salute. "So, 'tis as our original plan? I shall return here to meet you with all haste, once the chieftain grants his aye or nay?"

"Aye."

But Rodney hesitated. "You are certain 'tis wise to insist upon ransoming the woman still? Once I depart, naught can be changed."

"I see no reason to abandon our plan."

Rodney's smile was wry. "Even though she is not Mhairi?"

"If all she tells of Duncan is true, then he will pay as readily as Cormac."

"If indeed he is fully heir to the chiefdom."

Angus shrugged. " 'Tis time for answers, Rodney, not more questions. There is only one way to know the truth for certain. You will have to go there."

"And you will keep the wench for yourself," Rodney

teased, no doubt as startled as Angus when the lady in question called a merry greeting.

"Good morning to you," she continued cheerfully, swinging an empty bucket as she came. Angus stared, astonished by her manner. Indeed, she might have been comfortably at home, arising to do a few small chores. He blinked when she smiled at him, momentarily struck silent.

Rodney, fortunately, shared no such liability.

Chapter Seven

HE OLDER MAN CLICKED HIS TEETH WITH ANNOY-
ance. "What madness is this?" he muttered. "If you
are going to take a captive, boy, 'tis important that
she does not run free, doing whatsoever she will. Seeing as
you have not done a deed so bold before, perhaps that detail
of *captivity* escaped you—"

"There is nowhere for her to flee, Rodney."

He snorted. "As if that halted her yesterday. The woman
has no sense at all. What manner of fool would choose to
risk a night alone in the woods over what security a knight
might offer?"

Only a very frightened woman. Angus thought again of the
terror the woman had shown of him and wondered at its root.

She halted beside Angus and Rodney, evidently unaware
of any dissent between them, or else choosing to ignore it.
Rodney glowered at her, while Angus contented himself with
watching her. She was more fetching than most, but 'twas
her manner that enchanted him as much as her appearance.

The lady seemed to sparkle—like a jewel, beauteous
enough in itself but brought to life by a chance ray of sunlight.

"And what happens next?" She looked between them as
pertly as a sparrow. "I must confess that I have never been

held hostage before. Do I have an opportunity to break my fast? And what of this day? Do we remain here, or do we move to another more secret locale? When do you demand the ransom? And what *is* the ransom?"

The two men exchanged a glance. "You ask many questions," Rodney huffed.

She smiled. "I am said to be overly burdened with curiosity."

" 'Tis a strange trait for a novitiate," Angus commented, and she flushed crimson.

"I shall pray for aid in overcoming my weakness," she muttered, though he doubted she would do any such thing— no less that she might succeed. He chuckled at the prospect, though it earned him a dark look. " 'Tis not so amusing as that to pray for aid!"

" 'Tis the remote possibility of your losing such a characteristic trait that amuses," he said.

Though he would not have thought it possible, her blush deepened. "A person can do much if they have the will," she replied, setting her lips with resolve.

"Indeed." 'Twas odd to have his own conviction cast at him from this maiden, and Angus felt a strange kinship with her. She had said that her mother did not approve of her choice, but still she pursued it.

Perhaps they both knew what 'twas to face adversity of a kind. Angus was embarrassed to realize that he had offered her no food sooner.

"If you are hungry, there is bread," he said gruffly, opening his saddlebag. "Though 'tis somewhat stale."

She pinched a loaf and grimaced. " 'Tis nigh as hard as rock."

" 'Tis better than naught." Once the crust was removed, it would suffice to keep a man from starving. He and Rodney had halted en route at Templar foundations and been housed with the hospitality shown to guests and those who had served with the order in Outremer, although the Templars kept simple fare.

The demoiselle's expression made Angus realize how coarse his fare had become—and wonder how long it had been since he had dined in the splendor to which she was undoubtedly accustomed.

'Twas a fitting reminder that they two had little in common. His experience was as far from what this maiden knew than it could be—and his experience had made him what he was.

He should feel no sympathy for her or her plight, especially as all would be resolved shortly.

"And there are apples," Rodney contributed. "Though they are ridden with worms. You probably have no desire for them. I know well enough how particular women are about worms." He opened his saddlebag and she rummaged through the dozen apples there, pinching and sniffing them like a housewife buying produce.

"This one," she announced, choosing a rosy specimen.

" 'Tis yours," Rodney said. "Though do not cry to me when you find a wee worm caught between your teeth." He wiggled his finger to illustrate his threat.

Surprisingly she did not flinch. "I would cut it into four first."

Rodney grinned at her. "Afraid to simply bite?"

She rolled her eyes. "I always eat apples thus. May I have a knife?"

"Nay." Angus took the fruit and quartered it for her, offering it on his palm. He took no trouble to hide or remove the small green worm wriggling in the core.

To his astonishment, the maiden considered the worm solemnly, then lifted it onto her finger. She carried it to the nearest shrub and laid it carefully upon a leaf, then returned to take the apple from him.

She smiled and bit into a piece, apparently unconcerned. "Naught else? You will scarce be prepared to wage war if you eat so poorly."

The men again exchanged a look, and Angus knew he had not been alone in expecting a more noisy response.

"Are you not afeared of a worm?" Rodney challenged.

She gave that man a look that made Angus want to smile. "Why would I be afraid of a worm no bigger than the end of my finger?" Scorn dripped from her tone. "He has no teeth with which to bite me, and indeed, he favors apples over my flesh." She rolled her eyes. "I am not such an idiot as that."

"But there could be another. You could eat it and 'twould wriggle in your belly. Perhaps 'twould grow . . ."

"Rodney!" The man was so bent on making mischief that Angus had to intervene.

"What nonsense!" she declared, clearly not needing Angus to defend her tender sensibilities. "We have these at Ceinnbeithe oftentimes. They do not like to share their homes." She smiled with sudden impishness. " 'Tis far better to find one before you eat or even none at all, than to discover half of one in the midst of eating."

Even Rodney grimaced at that and Angus had to fight to keep from chuckling. She had an earthiness he had not expected. Truth be told, he found it quite fetching.

Aye, there was much of this woman he found alluring, though that was the last realization he needed on this morn. Indeed, Rodney could not ride fast enough to suit him.

"Why would you carry apples filled with worms? These are no better than those that fall from the trees in the autumn."

" 'Tis a dark trait of human nature to take advantage of strangers in our midst," Rodney declared. "And we were tricked in a market in Lincoln where they were overly wary of travelers."

"We?" Angus felt obliged to ask.

The older man colored. "The apples I chose were fine indeed. I thought 'twas only courtesy to two men of war returned from fighting the infidel that the seller offered to pack the apples into my bag." Rodney's brow furrowed. "He changed good for ill, 'twas what he did. 'Twas a faithless bit of treachery, though I knew it naught until we were much farther on."

The maiden shrugged, her eyes bright. "You do not have to eat them. Feed them to the steeds and buy more."

"There is an issue with coin, lass." Rodney muttered through gritted teeth, omitting his role in that circumstance as well. " 'Tis not falling from the trees hereabouts, in case you have not deigned to notice as much."

Angus groaned inwardly at the maiden's evident interest in this. 'Twas better if she knew naught of them and their motives.

"I thought all knights were rich."

"You thought wrongly, but then who would expect much different from a lass as pampered and sheltered as you must be." The older man warmed to his theme. "As poor as church mice is what we are—"

"Are you not already overly late in departing?" Angus interrupted, and his companion straightened.

"Aye, indeed I am." He made a mock bow to the maiden. "Until we meet again, my lady fair," he said with no small measure of humor. He saluted Angus, then turned his steed and galloped through the forest.

The hoofbeats had barely faded before the woman turned upon Angus. "But where is he going?"

It seemed that she had lost far too much of her fear of him. He scowled at her, to no discernible effect. "Away."

"But *where* does he go?"

Angus took a steadying breath, though he was not truly surprised that she did not abandon her inquiry. " 'Tis not for you to know."

"Whyever not? What might I do about the matter?"

"You will know what I decide you shall know, and no more than that," Angus said flatly. She frowned, but he turned to groom his steed again, for 'twas a good excuse to ignore her. Perhaps if fear could dissuade her from asking questions, so too could rudeness.

He already knew better than to truly believe that.

❊

'Twas a surprise to Jacqueline to learn that Angus groomed his own steed. He ignored her completely as he shed his tabard and mail tunic, then brushed away the stallion's nibbling of his hair. Clad in only his linen shirt, dark chausses, and boots, he began to brush down the beast, his movements filled with both vigor and grace. He still wore his belt, the scabbard, weighted with his sword on one side, his knife on the other.

She was struck by the gentleness Angus could exhibit. He scratched his beast's ears, murmured to it, and brushed it with a thoroughness that spoke of affection. And truly, the steed had no fear of him, as animals oft did of those of malicious intent.

Was he truly as wicked as she first believed? Jacqueline watched, recalling Edana's tale, and wondered. She certainly sensed that Angus wanted her to *believe* he was evil, but she was beginning to have her doubts.

If Edana told her rightly, then he had tried to aid his family and come home to find them all dead. That could not be an easy burden to bear.

She knew, however, that he did not wish to discuss his tale with her. She watched him and nibbled her lip, wondering how best to discover the story.

There could be no doubt that knight and steed were wrought for each other, for these two were larger, darker, and more mysterious than any man or steed she had ever known. Jacqueline stared, knowing she should go to the well, but felt rooted to the spot. Angus worked with such easy deliberation, the rhythm of his movements calming her anxiety and making her want to linger.

'Twas as if she no longer stood here, or that Angus had forgotten her presence, for he did not so much as glance her way.

Though she did not doubt that if she chose to flee, she would have his attention quickly enough.

'Twas the great black steed that offered her a chance to speak. He lifted his head and fixed his gaze upon her, his eyes as black and filled with secrets as those of his master. His darkness was touched by only a small white star over one eye.

The steed whinnied, stretching his neck toward her. Jacqueline, unable to resist, stepped closer and offered the last quarter of the apple. When she stood directly before the horse, she was doubly certain that there had never been a larger and more fearsome beast in all of Christendom. But Jacqueline, mindful of the knight's watchful gaze, refused to show her fear.

She offered her open hand to the stallion, the apple perched upon it. His nose was as soft as silken velvet when he accepted the gift. He chewed noisily, then his nose moved over her hand once again. Jacqueline smiled when the steed snorted and tossed his head. Disdainful that she brought him no further treat, he deigned to ignore her. Perhaps he was not so different from her mother's palfreys.

"What is his name?" The question left her lips before she could consider the wisdom of asking it.

"Lucifer." Angus moved to the other side of the horse.

Jacqueline was reassured to have the beast between them, even though Angus watched her more openly now. "Because he rides like the devil?" she asked pertly.

Angus fixed her with a steady look. "Nay. Because he was spawned in hell."

He returned to his labor, leaving Jacqueline to wonder at his words. Lucifer seemed untroubled by this recounting of his origins. He shook his mane, his nostrils moving as he assessed the breeze.

Jacqueline dared to be bold. "But Lucifer was not spawned in hell. He was said to have been God's favored of the angels, though he fell from grace by dint of his pride."

Angus flicked her a glance. "In the East, a different tale is told of Lucifer."

"Indeed?"

"Indeed." Angus did not look her way, but bent to brush the stallion's haunch. "He was said to have been the King of Babylon, otherwise known as Nebuchadnezzar."

Jacqueline vaguely recalled Babylon from the tales of the Old Testament and was certain little good had happened in that city with its tower built to touch the face of God.

She peeked around the horse to watch Angus work. "I do not understand what connection there might be."

"Nebuchadnezzar was a man of much ambition, 'tis said, and one who declared his power so great that he would ascend to the heavens upon his demise, to rule alongside God himself."

Angus brushed the stallion's rump, then slipped behind him and appeared beside Jacqueline. She jumped, as much from his abrupt appearance as the wicked gleam in his eye.

" 'Twas said that the morning star did indeed appear in the sky after his demise but that it sinks low each day as a sign that this king's ambitions were too great in the end. The name itself means bearer of light."

She stared at him, uncertain whether he told a true tale. "I have never heard this tale."

"Of course not. A demon wrought of earthly sin is a simpler tale both to recount and to understand."

"Is that a comment upon women being slight of intellect?" Jacqueline demanded, then clapped one hand over her mouth for her foolishness. Oh, she was said to become vexed too quickly with those who assumed much from her looks alone!

But Angus smiled fleetingly. "Even I would not be so bold as to suggest you witless."

Jacqueline flushed, uncertain how to reply to the unexpected warmth in his words. Did he mean to compliment her?

She returned to the safer ground of the steed. "So, you named him for the star on his brow."

"And for his origins. He was bred in Damascus, not so very far from Babylon."

Jacqueline frowned in confusion. "But you said he was wrought in hell. Is Damascus hell?"

Angus turned away, ignoring her question so thoroughly that she knew she had a found a truth about him.

Jacqueline took a single step after him. "Was it there that you sipped from the cup of wickedness?"

Angus's head snapped up. "What is this?"

Jacqueline's mouth went dry, but she was not one to leave what she had started half done. "Edana says you have known wickedness since last she saw you and that you now wear its taint. Was it in Damascus that you made its acquaintance?"

Angus's lips tightened to the grim line so typical of his expression, and he began to brush the steed with greater vigor. "Edana knows naught of what she speaks."

"Aye? Then what else would explain the change she sees in you?"

"What change?" he demanded coldly, fixing his stare upon her.

Jacqueline took a step back. "I merely was curious—"

" 'Tis not for you to know what has brought me to this place." He spoke tightly and without raising his voice, but there was no doubt of the anger that thrummed beneath his words. He cast down the brush and Jacqueline realized too late that she had provoked him.

Curse her curiosity! Her fear of his intent easily conquered her desire to appear fearless. She took another step back and his eye narrowed, though he followed her immediately.

"You will ask no more questions of me, or of Edana, whether you are curious or not. Are we understood?" He loomed over her, size and expression menacing.

Jacqueline swallowed and nodded. "I have to leave," she said hastily, which did naught to diminish his vexation with her.

"To go where?" he demanded irritably.

"I go to the well to make an offering to the lady," Jacqueline explained, more breathless than she might have preferred. And in truth she was much more anxious to fulfill this pagan debt of gratitude now that it granted her the chance to evade his wrath.

She waved her cloutie at Angus, backing away with haste as his brow darkened. "I shall return shortly."

"You are a captive! You will go nowhere alone!"

But Jacqueline turned and did precisely that.

Indeed, she ran.

For a woman of apparent sense, she could be rid of it quickly enough. She ran now, like a mad hare, through the undergrowth where any manner of twig or root or hole could twist her ankle again, if not see it broken.

'Twas as if she would challenge his intent to return her to her father unscathed.

Angus shouted for her to halt but did not truly expect that

she would. Nay, she would insist that she replied only to her own name, and he would not suffer it to cross his lips. She did not even slow her pace, though he did not doubt that she heard him.

A most troublesome woman, that was what she was. No maiden bound for a convent would so adamantly refuse to be biddable, of that he was certain. She was bold and proud and foolish and clever, and he was nigh certain her family had agreed to support her vocation because they feared they might throttle her otherwise.

As before, she was fleet of foot, and he did not catch her as quickly as he might have liked. He snatched at her once, but she ducked beneath a branch he had not seen and he nearly took the limb between the eyes.

He swore then in truth, exhausting every phrase he had learned in fifteen years of living among fighting men. 'Twas a considerable arsenal, but it fell short of expressing his frustration.

Finally Angus strode impatiently through the undergrowth in a straight line, ignoring the winding path she followed. She glanced back, terror in her gaze, then slipped on the muddied trail and disappeared with a splash.

Angus lunged forward and nigh stepped into the hidden well directly behind her.

He caught at a branch and steadied his footing in the nick of time. The rocks were so slick surrounding the pool that 'twas easy to see how she had slipped. A man could not see the spring until he was upon it, and certainly there had been no chance of hearing its burble in the din they had made.

He braced his boots against the treacherous ground and, propping his hands upon his hips, granted a stern glance to the lady. He fully intended to recount the foolishness of her actions to her, then demand a change in her behavior. He met her gaze to begin.

But she, to his astonishment, smiled.

The words froze on Angus's lips. Zounds, but the woman's moods changed like a spring sky!

She was sprawled on her backside in the shallow water, only her face and the wool of her kirtle visible. Her hair was escaping from her braid and a healthy smear of mud adorned one cheek.

And she looked on the verge of laughter. Surely any woman would be infuriated to find herself in such circumstance?

He scowled, assuming that she mocked him. "And what so amuses you about this?"

"I feared I would not be able to find the well," she confessed, her lips quirking and her eyes sparkling. "But it seems the lady will have her due, one way or the other."

He knew not what to say to that. She straightened and he caught his breath, for her kirtle clung to her curves in a most distracting fashion. The chill in the air was revealed by the pert tightening of her nipples—and proved the lady to be as innocent as she claimed, for she was clearly unaware of the provocative sight she presented.

Aye, he recalled the sweet heat of her kiss rather too well.

Some hint of his desire must have appeared in his expression, for her laughter faded and her eyes narrowed. Angus stepped toward her, noting that though she still recoiled from his outstretched hand, she did not flinch from holding his regard.

"Is this where you will take what you will of me?" she demanded, her voice unnaturally high. Her gaze flicked to his chausses and back to his face in her obvious quest for reassurance. "Where none can aid me and none might witness your crime?"

" 'Twas you who fled here," he felt compelled to observe.

"I fled you and your anger."

"I was angered only by your insistence upon risking your own good health. Did you learn naught yesterday?"

She flushed, but her lips set stubbornly and still she did not take his hand. "Why will you not release me? You could leave me at Inveresbeinn and none would know the truth of what you have done."

Angus was surprised that she offered him such a simple solution. "I did not capture you to set you free for naught."

"If not for naught, then for what?"

"No less than my sole desire."

"Which is?"

"Not of import to you."

She shivered at that and looked away, her concern more than clear. She wrapped her arms about herself but still did not stand. "But of sufficient import to you that you will release me in exchange for it?"

Angus could not deny her anything so simple as reassurance. "Aye."

"Unscathed?"

In other circumstance, her suspicion might have been insulting, though Angus could not help recalling that she alone was responsible for the injuries she had sustained. He glanced pointedly to her ankle. "Unless you insist upon continuing to wound yourself."

She flushed anew, looking young and fetching as a result. She was most agitated, though, and her uncertainty loosed his tongue when he had no intention of saying anything at all.

"Your ransom is contingent upon the name of your father," he asserted gently, "not the beauty of your face, nor even the desirability of your form."

She was visibly startled by this claim, but Angus held her regard steadily. "You pledge that you do not mean to rape me?"

Angus told himself that he had no interest in the details of her tale, though, in truth, a dull anger of suspicion rose within him. She was too quick to fret about rape to have been completely spared its ugliness.

He stepped closer and squatted beside the pool, unwilling to examine his determination to reassure this convent-bound maiden who seemed too lively to abandon the world. "I have told you that I take naught that is not offered to me willingly."

"I will not cede to you willingly," she retorted. Though she spoke boldly, her breathing was quick, as if again she sought to hide her fear of him.

"Then you have no coupling to fear." He watched her eyes narrow as she studied him, her uncertainty as interesting as her unflinching regard.

"You will say that I tempted you with my looks," she said with no small measure of bitterness.

"As others have maintained?" he guessed, seeing more of the truth that he expected she knew.

Her lips tightened and she looked away. "I will be no man's prize."

Angus nodded, noting how she evaded his charge. " 'Tis true as far as I can see." When she glanced up in surprise, he held her gaze. "Indeed, you have no fear of becoming mine."

She studied him for a long moment and he let her look, knowing she would find no hint that he lied. Then she frowned. "Why should I believe you?"

"Because the deed could have been done a hundred times by now, if it had been my intention to do it."

That truth was unassailable and she did not argue it further. The silence stretched between them, and he would have given a silver *denier* to know what she was thinking.

But Angus cleared his throat and laced his fingers together, intent upon finishing what he had begun. "This madness must halt, if I am indeed to ensure that you are returned to your family unscathed. I shall make you a wager, my beauty. An exchange, if you will."

"Aye?"

"Aye. I shall pledge to take naught from you if you pledge not to escape."

Her eyes lit with hope, a most beguiling sight, though she was not yet persuaded. "Would you leave me untrussed?"

Angus inclined his head. "I would accept the sworn pledge of one intent upon becoming a novitiate."

Her lips quirked with surprising humor. "For a greater authority than your own should strike me down if I lied."

"Perhaps so." Angus offered his hand again, and this time she hesitated for only a heartbeat before putting her delicate hand into his own. He aided her to climb from the water, then was surprised by the decisive glance she gave him.

"We shall swear it upon your father's blade," she said firmly.

Angus froze. "How do you know that I carry my father's sword?"

She blinked, blushed, then smiled so brightly that he was momentarily dazzled. "You must have told me so."

Angus folded his arms across his chest and glared down at her. A suspicion glimmered, but he would know the truth before he responded. He did not like that she knew anything of him, not even this small detail.

And he knew that he had told her naught.

"Nay. I told your guardians, but you had fainted." He arched a brow. "Unless that was a lie?"

"Nay, I . . ." She blushed the deepest shade of crimson he had ever seen and nigh fidgeted before him. "Edana must have mentioned it."

This irked Angus beyond all. "And what else did Edana tell you of me?" he demanded tightly.

"Naught. Naught at all." She spoke so quickly and her

voice was pitched so high that Angus was not convinced. He noted how hastily she tried to divert his attention. "You do not draw the blade for our vow," she challenged. "Perhaps you do not truly intend to keep your word."

Oh, he would keep his word and he would see this matter finished. But he would have something to say to Edana.

Angus pulled the blade then and made his pledge upon it, offering the hilt to her that she might do the same. She could not bear the weight of the sword, though she made a valiant effort to do so. Angus found himself supporting the blade where she could not see his touch.

This demoiselle had a merry laugh, one that put him in mind of sparkling brooks and sunlight dancing on the sea. Yet she had expected the worst from the first moment she had glimpsed him, then refused to believe his every assertion to the contrary.

Angus found it too easy to guess what had happened to make her so fearful of men. Perhaps her desire to join a convent masked an older crime. Perhaps there were men in her family's dwelling who presumed too much and she sought to be free of them.

Perhaps her stepfather himself.

Anger rolled within Angus, anger that he had no right to feel. Had he not kidnapped the woman himself? Aye, he had no claim of honorable deeds in this!

Who was he to feel the urge to protect her?

She addled his wits, that was the simple truth of it, and he had called the matter right when he had decided to avoid her company for the sake of his sense. He scowled at her, but she was too dissuaded of her fear of him.

Indeed, she laid her hand upon his arm in a most familiar manner. "Why are you angered with me?"

"Why do you believe my pledge so readily as that?" he demanded.

She blinked, then unwittingly told him more than he wanted to know. "Because you are a knight and a man who undertook a crusade to Outremer for the goodwill of his family—"

"EDANA!" Angus roared, furious that so much of his tale had been shared. He had no doubt that this maiden would be coaxed to recall all she could once she was ransomed. Aye, this Duncan MacLaren would seek every detail he could find of where his daughter had been held captive.

And then a penance would be demanded of any who had aided Angus in this. Edana undermined all his efforts to protect her by sharing too much with the maid. Indeed, the old woman risked her own safety.

Angus was livid. He could not bear to think of how a wrathful chieftain might take his due of the elderly woman, a woman who had been good to him and deserved no ill treatment. He should have made her take a vow of silence!

'Twas another error he had made, another failure to protect those whom he held dear. He hoped 'twas not too late to ensure that damage was not done.

"Hasten yourself," he said harshly to the maiden. "We return to the hut now."

"But I have to fill the bucket. And I have to thank the lady of the well."

Angus glowered at her.

She smiled at him, undaunted. "You need not wait for me. I have given my word to you."

Ah, so now he was harmless as well.

Angus swore in frustration and began to march back to Edana's hut, his mood dark.

His had been a good plan, a simple plan destined to be effective, and he knew it well. In hindsight, though, it seemed the most ill-fated decision he might have made.

He willed Rodney to ride yet more quickly, that the matter might be resolved as soon as possible.

Perhaps that man spoke rightly when he said Angus had not sufficient experience of women. He certainly had never met one like this demoiselle. He paused and looked back, watching as she dipped the bucket into the well.

Perhaps Rodney was also correct in insisting that only a fool trusted a woman, even one who had given her word. Angus folded his arms across his chest, stepped into the shadows, and watched to see what this unpredictable vixen would do.

Chapter Eight

FTER JACQUELINE FILLED THE BUCKET, SHE TENDED
to her original mission. She unfurled the cloutie
that had been bound around her ankle and sought a
likely branch. There were so many clouties that 'twas hard to
find a limb not only empty but sufficiently low that she could
reach it. Then she reached up and knotted the rag securely
around the branch, then bowed low to the burbling well.

"I thank you, lady of the well, for healing my wound. And
in my gratitude, I surrender to you—" Jacqueline's voice faltered, for she was not certain what to offer this pagan deity.
She surveyed herself. She wore no jewels, she had no trinket
to cast aside. She had no coin, no steed, naught to sacrifice
at all.

Suddenly she realized what she had learned this morning
and straightened with the surety of what she must do.

"I surrender to you my conviction that all men other than
my stepfather are of the ilk of Reynaud de Charmonte," she
said firmly. "And if you had a part in showing me here that
that much was true, I owe you thanks yet again."

She bowed low as it seemed appropriate, marveling at her
lack of unease in fulfilling this ritual. In surroundings of
such tranquility, 'twas hard to believe the wickedness that
the church ascribed to pagans and their ceremonies.

Her ankle *was* healed, by some miracle. Angus had

pledged not to touch her. And he was no demon, but a knight who tried to aid his family's woes and had evidently paid a terrible price in the East for his noble intent. What ransom would Angus demand for her safe release? Jacqueline nibbled at her lip and stared toward the distant hut. He would want coin, without a doubt, for Rodney had said they lacked coin.

But Jacqueline's family had no coin, because they had gathered every one to make the donation to Inveresbeinn that she might become a novitiate. The convent would never surrender the donation made to them.

Jacqueline swallowed in new fear. A true brigand, denied his ransom, would kill his captive. One heard such tales. But Angus, Jacqueline was certain, was more a disappointed and grieving man than a true brigand. He fully expected to win his way in this, oblivious to the truth of her family's circumstance.

'Twas then that she understood at least some small bit of the divine plan at work. Though Angus had captured her in error, he had ensured that she was in his company. Which could only mean that she had been chosen to aid him. She had to keep him from plunging down a path of lawlessness, where each poor choice could only lead to a greater crime. She had to help him to see past his grief.

Somehow.

Aye, Jacqueline had to save herself—and the only way she might accomplish that was by persuading Angus to abandon the course of wickedness before he truly embarked upon it.

It did indeed seem a divinely inspired plan; she had to save his errant soul in return for her own earthly release. She had to tell Angus the truth of her family's resources, and then she had to persuade him to take her to Inveresbeinn without his ever receiving his ransom.

Jacqueline was not entirely certain how she would manage

that deed, for Angus seemed to have no lack of resolve. But she had been chosen for the task and she did not dare to fail.

Her own fate, most certainly, hung in the balance.

Jacqueline hefted the pail with a grunt and began to walk back up the hill. She realized that she truly had been mad to run down this twisted path. Roots stuck out at every angle, ferns hung so low that the uneven terrain was hidden beneath their fronds. She might have sorely injured herself.

Duncan would have been furious with her for her carelessness alone—which made her reconsider the cause of Angus's anger. Aye, he had accused her of risking too much as soon as he arrived at the pool.

'Twas reassuring to have his behavior now make some sense, let alone to discover that his objectives were as noble as one might expect from a knight.

Aye, she would change his thinking in this, without doubt.

She rounded a tree and jumped to find that knight himself standing in the shadows just ahead. She squeaked at his forbidding expression and nearly dropped her burden.

But Angus snatched the bucket before the water could spill. He cupped Jacqueline's elbow in his other hand and fairly marched her back to the hut.

Jacqueline was touched by his gallantry. The bucket was cursedly heavy when full and the hill was steep. Her heart warmed even more to this reticent man.

"I thank you for your aid—" Jacqueline began, but Angus interrupted her tersely.

"Do not be so hasty to credit me with chivalrous motives," he said through clenched teeth. "At this point, I have no means of knowing the value of your pledge."

"But—"

"But you lied in saying that Edana had told you naught. We shall discover shortly what other lies you have told."

Jacqueline opened her mouth to argue with him, then judged the moment not the best one to challenge him. Aye, she was content to try to match his pace.

✹

Angus could have spit sparks. This woman had no understanding of the dangerous situation in which she found herself, nor indeed of the forces that drove him to seek vengeance. He showed her a small measure of kindness and she decided that he was harmless.

She knew naught of him. She knew naught of what he had seen and what he had done and what he had endured. She knew naught of what he was capable.

He hoped she had no reason to learn of it.

He kicked open the door of the hut and set the bucket down with a thump. Edana did not so much as glance up from sorting her leaves.

"Have you no care for your own welfare?" Angus demanded of her. "Or have you lost your wits in the years I have been gone?"

"I have no less care for my survival than any other sensible soul," Edana said tartly. " 'Tis you who seem bent upon ensuring your own demise. 'Tis a strange manner of homecoming you have made for yourself, Angus MacGillivray."

He released the maiden and folded his arms across his chest. "What have you told her?"

"I see no reason why it should trouble you to know. You left we two alone."

"I thought you would have the sense to hold your tongue!" He paced the width of the cabin restlessly. "You have always been most circumspect in the past."

She granted him a strange glance, one that did naught to ease his irritation with her. "Fifteen years is a long time. Much can change in so many days and nights."

Angus crouched down beside her stool and granted her his most quelling glance, his words falling low. "Why did you tell her of the origin of my blade?"

Edana blinked. "Did I?"

"How else would she know of it?"

The old woman smiled. "Then I must have told her. Undoubtedly I did so because she asked."

"If you answered every question the maid asks, then she knows more of us than we know ourselves!" Angus retorted, then rose to his feet. He paced the hut again and shoved one hand through his hair.

Edana laughed. "Aye, Jacqueline is most curious." The women shared a smile, which did naught to ease Angus's annoyance.

Angus spun to face Edana, jabbing one finger through the air to emphasize his point. "There is naught amusing in this!"

"There is no harm in entertaining the maid!"

"Is there not?" Angus pinched the bridge of his nose, counted to a dozen, then pivoted to face the old woman again. "Perhaps I might recount the truth of it to you," he said silkily, and both women drew back at the heat underlying his words. "Even if all goes well and her ransom is paid, then her stepfather will undoubtedly yearn for vengeance after this deed. The MacQuarries are known to be a vengeful lot, and I know the price of their quest for vengeance better than most."

He leaned over the older woman, who held his stare unswervingly though she blinked rapidly. His voice rose with each statement, despite his desire to remain calm. "I knew full well the risk in this, but we had need of sanctuary. I ensured she knew naught of you, I ensured that she did not know where she had been brought, I ensured that there was no way she might retrace her footsteps and lead her clan to you, but you, you have undermined all of that by telling her tales."

Angus flung out his hands and roared, both women flinching. "Of course there is harm in sharing what you know with her! I will not have your demise upon my conscience! Do you not think there is sufficient burden upon me without another load to bear?"

He glared at the older woman, his hands clenching and unclenching.

Edana clicked her tongue. "You must use more caution, Angus MacGillivray, if 'tis your intent to make all believe your heart is lost for all time."

Angus growled, hating that he had lost his temper, then spun and eyed the attentive demoiselle. Her eyes were wide and her expression dismayed.

"Where has Rodney gone?" she asked quietly, though she already knew the answer.

"To Ceinn-beithe, to demand your ransom, of course." Angus spoke crisply. He took a deep breath and reined in his temper. "You may shortly be freed of our companionship, my beauty."

His attempt to cheer her failed. She stepped farther into the hut, her expression earnest. "But this is madness," she argued. "No payment of coin will repair the damage done to you. And truly, my family has no coin with which they might pay your ransom—"

Edana caught her breath and Angus froze. "What is this you say?" he asked, his words dangerously soft. He felt Edana rise to her feet behind him, but he ignored her.

The maiden evidently took his quietude for encouragement, for she stepped forward, a tentative smile curving her lips. She looked young and soft, yet resolute in her certainty that she was right.

The woman could tempt a saint, of that Angus was certain.

"My family sent all their coin to the convent. There is no

wealth at Ceinn-beithe, though many a man has thought it must have a full treasury. When there is coin, my family build—"

"Not that," Angus interrupted impatiently.

But the maiden was determined to appeal to him. "You should cease this madness before it proceeds further. You are a man of honor, a knight, a crusader."

Her insistence upon believing good of him was nigh as tempting as she was.

"Am I?" Angus demanded coldly, intent upon destroying her illusions about him. If naught else, she would reveal herself more fully if she continued talking.

"Of course you are! You wear the cross, you rode to crusade, you sacrificed your own desires. This change of course will win you naught. Take me to Inveresbeinn while all can yet be forgotten. Do not cast away all your noble deeds for a life of banditry!"

Angus smiled the predatory smile that so troubled her, knowing that alone would shake her determination. "Is that what I do, vixen?"

She faltered and seemed startled. Already he could see her flush rising. "But—but I am no vixen. I am no temptress. I . . . I . . ."

"Are you not?" Angus purred and leaned closer. "Then how is it that you tempt a man so well? Is this the manner of most novitiates in these days?"

She shook her head, licked her lips, then flushed more deeply when Angus watched the movement of her tongue avidly.

To her credit, she tried to continue with her entreaty. "What shall you do if the ransom cannot be paid? I have no doubt that you believe your success assured, but what if 'tis not?"

"Then a captive will be of no use to me," he threatened, but she was not dissuaded.

"One hears of knights driven to banditry to see their purses filled again, and yet of others driven to criminal deeds out of grief for their losses, but there are other choices . . ."

"Losses? Exactly what losses would those be?" he asked with a care that should have warned her.

But the maiden did not heed his manner in time and Edana was too slow to intervene. "Why, the deaths of your family," she declared. "Especially since you rode to crusade to save them from the ill fortune that befell them after your father's refusal to go! Any man might find their demise disheartening, but 'tis not reason enough to become a villain, and I fear that when your ransom is not met, you will feel obliged to worsen your crimes—" She closed her mouth suddenly, realizing that she had revealed too much.

Angus watched her, his countenance set to stone. "How is it that you know so much of my family?"

Her gaze flicked to the older woman in appeal.

Angus's words fell harshly from his tongue. "The tale was not Edana's to tell."

"She sought only to aid you! She sought to make me understand."

"You have no need to understand."

"But . . . but . . ."

She managed no more before Edana herself spoke in her own defense. "Did you not call me *seanchaidh*, lad? Stories are my wares and I shall tell them wheresoever I will, regardless of what you might say of the matter."

"You should not have told her."

The old woman shrugged, unrepentant. "But I did and there is naught that can change the fact of it now."

They stared at each other for a long moment. "I do not

recall you being so defiant of the wills of others. You have changed, Edana."

The old woman laughed. "Aye, I have changed, and changed more than you know, but that is of little import now."

" 'Tis of much import," he corrected. "For your doing this compels me now to leave." He turned toward the demoiselle. "With my captive, of course."

"What is this?" the maiden cried. "Where do we go?"

"It matters naught." Angus gave Edana a harsh look. "We will leave immediately. Perhaps the *seanchaidh* would do me the honor of forgetting that this particular story transpired."

The old woman lifted her chin and he saw that he had irked her. "I should like naught better. You are not the man I remember, Angus of Airdfinnan."

"You remember a boy," he retorted.

"I remember a boy, 'tis true, but one with honor in his soul." Edana leaned in her door. "I see he has been abandoned in the course of your journey. Tell me, do you mourn his loss?"

Angus paused to meet the elderly woman's gaze again. "Much has been lost beyond retrieval in this journey. You may be certain that I mourn the loss of the only thing I truly desire. I shall reclaim it or die in the trying."

"You should not have come here."

"Nay, 'tis clear that choice was yet another error on my part." Angus marched out of the hut, moving with haste to saddle Lucifer.

"Go then! You will find no better sanctuary than this!" Edana cried.

The steed stamped, echoing his master's impatience to be gone. Angus fastened the saddlebags, with savage gestures, then fetched a length of linen from within them. His lips tightened grimly and he blindfolded the maiden, ignoring the older woman's words.

"But—" the demoiselle protested.

"You already know too much," he snapped. "You will not find your way back here or lead another to this place."

She had the sense to hold her tongue. He lifted the maiden to the saddle, with terse movements, well aware that the old seer trailed behind him.

"You ride on a fool's errand, lad, and with a burden of wickedness that can do naught but draw more of its kind to *you*. I would wager that you would die in the attempt to regain what you have lost, were I a gambling woman."

Angus pivoted and smiled. Edana shivered at the sight of it. "I fear naught, Edana *Seanchaidh*, for I have naught left to fear. Every event I have ever dreaded has come to pass, regardless of my efforts to the contrary. And even if you should win your wager, I for one should not mourn the loss of this knight."

The maiden gasped, but he ignored her response and swung into the saddle. He drew her tightly against him and she had the wits not to challenge him.

"Do not draw her into this trouble," the old woman commanded.

" 'Tis too late! She is mine, and I shall do with her whatsoever I will." The demoiselle shivered, but he held her fast.

"You do not fool me," Edana retorted. She strode forward, shaking a finger in recrimination. "There is more honor left in you than that. You may feel that the world owes you much, but be careful, Angus MacGillivray. You would not be the first to become what you despise."

Angus granted her a cold glance but she held his regard unswervingly. "You know naught of what you speak." With that he spurred the beast on, feeling the weight of the old woman's gaze upon them.

He dared not say more. It had long been said that Edana could see the future, and in this he feared she was right.

And Angus knew he was becoming a man no better than

his father's archfoe, a man who would pay any price or demand any price to see his goal achieved. He deliberately did
not look to the woman before him, for he knew what he had
done and was not proud of the result.

He could only hope that his father would believe as he did,
that his family legacy was worth the price to be paid by himself and this woman.

✷

They rode hard along the narrow, twisting path, the steed evidently as anxious to be gone as the knight who rode him.
The forest was still wet with rain, the leaves verdant with
new spring growth.

Angus of Airdfinnan, Edana had called the knight, and the
name of the holding rang familiar in Jacqueline's ears. 'Twas
a keep, an old stronghold, and one but a few days' ride from
Ceinn-beithe. Beyond that, she knew little of it.

Save that she thought 'twas held by the church.

Jacqueline's thoughts flew. If Angus was the son of
Airdfinnan, then he was of the local nobility. It would make
sense if his family lost their riches as well as their lives and
thus that he would seek coin in compensation.

Though she could not imagine why he thought those at
Ceinn-beithe ought to render his due. 'Twas clear there was
more to the tale than Edana had told her, and Jacqueline's curiosity began to plague her.

Angus did not seem inclined to confide his secrets in her.
Indeed, he had moved brusquely, as if the old woman had betrayed his trust. Jacqueline knew that Edana only meant to
help, though this was not the moment to make such an argument.

And she appreciated his concern for the old woman's welfare. She knew Duncan would not demand any restitution
from Edana, but Angus had not the luxury of knowing that
the chieftain of Clan MacQuarrie was a just man.

She would have plenty of opportunity to choose a moment to plead the old seer's case. Aye, the two were utterly alone together, and she knew not how long 'twould be thus. That fact made her innards chill with mingled anticipation and dread.

Angus kept one arm clamped around Jacqueline's waist like a vise and she held her tongue, not even daring to gasp when Lucifer leapt over a narrow stream.

He must have felt her body clench, for he chuckled darkly. "You test my lack of faith in miracles by remaining silent for so long."

'Twas hardly a compliment. Jacqueline held herself stiffly, noting that his anger seemed to have faded as quickly as it had arisen. "I have naught to say."

"Another miracle," he muttered, though there was a thread of humor in his tone. "Have you decided then that I am no longer worthy of salvation? Or are you persuaded that the deed cannot be done?"

"You are not so wicked as you would have Edana believe," Jacqueline retorted. "Only a fool would take the falsity of your claims over the truth of your deeds."

"I had not realized that the capture of virgins was no longer a lawless deed," he murmured, his lips against her hair. "Perhaps I should begin a collection."

Jacqueline opened her mouth and closed it again, momentarily confused. She decided to feign insouciance. " 'Tis true there is little crime in the capture of virgins," she declared as calmly as she could. " 'Tis the subsequent ravishing of them that troubles fathers everywhere."

He was silent, as if she had surprised him again. "Is that an invitation, vixen?"

"Nay, of course not!"

To her consternation, something stirred against her buttocks. She wriggled, which only made matters worse, and

Angus began to chuckle. She tried to put some distance between them, but he deliberately drew her closer, then bent to kiss her neck beneath her ear.

"Patience, vixen," he whispered. "We shall put these woods behind us soon enough, and then you may have all you desire of me in privacy."

"I desire naught of you!" she squeaked.

"Only a fool would take the falsity of your claims over the truth of your deeds," he teased, sounding as if he were on the verge of laughter. "Perhaps you are no virgin, after all."

"But I am!"

" 'Tis clear that you know how to tempt a man, for I am tempted. Perhaps you make an invitation." He drew her yet more firmly against him, so that she could have no doubt of his state. "And there is only one way to know for certain that a woman is indeed a maiden."

She twisted to regard him in horror, pushing the blindfold from her face. His set features revealed naught to her. "You would *not* steal my chastity!"

"It seems to me that you offer it willingly."

"Nay. I . . . I would never! I—" Jacqueline halted and mustered her thoughts. She only amused him when she responded in outrage, and she saw the telltale gleam in his eye. "You gave me your word."

"My word to not ravish you." He arched his dark brow, looking rakish once again. "To take what you offer is another issue altogether."

"But—"

They reached a larger road and Angus indicated that she should be silent. They hovered in the shadows for a moment. Naught carried to their ears but the echo of birdsong. Finally, persuaded that the road was indeed deserted, Angus urged the stallion onward.

Lucifer tossed his dark mane, apparently preferring the more level road, and increased his pace to a canter.

"But?" Jacqueline demanded.

"But you continue to tempt me, and now you yourself have declared that your family would not be able to spare any coin." Angus paused, a hint of mischief lighting his tone. "Perhaps you would prefer to offer other compensation to me to see your release."

Jacqueline twisted in his grip, not surprised to find him watching her intently. "Would you release me in exchange for my maidenhead?"

"There are no guarantees in this world, vixen, though there is naught ignoble in trying to influence one's fate." He smiled wolfishly. "Indeed, you might find that the joys of the convent lose some of their luster when compared to more earthly delights." His brow arched high. "You might not wish to abandon my side, after all."

"Rogue!" Jacqueline spun to face the road ahead as he laughed. Aye, if any man could make her forget her desire to be a bride of Christ, 'twould be this man. Perhaps her mother had spoken aright in advising that she cast away too much in joining the convent.

She wondered what 'twould be like to be sampled by a man.

She wondered what 'twould be like to be sampled by Angus, a man of passion and tenderness, a man disserved by the world but still gallant in his manner. Angus could enflame her with a mere glance, and his touch awakened an answering fire within her with disconcerting speed. He was not the only one tempted to do what he should not.

But Jacqueline knew better than to welcome temptation.

She heaved a sigh. "I know you are angered that Edana told me of your family, but I am sorry that they are lost to you."

Angus's words were cold. "You know naught of my family. Edana knows naught of the truth."

"Who is she?"

"She is but an old madwoman who has not left the forest in decades."

"Then how do you know her?"

"All know Edana."

"I do not."

He made some sound in his throat that might have indicated exasperation. "All raised hereabouts know Edana, or did."

Jacqueline shook her head. "That makes little sense. She lives in the forest, far from all. How could any know her?"

"All go to the cloutie well for injuries and blessings. And many go to Edana for tales."

"She is more than a storyteller," Jacqueline guessed.

"There are those who believe she has the Sight."

"Like whom?"

"Do your questions ever cease?"

"I am curious. Who took you to Edana?"

He sighed. "I suppose 'tis harmless to admit 'twas my father. He had much faith in the old seer and oft consulted her. My mother called it pagan sorcery and would neither go nor permit us to go."

"Then—"

Angus interrupted her firmly. "As you might well understand, I was sufficiently curious to follow my father secretly and thus came to know the old woman."

"She is old."

"Beyond ancient, my father said. He declared she had been old when he first visited her and hinted that she was immortal."

Jacqueline rolled her eyes at that nonsensical claim. "Immortal or not, her tale of your family made sense to me."

"Tales oft make more sense than the truth," Angus said mildly. "I tell you that Edana lies. Who would know my tale better than me?"

"You argue overmuch." Jacqueline shook her head stubbornly. "There was a truth in her tale, and I believe her, regardless of what you say. You seek compensation you deem due, but you seek it in the wrong way."

Now his words were tight. "You know naught of compensation due."

"I believe you know you pursue this matter wrongly," Jacqueline insisted. "Did you not yourself vow that you would take naught that was not yours to take?"

"And what do you offer me in compensation for my losses of which you know so much?"

Jacqueline lifted her chin. "I will listen to your tale. Set the matter to rights if you are so certain that Edana told it incorrectly."

He chuckled. "Sadly, I do not wish to tell the tale. And I shall never tell it to you, not even to satisfy your cursed curiosity. It has naught to do with you—you are but a tool for me."

"Then the truth of your tale will haunt you forever. The only way to loose its power over you is to tell it."

"Nay. The only way to loose the power of a ghost is to see it avenged."

Jacqueline shook her head. "People die, Angus. 'Tis part of life that cannot be denied. There is no compensation due for the loss of a loved one taken in their own time to God's reward."

"Nay? What of those *dispatched* to their own reward?"

She twisted around to study him again, uncertain of his meaning. He fairly thrummed with annoyance, his expression tellingly intent.

"My father was murdered; my brother as well." Angus

spoke dispassionately, though his eye glittered with an anger that ran deep. "There is a payment due for murder in every man's code of law, is there not?"

"Murdered!" Jacqueline felt her eyes widen in mingled shock and dismay. "But who killed them?"

Angus's smile was far from reassuring. "None other than the chieftain of Clan MacQuarrie."

Chapter Nine

AY!" JACQUELINE CRIED OUT IN SHOCK AND DISMAY. Angus, though, was resolute. "Aye. If not with his own hand then as surely as if 'twas."

"But this cannot be! It makes little sense at all."

"It makes perfect sense. Airdfinnan was the prize." Angus breathed the name of the holding as if 'twas an incantation. He granted her a quelling look. "Do not suggest to me that that old feud is forgotten."

"What feud?"

Angus's gaze flicked over her features and his eye narrowed. His voice dropped low. "I have no obligation to tell you of your clan's wicked deeds. The chieftain of Clan MacQuarrie will surrender Airdfinnan to see you safely home again, and that is all you need to know." With that he stared grimly at the road ahead and evidently thought all discussion complete.

But Jacqueline shook her head. " 'Tis no lie that this makes little sense. How can Duncan surrender what he does not hold? I do not even know for certain where Airdfinnan lies! Its governance has naught to do with my family."

Angus frowned, answering her with evident reluctance. "Aye, it does, for Cormac MacQuarrie was an old foe of my father's."

"That has naught to do with Duncan."

Angus's expression turned fierce. "Men bound together by blood or by vow do not forget each other's pledges. Cormac swore that he would hold Airdfinnan if 'twas the last deed he did or if that could not be done, he would see it ripped from my father's hands."

Jacqueline blinked in astonishment. "But why?"

He watched her carefully. "Because Cormac believed the guardianship of Airdfinnan should have been entrusted to him by the King of the Isles instead of to my father." Angus shook his head in impatience. "But why do you insist that I tell you what you must already know?"

"I do not know this tale. Cormac, after all, is long dead," Jacqueline reminded him.

"But an old oath does not die so readily as that. Whosoever the chieftain of Clan MacQuarrie might be, that man will uphold the command of his forebear."

"Nay, not Duncan!"

"Nay? Does he uphold no interests of the man who granted him the power he holds?"

Jacqueline could not help but think of Cormac's son Iain and how Duncan treated him with all the affection of a brother.

And Angus, curse him, guessed the reason for her hesitation. "Does he?" he prompted.

"He has seen Cormac's son wed to my half-sister."

Angus nodded. "A dynastic alliance, 'tis clear." He frowned. "And you believe this man does not tend to old pledges? You are not so witless as that."

"You do not know Alienor," Jacqueline could not help but observe. "There are those who would think it a curse to be wedded to her. She has a wickedly sharp tongue."

He chuckled suddenly and regarded her with a warmth that surprised her. "Yours is not without its barbs, vixen."

Jacqueline straightened. "Do you mean to silence me again so that you might be untroubled?"

"Nay. There is none who might hear you cry for aid in this remote place, and truly"—his gaze darkened as his gaze lingered upon her mouth—"there are advantages in having your lips freed."

'Twas only too easy to discern the direction of his thoughts now. "You seek only to frighten me," she charged.

That dark brow arched, giving him a diabolical air. "And do I?"

"Nay." 'Twas only half a lie, though Jacqueline did not doubt he knew the truth of it.

Angus leaned closer, his fingers splaying across her belly. "Then perhaps I should make a more diligent effort," he whispered.

Her heart had time to skip one beat, though whether 'twas due to dread or anticipation, even Jacqueline could not say. Angus's silhouette blocked out the pale sunlight as he leaned closer. He dropped the reins as his lips closed over hers in a resolute kiss.

Jacqueline refused to give him the satisfaction of a fearful response. Indeed, the only way to dissuade him of his conviction that she could be terrorized with his touch was to welcome it.

'Twas surprisingly simple to do. Jacqueline parted her lips, as if inviting his embrace. He gasped in surprise, and she felt as if the power had shifted in their exchange. Aye, he was not immune to her touch either!

That realization emboldened her further. She arched against him like a wanton and opened her mouth to him, then touched her tongue to his.

She did not win precisely the response she had expected. Angus fairly tore his lips from hers, swore and pushed her away from him. She felt the heat of him against her buttocks and knew not what she had done amiss.

Though 'twas more than clear that Angus was angered with her. She might have asked him what she had done awry, but he silenced her question with a glare that shook her to the core.

Clearly, her response had offended him. And truly, what madness had seized her that she invited his embrace so boldly?

"I am sorry." She felt his gaze as surely as a touch, but she did not look over her shoulder to him. A long silence stretched between them and she felt her cheeks burn with embarrassment.

"How sorry?" Angus asked silkily.

Jacqueline's pulse leapt and she could not keep herself from glancing at him. "What do you mean?"

His expression was impassive, but his words surprised her. "In lieu of an apology, I would hear your tale."

"What tale? I have no tale to tell."

"Liar," Angus murmured, unexpected affection in his tone. His gaze was unswerving, making her feel cornered yet again. "Tell me what happened to make you fear men as you do."

"I offered an apology," she said stiffly, "which should suffice."

"Aye, it should," he said ruefully, "but I am a bandit now by your own recounting and must therefore adopt the unjust means of a lawless man."

Jacqueline regarded him warily, not in the least bit certain that he did not mock her conclusions. Aye, there was that mischievous gleam in his eye again.

"And what if I do tell you?" she demanded, knowing that he expected just the opposite.

"Then the wager should be even. You have a tale of me and I would have a tale of you."

"But we should be no closer to my release."

"Of course not. Only your family can see to that, for only they can surrender Airdfinnan in exchange."

Jacqueline nibbled her lip as she considered his assertion. Her family could not ensure her freedom, contrary to Angus's expectation, for they had no claim over Airdfinnan. She wondered what she might do to see that he won his objective—and thus see to her own release.

"You see now how difficult 'tis to surrender a tale of oneself to another," he said quietly, evidently misunderstanding the reason for her silence. "You have until this evening to decide your course, for this evening I would have your tale."

"And if I choose not to tell it?"

He smiled coolly, aloof and dangerous once again. "Then we shall negotiate other compensation for the tale of me that you have already claimed," he murmured, no small measure of threat in his tone.

They rode in silence for the remainder of that day and made a camp at dusk. Angus found a clearing sufficiently deep in the woods where his fire would not be spied easily from the road. He bound his captive's hands and ankles, ignored her displeasure, and left her with Lucifer while he snared a rabbit for their meal.

'Twould be simple fare, naught but meat and a thin broth of water, but 'twould be hot and not unwelcome. The maiden averted her face as he kindled the fire and he knew Rodney would have had some comment upon her silence.

While the meat stewed, Angus strode half a dozen paces into the forest and walked in a circle around their camp, breaking the undergrowth deliberately. He did this until he was certain his scent was well established, then urinated at intervals on his last walk around the perimeter. 'Twas not much of a defense, but the woods were bountiful this spring—perhaps 'twould be enough to deter the wolves.

Men, however, would not even see this obstacle. Angus listened, but the hills echoed only with silence. Rodney could not have arrived at Ceinn-beithe as yet. Even if they rode in pursuit on the moment of his arrival, and even if they persuaded Rodney to aid them, they would have to retrace that man's steps. He would take them to Edana's hut, if he could be coerced to do so, unaware that Angus had departed. Then they would have to follow his course of this day.

On this night, Angus could sleep with the certainty of not being disturbed. Indeed, it might be his last night of such conviction.

His captive wore a mutinous expression when he returned, though it did not mask her own exhaustion. "The meat burns," she said accusingly, then lifted her bound hands. "And there was naught I could do about the matter."

She had spirit, he would grant her that. Indeed, she had a gift for making him smile, though Angus would not admit such a weakness aloud. He stirred the meat and turned it, his dagger and spoon the only cooking utensils he had. He sat down, his back against a tree opposite the maiden, close enough to the fire that he could tend to the food. The sky had darkened overhead and the fire snapped and crackled, casting lights on the surrounding trees.

And upon the woman's face. He watched her as she watched him, having no doubt that he looked as wary as she. "Well?" he prompted quietly. "What of your tale? Will you tell it or nay?"

She wriggled. "Will you unbind me?"

"Nay."

Indignation made her eyes flash. "Not even for the tale?"

"The tale is owed for your knowing my tale. What you would wager to see your bounds loosened is another matter altogether."

She visibly gritted her teeth and glared at him. "You are a most vexing man."

He braced one elbow on his knee and smiled. "You expect otherwise from a man who captured you to serve his own ends alone?"

She laughed, most unexpectedly to his thinking, yet the sound was a delight. "I suppose 'twould be unfitting, though I know little of brigands and their ways."

"I know too much of villains," Angus said grimly. "Count yourself fortunate in your ignorance."

Her laughter stilled and her smile faded. "Have you truly been to hell?" she whispered, her gaze bright with curiosity.

He moved forward to survey the cooking meat. " 'Tis you who are to tell tales this night," he chided gently. "Not I." He flicked a glance to her. "If indeed that is the offering you choose to make."

She looked at the ground before herself, her words falling softly. "I would tell you the tale, if I knew whence to begin."

"Why did you choose the cloistered life?" Angus asked, equally quietly. "And tell me no tale of your calling to serve Christ."

Her smile was fleeting. "I believe I have such a vocation, but my mother says 'tis naught but an excuse. She speaks wrongly, for I know that the convent is the place for me." Her brows drew together fleetingly. "If naught else, I do have a choice and I would make the most of it."

Angus said naught.

Her lips tightened as she met his gaze. "I was born a woman. So be it. And by dint of my gender, I am compelled to select from meager range of choices. So be it, again. The fact of the matter is that there are but two courses for my life—marriage or the convent. Marriage to an earthly spouse or a divine one. So be it. I have chosen. What is so irksome about men is that not a one of them permits me to make the single choice that is mine."

"You still have suitors," he guessed.

"Aye, but worse than that." She stared off into the shadows of the forest for a moment, eyes narrowed in concentration. "I was betrothed virtually upon my birth, to a man who was a comrade of my father's. As my mother tells it, my father made this arrangement upon her father's comment that I would one day be a beauty. Perhaps my father wished to ensure my safety, perhaps he merely wished to pay some debt owed his comrade. I do not know."

'Twas interesting how dispassionately she recounted these facts. "Did you not ask him?"

"He died when I was too young to care for such matters. My mother wed again and was widowed again when I was fourteen summers of age. My betrothed had since made himself familiar to me and made it clear that he intended that we should wed shortly. I suppose he was of an age that made him disinclined to wait longer than necessary."

"How old was he?"

"At that time, he was some sixty summers of age." She laughed under her breath and her eyes sparkled with mischief, though Angus could not imagine why. "I must confess that I thought him more ancient than God himself, though 'twas an uncharitable thought, and worse, I called him 'the old toad.' My sisters and I mimicked him most wickedly."

Angus felt his lips quirk before he could stop them.

" 'Twas not simply that he was so aged, 'twas his manner. I thought perhaps that if I talked with him, if I came to know him as a man with whom one might converse, then his looks would not trouble me. 'Tis oft this way—when one cares for another, one overlooks the other's faults."

Her lips tightened. "But he would not talk to me. He said 'twas unfitting for women to be heard. He spoke always of *possessing* me, as if I were some desirable chattel that he would add to his household." She shuddered. "And he touched me, oft in most familiar and unwelcome ways. I came very quickly to loathe him."

Angus could readily understand this, though he said naught to interrupt her.

She shook her head in exasperation. "But if a man desires a woman to be his wife by virtue of her appearance alone, what does that say of that man? I am unimpressed by a man with a pretty bride. It says naught good of his character, in my estimation. If his wife is clever, or kind, or uncommonly pious, these traits reflect well upon the man who wedded her. But beauty?"

She shrugged before he could reply. " 'Tis naught but an ornament, and one that does not endure. A sensible woman can only wonder what this ardent suitor will do when she ages, as we all must do. What merit will she hold in her spouse's eyes when her beauty fades?"

"He might become fond of her," Angus suggested, intrigued that her beauteous features meant so little to her.

The lady scoffed. "I am unpersuaded that a man who weds only for appearances is capable of feeling much for another. Certainly my experience has not shown me otherwise, and, truly, I would not hang my fate upon so slender a thread."

"So you defied this betrothed?"

"Not I. I knew little of such matters then and merely disliked the man. My mother had been against the match from the first, and when my distaste became clear to her, she tried to have the contract broken. But my betrothed would not desist. So, when my mother was widowed again, she chose to flee to Scotland rather than cede me to this betrothal. She wished to grant myself and my sisters the chance to wed for love, though, indeed, she herself was the first to do so."

"To this new chieftain of Clan MacQuarrie." Angus supplied.

"Aye." She tilted her head to regard him suddenly. "And you remind me of him, truth be told."

The comparison startled Angus, and his response evidently showed, for the maiden smiled. "Aye, you do. He has a fearsome temper, though it is never long-lived, and he never would wound another willingly. He loves my mother as never a man had loved her before, as she deserves and for the woman that she is, not for her beauty or her possessions or her ability to grant him a child. They are very happy."

She fell silent, and Angus fully expected her to confess to this man's betrayal of her mother's trust and affection.

"But my mother's plan went awry in my case, for my betrothed was not so readily swayed as that. Reynaud followed us to Scotland and attacked me. He would have raped me in my own bed—for he made certain that I was helpless to save myself—and done so gladly had it not been for my mother's timely intervention."

She took a shuddering breath but continued with vigor. "He would have done so purely to see that he was not cheated of what he believed to be his own. He did not care for me as my mother says a man should care for his bride—he saw naught but my face and his contract, which granted him the right to claim me."

"Because you are beautiful," Angus said.

She nodded, then mused for a moment, as devoid of airs as he could imagine a woman might be. "Perhaps 'twould have been different if I had always been fair of face, like my sister. Esmeraude is accustomed to attention won by her appearance alone, and she has a comfort with that which I cannot emulate. She knows how to win her desire, how to turn the perceptions of others to her advantage. I have no such skill and I desire none. When I was younger and plain of countenance, people talked to me and they listened to me.

"But since my shape has changed and my features became what they would be, no one talks to me. No one listens to me and all assume that I have naught to say. All guess they know my character, my hopes, and this without permitting me to speak. And men"—she rolled her eyes in frustration—"these men who come to plea for my hand, they speak about me as if I am not present or stare at me with their mouths gaping. 'Tis a poor exchange for conversation, for laughter and wit, and 'tis one for which I have no taste."

Angus could understand this. The maiden before him, although a beauty, was not conventionally pretty. She would not have been a fetching child, but likely a solemn one, much interested in the world and its workings. 'Twas certain her curiosity had not arrived with her winsome curves. She was not slow of wit, and he could imagine well that 'twould be most tiresome to have others presume her to be so foolish as so many lovely demoiselles tended to be.

She frowned at the ground. "Reynaud's assault is the reason why your capture so terrified me. I feared you were of his ilk, and knew that there was none to rescue me this time from my fate." She glanced up, what might have been admiration shining in her gaze, and Angus was startled again. "But you defied my expectation."

The fire crackled between them, the meat sizzled. Still they stared at each other, Angus uncertain what she would credit to him but desperately wanting to know.

He could not ask, but he did not have to do so.

"You did not force yourself upon me, as you could have

done more than once. You put me in mind of my stepfather in this way as well, for I have no fear in his presence. Indeed, 'twas he who killed Reynaud."

She nodded as if to add even more conviction to her words. "I would trust Duncan with my very life and know that my trust would not be misplaced. I trust *you*, for your deeds have proven the manner of man that you are, though you would try to dissuade me with your words from thinking good of you."

"You know little of me."

She shook her head and regarded him with shining eyes. "You will not change my thinking."

Her trust was most unsettling. "Do you dare me?" he challenged.

"Nay." She held his gaze steadily. "Though it matters not. You have not that thirst for violence within you. If you had, you would not speak to me as you do, as Duncan does—you would not argue with me, you would not tease me, you would not ensure my safety. You would not kiss me as though you sought permission to continue."

Angus frowned and shoved to his feet, troubled more than he would have preferred by her insight. He made much of turning the meat and checking its readiness. "You seek only to keep that chastity you so prize, by lavishing compliments upon me."

" 'Tis safe in your presence. I know it as well as you do."

"You know naught, and even less of me," he said with deliberate harshness. " 'Tis only good sense to protect one's captive when one seeks ransom from a hot-blooded chieftain. That alone is the reason you have not been injured, at least as yet. If Rodney returns with a poor response, you may be certain that you will pay the price."

"Liar," she charged softly, showing no inclination to be frightened of him. "I would wager that you know what 'tis to have only poor choices and, worse, to have even those choices stolen away. You understand more than you care to admit, and because of that, I will have my choice in the end. I trust you to see it so."

"Your trust is sorely misplaced. I care naught for your objectives, only for my own." He spoke tightly and quickly, but there was a ring of falsity to his claims.

Indeed, the lady merely smiled at him.

He ignored her, letting the forest fill the silence between them with its nocturnal sounds. The meat was cooked through, so he pulled the pot from the fire, letting it cool on the earth for a few minutes.

He stoked up the fire and busied himself, well aware that she watched him. When the meat had cooled, he boned it, leaving only flesh in small pieces and a thin sauce. He fetched his cup and handed it to her, setting the pot before her.

"Eat whatsoever you will."

"What of you?"

"I shall finish it, once you have had your fill."

Her smile had all the brilliance of the sun appearing suddenly from behind the clouds, and the sight made him take a step back. "I thank you." She had some difficulty scooping the cup into the pot with her hands bound, but she managed the deed.

And was too proud to ask him again to release her.

He felt like a cur for pretending not to notice.

" 'Tis good," she said appreciatively. "And most welcome. Though what we might have done for an onion, and a few pot herbs, I cannot guess." Again she smiled, but Angus turned away, content that she was able to eat and would do so.

He left her there while he fetched more wood for the fire, letting Lucifer keep watch, even as he listened with care.

Aye, he needed time to bolster his determination to finish

what he had begun. She had touched him with her appeal, more deeply than he would have her know. 'Twas better he left her alone, this woman who could so readily beguile him.

Angus could nigh hear all Rodney would have to say of that.

Chapter Ten

T WAS LONG BEFORE ANGUS SHOWED HIMSELF WITHIN the clearing again, and the maiden had succumbed to the warmth of the meat and her own exhaustion. She had stretched out to sleep, though her eyelids fluttered when he approached.

"I feared you gone," she murmured, her voice drowsily low.

Angus was still shaken by her conviction that she understood him. He took refuge in teasing her as if she were a child, not a woman who tempted him in ways he would prefer not to be tempted. "And leave you with all the stew, such as it is?"

She smiled and he shed his cloak, helping her to sit up while he wrapped it around her. She yawned luxuriously, then lay down, thanking him once more for the meal. He took the pot silently and returned to his favored tree from across the fire, watching her eyelids droop.

'Twas not long before she was asleep. He watched her as he ate without tasting the meat, his thoughts churning. Then he cleaned up. He discarded the bones far from where they slept, and washed his knife, cup, and pot in a thin trickle of a stream.

Upon finishing, he returned to sit and watch his captive. The fire burned low between them, casting its flickering

golden light over her features. She looked so soft, so innocent and young.

Angus thought of her tale, of her fear, of her efforts to be
valiant despite the memory of her betrothed's deed. The
man's presumption angered him. 'Twas not his affair, though
she spoke aright when she guessed that he had a distaste of
such violence. She had left much left unsaid, he was certain,
and he did not doubt that "the old toad" had earned her disgust by more than his refusal to listen to what she said.

He was ridiculously glad that this Reynaud, a man he had
never known and against whom he had no complaints in his
own right, was dead.

Perhaps 'twas because it had been long since any had
trusted him as this maiden claimed to do, any save Rodney.

This trust she granted him was a curious burden. It made
Angus sit in the woods, sleepless despite his exhaustion, and
consider the merit of what he did. She trusted him with her
life, her chastity, her protection, but he trusted her with
naught in return.

Indeed, Angus lied to this woman when he said he took
naught that was not his to take. Perhaps he insisted upon that
claim because he knew deep inside himself that 'twas untrue.
He took her freedom. He took her right to choose. He broke
her commitment to the convent that was already sealed with
coin. He awakened urges within her that would best be left
dormant if she was destined for that novitiate's life.

He was a thief.

He was little better than Reynaud, who thought of her as
chattel. Had he not considered her a burden that would win
him his due? Had he not insisted upon thinking of her that
way?

But she was not chattel. She was a clever and determined
young woman, a beauty to be sure, but one with a character
that would have shone whatever her countenance had been.

She was Jacqueline.

He whispered her name beneath his breath.

Yet despite his crimes against her, she trusted him, and that trust humbled him. She curled up like a child and slept before him, her wrists and ankles bound, trusting him not to presume overmuch. She offered her pledge not to flee if he unbound her. She shared with him the story of the abuse she had suffered, a tale that filled him with a need for vengeance upon her behalf.

'Twas a tale that made Angus feel a knave for what he took of her in his turn.

He frowned and pushed to his feet, then kicked another log onto the fire, watching her all the while.

For a long time, he had been certain that he had been to hell and that what he had endured and seen had been a madness wrought by the Holy Land. It had seemed to Angus that the wickedness had indeed left its taint upon him, as Edana claimed. All across Christendom, he had been convinced that the shadows he had seen followed him, dogging his footsteps with ill fortune and malice.

But now it appeared that wickedness had no exclusive tie to him. Nay, it dwelt everywhere, in many hearts and many deeds. Now that he had become aware of it, he saw its taint where he had never thought to look.

It had been there, in the intent of men like Reynaud, though once Angus himself had been too innocent to see evil's stain.

As Jacqueline had been.

He could not again be the boy he had been fifteen years ago, but he could ensure that Jacqueline did not become so embittered as he. Angus crouched beside his captive, hesitated for a moment, then gently untied the rope knotted about her wrists.

The soft flesh had chafed and he slid his thumb across the

abrasion in mute apology. She stirred at his touch and he froze momentarily, afraid to be caught in this small act of kindness. Then he tucked his cloak over her hands and bent closer.

"Hush, 'tis naught," he whispered. "Go to sleep, Jacqueline."

She smiled in her sleep and sighed, folding her hands together and tucking them beneath her cheek. Angus crouched there motionless, watching the firelight caress her features, until her breathing deepened again. Then he moved to unbind her ankles, tucking the wool about her carefully.

There was no question of his abusing her trust.

Angus returned to the other side of the fire, bracing his back against the same tree once again. Lucifer snorted, then dropped his head, nuzzling in the undergrowth.

The sounds of the night forest echoed around them, the firelight keeping any intruders at bay. Angus closed his eyes, a mistake, since the memories were always lurking there, waiting for him to grant them a chance to live again.

He shuddered and forced his eyes open, though he was tired to the bone. He frowned and studied the woman, wanting naught but to lie down beside her and hold her close against his warmth.

But he had no right and he knew it well. His argument, after all, was not with this woman.

It was with whoever had ensured that Airdfinnan was stolen, whoever had seen Angus's father and brother dead. He had been certain 'twas Cormac MacQuarrie behind the matter, but Jacqueline's protests made him wonder. While Cormac might have ensured the deed was done, if Cormac was dead, his heir might know naught of it. Certainly this Duncan had not been at Ceinn-beithe when Angus's brother and father fell ill.

What if the truth had died with Cormac? What if these

people knew naught of that wickedness? What if they truly could not surrender Airdfinnan in exchange for Jacqueline? Rodney had been right—the scheme that had seemed so infallible was now ridden with holes.

'Twas not this woman who knew who was responsible for the death of the MacGillivray family. The man who currently held Airdfinnan's seal was certain to know the truth but Angus knew his query would not be welcomed at Airdfinnan.

Even if 'twas proven that this Duncan of Ceinn-beithe *was* the man owing restitution to Angus, Angus no longer had any desire to use Jacqueline in his plans.

Let her flee him in the night if she so chose.

If she did not, he would take her to Ceinn-beithe, or to Inveresbeinn, whichever was her choice. And she would be readily persuaded to quit his side, if not for the sake of her freedom than for the fear of her own safety.

Or of fear alone.

He smiled wryly to himself. Truly, if he wished to frighten her, he need not do so with his touch. Angus unbound the patch over his eye and laid it aside. One look at the monstrosity that had been wrought on his face and she would beg to be released.

Angus was certain of it. He rubbed the scarred flesh where his eye had been and leaned his head back against the tree trunk. He braced his hands upon his knees and looked once more about the forest, filled with familiar peaceful sounds.

He had thought that coming home would be the simplest part. He had spent years dreaming of Airdfinnan, of what good fortune his family must enjoy for his willing sacrifice, of how he would be welcomed back to all he had known before. He had thought this place to be innocent, to be safe, to be a refuge.

But Airdfinnan was lost, his family ashes, his home naught but a haunting memory. There were no true refuges, not from whatever darkness a man carried in his memory. And there were no survivors here, no family to welcome him, no one even to herald his return after all he had endured.

They were not tears upon his face, nay, they could not have been. Angus of Airdfinnan knew he had forgotten how to weep.

✳

Jacqueline awakened and stretched before she realized that her wrists and ankles were no longer bound. She sat up hastily, half certain she had been abandoned in the forest, then took a steadying breath when she spied Angus sleeping across from her. His stallion nickered and she turned to find the beast regarding her expectantly, ears flicking.

Angus did not stir. The fire had burned down to glowing coals, so Jacqueline rose and stretched again, then stirred the coals to life. There were clouds gathering overhead and 'twas early, by the sound of the birds, though the sky was faintly light. 'Twould rain before midday, she guessed.

And 'twas damp now, chill enough to make one shiver to the bone. She coaxed more of the collected wood to burn, then went to greet the horse. He nuzzled her ear, sniffing for treats of which she had none, and she chuckled at the way his nose tickled.

Still Angus did not move, and Jacqueline eyed him. He gave no impression of coiled strength this morn. His head had fallen forward and slightly to one side, hiding the patch over his eye and leaving his hair tousled. His booted ankles were crossed and his arms folded across his chest, his mouth as grim a line as ever. Despite that, he seemed soundly asleep.

Or perhaps worse. She frowned and abandoned the horse, stepping quietly across the camp until she was before the knight. She crept closer, searching for signs that he drew breath, yet unwilling to awaken him.

To her relief, his chest rose and fell with the even rhythm of sleep. She crouched and leaned toward him, just to be certain, and 'twas then she realized that he had removed his patch.

It lay upon his lap, as if discarded there. A lump rose in her throat even as she knew she could not resist the urge to look.

Angus stirred, murmuring something. He frowned and moved suddenly, making Jacqueline dart out of his way. He refolded his arms and crossed his legs the other way, restless with the impatience of one snared in an unpleasant dream.

Certainly his expression was forbidding.

But Jacqueline, undeterred, crept closer.

There was no eye there any longer, she saw that quickly, for his flesh was scarred over the empty socket. It made her belly clench to see the angry furrows left there, for 'twas clear even to her that his face had been burned. The stretched skin could not be mistaken for anything else.

Whether it had been by accident or by design, she did not know. But she could guess. He had been to Outremer, to holy wars more unholy than any ever witnessed. Aye, she could guess, and her heart ached for the agony he must have suffered.

The wound had been sealed shut, whether by the original injury or a healer's choice. His lashes were gone on that side, singed away so surely that they had not grown again. His brow had a quirk in it, by virtue of the way the wound had healed, and she saw that the straight scar on his cheek was just the final ripple in his greater injury.

She could not begin to imagine what could leave a man's face so marred. Indeed, this must have happened long ago, but the flesh was still red in places, angered if not raw. Jacqueline stretched out one hand, sorely tempted to soothe away this wound with her fingertips.

If only it could be done. Her fingers hovered before his

face, where she could feel the heat of his skin. Her fingers were halted by the realization that a man who did not like the tale of his family shared would like even less that she had seen the fullness of his scarred face while he slept.

She sat back on her heels and studied him. Although the damage was terrible, already she grew accustomed to it. He did not repulse her, though she certainly would have been shocked if he had removed his eye patch suddenly and while awake. She watched him sleep, felt her compassion for him grow, and decided that she still found him a very handsome man.

She would not recoil if he made to kiss her again. Her gaze dropped to the firm line of his lips, and that telltale warmth spread within her.

Nay, she would not deny Angus another kiss.

She got up and fetched his cloak, easing it over his legs so that he would not be chilled. It had been gallant of him to offer it to her, but after fifteen years in more exotic climes, he would be the one unaccustomed to such cool mornings.

From this closer vantage point, she saw the faint shadows beneath his eyes, the lines of exhaustion drawn to the corners of his mouth. When he was awake, she never noticed these signs of strain. Perhaps she had called it aright when she declared that banditry did not suit him.

He muttered again, and she slipped away, not wanting to be caught so close at hand. She decided to pretend that she had not noticed that his patch was removed and thus grant him the chance to hide himself once more.

Jacqueline looked around the clearing. She would position herself so that she was on his "good" side, so that 'twas possible that she had not observed his eye. Thus he could not so readily see through her claim to the contrary.

After all, he had unbound her and surrendered his cloak to

her. He had kept his pledge. And she had given him her word that she would not betray his trust if he released her. Jacqueline did not intend to break her vow.

She would not flee, though she had the chance. She would show him that those at Ceinn-beithe knew how to hold their pledges. Perhaps that would dissuade him from seeking vengeance from those who owed him naught.

Angus had cooked for her the night before, so she would cook something to break their fast. She would prove that she was more than a pretty face and a shapely figure—that she, like him, had the wits to survive.

Jacqueline had a sense that this man, unlike other men, might see past the surface to the woman she was in truth.

✷

Jacqueline rummaged through Angus's saddlebags and found that there was precious little to eat. A small piece of some ancient cheese was wrapped carefully there, though it was of so ripe an odor that she doubted anyone possessed of their senses could have forgotten its presence. There were several of the apples for which Rodney had bargained and an empty flask of ornate design that smelled strongly of eau de vie.

There was some small quantity of what might have been flour, though she could not guess from what grain it had been ground. 'Twas coarse and heavy and would have need of leavening to make anything of merit. There was one large spoon carved of wood and there was the pot Angus had used the night before, though well cleaned.

Other than that, two plain linen chemises were carefully folded within one bag, though they had become jumbled with a spare horseshoe, as yet unused, and several brushes that she had seen him use on Lucifer. She supposed as choices went, 'twas better to have his clean chemises with the steed's effects than with that cheese. Indeed, his belongings were quite orderly and clean, a fact of which she heartily approved.

There were also a few tools in the bottom of that bag and miscellany that would be useful for pitching a tent, though no tent was to be found. Angus would seem to be a man of few possessions.

Jacqueline surveyed her potential ingredients and decided that a bannock was the best that she might hope to concoct, though the flour was almost certainly not wrought of oats. On impulse, she ducked into the woods, hoping it was early enough in the spring that she might find an egg or two.

After considerable hunting, she found a pheasant nest. If the parent bird had not panicked and dashed away, Jacqueline might have stepped directly past it, for 'twas well camouflaged.

There were six eggs, very tiny, each the size of the last half of her thumb. She could not bear to take them all and leave the bird without offspring. After wrapping her hand in leaves from the forest floor so as not to leave her scent, she took three.

There was no fat for the pot, so she took Angus's knife from his belt—stealthily so as not to wake him—and diced one of the apples, keeping a keen eye for small green intruders. 'Twould add some moisture to the pan and perhaps keep her creation from sticking. She mixed the flour with the broken eggs as best she was able and dumped it all into the pot, stirring mightily with the spoon, then she placed it over the fire where the flames were lower and hoped for some success.

To be certain, she was hungered enough that she did not care what it tasted like. Angus stirred when the concoction began to burn. Jacqueline was aware that he moved, but she was desperately trying to loosen their meal from the bottom of the pot before it burned to cinders.

"Can you cook in truth?"

"I can, when there is aught to cook." She scraped a stubborn apple from the bottom and moved the pot to a cooler part of the fire.

She rubbed the back of her hand across her brow, irritable that he had awakened just when matters looked their worst. *Now* it sizzled calmly, curse the mixture! "Had you saved some of the fat from the rabbit last eve, 'twould have been easier."

"I did not want to attract guests to our camp." 'Twas most reasonable, though Jacqueline would have given her left hand for a morsel of butter in this moment. Angus rose and stretched and crossed to the fire, holding out his hands to warm them. She watched her bannock like a hawk.

"Do you need aid?"

"Nay, but the giblets would have also been welcome. Was that flour?"

"Aye. 'Tis coarse but better than naught. What have you mixed with it?" He sniffed with an appreciation that soothed her pride.

"Eggs."

"Eggs? Where did you find eggs?"

"Beneath a pheasant who is undoubtedly quite irked with me. I left her the other three."

She glanced up in time to see his surprise, then was startled herself to note that he had not replaced his patch. Indeed, Angus stared directly at her, as if he would dare her to be shocked.

Jacqueline deliberately spoke as if naught was amiss. "Did you sleep well?"

His good eye narrowed and she looked back at her

bannock, unable to hold that piercing gaze. The last thing she wanted to do was flinch, for he would interpret it badly, but 'twas nigh impossible to hold his glare.

"As well as ever." He moved closer, as if to compel her to move by his very presence. Jacqueline held her ground, though gooseflesh rose on her neck when he leaned close to whisper. "And you?"

She would not grant him the satisfaction of a visible response. Jacqueline dug the spoon beneath the browning bannock and carefully gave it a nudge so that it flipped over neatly. She threw him a triumphant grin before remembering what she would see.

He smiled back at her, challenge bright in his expression. "Well done. And it smells good."

"It does not smell that good," Jacqueline corrected. "But beggars cannot be choosers."

"Perhaps I should show proper appreciation for your skills."

Jacqueline took his dagger and cut her creation in two parts, one much larger for Angus and a smaller one for herself. She handed him back the blade and offered the pan to him. "Later, if you will. If you are as famished as I, then we will undoubtedly finish it, regardless of whether 'tis good or ill."

"Is this some ploy to be rid of me, by making me sample the fare first?" he said solemnly, though she knew he teased her again.

"I was being polite, as you were last evening." She wrinkled her nose and surveyed the sorry contents of the pot. "Though truly, I make no guarantees."

"It cannot be so bad as that, so long as you remembered to remove the worms from the apples." Angus neatly cut a piece with his knife and lifted it to his mouth.

"Oh, nay!" Jacqueline cried, as if she had indeed forgotten

the worms. He bit down on the bannock then froze at her words, his expression of such dismay that she laughed.

"I remembered," she chided, and nudged his arm. "How could I forget such a thing? Give me a piece before I faint of hunger. How bad is it?"

" 'Tis not fare for a king, but 'tis good." He waited until she had taken a bite, watching her so carefully that she should have expected his jest. "Perhaps the worms add a certain spice."

Jacqueline began to laugh again, and had to clamp one hand over her mouth lest she lose her precious mouthful of bannock. He smiled slightly as he watched her, though with an affection that was lacking in his usual chilly smile.

"You are wicked," she informed him archly.

"You knew that from the first moment you saw me," he retorted. He gave her a sharp look. "And who would not know the same, with just one glance?"

Jacqueline supposed 'twas inevitable that they discuss his wound this morn. "Nay, you are wrong in this." She took another bite and decided she had not done so very badly. "A man's visage and his character have naught to do with each other." She gave Angus a steady look, unflinching even as he turned his face slightly so that she could not miss his scar. "You are trying to frighten me."

His lips quirked. "Is that why you refuse to appear frightened? Merely to spite my intent?"

"Nay, I am not afraid of you. 'Tis as simple as that."

He frowned. "You should be."

"Why? Because you have sustained a horrible wound? Because you have treated me with care?" Jacqueline scoffed. "Why should I fear you?"

"Because I have taken you hostage and am thus a violent and unpredictable man." He regarded her steadily. "Because you know that I might have to kill you should this plan go awry."

Jacqueline was not quite as certain of her words as she would like him to believe. "Another attempt to frighten me, no doubt."

"It worked before."

"Then perhaps. Now it does not." She poked him in the chest with one fingertip. "If ever there was a woman unpersuaded that appearance dictates character, you should know that you stand in her company this morn."

"That does not mean she is right," he said softly. "She is a woman who has seen little of banditry, by her own confession."

Jacqueline rolled her eyes in exasperation. "But enough to know you are an honorable man, Angus, regardless of what you would like to have me believe. I know this in my heart."

Angus glared at her, a surprising response. "At least one of us has confidence in my character, however undeserved it might be," he finally said, his tone harsh.

Before she could reply, he offered her the last of the bannock; their portions had disappeared with remarkable speed.

"I thank you for this," he said stiffly. " 'Twas most satisfying." With evident impatience, he gathered all the implements she had used and strode toward the small stream to wash them.

Jacqueline had to believe 'twas the first time she had ever seen a man insulted when his noble intent was named and praised. But then, she knew already that Angus was not like other men.

She trailed behind him, not prepared to let him believe ill of himself so readily as that. He did not look up when she paused beside him, though he scrubbed the pot with greater vigor so she knew he was not unaware of her presence.

She knew she would have to begin any conversation. "I thank you for your praise, but 'twould have been better with a bit of butter, and perhaps a finer pot. One wrought thicker and with copper, as they oft have in the South."

Angus shook his head as he crouched beside the running water. "What do you know of such pots?"

"The cooks at Ceinn-beithe have two and profess them to be the finest. They are always suggesting that someone should go South, if only to fetch them another." She wagged a finger at Angus. "They would be most dismayed to know that you passed twice through those lands and did not fetch so much as a single saucepot."

He snorted. "And what use would I have for a fine pot?"

" 'Twould make an excellent gift. For your mother, for example, on your return."

"My mother is dead, if you recall."

"But you did not know that when you rode for home."

"All the better that I did not carry a pot several thousand miles," he said grimly, "for there would have been none to want it once I arrived."

"Nonsense! You might have granted it as a betrothal gift, for the woman you would take to wife. Many a bride would be delighted to have a fine pot from afar, especially one brought to her by her spouse-to-be. No doubt 'twould be set in a place of honor, as a marvel from distant lands—"

Angus stood then with alarming speed, spun and caught her shoulders in his hands. He leaned toward her and her gaze flicked between his good eye and the one that was no more. "What bride would have a man like me, Jacqueline?" he demanded. She jumped at his ready use of her name. "Even if I had a *denier* to my name?"

Jacqueline squared her shoulders. "An eye or lack of one does not make a man all he is, Angus. Any woman who believed as much would be a fool."

"Any woman who believed otherwise is a fool," he corrected sharply. Jacqueline knew her confusion showed. His expression turned harsh. "If my father were yet alive, he would refuse to grant Airdfinnan to me though my sole brother is dead. Do you know why?"

"Nay."

"Because my father would believe that I am not worthy to rule. Under the old laws, a man is not fit to lead unless he has two hands, two feet, two eyes, and his wits about him."

She was outraged on his behalf. "What foolery! You have enough wit to compensate for that eye!"

"Nay, Jacqueline, I am not whole. My father lived by the laws of the Celts, and no Celt king was ever made of a man half blind."

Jacqueline propped her hands upon her hips in indignation. "Then the laws are wrong. You would make a fine chieftain—"

"You must concede that there is sense here. I cannot do battle alone, for 'tis overly easy to surprise me. And there would be no heir, for any woman would fear to couple with a demon and thus pass this disfigurement on to her child."

Jacqueline shook her head with impatience. "That is ridiculous. A scar from battle cannot be passed to a child. Any woman so witless as to believe as much should not be worthy of your attention."

"Look at me, Jacqueline." Angus caught her chin in his hand and forced her to look upon him fully. He was deadly serious. "Look at this and tell me—what woman would welcome me to her bed?"

Jacqueline lifted her chin and stared deliberately at his wound. She studied it slowly, as if memorizing every whorl and mark, seeing the man behind the scar more clearly than the scar itself. "I would."

"You lie again." He released her and turned away in disgust. " 'Twould be crowded in your bed, since you have already made your intention clear to become a bride of Christ."

"You know what I mean!"

Angus spun angrily. "I know that you lie. Perhaps 'tis done out of kindness or worse, out of pity, but neither cannot change the fact that 'tis a lie."

She stared into his dark gaze, willing him to believe her. "Nay, Angus, 'tis no lie. I find you most alluring."

His laughter was short and cold. "Liar, liar. Jacqueline, you must be rid of your bad habits before you join the nuns."

He argued no further, for Jacqueline knew there was but one way to persuade him of the truth. She framed his face in her hands, stretched to her toes, and kissed him as if her life depended upon it. She felt him jump, felt his lips soften as if he would return her kiss.

Then Angus abruptly broke away and his mouth drew to a taut line. " 'Tis pity then that compels you to offer your wares. I have never understood its merit."

Jacqueline could not believe that she had summoned the audacity to kiss him of her own volition and, worse, that he had spurned her touch.

"You must not agree with your father's conclusion," she charged. "You are intent, after all, upon regaining your family's holding."

"You know naught of my intent."

"I know that you love Airdfinnan enough to see it restored to you. And I know that you will not grant it to another once its seal is in your hand again."

Angus sighed with exasperation. "Aye, 'tis true, I have hopes of proving my father wrong, at least in my ability to rule the holding," he admitted tightly before his tone turned bitter. "But it has oft been said that I am overly familiar with the bottom of an infidel's boot."

"When did that happen?" Jacqueline demanded. "And where?"

Angus gathered the pot and utensils, clanging them together in his annoyance, and stepped past her to his saddlebags. "You have a choice to make this morn," he said, casting the words over his shoulder. "I will return you either to Ceinn-beithe or escort you to Inveresbeinn."

She trotted after him, certain she had heard him incorrectly. "What is this?"

Angus shoved his belongings into his saddlebag, then stared at her hard. "I am releasing you as my hostage and 'tis to you to decide your destination. I will escort you there today. Choose."

Jacqueline folded her arms across her chest and glared at him, in no mood to be cast aside. "I choose Airdfinnan."

"What nonsense is this? I gave you no such choice!"

"You gave me choice and I have made it. I would see this place that so haunts you. I would know the rest of the tale."

Angus kicked at the fire, spreading the logs then stamping on the embers. "You will not go to Airdfinnan. I will not take you there."

"What do you intend to do after you release me? Where do you intend to ride then? Back to Outremer?"

"You know I will not."

"Nay, you will go to Airdfinnan."

The set of his features confirmed what Jacqueline had guessed though Angus would not say so in words. " 'Tis not your affair."

"I say 'tis. I am part of this matter, by your choice, and I will not be cloistered before I have seen Airdfinnan. I will not be so much baggage that can be captured, then abandoned to suit your will alone."

He looked up then. "Is that what you believe I do?"

"Clearly." 'Twas Jacqueline's turn to challenge him. "It seems you are not so different from Reynaud after all."

He strode back to her, the sparks nigh flying from him. "You know that is not true!" Angus flung out his hand. "I grant you a choice, as other men have not granted you choice, as you insist is your sole desire."

Jacqueline's heart warmed at his determination to treat her fairly, but she was not prepared to cede to him. "Aye? But I have made a choice and you would deny it to me. It seems to me that you offer only the choice of the choices you have already made, which is not so different in the end."

He muttered something beneath his breath, then impaled her with a glance. "Why? Why would you see Airdfinnan?"

Because he loved it.

Jacqueline bit back the confusing assertion that rose to her lips, then shrugged. "Because I am curious. Is that not said to be the curse of women?"

" 'Tis indeed, if one listens overmuch to Rodney." He surveyed her, then shook his head in turn. "You are determined in this?"

Jacqueline nodded, realizing that she truly was.

He slapped his gloves against his palm, granting her a smoldering glance that nigh melted her bones. "Then I shall take you there, but be warned that whatsoever comes of this will be as much your responsibility as mine."

"But what could come of this?" she asked, her voice rising higher than she might have preferred.

Angus stepped closer and caught her chin in his grip, the smooth leather of his glove beneath her chin. "Anything, vixen, anything at all. Airdfinnan has been known to stir unruly passion within men who desire it. I do not count myself immune to worldly temptation."

He claimed her lips with his in a possessive kiss. His

tongue slid between her teeth, his hand slipped into her hair, and it seemed she hung boneless from his grip. She was helpless to pull away and had no desire to do so.

An eternity of pleasure later, Angus lifted his head. He waited until her eyes opened, then rubbed his thumb across her bottom lip in a rough caress that left her trembling.

He smiled down at her, once again the lawless rogue, then turned to saddle his steed.

And 'twas only when he ceased to touch her that Jacqueline wondered whether those unruly desires were roused by his family estate or by her.

She remembered suddenly her mother's insistence that she not depart immediately for the convent. Her mother was right, yet again.

A man of honor was worth both the wait and the challenge.

Chapter Eleven

RODNEY ARRIVED AT CEINN-BEITHE AT MIDDAY ON THE day after leaving the witch's forest glade.

Indeed, he had planned as much, for he knew that all would be gathered for the midday meal. And he wanted the largest audience he might have. 'Twould ensure that the chieftain could not pretend that he had never received the missive—an old ploy, which was taken as justification for retaliation in many a feud—and also would see to Rodney's own safety. Few chieftains were so assured of the alliance of every man in their hall that they would attack a messenger before them.

In a smaller conference, however, 'twas not uncommon for a chieftain to have only his most trusted men present. Then any deed might occur and any tale might be told of what few had witnessed.

Midday suited Rodney better.

He had not known what to expect of Ceinn-beithe, for these lands were not familiar to him. Angus had told him of the legendary great standing stone upon the site, though Angus had never visited Ceinn-beithe either. Rodney reined in his steed at the apex of the path, startled by the stunning sight spread before his eyes.

The location of Ceinn-beithe was magnificent. The sea surrounded the jut of land on three sides, sparkling in sunlight even while it held distant islands in its embrace. Out there, Rodney knew, lay the hall of the King of the Isles himself.

A commanding site and one that would be readily defended, Ceinn-beithe was a carefully chosen point, of the same sound scheme of strategic defense as Airdfinnan. 'Twas Ceinn-beithe before him, of that Rodney had no doubt, for the standing stone was there, beyond the village palisades, as was the broch Angus had mentioned on the lip of the point itself. The broch was in surprisingly good condition for its age. Apparently the resident chieftain had seen to its repair.

Just as that man had created a prospering village. Angus had said naught of such a settlement, though he and Rodney both had anticipated a hall of some sort. This far surpassed such a simple dwelling and put Rodney in mind of walled villages they had passed on the continent.

This one was wrought primarily of wood. The mud walls were capped with wooden palisades, those walls encircling both a large hall and a variety of smaller dwellings. Smoke curled into the sky from a dozen fires, and the scent of burning peat tinged Rodney's nostrils. Fields were tilled beyond those walls, both sheep and goats grazing in enclosures. The gates to the village were closed.

Wary of what might greet him, Rodney continued onward. He had ridden past the place where they had captured the woman, and there had been no sign of her guards between there and here. Rodney had to believe they had managed to return and share the news of their charge's fate.

Unless they had fled into the hills rather than face the wrath of their chieftain. 'Twas impossible to be certain without knowing the man himself, whether he be Cormac or Duncan.

A cock crowed as Rodney drew near the gates and dogs barked within the walls. If not for the closed palisade, he might have happened upon a pastoral village with complete surety of its borders being well defended and its peace being maintained.

He was considering how best to announce his presence, when one gate opened slightly. Chickens spilled through the gap, followed by hounds and inquisitive boys who were probably supposed to tend them all. They looked well fed as well as mischievous, and Rodney was delighted to note another sign of Ceinn-beithe's prosperity.

This chieftain, whatever his name, could afford to relinquish distant Airdfinnan, even though Airdfinnan was a rich prize.

A man shouted from inside and the boys, unaware of Rodney, hooted in playful defiance. 'Twas clear that one tall fair lad was the leader of them. A heavyset man stepped through the gates. Rodney halted his horse, recognizing the man even at a distance and smiling in anticipation of the moment he looked up.

"Hoy! I left you to mind the gate while I had my meal!" The man wiped his mouth and scowled at the boy. "You pledged to remain within, as Duncan decreed. 'Tis not the time for frivolity, for the hills are rife with brigands."

The boys scoffed and mimicked the sentry.

"I should like to meet these brigands," the tall boy declared. "I should make them give back Jacqueline."

The sentry reddened, clearly interpreting this as an accusation, but Rodney quickly spoke up.

"And here is just that opportunity," he said smoothly. Man and boys pivoted to stare at him, and he smiled. " 'Tis oft said that one should be wary of what one asks to be given, lest one receive it in truth."

The sentry shook his fist and strode closer. "I should see you dead for how you shamed me! I should see you sorely injured for the loss of our Jacqueline!"

"Perhaps." Rodney enjoyed the advantage of his height.

"If you could." He clicked his teeth to the horse, which strolled forward. The boys fell back, their eyes wide, though the sentry did not step aside.

"I am charged with keeping all foreigners from passing these gates."

Rodney shrugged. "In your place, I would be more anxious to know the terms governing the maiden's release." He met the man's gaze. "I could leave and you would never know her fate. What then would your chieftain say—if you had not only failed to protect his child, but lost the sole opportunity to regain her?"

The man swore. "Surrender your weapons first! You shall not pass this way armed."

'Twas not unreasonable, and truly Rodney had no need of a blade to best this man. He had learned how to fight with his hands and his feet if need be. Rodney pulled his dagger from its scabbard, but presented it to the tall boy instead of the sentry.

The guard inhaled sharply.

" 'Tis irresponsible," Rodney declared, "to entrust a weapon to one who knows not how to use it." He looked the boy in the eye. "You will pledge to me that you will not use mine own blade against me, and further that you will return it to me on my departure."

"We need make no such guarantee," the sentry huffed.

But the boy's eyes were filled with awe. "Aye, sir." He accepted the blade and held it with a care akin to reverence. The other boys clustered closer to him, impressed by his responsibility. One stretched out a cautious finger to touch the blade. Rodney scowled and said but one sharp word and they all stepped back.

He smiled. "Take me to your chieftain, lad, and I shall also entrust you with the custody of my horse. I come with ransom terms, and the sooner they are heard, the sooner this may all be resolved."

'Twas all the temptation the boy needed. Indeed, his feet might have been winged, so great was his enthusiasm.

The sentry roared in protest, but Rodney and the boy quickly left him behind.

❋

Eglantine was startled when a man rode a prancing horse directly into Ceinn-beithe's hall. She stared in astonishment as the man smiled and continued cockily to the middle of the hall.

"What madness is this?" Duncan, beside her, was on his feet in a moment, his blade drawn.

His men quickly followed suit, the assembly bristling with knives. Esmeraude regarded the guest with mingled awe and admiration, yet another signal to a protective mother that this daughter should be wed sooner rather than later.

Which made her think again of Jacqueline and the dreadful word that had come of her fate. She drummed her fingers and eyed the man before her, guessing that he brought yet more news.

The sight of him did naught to ease her fears. Eglantine judged him to be a mercenary by the rough utility of his garb and a Norman by the cut of his beard. She had not seen a beard trimmed to so meticulous a point, nor so carefully shaved to be no wider than his lip, not since she left France's shores—and there 'twas only the Normans who had such fondness for the style.

This man was as bald as an egg, though he moved with a certainty that revealed his affection for holding every eye. And hold it he did, as he dismounted and cast his reins to one of the boys who usually tended the sheep.

Fortunately the steed was too well trained to move so

much as one hoof once his master left the saddle. Eglantine could not imagine that this shepherd boy would have any idea how to keep such a horse from doing whatsoever it desired.

Despite herself, she admired the man's taste in horseflesh. 'Twas a fine chestnut stallion he rode, and one well tended. The beast tossed its head in a small show of temper.

She considered the swaggering mercenary and decided the steed had been stolen.

"Name yourself," Duncan roared. "And explain your mockery of my hall."

The man made no haste to respond. He surveyed the assembly, as if amused by their weapons and aggressive stances. Then he scanned the hall itself as if 'twas so backward that he had never seen the like.

His mocking gaze finally fell upon Duncan. "I seek Cormac MacQuarrie, chieftain of Clan MacQuarrie."

"He is dead and I am chieftain by his command."

"And who are you?"

"I am Duncan MacLaren. I at least have no fear of giving my name to a stranger."

The man smiled. "I am Rodney of Dunsyre and I have no fear of speaking the truth when I know the company I share. 'Tis a caution, no doubt, born of experience in lands where a man would not be so bold as to leave his gate unguarded."

Duncan's eyes narrowed and Eglantine knew that Malcolm had made his second and perhaps his last mistake in Ceinn-beithe.

Malcolm himself appeared in the portal, out of breath, then hastened through the hall. "I tried to halt him, Duncan, I did, but he refused to heed me."

"Aye, I could not hear your command, seeing as you were at the board inside a hut," this Rodney replied sourly. "In my experience, a gatekeeper keeps his place by the gate." He bowed mockingly to Duncan. "You must forgive my unfamiliarity with your quaint custom."

Duncan's features might have been wrought of stone. "Why are you here, Rodney of Dunsyre?"

"He is here to command a ransom for Jacqueline!" Malcolm cried. "This is the man who so humiliated us. This is the man who should pay a penance for the insult to your family, Duncan."

"This is the man, Malcolm, who knows the fate of Jacqueline," Duncan snapped.

Malcolm colored and cast a baleful look at the visitor.

That man smiled. "I do so prefer clever men. Their presence makes matters much simpler." He spared a telling glance at Malcolm, then looked around himself in apparent amazement. "Is there not a bench in your hall for a guest? For shame, Duncan MacLaren—one hears so much of Gael hospitality and yet, in the truth of it, I find something lacking."

"We are not accustomed to hosting brigands and thieves."

Rodney eyed him coolly. "What of those seeking justice?"

Duncan lowered his blade warily. "Justice for what?"

"For the murder of two innocent men and the return of a holding that was never yours to claim."

By the expression on her spouse's face, Eglantine knew he did not understand what this man meant. Fear lit her heart, for she doubted that this Rodney could easily be persuaded that he was wrong.

Which could be most dire for her Jacqueline.

"Where is my daughter?" she demanded, hating how high her voice rose in her fear. "What have you done with Jacqueline?"

"She is well enough, whoever you might be."

"I am her mother, Eglantine de Crevy." She glared at him.

"Then know that she is safe, if only for the moment."

"What estate and what murders?" Duncan asked impatiently. "And what have they to do with Jacqueline?"

"Do not mock me, Duncan MacLaren. We both know that Cormac MacQuarrie swore to possess a certain keep for his own, regardless of what the price might be."

Duncan blinked, clearly knowing no such thing. He had no chance to speak, though, for Iain, Cormac's own son, intervened. "Aye, there was a time when he would have done anything to hold Airdfinnan as his own."

"Aye!" their visitor replied. "And who might this be?"

"Iain MacCormac," the fair man supplied. "My father believed that he had been cheated by the King of the Isles, that Airdfinnan should have been granted to him."

"And what did he do of it?" Rodney asked smoothly, his manner that of a man who knew the answer to his own question.

Iain shrugged. "Naught. He had not the time. Duncan came shortly thereafter. My father argued with another chieftain, for he was wont to be quarrelsome. Then Mhairi died on the day of her nuptials and not much later, my father himself died. Like so many of his hot words, naught ever came of his oath."

"You lie!" Rodney cried, stepping forward to shake his fist. "A family is dead. 'Twas the fault of Cormac MacQuarrie, and now the blood son of Airdfinnan would have his due."

"My men who guarded Jacqueline said that you were two," Duncan said. "And that your companion was garbed as a knight."

Eglantine feared the arrival of another like the rogue knight Jacqueline had already known, and her heart pounded anew in fear for her child.

"He is a knight in truth!" Rodney snapped. "I saw him train and win his spurs with my own eyes. I have served with him and know the merit of his valor and his skill."

"And that he claimed his name was Angus MacGillivray."

" 'Tis no claim. 'Tis his name, for all the woe it has brought him."

A murmur rolled through the assembly and Eglantine frowned. "Why does this trouble so many in this hall? Who is Angus MacGillivray and where is Airdfinnan and why are either our concern?" She stood up and flung out her hands. "What about my daughter?"

"Angus MacGillivray has long been said to be dead," Duncan said quietly, his gaze fixed upon Rodney.

"Fergus MacGillivray was the chieftain entrusted with guardianship of Airdfinnan," Iain supplied, "which was held by the King of the Isles and considered to be key to the defense of the West. He had two sons, the eldest of which fell ill when he stood on the verge of manhood. Angus, the younger, departed on crusade to win his brother's salvation and was never heard of again."

"And both father and brother died shortly thereafter," Duncan told her, "leaving Airdfinnan in the trusteeship of the local monastery that Fergus had seen founded and well endowed."

Eglantine shook her head in confusion. "But what has this to do with Jacqueline?"

"It has more to do with your spouse, my lady, and the bloodthirsty clan into which you foolishly chose to wed," Rodney said with determination. "For Angus is not dead, and he has returned. He knows that his father and brother were murdered, and this by the dictate of Cormac MacQuarrie. He knows that Clan MacQuarrie are the true holders of Airdfinnan, though they hide behind the mask of the monks who perform their will."

"Why would anyone do as much?" Duncan asked, his tone dripping with skepticism.

"To avoid intervention by the King of the Isles, of course. 'Twas he who granted it to Fergus, after all. But that king will not attack a monastery to reclaim the holding, especially if the monks insist they hold the estate in trust for its legal heir. On the other hand, if Clan MacQuarrie were to make an overt claim upon the property, 'twould be short-lived, from what I know of this king."

"Nonsense!" Duncan sheathed his blade. "I know naught of such a scheme."

"Nor do I," Iain claimed.

"And if such a plot ever existed, then I had no part in it then and have no influence in its outcome now."

"You lie!" Rodney shouted.

Duncan opened his mouth to argue the matter, his hand falling to his hilt again. The mercenary reached for his own blade, but Eglantine placed a hand on her husband's arm. She rose and addressed Rodney. "If the monks hold the estate in trust for Angus MacGillivray, why does he not petition them for its release?"

"He has done so," Rodney declared. "And was turned from the gates. They insisted he could not be who he is, and when he insisted upon it, weapons were drawn upon us. We barely escaped with our lives, which says much indeed about the honest intent of peoples in this land." He stepped forward and shook his fist. " 'Tis this that shows the lie behind their deed! If they held Airdfinnan for him in truth, then 'twould already have been surrendered to him. Nay, there is another in command who does not wish Angus alive, one who sees much gain from this ruse, this much is clear!"

"And where is this Angus now?" Eglantine demanded tightly. "Why does he not plead his own case?"

Rodney smiled. "I would not expect a woman to understand the complexities haunting a hunted man. If 'tis easier
for Angus to be dead, and if 'tis the MacQuarrie clan who
would prefer him to be so, he would have to be much slower
of wit than he is to walk directly into that clan's own hall."

"So he seized my daughter, like a common brigand, to see
his holding surrendered to him in exchange," Eglantine
guessed.

Rodney bowed mockingly. "You are most astute for a
woman."

"I thought you said he was a knight."

"He is."

"Yet, if I recall, the vows made by a knight involve the
protection of those unable to protect themselves and the defense of women."

The mercenary's eyes narrowed. "Your daughter is unin-
jured."

"I do not share your faith in the honor of criminals. Nor do
I put much credence in your word."

Rodney's eyes flashed. "My companion is a knight, a man
of valor and honor, a man who departed upon crusade to save
his family from ill fortune and instead found only more for
himself."

He turned, appealing to the assembly who hung on his
every word. "Angus MacGillivray fought valiantly in the
Holy Land, believing he guaranteed his family's salvation.
He was imprisoned and tormented, yet when he finally found
his way home again, 'twas to find his legacy stolen and his
family murdered without remorse."

He held out his hands. "What reward has he for all his sacrifice? Can any man blame Angus for pursuing justice for his
own blood, for seeking vengeance against those who murdered his family and stole his inheritance?"

Rodney spun and jabbed a finger through the air at Eglantine. "Barring any foolishness on her own part, your daughter is as safe with him as by your own side, but she will remain with him until he wins the justice that he seeks. How dare you deny him the restoration of his rightful due?"

"But—" Duncan began to protest, though Eglantine silenced him with a glance.

"How do we know you can be trusted?" she asked.

"I knew the MacGillivray family," Iain supplied. "If indeed 'tis Angus returned, he was always said to be most like his father. That man was one who gave his word and clung to it, for better or for worse. Even my father acknowledged that Fergus was worthy of admiration, for the surety of his pledges if not his claims to property."

"Oh." Eglantine sat back and considered the cold-eyed mercenary before her. She had a sudden sense that something good might come of this, that Jacqueline being alone with a man of upright character might not be something that should be hastened to its end.

To be sure, she was still worried about her daughter's welfare, though she could not help but wonder whether there had been some miraculous intervention in Jacqueline's plans.

In her own homeland, 'twas not uncommon for knights to seize a woman of their choice. Once they had bedded the demoiselle, the woman's father had no choice but to permit a marriage. Oft such marriages would not have happened otherwise, the father of the bride more intent upon the wealth of the potential husband, not his age.

Young knights seldom were granted permission to wed, purely because their holdings were as yet small—and 'twas not unknown for the woman in question to have departed willingly with her captor. Many such events were less a rape than a merry liaison intended to achieve the couple's own ends.

Eglantine did not imagine that her daughter would have welcomed any knight's advances, nor that Jacqueline would willingly warm the man's bed, but she did wonder about the knight in question.

Would it not be perfect if the last man Jacqueline met before her retreat to the convent was the one man of honor who could open her heart?

Eglantine had to know more to assess whether hers was just a mother's hopeful conclusion.

"Do come to the board, Rodney, and partake of a cup of ale." She smiled even as Duncan eyed her uncertainly. "I would have you tell me more of this knight you serve." Two men escorted Rodney to the barrel of ale and ensured he was served, thus giving Eglantine and Duncan a moment to converse.

"To better measure this mercenary's worth?" Duncan mused in an undertone.

"To better know this knight Angus MacGillivray," she whispered. "He sounds to have a certain promise."

Duncan shook his head. "Eglantine, you are much concerned with matters of nuptials and happiness, perhaps *too* concerned."

"You know my view of this convent choice."

"Aye, and you may speak aright. But you may not. The proof will lie in Angus's deeds, not in the words of his man," Duncan muttered.

"But you cannot surrender Airdfinnan, for we do not hold it."

"If this one speaks aright, then this Angus has a legitimate cause for complaint. If that is so, then I shall find a way to aid him in regaining his legacy."

Eglantine watched her spouse, admiring yet again his uncommon desire to see matters resolved fairly. "It may cost us dearly."

"Justice seldom comes to those unprepared to strive for it."

"But I would not have you harmed! And I would have Jacqueline safe."

Duncan clasped her hand in his and gave her fingers a tight squeeze. "He will take me to Jacqueline afore I tell him anything further, and I shall ensure her health and welfare myself. That is the first matter to be resolved, and 'tis only once that is resolved that we will see what else we might do in aid."

"I will go with you."

"You will not." Duncan granted Eglantine a stern look. "Rest assured that if so much as a single hair of Jacqueline's is harmed, neither of these men will live to see another dawn."

"You are most fiercely protective of your women, Duncan." Eglantine smiled at her spouse. "I knew there was a reason I loved you so."

"It shall all end aright, Eglantine," he murmured as Rodney approached the board. "I shall ensure it."

And she knew that he would, for her spouse was a man of uncommon resolve.

Chapter Twelve

AS JACQUELINE HAD SUSPECTED IT WOULD, IT BEGAN to rain before midday. The first drops fell heavily, splattering cold against their faces. They bowed their heads against the rising wind and rode onward. Jacqueline did not ask for shelter for 'twas clear there was none on this empty road.

'Twas not long before they were soaked. Indeed, the wind rose with such vigor that 'twas difficult to see much of the road ahead. Lucifer did not falter, though Jacqueline could feel displeasure with the circumstances in the beast's tight gait.

Jacqueline shivered and Angus drew his cloak around her. Enfolding her in the wet wool did little to ease her woes, though the heat of his own body was most welcome. He wrapped his arm around her and she buried her face in his shoulder. She huddled against him and hoped that 'twas not far to Airdfinnan.

They rode in silence for the better part of the day, and 'twas only when the sky darkened that Angus slowed Lucifer. Jacqueline glanced up to find Angus scanning the undergrowth on either side and dared to hope for shelter.

"Is Airdfinnan near?"

"Nay."

"Then what do you seek?"

"A path."

Jacqueline gritted her teeth, for he was clearly not in a mood to share any of his carefully guarded secrets. "A path to what?"

A smile touched his lips fleetingly. "You will see."

He clicked his tongue and urged the steed to one side of the road. There was no discernible path, but once the beast stepped through the first barrier of thickly meshed undergrowth, Jacqueline did see a faint thinning of plants. It looked to have been trodden by many footsteps, though the wild state of the surrounding vegetation hinted that it had been long since any had come this way.

Indeed, Angus dismounted to peer more closely at the ground and guide the horse onward. More than once Jacqueline could not guess whether the way branched left or right. She wondered whether Angus could see the truth either, for he tended to straighten at these places and look, as if seeking a recollection in the shape of the trees.

It seemed the rain halted when they entered the forest, though 'twas only that the canopy of leaves far overhead broke the onslaught. 'Twas a relief nonetheless, and the sound of dripping water echoed from all sides.

The land rose rapidly once they left the main road, and stones quickly intermingled with the dirt underfoot. They ascended with every step, Lucifer needing encouragement from his master when the way was very steep.

Jacqueline watched Angus, impressed by the care he showed in seeing that the steed always had a solid footing. Indeed, the way behind them was precariously steep, and she resolved not to look back. Angus spoke to the destrier constantly, his words so low that Jacqueline could not make them out, though his tone soothed her uncertainties as well. 'Twas no wonder the beast would follow his master wherever he led.

The wind began to buffet them as they climbed, and Jacqueline had glimpses of the brooding sky through the thinning tops of the trees. A sheer rock face appeared suddenly before them, and she feared they had taken the wrong course. But Angus led the stallion to the right and now she saw a path clearly etched in the stone. It ran along the face of the rock, dropping away to the forest floor to the right.

Lucifer saw it as well, though he balked at continuing upon it. Angus stroked the steed's nose and murmured in its ear. The beast shuddered, but when Angus stepped forward again, Lucifer folded his ears back and followed dutifully. Not a dozen steps later the rock face opened into a cave. Lucifer needed no encouragement to duck inside, and Jacqueline herself smiled in relief.

"You knew this place!"

"Aye, I remembered it."

"But it must be years since you have been here."

"Or anyone else, for that matter." He lifted her from the saddle, then peered around the cave. It was of a fair size, though it had no ending, for clearly it was but a gateway to a tunnel. Jacqueline eyed the shadowed opening, noting how it dipped downward, and shivered.

"It could be a portal to hell," she muttered.

" 'Twas what my brother always said."

"You came here with him?"

"We played here as boys." He winked at her with unexpected mischief. "Though we were forbidden to do so."

Jacqueline studied the tunnel opening again. "I would imagine you dared each other to enter that tunnel and that you told each other tall tales of what you found there."

Angus snorted and smiled briefly, as if in recollection, though he admitted naught. He unsaddled the destrier, running a hand over the beast's wet flesh with evident concern.

His gaze flicked over the barren cave and Jacqueline guessed his dilemma.

"Will Lucifer let me wield the brush?"

"I beg your pardon?"

"I know how to brush down a horse, and I know that this one has need of such grooming. He might become ill after working in such foul weather. My mother always says 'tis easier to keep a horse healthy than to heal it once it falls ill."

" 'Tis true enough."

"And we all have need of a fire. If I tend your steed, you might light one."

Her practicality seemed to amuse Angus, though Jacqueline could not imagine why. 'Twas only good sense.

"Are you ordering my labor?"

"Nay, I am offering my aid, that we all might rest in comfort sooner." She stretched out her hand, in silent request for the brush. Lucifer snuffled her palm, mistaking her gesture, then snorted to find no treat for him there.

Angus placed the brush within her palm, eyeing the difference between her stature and that of the destrier. "I shall finish what you cannot reach," he said. A gleam of something flickered in his gaze and she thought he might tease her again, but then he sobered, drew his cloak about him, and stepped out into the rain once more.

Jacqueline, intent on proving herself useful, set to her task. She need not have feared the destrier's disapproval, for 'twas clear he loved to be groomed. He leaned into the brush with such vigor that he nigh flattened her against the wall of the cave.

Jacqueline worked diligently, more aware of her solitude in this chilly cave than she had expected. 'Twas that dark hole that drew her gaze time and again. She recalled more than one fireside tale of ogres lurking in the shadows, waiting only for their intended victims to fall asleep before revealing themselves.

It seemed that Angus was gone overlong. Aye, in a moment like this, all of Duncan's tales seemed more a liability than ever they had before.

Angus returned when Jacqueline was standing on the removed saddle so that she might reach Lucifer's back. The leather was slick, both with use and moisture, and her footing precarious. He startled her when he abruptly dumped wood upon the rocky floor. She jumped, yelped, and slipped.

Angus swore even as he caught her around the waist. "I told you that I would finish the task."

"What else was I to do?" she snapped, as troubled by his touch as that he had seen her fall.

"Wait?" he suggested, a suspicious thread of humor in his tone.

Jacqueline pushed his hands away and turned to survey him. "Did you find dry wood in this storm?"

"Nay, but some that is dryer than most. 'Twill smoke, no doubt, but . . ."

" 'Twill be better than naught," she concluded, knowing full well what he intended to say. Angus looked startled and she shrugged. " 'Tis what you always say. Clearly you have made do with what you had on more than one occasion and learned to be grateful for it. 'Tis not such a bad trait to be resourceful."

If he was pleased or insulted by her words, Jacqueline could not tell. He then proved to be more resourceful than she had believed. He removed a collection of kindling from his saddlebag that had not been there when she checked his supplies this morn.

"There was rain in the wind," he said at her questioning glance, then set to shredding it with his knife.

'Twas not long before he struck the flint, and not long after that a fire burned. The newly collected wood did smoke, but it continued to burn. Angus arranged the other logs around the fire that they might dry somewhat before they were needed.

Then he straightened and brushed his hands together. "There are two chemises in the saddlebag. Shed your wet clothes and don one while I am gone."

"What of you?"

"I have a snare to check."

And he was gone once more.

But Jacqueline had one task to do while she was still sodden. She ducked out into the rain to gather plants. She had recognized a number that also grew at Ceinn-beithe and that her mother favored for fodder for their palfreys and ponies. She collected as much as she could carry, dropped them inside the cave, then repeated her task twice more, for she knew that a stallion could eat a fearsome amount.

Only when a great mound lay before Lucifer and he had begun to nuzzle through it selectively did she follow Angus's bidding. Jacqueline wrung out her kirtle and laid it to dry, then did the same with her chemise and her shoes. She took his longer chemise for her use, unbound her hair and gave it a squeeze, then leaned close to the fire to dry it.

Angus's sneeze announced his return, and Jacqueline met him at the cave opening. His gaze flicked over her and she realized belatedly that his chemise was probably quite sheer. She glanced down and flushed, for the ruddiness of her nipples and darkness of her pubic hair showed through.

"Your hair is a marvel," he said, and tucked a strand behind her ear, as if he had not noticed her other displayed charms. Jacqueline's cheeks burned and she could not meet his gaze. "Come back to the fire," he advised, his tone almost paternal. "The air is chill this night. 'Twas good of you to tend Lucifer and illness would be a poor reward."

He stepped past her, laying the meat he had brought into the pot, then shedding his gloves. He shook the rain out of his hair and cast aside his wet cloak. Jacqueline watched him through her lashes, sorely tempted to see more of him.

The man wore a cursed amount of garb and 'twas all sodden. He unfastened his belt, carefully laying aside both sword and dagger. His tunic was hauled over his head next, followed by his mail surcoat, which hit the rock floor with a clatter. He kicked off his boots and turned his back to her when he pulled his chemise over his head.

She saw the tanned and muscled expanse of his back for only an instant before he donned the dry chemise. He did not shed his chausses. To her surprise, he removed a dark sleeveless tunic from his saddlebag that she had not realized was there and pulled it over the chemise.

Only then did he turn to face her. He knotted his belt once again, though he left his sword where it lay, then came to crouch beside her.

"Squirrel on this night," he told her. "In case you are curious."

Jacqueline noticed that his kill was fastidiously dressed, as before, both offal and fur already discarded. "You do not leave the skin," she complained.

"I have no taste for flesh," he said grimly, setting the pot over the fire with a measure of water in it.

" 'Tis not a matter of taste, 'tis simply easier cooking. If you were to leave a bit of the flesh, 'twould sizzle and the fat would keep the meat from sticking to the pot."

"Let the meat stick."

"Do not be ridiculous."

He gave her a chilling glance. "I cannot bear the smell of burning flesh."

"That makes no sense at all, and I have already witnessed that you are a sensible man . . ."

"What else have you witnessed?" Angus demanded.

Jacqueline looked up at his tone, met his steady glance, then noted anew his scar.

And what had wrought that scar.

"Oh!" She recoiled, horrified by her sudden understanding of why he could not bear the smell of burning flesh. "Oh. Oh." She stammered to silence, wishing that the tunnel truly did offer a gate to hell and would swallow her up that she might be saved from such mortification.

"Oh," he echoed, his tone mocking.

And there was naught she could say to that. The silence between them was oppressive, though Angus seemed untroubled by it. He tended the meat, turning it at intervals, evidently having perfected the art of cooking without fat.

At length, Jacqueline decided she had naught to lose. Truly, he could not be any more irked with her than he was now. "Will you tell of it?"

His quick glance could have left a wound, 'twas so cutting. "Of what?" he asked with feigned idleness, looking again at the meat.

"Of your wound. Of how you were so scarred."

"Nay."

His tone did not invite further discussion, but Jacqueline was not prepared to surrender her inquiry as yet. "Rodney said you had been in a Saracen prison," she said, matching his diffident manner. "Will you tell me of that?"

His lips tightened. "Nay."

"Whyever not?"

He braced his elbow upon his knees and gave her a smoldering glance. "Because 'tis not a tale suitable for the ears of an innocent."

"I am not so innocent as that!"

"Aye, you are." He turned the meat, frowning slightly as

he did so. His voice softened. "Count yourself fortunate in that, Jacqueline. There are things no one should be compelled to learn."

The meat sizzled in the quietude between them and Jacqueline watched him work. She might not have been there, for all the attention he granted her. She sighed, sparing another glance to the yawning cave.

"Will you tell me of Jerusalem, then? Is it true that the streets are paved with gold and the walls of the city wrought of gemstones?"

He laughed under his breath. "Where did you hear such a tale?"

" 'Tis the City of God, it should be wrought of every finery. And 'tis writ that the new Jerusalem will be made of every treasure known to man—"

"The old Jerusalem is wrought of mud and dirt and quarreling neighbors, just as any other city of men."

"Truly?"

Angus smiled at her across the fire. "Truly."

Jacqueline was unaccountably disappointed by this. She frowned and stared into the fire. "I had thought 'twould be different somehow, that 'twould show the mark of God's favor in some way. I suppose that is no more than the whimsy of one never destined to see it."

" 'Tis a whimsy held by many," he admitted. "And to be sure, there *is* something different about Jerusalem. 'Tis a city like any other, as I said, but 'tis also unlike any other, for every rock within it, every corner, every river, every ford is marked by an event from the Bible. There is the rock where Abraham made to sacrifice his son, there is the stone upon which the angel Gabriel set his foot."

He shook his head and smiled. "People say, for example, that they shall meet you at the ford where Jacob baptised his child. Every stone seems fraught with import and history, and there are many of them. In a curious way, it gives credence to all the tales we were taught as children, tales that seemed of another world. Yet at the same time, the Holy Land itself seems not a part of our own world because so many legendary deeds occurred there."

Jacqueline hugged her knees. "I should like to see it."

"I would not advise it. You would be disappointed, and you might very well not return."

"I would go as a pilgrim, not a crusader."

"Pilgrims are robbed and left for dead all the time. 'Tis a cruel land, for all the sanctity of its history. Indeed, I have heard it said that very sanctity makes a madness in the blood of men."

"Why?"

"All the faiths claim Jerusalem as sacred ground—the Saracens, the Christians, and the Jews—and all desire to possess it. More than one man, regardless of his creed, has been willing to do much wickedness to see the aim of his faith fulfilled."

"Perhaps 'tis a grand test of faith."

"If so, most fail the test."

"Was your faith strengthened or weakened by your journey?"

He shrugged, noncommittally. " 'Twas changed."

"Then it must have been weakened, for a man rides to crusade for the ardor of faith alone."

He smiled then, amused by her once again. "Does he?"

"Why else?"

"There are as many reasons as there are men."

"Like what?"

"A desire for the adventure to be found in war. A pursuit of opportunity, for conquested lands are divided among the victors. A lust to see more of the world, to shape one's own destiny." He paused, and she knew the last reason would be his own. "A sense of duty to one's family."

Aye, she recalled Edana's tale. Angus had gone to redress his father's error and save his family from their misfortune.

Though his departure had not achieved that end.

"Which was your reason?"

"I shall let you guess."

"Why did you leave there after so much time?"

"Why would any man stay?"

She smiled. "But you were gone for years, were you not?"

"Fifteen years, nigh to the day."

"Then you *did* stay for a time. What changed? Did you have news of your family? Or did you simply yearn to see them?"

He offered the pot to her along with his dagger and spoon. "Eat your meat afore it grows cold." The moment she took it, he turned and walked to the opening of the cave, standing with his back to her as he stared out at the falling rain.

She watched him as she ate, being careful to eat only a third of what he had prepared. He was accustomed to making do with what he had, and she for one wished she could offer him more.

And truly, in his rare talkative mood, Angus had told her more than she had expected him to. Perhaps she too should be satisfied with what she had.

She might have been an angel, so brightly did she shimmer.

Angus found his eye drawn to Jacqueline time and again, not only because her charms were so visible through his chemise but because she shone like a ray of sunshine in this place.

Aye, he was more troubled by the yawning cavern at the

rear of the cave than he would have her know. His own night terrors were lurking there, sheltered by the cold darkness of the stone, waiting to remind him of the past. They tormented him every night, though he had learned to sleep reasonably well in the open air.

This cave though, so cold, so dank, so dark, gave those horrors new strength. He could hear the clink of chains, the screams of the tormented, the wails of the dying. He could smell rot and disease and burning flesh as surely as if 'twas right before him.

Those memories would erupt with a vengeance once the fire died. He knew not what he would do when he was assaulted by the demons again.

And he feared for Jacqueline in his presence.

He should have frightened her when she met him at the cave opening. He should have kept her at a distance. But Angus had not the heart to do so. There was enough fear in this place, enough terror gnawing at the periphery of his thoughts to suffice for two.

He was glad of her company, perhaps that was the extent of it. She had left her hair unbound, and a marvel of gold 'twas. It hung to her hips as straight as could be, more thick and luxuriant than he had ever imagined a woman's hair might be. He was sorely tempted to plunge his hands into it, to feel its softness, to let its glimmering light caress his flesh.

And even better, she chattered almost incessantly. She asked him questions and was unoffended when he did not reply—indeed, she merely asked another question. She was a charming companion, far better than his nightmares alone, and her presence seemed to consign those dark memories to the shadows.

Jacqueline laughed as she tried to coax Lucifer to eat what she had gathered, and Angus decided she might have been wrought of sunlight and happiness. Indeed, she even made him smile, something he had been certain he had forgotten how to do.

For Lucifer, the world was simple. The destrier acknowledged two types of people—those who cared for him and those not worthy of his attention. Jacqueline, having brushed the beast, had won the former status. She offered him morsels of herbs by her own hand, but the beast was more interested in nibbling at her hair, his own sign of affection.

Angus brushed the stallion's back and neck, coaxing the tangles from his mane, in an effort to redeem himself. Lucifer ignored him, smitten as he was with the damsel.

Jacqueline suddenly fixed Angus with a bright look and evidently misinterpreted his expression as encouragement. "And where in Christendom did you find hell?"

"I beg your pardon?"

"You said Lucifer had come from hell, that you found him there. By what other name was that place known?"

"Hell has many names in the realm of men."

" 'Tis only where you acquired a horse," she chided in disgust. "I am not asking for the deepest secrets of your heart. I merely try to make conversation." Lucifer nuzzled her neck playfully, discontent with the loss of her attention.

"If I bade you not to ask me such questions, would you do it?"

She laughed. "You have made it most clear that you do not welcome any questions," she said, merriment in her eyes. "But that has not halted me."

"Indeed it has not."

"Then you have your response."

"But do you know the three pledges a novitiate must make?"

"Of course. Poverty, chastity, and obedience."

"And even knowing that, you are determined to join the convent."

"Aye." Wariness dawned in her eyes. "What of it?"

"Have you considered the burden of those pledges?"

"In what way?"

He met her gaze steadily. "Can you *keep* them?"

"Do you doubt my word?"

"Nay, but I do doubt that you will ever be obedient to anyone. I suspect that you will have considerable difficulties with that pledge, above all." He gave her a quelling look. "Curiosity and obedience do not make good bedfellows."

She smiled impishly. "Then I had best exhaust my curiosity before I join the convent. And I had best make haste, for you are determined to be rid of me."

"On the morrow you shall see Airdfinnan."

"And then?"

" 'Tis a long day's ride to Inveresbeinn. If Fortune smiles upon us, you will be there late tomorrow evening."

Her smile faded. "You *are* anxious to be rid of me."

"I am anxious to pursue my own objectives. I erred in capturing you, and for that you have my apology. There can be no delay in setting that matter to rights before resuming my own quest."

"But Rodney has gone to Ceinn-beithe. My parents will be troubled by his demands."

"So I shall ride from Inveresbeinn to Ceinn-beithe, collect him, and take word from the abbess regarding your safety. Your parents will rest easily then."

She came to stand beside him. "And then what shall you do?"

"Whatever must be done." He had no intent of sharing his plans with her. In truth, he had no good plan as yet, though he believed 'twould come.

"You are not going to tell me."

Angus shook his head, smiling. "Despite your curiosity."

"You could send word to the convent once 'tis done," she suggested hopefully.

He shook a finger at her. "Nay, I cannot. For you will have left the realm of the living and have surrendered any interest in secular affairs."

She rolled her eyes and stepped away. "So I have heard." She folded her arms about herself and stood before the dwindling fire, the light silhouetting her curves in a most interesting way. Angus ceased his brushing and stared, unable to look away.

She caught him, glancing up suddenly as if she felt the weight of his gaze. They stared at each other for a moment stretched taut. She pinkened and covered her breasts, evidently mistaking what he had noted.

" 'Tis cold." She shivered elaborately. "I am surprised that you kept your own tunic, for you have been most chivalrous to date."

"Perhaps 'tis also chivalrous to hide what it conceals," he suggested quietly.

She swallowed. "Your eye is not all of it?"

He shook his head, embarrassed that he should have to deny her the courtesy of warmth to protect her from the horror of him. He turned back to brush the stallion, though the deed was well and truly done.

Her hand on his arm surprised him. She smiled tremulously when he looked down at her. "Would you be gallant enough to keep me warm another way?"

He laughed beneath his breath. "Perhaps I wrongly named the vow that would vex you."

She blushed as he had known she would, and her lips worked in indignation as she sought the words. "Not that! I meant only that we might sleep beside each other, that we would be warmer that way, that . . ."

He touched her chin with affection. "Of course. I would not leave you be cold, though I will not sleep this night."

She tilted her head, ever inquisitive. "Whyever not?"

"Because I will not, and that is all you need to know."

Her lips pinched and she glared at him, as irked as he had ever seen her. "You are a most vexing man, Angus MacGillivray."

He bowed low, pressing a kiss to the back of her hand. "Then I am in most auspicious company, Jacqueline of Ceinn-beithe." Angus permitted himself a smile of satisfaction when the peal of her laughter echoed in the cavern.

✵

Much later Jacqueline curled beside him, all gold and white, an angel of mercy who might keep his demons at bay. Angus wrapped one arm around her waist and cradled her against his chest, smiling when she snuggled against him like a contented cat. Her hair spilled over his arm, her lips softened as her breathing deepened. He stared down at her, as transfixed by her beauty as by her determination to see the good of all around her.

She even found good in him, which was no small feat in his estimation.

The night darkened outside the cave, and the rain still pattered in the trees. He had added the last of the wood to the fire and, though he willed it to burn long, eventually the shadows beat back the fire's glow. Angus watched the blaze, knowing he could not escape the dread that rose within him.

When finally the embers died and the darkness engulfed him, cold sweat trickled down his spine. Angus held fast to Jacqueline and slid fingers through the sunlight of her hair. He breathed deeply of her sweet scent and tried to draw some of her optimism into himself. He fought to endure the night in this place, and fixed his gaze on the comparatively lesser darkness of the night sky.

To be sure, he had survived worse. That was what tormented him. His every muscle was tight with tension, his innards were tied in knots. Memories flashed through his thoughts, unwelcome and unwanted but persistent all the same.

Oh, Angus remembered. He remembered men reduced to little more than skin and bones, he remembered suffering and fetters and oozing wounds. He remembered the sounds of men being tortured to surrender whatever they knew, he remembered the terror of knowing naught and being powerless to persuade anyone of it. He swallowed, remembering the heat of a poker searing his own flesh, the sight of his own eye removed, the sound of his own voice as he screamed in agony.

He remembered the sound of a guard's footsteps in the corridor, the scrape of a key in a lock and how it could make one's heart stop beating in fear. He recalled the terror of wondering whether they came for him this time, the dreadful certainty that the man dragged away would not return. He knew the sound of limbs being removed, of execution, of jailor's keys and scurrying rats. He knew all these things and he would never forget them.

Especially when he was surrounded by darkness and stone. His heart raced in the darkness, his guts might have been tied in knots, a thread of sweat trickled down his back. He recalled the men he had known, the valiant knights and squires with whom he had been captured. He knew the order in which they had died, some in his presence, some distant but audible. It had been a year and a half since his release, and the torment did not ease.

He expected it never would.

And she thought he would tell her of it.

What innocent faith she had that his tale could not be so terrible! Angus cupped Jacqueline's face in his palm and laid his cheek against the softness of her own, taking comfort in her presence. When he was weakened like this, he would take solace where it could be found.

He felt her breathing change, though not in time to draw back. He began to apologize, but she touched his lips with her fingertips, mimicking his earlier gesture. He saw her smile, then she stretched up and touched her lips to his own.

Angus froze, knowing he had no right to partake of what feast she offered. But Jacqueline had learned too quickly, and she slipped her tongue across his lips, coaxing him to join her.

He shuddered with desire but shook his head. "You go to the convent," he whispered. "In but one more day you will be there, your maidenhead intact."

"I care naught for my maidenhead, and none will know 'tis lacking unless I tell them," she replied, as ardent in her determination as he fought to be in his own. "Show me, Angus, show me what 'tis I surrender in this."

"I cannot," he insisted, though his will was not so vehement as his words.

She laid a hand upon his hardness with a surety that was far from innocent. "Aye, you can. Was it not you who told me that a chivalrous man must grant a woman her desire?" He heard the laughter in her voice and yearned anew for a taste of her sunshine. "I have but one opportunity to know the truth of what happens betwixt men and women. I would know of it now, Angus, and I would learn of it with you."

He shook his head, yet clinging to his certainty that 'twould make him a knave to take what she offered. "You do not understand . . ."

"And I do not care." Jacqueline kissed the corners of his

mouth in quick succession, then whispered against his lips, the fan of her breath melting his resistance. "Love me, Angus, and let the once suffice for all."

When she kissed him fully, his resistance abandoned him, like the pollen of a flower scattered in the wind.

Chapter Thirteen

ACQUELINE KNEW THE VERY MOMENT THAT ANGUS surrendered to her. His touch changed, the restraint in his manner dissolved, and she felt his passion unleashed. Angus had introduced her to such tenderness and sensation that she was anxious to know more.

She was curious.

And she desired Angus as well. There was something about this man that made her aware of her femininity, that made her yearn to understand what intimacy passed between men and women. She had decided impulsively that 'twas a sign that she should discover the truth of it with him.

Perhaps that was but an excuse. Either way, there was a quickening in her blood when he kissed her so ardently as he did now, as if her own flesh knew more of what would come than she did herself. His hands roved over her as he tasted her and she echoed his gestures, determined to give as much as she was granted. She felt the span of his shoulders, the muscles in his upper arms, the corded strength of his neck. She matched him, touch for touch, savoring every sensation even as 'twas excelled by the next.

Angus caught her close. Jacqueline felt the chill of the stone against her back and smiled when he was stretched out beside her. 'Twas as if they lay abed, though the rock was not the softest pallet they might have known. Jacqueline did not care.

There was naught but they two. If they had lain in a palace of richest ornament, upon pillows of fine silk and amid expensive perfumes, his touch would not have pleased her more.

Angus slid one broad palm slowly down the length of her. Jacqueline rose to his touch, feeling like a cat stroked before the fire. He chuckled and repeated his gesture, lingering upon her hip, the indent of her waist, the fullness of her breast. She twined her arms around his neck and arched against him, tangling her fingers in his hair and offering her lips for his kiss.

He held her nape in one hand, his other cupping her breast as he kissed her deeply. The teasing of his fingers made her gasp and she felt him smile. He eased the neck of the chemise open, and the heat of his hand suddenly caressed her bared flesh. Jacqueline had never felt so aflame, nor had she felt such urgency within her belly for more before.

Angus loosed the drawstring further, his hand sliding lower even as his teeth drew the neckline wider. He nuzzled her neck and kissed her ear, his hand sliding over her belly, before his fingers slipped into the nest of curls below.

'Twas more wondrous than she could have imagined. She reveled in his touch and the rising tide within herself, running her hands over him. She wanted to please him as he pleased her, but hesitated to reach beneath his own chemise. Sensation overwhelmed her all too soon, leaving her powerless to think, let alone respond.

Angus took her to the brink of release, then let his fingers slip over her thighs. Jacqueline moaned that he denied her such pleasure and wriggled against his hand impatiently.

Angus laughed quietly. " 'Twill be all the better for the

wait, vixen," he promised, then coaxed her to the precipice once again.

When he withdrew this time, she cursed him in jest and they laughed together, as if they coupled thus all the time. Indeed, his ploy fed her hunger for him and loosed her inhibitions as surely as the tie of that chemise. Jacqueline became bolder and more demanding.

She could feel his response to that, straining against her hip.

Angus spoke the truth, for each time she danced higher and more breathlessly. She clung to him and kissed him and ran her teeth across his neck. She twined her legs with his, she entreated him, she kissed him anew.

He shivered and growled deep in his throat. She caught hold of his erection through his chausses and caressed him with gentle persistence.

He gasped in a most satisfactory way, then hauled her against his length. His fingertips danced with new vigor, his tongue cavorted with hers as if he might swallow her whole. Jacqueline ascended that peak with dizzying speed, and she screamed aloud as she abruptly found release.

"Angus!" she cried, her voice echoing in the cavern. He held her fast while the passion exploded within her, then clasped her tightly while the tremors subsided.

Jacqueline clung to him, closing her eyes against the thunder of her heartbeat. When she caught her breath, she realized her fingernails were nigh embedded in his shoulders.

"I have hurt you!" she whispered. She rained kisses upon the flesh that must be marked by her nails, then glanced up to his face.

Contrary to her fears, she saw the rare flash of his smile.

"And?" There was a wealth of pride in that single word, a faith in his own ability to please that made Jacqueline smile in turn.

"You did not mislead me, Angus," she declared, cupping his face in her hands. "For 'twas indeed all the finer for having waited." She kissed him and noted now the tremor of his own desire.

'Twas time she paid her own due.

"But then, you never have misled me," she whispered, liking very well that this was the man who would first know her fully.

Jacqueline kissed Angus anew, even as his hands slid beneath the chemise to cup her buttocks. He squeezed them, then lifted the linen garment away, breaking their kiss that the garment might be cast over her head.

Jacqueline found the hem of his tunic and made to remove it as well, but Angus seized her wrists. "Nay." He punctuated his denial with a kiss to her temple.

He wanted only to protect her from the sight of him. " 'Tis dark, Angus. You need not fear what I might see."

Still he was resolute. "Nay, Jacqueline."

"I would touch you in truth. I would know how a man is wrought." She curled against him and heard his quick intake of breath. "I would feel your flesh against my own."

Aye, he was not indifferent to what she offered. Jacqueline kissed him in her own turn, using her teeth and her tongue until he moaned beneath her caress. She kissed his ear and felt him shiver, then reached for the hem anew.

"Stubborn wench," he whispered, though he did not fight her.

"Aye, most stubborn indeed." Jacqueline flung the tunic aside, sending his chemise after it in short order.

"You will regret this course."

"Nay, not I."

His flesh was smooth beneath her hands, though he stiffened when her fingers strayed toward his right chest. She did not touch him further there, understanding that he would not find such a caress pleasurable.

She spread her hands flat against him, intrigued by the smoothness of his skin, the wiry hair she found in the midst of his chest and on his forearms, the sinew of muscle beneath. Her hands slid down his torso to his waist, over his flat taut belly.

Then she hesitated, her hands stilling upon him.

Angus chuckled. "But you are not so bold as you would have others believe."

Jacqueline felt herself blush. "I do not know how men's chausses are fastened," she insisted, though that was not entirely true. She had never unfastened a man's chausses, but she had eyes in her head. It seemed impossibly bold to simply disrobe him.

But Angus was either unaware of her shyness or untroubled by it.

"The lace is in the front," he purred, taking her hands in his. "Let me help you find it." Again, she thought she heard a thread of laughter in his words.

But he laid her hands upon the front of his chausses and she forgot all else than what was beneath her fingers. She felt the lace, but she was more aware of the strength of him beneath the barrier of the wool. Indeed, he seemed to grow beneath her touch.

Her cheeks might have been aflame, but she did not take her hands away. Indeed, she was curious enough to explore. Angus caught his breath when she moved her fingers. She caressed him gently through the cloth, sliding her fingertips up and down his length. He gasped and shuddered, and she could feel his muscles tightening.

" 'Tis large," she said, trying to sound nonchalant.

"I suspect you have had a part in that."

She plucked at the lace, for 'twas clear Angus had no intent to aid her in this task. And when his chausses were unfastened, she slipped her hands beneath the wool, caressing him gently, much as he had touched her. His erection grew and hardened until he sat up abruptly and discarded his chausses himself. He flung them across the cave then drew her into his arms once again.

"Vixen," he muttered, then kissed her soundly.

Jacqueline melted against him. She loved the feel of him against her, the tickle of his hair against her skin, his strength against her softness. 'Twas all new yet wondrous. She tangled her legs with his and found herself on her back once more, the shadow of Angus leaning over her.

"How did Reynaud assault you?" he murmured. Jacqueline blinked, for she had nigh forgotten that abuse and certainly did not feel it had any link to what they did together now.

"He was atop me, holding my wrists while I lay on my back."

Angus kissed her cheek. "I apologize for reminding you of that, however inadvertently."

" 'Twas not the same." She smiled, though she knew he could not see it. " 'Twas never the same with you."

"But you were fearful of me from the first."

Jacqueline took a deep breath. "I feared 'twould be the same and 'twas that fear that fed my response." She touched his jaw, feeling the tension of uncertainty in him and loving that he was so protective of her. "But you never touched me roughly as he did, Angus, and I was quick to see that I had naught to fear from you."

Angus kissed the tip of her nose. "Nonetheless, I will not risk a sudden memory."

He clasped her waist, then deftly rolled to his back.

Jacqueline gasped then laughed, for she sat astride him. She was kneeling, her heat close to his hardness, her hands upon his belly.

"This time," he declared in a low voice, " 'twill be you who assaults me."

"It can be done this way?"

He laughed. "It can be done many ways, my vixen." She felt his fingertip brush her cheek even as his voice dropped lower. "But this way, the deed is the lady's to command."

Jacqueline's heart warmed with this sign of his consideration. Truly, she had found a man of rare honor with whom to share this deed. "But I do not know what to do," she admitted, laughing.

Angus cupped her buttocks and coaxed her over him, moving until the tip of his hardness nudged at her.

"Oh." There was a twinge, enough to make her wince but no more than that, then she felt his heat ease slightly inside her. "Oh!"

"Are you pained?" He froze, anxious for her answer.

"Nay, naught but a twinge." Jacqueline leaned down and kissed him, not wanting him to misunderstand. " 'Tis fine."

"Then we shall continue," Angus whispered huskily. He eased her lower, letting another increment of him slide within her, and Jacqueline felt her knees weaken at the sensation.

"Oh!"

"Oh, indeed," he echoed, letting his hands slide down her thighs. She felt a shiver run over him and knew that such control was not so readily won. " 'Tis for you to set the pace, Jacqueline."

"But you must aid me."

"Not now. 'Tis all at your command."

"But, but, you will not fit within me."

Again he chuckled. "Aye, I will. But if the deed is not pleasurable, 'tis in your power to halt."

Trusting his conviction, Jacqueline took him within her in small measures that left him gasping beneath her. He seemed to grow tighter and quieter each time she moved, his muscles as hard as the rock beneath her knees. To her amazement, 'twas not long before she sat fully on him.

"And?" Angus's question was as taut as the rest of him.

Jacqueline laughed lightly, her eyes widening at the sensation that resulted. "I am full of you, nigh filled to bursting."

"How does that feel?"

"Well enough, but less remarkable than I had expected," she admitted honestly.

"Indeed?" There was that hint of laughter again.

"Indeed," she agreed. "I would not have you offended, but there should be truth between us in this moment."

"Aye, that is a good impulse. Tell me more."

" 'Tis not an unpleasant sensation, but hardly worth much sacrifice." Jacqueline frowned. "People risk so much with such relations, I had expected the deed to be at least as pleasurable as what we did before."

"But we have only just begun, my Jacqueline," Angus said silkily. He fitted his hands about her waist and lifted her until he was only just within her, then lowered her again.

"Oh!" Jacqueline whispered, the move awakening a new army of tingles within her.

"Oh," Angus mimicked, then repeated his move. Jacqueline rocked her hips as she became accustomed to him, and he inhaled sharply though he did not halt.

Feeling in command of this delight and bold with her power, Jacqueline moved of her own volition. The tender part of her that he had already pleasured was rubbed in a most intriguing way when she arched her back. She leaned forward to kiss him and 'twas yet better.

He caught her around the waist, then moved within her with increasing ardor. She could not have said who led their dance for they found a rhythm together. She felt that heat gathering beneath her flesh once more and wanted all that he might surrender to her. And then Jacqueline knew she would need more. 'Twas not a deed any woman could do only once.

She did not want to do this only to know what 'twas like. She wanted this because she wanted this man. And she did not desire him only once. Nay, Jacqueline wanted to meet Angus MacGillivray abed like this every night of her life and perhaps on more than a few afternoons.

She wanted to hold his secrets and be there when he faced his fears, she wanted to see justice wrought for him and his family. She wanted to ride by his side for all her life. She wanted to see that half smile when first she awakened in the morning, she wanted to bear him sons.

Because she loved him.

That understanding made this even more exhilarating. She coupled with the man who held her heart. She writhed against Angus like a wanton but was powerless to stop.

Indeed, she did not wish to stop. She wanted him to know how he made her feel—she wanted to know that he felt the same way. She made to tell him of her love with her touch.

Jacqueline felt Angus watching her, as if he too had made such a realization. Inordinately pleased by the prospect, Jacqueline touched him as she had never imagined she would be bold enough to touch a man. She felt his own body grow taut and knew that he too rode in pursuit of a release.

Aye, they always would be together thus.

"Jacqueline," he whispered, a question hovering in the strained word.

She had no chance to tell him that his regard was returned before the tide broke over her with astounding vigor. Jacqueline cried his name and shook like a leaf in the wind, then heard Angus roar as the heat of his seed spilled within her.

She tumbled into his embrace and he held her against his chest, their hearts hammering in rhythm. He caught her nape in one hand and cupped her against him, his thumb moving in a ceaseless caress.

Exhausted by their deed and wanting to be nowhere else than in his embrace, Jacqueline let her eyes close. Her breathing was ragged and a sheen of perspiration over her skin made her shiver.

Angus drew his cloak over them both, then hugged her against him. "Still less remarkable than expected?" he mused, his lips against her temple.

Jacqueline laughed. "Nay, 'twas wondrous indeed. I thank you, Angus, I thank you for showing me the marvel this deed can be." She kissed him sweetly and curled against his heat, smiling at his snort of satisfaction.

Jacqueline did not find sleep so readily as she expected, though she was content to lie, limbs entangled, with Angus. His breathing slowed though he did not relinquish his sheltering grip upon her, even in sleep. She listened to the pounding of his heart and thought about the man he was.

A man who had been cheated of much yet still did not lose his honor. A man who pursued justice for his family, who could not seek their own justice. A man who sacrificed years and opportunities for the greater good, then was cheated of it. A man who fought his own desire to see a virgin left chaste, a man who had treated her with more gallantry and care than any she had known before.

A man she could trust to keep her person and her heart safe.

The sky was beginning to lighten and the rain was slowing. Jacqueline sat up to study Angus as he slept. He was an uncompromising man, to be sure, but a man of principle and honor.

He frowned and stirred restlessly, haunted by some demon from his past. Jacqueline eased yet closer, wanting to comfort him but not awaken him. His other hand rose to her shoulder, then his fingers curled into the ends of her hair.

He seized a fistful of it and the anxiety eased from his features. He lifted the hair to his lips without opening his eyes, running the tresses across his face and inhaling of their scent. He seemed to find some respite there, then he grimaced as if snared in pain. His grip tightened around her hair.

Her heart ached that he should be so tormented. She kissed his shoulder, tears of sympathy in her eyes, then pulled back slightly and studied him anew. But Angus slept, unaware of the new day dawning, unaware of the uncertainties dawning in his lover's thoughts.

Did he love her? Only now did Jacqueline fear the truth. Her mother had oft said that a man could welcome a woman to his bed without affection between them. Did Angus merely accept what she had offered, what she had insisted upon giving to him? Or was he simply reticent in claiming his feelings?

Though, indeed, she had yet to tell him of her own. Surely all would come aright when she did?

Without a doubt, she would know the truth when she told him.

Light crept over the threshold of the cavern, the first glow of sunlight touching his dark hair. Jacqueline, certain there need be no secrets between them after the night before, eased away from him. He had claimed her hair near the ends of the long strands, so he did not limit her ability to move. She sat up, her hair spilling around her, and looked fully upon him.

The morning sunlight touched his face gently, as if it would not make the truth more harsh than it was. The soft light did not flinch from the scar surrounding his lost eye. In the sharp shadows cast by a flickering candle, he might have looked demonic—certainly, if he had been scowling, the look of him would have made any soul take a step back. But now he slept, his features at ease.

And truly, Jacqueline had seen his face before. Though she knew she would never tire of looking upon him, in this moment there was something else she would look upon. She eased his cloak lower, half certain Angus would awaken and be displeased, but wanting to know all of him.

The scar he had tried to hide from her was fearsome indeed. It began below his shoulder and continued over his chest, every increment of it making Jacqueline shake her head.

Here she identified a stab wound, the pucker of skin and the heaviness of the stitches molded into his flesh forever hinting at its initial severity. And all around it there were burns, healed but still disfiguring him so that her tears of sympathy rose anew.

'Twas an enduring testament to the pain he had endured, though Jacqueline could not imagine for what reason. But he neither catered to it nor let another guess at its presence.

He had said he had no need of pity.

'Twas not so hideous as Angus believed, though she did not doubt that some would spurn him. As a woman who had been judged for years by the merit of her beauty alone, Jacqueline knew the emptiness that appearances could hide. Angus had no such hollow within him and so his physical scars were as naught to her.

Indeed, they hinted at the valor of the heart they concealed. With reverence and respect, she bent, and kissed the tip of the wound made by a blade. She touched her lips along the scar in a dozen tiny kisses, her own heart swelling with the weight of the love she felt for this man. She thought of the family he would never see again, the holding he had lost, the pain he had tolerated, and one of her tears slipped free to splash upon his flesh.

Angus awakened with a start, his eye wide for a heart-stopping moment as he surveyed her.

And then his countenance darkened. "I bade you not to look upon me," he said sharply, casting aside his fistful of her hair. He averted his face and rose, retrieving his garb, with quick gestures.

Jacqueline spoke calmly, hoping to ease his embarrassment. "You are too shy. I do not think 'tis so dreadful as that."

"No one has asked for your opinion."

"Angus . . ."

"I will not have your pity," he declared fiercely. He donned his chausses with a haste born of anger, his back toward her. "Even if 'tis the reason you came to my bed, I will have no more of it. Do you understand? Save your pity for one who deserves it."

"I do not pity you."

"Liar!"

Jacqueline smiled. "Nay, Angus, 'tis no lie. I love you."

He must have heard her, but he did not turn to face her. He found his boots and hauled them on, shaking out his crusading tunic with impatience.

'Twas as if she had ceased to be.

He could have chosen no response more irksome. She confessed a love for him, she was prepared to change the course of her life if her regard was returned! How dare he not grace her with a reply?

Jacqueline strode after him, infuriated. "Did you hear me? I said that I love you! That and that alone is why I welcomed you between my thighs."

"Then I suggest you cease," he declared through gritted teeth.

Jacqueline felt her eyes round. Nay! It could not be so! Angus was too much of a man of honor to treat her poorly.

Was he not? Jacqueline recalled all too well how she had begged him to take her maidenhead.

With no request for tender feelings.

"What nonsense is this?" Her words were uneven in her distress. Surely she could not have misjudged him?

Angus turned to face her only when he was fully dressed, even to the patch over his eye. He might have been a stranger, for all the warmth in his expression, the same remorseless stranger who had swooped down upon her only days past.

Jacqueline's conviction that she knew him faltered.

"I would not recommend your course," he said coldly.

"Whyever not?"

" 'Twill only bring you grief." He gave her a hard look, and she could not find the words to hurl before this knight who so little resembled the man who had granted her such pleasure. "See yourself dressed. We depart immediately." And he left her there, concealed only by her hair, while he saddled his steed with unseemly haste.

'Twas as if he could not be rid of her soon enough, which told Jacqueline much of their coupling—and worse, of his reasons for it.

It seemed that men saw only her beauty and desired no more than the possession of it. She had made her choice, whatever its price might prove to be.

Her hands shook, but her determination was as resolute as that of her companion. If she conceived a child of his, she would bear the babe in the convent. She had not been raped and she would not shirk from whatever shame came of her own decision.

She had always insisted she wanted only a choice. Having made a bad one changed naught.

How could she regret what she had learned, both good and bad, this past night? Jacqueline dressed with similarly quick gestures, sparing not so much as a glance for the man with whom she had only moments past shared such intimacy.

For now she knew its worth. Angus might be anxious to see her gone from her side, but his repudiation of the love she offered made her equally anxious to find herself behind the convent's high walls.

She loved him still, but she would be damned to hell if she told him so again. 'Twas his loss, for she would beg no man to accept all that she might give.

✵

'Twas a particular irony that the one time Angus had not planned to convince Jacqueline to be angered with him, he had succeeded admirably. She was furious, nigh spitting sparks, though she did not deign to grant him so much as a glance. Her confession had terrified him, and he had responded from the grip of that fear.

Aye, 'twould be tempting to let this maiden love him, a balm to his pride if naught else, but 'twould be wicked. Jacqueline knew naught of the truth of his past or of his intent for the future. Angus knew he had no right to tie her fate to his in the face of that ignorance—and he had no right to pledge himself to a woman when his future was so uncertain.

Of course, he had had no right to take her maidenhead, though that had not halted him the night before. He was torn between the proposal that he knew he should offer and a determination to make the best choice for Jacqueline's future, regardless of how unconventional it might be.

The fact remained that he would probably not survive his attempt to reclaim Airdfinnan. Where would she be left then? Betrothed to an outlaw and a dead man, a penniless corpse whose deeds might draw repercussions to herself.

He could not allow that to happen.

Jacqueline did not know him, after all. Since she did not know him, her affection must be no more than a whimsy. As much as he would have liked to welcome a true love to his side, in this case 'twould be folly. They had been in each other's company but three days. Her attachment would fade before the obstacles yet before him, but not before it ruined the choice she had already made for herself.

Indeed, it had already led to a poor choice on both their parts. He should not have taken her maidenhead. He should not have touched her. He should not have weakened before her appeal. There were no excuses sufficient for his churlish behavior, so not a one of them made him feel less a knave.

Perhaps 'twas better this way. Angus would cherish the memory of her sweetness for all his days and nights. The recollection of the light she had brought into his deepest darkness would sustain him when the demons came again.

But that did not make it right. And it did not give him any right to feed her romantic illusions, or to take more from her than he had already been weak enough to accept. Even if she did love him in truth, 'twas far better for her to be angered with him and put that affection from her thoughts.

Every step closer to Airdfinnan made the prospects most clear. He had been chased from the gates when last he visited here, pursued with the claim that Angus MacGillivray was dead and that he lied in claiming his own name.

'Twould be easier for all involved if he were dead. And the more Angus thought of the matter, the more convinced he was that anyone who would murder twice to claim Airdfinnan would not hesitate to murder again to see that holding secured.

He could not leave the matter be, even knowing that his own death might ensure the result. He had to seek justice for his own blood.

Angus would leave none behind him to grieve. His family

was already gone. If Rodney survived, he would see to
Lucifer, though indeed the stallion was enough of a prize that
he would be sure to find a new master. But Angus would allow no others to fret for him, most especially not this woman
from whom he had already stolen so much.

'Twas a matter of principle, though he was honest enough
to admit to himself that he wished his circumstance might
have been otherwise. Indeed, this was yet another dream
stolen from him by the thief who had claimed Airdfinnan.

Angus looked forward to having restitution from that
man's hide, whoever he might be.

Chapter Fourteen

NGUS WAS EVEN MORE GRIM THAN WAS HIS CUS-tom—which said something indeed—though Jacqueline was far from merry herself. They rode in a silence so complete that even the birds seemed to cease their calls as they drew near.

Jacqueline refused to be the first to speak. She folded her arms across her chest and held herself apart from Angus, not caring if she bumped along awkwardly. She was tempted to ask him to take her immediately to the convent, but that would have involved speaking to him.

She preferred to ignore him and seethe at her own foolishness. She cursed her companion silently more than once, for he seemed untroubled by her censure.

Then she told herself that 'twas only proof that he was not the man she thought him to be. Nay, an honorable man would have apologized for granting insult, or for claiming what he should not have done, or for irking her at the very least.

Not Angus. He said naught.

They returned to the main road, then made good time along it, taking another side trail just before midday. The valley had closed in on either side that morning, the land becoming more rolling even as high hills rose from the road itself.

That side trail had risen crookedly, ascending steadily, oftentimes making the stallion hesitate to choose his footing among the rocks. Angus dismounted and led the steed at intervals, the trust between them so well established that Jacqueline imagined the horse would follow him into hell.

The land flattened and the trail completely disappeared. Angus led Lucifer into the surrounding forest, tethering him there. Angus held up one fingertip in a bid for continued silence, then offered Jacqueline his hand. She nodded understanding but spurned his hand, slipping from the saddle without aid, then picking up her skirts as if she would step past him.

"I thought you did not know the way," he muttered. Jacqueline knew he glared down at her, but she did not give him the satisfaction of glancing up. Indeed, she was all too aware of his proximity and would not let him see any spark of unruly desire in her eyes.

Cursed man! She held her ground and stared straight ahead, waiting for him to take the lead.

Angus murmured something that perhaps she was glad to have not fully heard, then abruptly turned. He led her through the forest, picking his course with care, and as they walked, the wind increased. Angus offered his hand repeatedly, despite her constant refusals.

They could not have gone more than a hundred paces when the trees suddenly thinned and there was naught beyond them. Angus dropped low and she followed suit, nigh crawling through the undergrowth to the lip of the cliff. They lay on their bellies and eased forward to the very edge.

Jacqueline caught her breath. Spread before her was a verdant valley, sheltered by the surrounding hills like a jewel protected by its setting. And in the very midst of that valley, perched on an isle in the midst of a rushing stream, stood a fortification.

"Airdfinnan," she whispered.

Angus merely nodded, his gaze fixed upon the activity below. Jacqueline watched him for a moment but could not guess his thoughts, so looked again.

There was none of the isle that was not encompassed by the keep. Indeed, the heavy walls seemed to rise directly from the stream, which was swollen and dirty with the waters of spring. Those walls were straight and wrought without so much as a chink on their faces. Heavy stone comprised their lower levels, expertly cut and fitted, while above that they seemed to be made of packed earth. They were high and wide, and breached by only one gate.

The river had been widened by artifice, she realized, seeing the rocks that dammed its course. A wooden bridge connected that gate to the shore, and its course bristled with men. Indeed, men paced the top of those wide walls.

Beyond the keep and well away from its main access was clustered a village of considerable size. 'Twas prosperous from the look of the homes there, and there was a wooden palisade around their perimeter. The tower of a chapel rose in its midst, and fields, already tilled, spread from there across the valley.

Jacqueline spied grazing stock, sheep and the occasional cow, and noted that they were plump beasts. In the distance a trio of men tilled a field with a pair of oxen. Half a dozen boys cavorted around the plow while marauding birds swooped low, hopeful of seed.

Airdfinnan seemed incomparably wealthy, reaping the gains of its sheltered locale. Any man would covet such a holding as this. She wondered anew at Angus's motivation and stole a sidelong glance.

He ignored her.

Within the keep's walls, Jacqueline could see little of interest. One square abode was there, as well as a chapel marked by a cross upon its roof and a variety of leaning wooden structures. There were many sentries: at the gate, on the bridge, on the top of the walls, inside the courtyard.

Curiosity had the better of her before Jacqueline knew it. "Airdfinnan is most heavily guarded. Is it frequently assaulted for its wealth?"

" 'Tis prosperous, indeed, but that is not all its merit."

"What then?"

Angus braced his chin on one hand, seemingly fascinated by the men pacing below. He pointed to the right, to a deep cleft in the surrounding hills. "There is an easy path to the east, one of the only easy courses from east to west in this land and thus one of the only weaknesses in the defense of the Kingdom of the Isles.

"From there"—He pointed to the left, Jacqueline seeing that the keep perched in the middle of a glen—"an army might ride to Skye.

"And from there"—He pointed harder to their right, back the way they had come, and she saw another breach in the surrounding mountains—"that army might ride to Mull and the very court of the King of the Isles. Of course, the King of Scotland sees Airdfinnan as a means of his western rival reaching his lands. Airdfinnan sits at the crossroads, positioned to halt an assault in either direction."

"Your family must have been trusted by the King of the Isles to win such a responsibility."

"My father saved the hide of Somerled once in battle and that king never forgot his debt. Airdfinnan was his payment, though a cynical man might perceive that the richness of the gift was his assurance of my father's continued loyalty."

"And Cormac of Clan MacQuarrie?"

"Believed that he too had served the king loyally, perhaps more loyally than my father. He desired Airdfinnan as his own reward, though he was granted Ceinn-beithe, a site held to have great import for his clan."

"Did he protest to the king?"

"He did not dare. But when Somerled died, Cormac made his intention clear. He marched once on Airdfinnan, though was repulsed and was consequently chided by Somerled's son and heir Dugall."

"Somerled had died in an assault on the Scottish king's defenses."

"Aye, and his son was disinclined to tolerate dissent within the ranks of his supporters, poised as they might be for war. Cormac made his threat to my father, though, and many of us doubted that he would bide his time for long. A chieftain's pledge of vengeance is not so readily forgotten."

They stared in silence for a moment, Jacqueline trying to determine how she might make the most of Angus's talkative mood. She clung to a winning theme. "Airdfinnan seems most formidably defended," she said, hoping he would expound upon military matters at least. She was interested in the keep, though she knew 'twas because she hoped to learn more of him in his recounting.

Aye, when he was not angered with her, 'twas difficult to remain angered with him. Jacqueline decided 'twas because Angus never spoke to her as if she were a witless fool.

" 'Tis indeed," he agreed. "The obstruction of the river was my father's pride. He maintained that Airdfinnan could never be taken by force but that 'twould fall only by treachery from within."

"Yet 'tis in the hands of another."

Angus said naught to that, his gaze slipping over the property that should have been his legacy in his brother's stead. Did he believe there was treachery from within, or had his father been wrong?

She knew better than to imagine he would answer her. "How do you know that your brother was murdered?"

His lips tightened. "I know it."

"But how? By Edana's telling, he was ill before you departed, and any man who has fallen ill may surely die. And you cannot have witnessed his death, for you had left for Outremer."

"Again, you put much credence in the ramblings of an old woman."

"How do you know?"

He turned to regard her with no less intensity than he had surveyed Airdfinnan. "You have many questions for one pledged to surrender secular life for the cloister."

Jacqueline smiled. "I am curious."

"And I am disinclined to entertain you." He pushed back from the ledge, ensuring that he was in the shadows of the forest before he stood. He offered her his hand. "You are late for your novitiate."

Jacqueline spurned his assistance, echoing his cautious retreat then rising to her feet unaided. "And I have only had half of the truth. Would you condemn me to never knowing the fullness of your tale?"

"Readily." He marched back toward his steed.

She resisted the urge to swat him and trudged behind. "Then you are witless enough to deserve your fate, just as Rodney would maintain," she charged, and won his attention in truth.

He spun to face her so quickly that she nearly ran directly into him. He caught her shoulders in his hands and glared down at her. "You know naught of what you speak!"

"And you clearly know naught of convents. Cloistered women are oft of influential families. Why, the abbess of Inveresbeinn is said to be a widowed cousin of Dugall, King of the Isles, himself. Though nuns surrender contact, all abbesses have correspondence with the world beyond the cloister walls."

Jacqueline lifted her chin in challenge, liking the rare sense of having surprised him. "Telling me your tale might lead to some aid in seeing Airdfinnan restored to you."

'Twas a feeble argument. Though the abbess's relations were a matter of fact, her inclinations were a matter of speculation. Jacqueline held Angus's gaze, watching him weigh the merit of telling her what he knew.

"You have no reason to aid me."

"Not if you continue to be so irksome."

Angus turned away, and Jacqueline was convinced for a heartbeat that he would tell her naught.

But he began to speak, his words low. "My brother fell ill most suddenly. Ewen was some eighteen summers of age, healthy and hale on one day and shaking in his bed on the next. 'Twas thought to be an ague that struck him or some nameless illness, though the priest was quick to name it as the vengeance of God."

"For your father's failure to depart on crusade."

Angus nodded. "In two days Ewen was barely recognizable as the man he had been. My parents were terrified that he might die, and there seemed to be naught any healer could do."

"So you pledged to crusade."

"'Twas a thin hope, but the only one we had." Angus frowned, his gaze flicking to the keep out of sight. "I learned on my return that he had died but two days after my hasty departure." His voice caught and he bowed his head, grieving.

Jacqueline's heart twisted with a sympathy that she knew he would not welcome. She did not offer it and likely sounded more stern than was her intent as a result. "And your father?"

"Faltered with the loss of his son. 'Twas said he took the same illness within a fortnight." Angus looked into the forest, away from Jacqueline. "He must have been dead before I even reached the shores of France."

He surely felt that he journeyed for naught. Indeed, it seemed that Angus had had little chance to influence his family's fate. Jacqueline laid a hand upon his arm, half certain he would decline her touch but needing to offer solace all the same. He left her fingers there but ignored them.

"And your mother?"

He swallowed and kept his gaze averted. " 'Twas said she was seized by madness and fled Airdfinnan in despair. She was later returned to the keep to be buried, having died of either her madness or her grief."

" 'Tis tragic, but still, I do not understand why you claim they were murdered."

He slanted a glance her way. "I never guessed it, until I met a man in Outremer. His skill was in assassination, and, indeed, he earned much coin by his endeavors."

"But if he was known to be a murderer, then surely he would have been punished for his crimes."

Angus shook off her grip and paced a distance away. He leaned against a tree, folded his arms across his chest as he regarded her, his eye glittering. "Only if he were to be caught at his deed, or if his hand could have been proven to be involved. All knew his reputation by name, though few knew which countenance matched the name of his reputation, and, truly, a man of such skills was most useful in the complicated alliances of Outremer."

"How would he know of your brother's murder?" Jacqueline could not understand the connection between Angus's family and this man. "Surely he could not have been responsible?"

Angus shook his head. "He knew naught of it, and I never

told him what I recalled. 'Twas he who had the need to boast, for he had finally been caught, and he desired to have another respect his cleverness before he was executed."

"A man unworthy of attention."

"But interesting all the same. He told of his favored way of dispatching a man. He was enamored of poison, though it grants a painful passing to whosoever ingests it. By dint of his experience, he had calculated how much of any given poison would make a man ill but not kill him."

"Truly? But why?"

"There are poisons, he told me, which gather in a man's innards—the first measure makes a man ill. The second measure adds to the first, and makes him more ill. This man could adjust the portion so that it took six, eight, even a dozen measures for there to be enough within his victim to see him finally dead. In this way the poison masked the murder, by appearing as an illness that defied treatment and grew increasingly worse."

Jacqueline, though appalled that any person could be so cruel, was fascinated by this gruesome tale. "But how did he make his victim willingly ingest poison?"

"He was fond of presenting himself as an ambassador of sorts, offering a gift of food from the one who had hired him to the intended victim. Though often a rich gift—some sweet dates, or candied elecampane from France, marzipan from Constantinople, a potion to ensure a man's vitality, even an unguent for the victim's skin—it held a hidden barb, for it had been treated with the toxin."

"And the victim took another measure of it every day," Jacqueline concluded in horror. "Thinking he adorned himself or indulged himself. 'Tis wicked indeed!"

"Aye. And this killer took delight in the small touches, in the victim, for example, understanding finally the truth of the gift when 'twas too late to change the outcome."

Angus continued. " 'Twas in his description of the symptoms of various poisons—supplied for my benefit, that I might recognize such a trick if 'twere ever practiced upon me—that I saw my brother's symptoms. Indeed, this man was not alone in knowing his craft, for another had done the same to my family."

"But who? But how?"

Angus smiled coldly. " 'Twas only then I realized the import of a gift brought to Airdfinnan shortly before my brother fell ill. 'Twas a basket of figs, a rare treasure in these parts indeed, brought to my father as a peace offering from another chieftain."

"From Cormac MacQuarrie," Jacqueline whispered.

"None other. My father loved figs, though my brother also adored them. My father surrendered the gift to Ewen, like the indulgent father he was. Thus the poison stole another victim than the one intended."

He offered Jacqueline his hand and took the remaining step to Lucifer. He might have been wrought of stone for all the emotion he showed, though Jacqueline now understood that such impassivity was a sign that he was sorely troubled.

"You have had your tale and you have seen Airdfinnan," he said curtly. "Now I will take you to the cloister."

Jacqueline moved reluctantly, disliking how determined he was to see her gone.

Indeed, just as matters became interesting. The prospect of recounting her rosary in silence for years and years seemed somewhat pallid in comparison to murders and blood feuds and vengeance and battles.

And intimacy.

'Twas only her innate dislike of half a tale, Jacqueline was certain. Aye, her inquisitive nature did not sit easily with the fact that she would probably never know what would come of Angus's quest for justice.

Which only made her doubly determined to learn as much as she could now. "Why do you surrender me as your hostage?"

Angus fitted his hands around her waist and lifted her to the saddle. "Because I see that capturing you achieves little but involve you in a struggle that has naught to do with you." He granted her a grim look. "My quarrel is with Cormac MacQuarrie and thus with his heir."

Jacqueline frowned and glanced back toward the keep. "But there is one thing that I do not understand."

"What?"

"How is it that Clan MacQuarrie does not occupy Airdfinnan? If indeed Cormac was responsible for these two deaths, why did he not claim the keep?"

"How do you know that he did not?"

"I knew naught of Airdfinnan. And we have never visited there."

"Which does not preclude the estate being held in trust by another. There is naught to say that revenue from Airdfinnan does not flow to Ceinn-beithe, or that missives are not exchanged."

Jacqueline frowned, for her parents were not secretive people and she could not imagine that she would not have heard of such a thing if 'twere true. But then, she had no evidence to present to this skeptical knight. "I am not certain—"

"Nay? Think of it," Angus commanded sharply. "If Cormac had boldly seized the keep, he doubtless would have been reprimanded again by the King of the Isles, perhaps more severely and at greater risk to his own wealth. Perhaps he would have lost Airdfinnan and then Ceinn-beithe as well. By allowing an apparently indifferent trustee to administer the holding, and one who insists that he but awaits my return, Cormac would have control of Airdfinnan without the king fearing his loyalty."

Angus silently challenged her to quarrel with that. " 'Tis so diabolically clever that 'tis nigh admirable."

Jacqueline pursed her lips and considered the matter. "But truly, it could have been anyone who sent the poisoned fruit to your father, anyone who wished to see Cormac blamed for the result. 'Twould have been all too easy to blame Cormac, if his oath of vengeance was well known."

"You have great faith in the honesty of men, a faith that I no longer share."

"Nonsense. This is not Outremer. Who holds Airdfinnan?"

"The MacQuarrie clan, as I have explained."

"Nay, who *administers* it?" Her own words were tinged with impatience. He reached again for the saddle. No incompetent rider, Jacqueline encouraged the steed to step away again. She smiled with feigned innocence. "Who is this apparently indifferent trustee?"

Angus was not fooled. Nay, he fairly growled his response, even as he snatched at the saddle again. "Father Aloysius."

Jacqueline blinked. She urged the stallion to trot in a circle around the knight, taking delight in infuriating Angus as he vexed her. "A priest?"

"Aye, a priest and abbot of the local monastery. He took command of Airdfinnan after my father's demise to ensure that 'twas not lost. Cease your game and bring that steed to a halt here!"

"That explains all!" Jacqueline declared, ignoring his command. "All one must do is explain the truth of the matter to Father Aloysius, for surely a man of God will not uphold any gain made by such deceitful means. You said yourself that he but awaits your return!"

"But—"

"But there is the weakness of your explanation!" Jacqueline declared. "Surely no trustee would willingly hold an estate that had been treacherously won—and no priest would deny you once he knew you returned in truth."

"Jacqueline, cease this nonsense!"

Jacqueline did not cease. "Nay, I am not convinced that 'twas Cormac MacQuarrie behind this matter, but whoever 'twas can be most readily found once Father Aloysius joins our course."

"Our course?" Angus glowered at her.

"Aye, *our* course. All we have to do is have an audience with the man. I am certain that all can be quickly set to rights."

"We will do no such deed!" Angus jabbed one finger through the air in Jacqueline's direction. "You are bound for a convent, and I am bound for Ceinn-beithe and thence to the court of the King of the Isles!"

"Nay, I am going to aid you."

"Nay, you are *not*!"

Angus lunged forward for the reins just as Jacqueline touched her heel to the stallion's side. Lucifer cantered in a broadening circle and tossed his mane impatiently.

"We shall talk to Father Aloysius!" she insisted.

"We shall *not*," Angus raged. "I will not be so foolish as to approach those gates, not without an army at my back!"

"Then I will do it for you," Jacqueline retorted. "There is no need for warfare when a simple discussion will suffice. I am certain 'twas no more than a misunderstanding." She gave Angus a hard look. "And I can well imagine that you may have lacked some diplomacy in your earlier appeal."

His expression turned thunderous, but Jacqueline was not afraid.

"Truly, Angus, let me see to this matter for you. I shall plead your case and Airdfinnan will be returned to you and then I shall retreat to the convent as planned." She smiled pertly, but Angus lunged after her.

"You will do no such thing!"

Jacqueline clicked her tongue and drove her heel hard into Lucifer's side. The steed took off like the wind. He was not a small beast and she nigh lost her seating, so unaccustomed was she to riding sidesaddle.

But she held on with a vengeance. She would see this repaired, she would see Angus regain his rightful holding, for she had perfect faith in her ability to discuss matters reasonably with a priest.

"Jacqueline!" Angus roared far behind her.

But he would see the merit of her plan soon enough, Jacqueline was certain. She simply could not retire to the convent without doing her part to ensure that justice was served. And this, she knew, could so readily be set to rights.

Jacqueline took the downward course of the larger path, Angus's cries fading behind her. At the main road, she halted the destrier just long enough to fling her leg over the saddle and arrange her skirts, then urged him onward.

She admitted to herself that this was far more exciting than recounting her rosary or even discussing the lessons of the Good Book with Ceinn-beithe's priest.

Angus swore as Lucifer's hoofbeats faded. Jacqueline was the most irksome woman who had ever drawn breath and if ever he caught her, he did not know whether he would kill or kiss her senseless.

Obedience. Ha! She would never manage to keep that oath. She was not remotely biddable, she did not even cede that there was any other point of view than her own, she was impulsive and a threat to the clear thinking of men everywhere.

Or perhaps just to Angus's own.

And his steed was a faithless wretch, one that should have

been sold in Sicily when he had the chance, or left for the wolves. Angus marched through the undergrowth, his cloak catching on burrs and branches, reached the road in a fury, and was not surprised to find it empty.

Even the dust raised by the beast's hooves was settling. He bellowed one last time but knew she would not heed him now. He could not run faster than the destrier when that beast desired to race.

He should never have let her brush him. Therein lay his error, for now Lucifer would permit Jacqueline to ride him.

Although the alternative was sobering. She was a vexing creature but he was glad that Lucifer had taken to her—'twas reassuring to be certain that the steed would not permit her to slip from his back.

And she was a skilled horsewoman. He had naught to worry about on that score.

Angus returned to their vantage point stealthily so that he would not be spotted by a sharp-eyed sentry. He lay on his stomach and had not long to wait before an unmistakably black steed galloped toward the bridge. The sunlight glinted golden in the rider's hair when she halted the horse with a flourish before the guards.

Angus was surprised and oddly proud as he watched Jacqueline. Lucifer was no means small and by no means un-opinionated. The stallion stomped and tossed his head, but she reined him in with impressive assurance.

There was far more to this seemingly demure maiden than met the eye.

Angus watched as she apparently declared her mission and the guards discussed their course. 'Twas only a moment before both she and the horse were led across the planked bridge and swallowed by the gates of Airdfinnan.

'Twas then he shivered with dread. He had no doubt that

Jacqueline would blurt out the truth of her mission, much as she had just declared it to him. Angus feared she would learn her own folly in the worst way possible.

Too late he realized that if 'twere convenient for him to be dead, 'twould also be convenient for any who claimed to know him—or worse, supported his cause—to be dead.

His blood ran cold at the prospect. He could not let Jacqueline die, not for her attempt to ensure Airdfinnan was restored to him.

Angus sat back, leaning against a tree, shrouded by shadows, while he considered his choices. There was no possibility of leaving Jacqueline within those walls. She was astute and would not take long to discern that she was within a den of thieves. Perhaps she would be more circumspect in claiming her intent.

Perhaps not. Angus could not fault her for not believing his skepticism, for he was not the most charitable soul alive. Indeed, he could not fault her for believing that right would prevail despite the odds.

But he had led her to this place, and he did not imagine that 'twas anything other than her desire to see justice meted out that had her charging to his defense. In better circumstance, he might have found it amusing that this maiden saw fit to defend a knight twice her size, but not on this day.

'Twas only a fortnight since he had crossed that bridge himself, seeking the same justice from Airdfinnan's guardian. 'Twas only a fortnight since he and Rodney had barely escaped with their lives.

Clearly, he was not welcome and just as clearly, any attempt he might make to plea Jacqueline's case would not be heard.

Not if it was made openly.

Angus pursed his lips. Lucifer, he was certain, would be remembered by the sentries. There were not many of his ilk in all of Christendom, fewer still in these hills. Perhaps that was why Jacqueline had been admitted so readily. Even if pursuing her meant his own demise, he had to try to see her free.

Angus would be remembered as well, which would compound the difficulties of retrieving the damsel from an impregnable fortress.

But he had once heard it said that men were more likely to remember the distinctive features of an individual than that man's face. His eye patch would be recalled, his tunic with its red cross, his flaring red cloak. The accoutrements of knighthood would also reveal Angus's rank and possibly his identity.

He hastily shed his spurs, his cloak, his broadsword, his tunic. His helm was in the stallion's saddlebags, so 'twas already accounted for. He cast his leather gloves into the pile, then pulled off his boots, for all were too fine to be unremarkable.

He knotted his simple belt again, this time over his chemise and dark tabard alone. He cast aside the scabbard for his dagger and stuck the blade into his belt. 'Twas old and honed many times, sturdy but without ornamentation.

Angus stood, barefoot and garbed in naught but his dark chausses and tabard and his white chemise. Even cleanliness could reveal his station, so he scooped up handfuls of mud and smeared himself with it. He rubbed it into his face and his hair, shoved it under his nails as if he had been filthy for a long time. He tore his chemise in a few places and worked the dirt into its weave as well, then rolled like a pig in the mud.

He separated the white tunic with its red cross, the broadsword, and his red cloak from his belongings. The rest he concealed in the undergrowth, hoping they would remain undiscovered. He stabbed his dagger into the tunic, then cut his hand and let the blood stain around the tear. He had to milk the blood from his own flesh that the mark would be large enough to be convincing, and even then he wished for more.

A weasel had the misfortune to peer at him inquisitively in that moment. The creature gave a merry chase, but it had not Angus's determination to see Jacqueline freed. Shortly thereafter the tunic boasted a bloodstain of a size sufficient to cast its wearer's survival in doubt.

Angus bundled it up, gripped his father's blade, and cast the cloak over his shoulders. He strode through the woods and stole down the steep path to the main road.

But when he stepped out of the shadow of the woods there, he was as a man transformed, so hobbled in one leg that he dragged it behind.

He also dragged his broadsword, as if unable to bear its weight. Angus was loath to lose the heirloom blade, but naught less would persuade his opponent that he ceased to draw breath.

He pledged with every step to see the blade sharpened anew if ever he regained it. Then Angus lurched away from Airdfinnan, knowing 'twould not be long before Father Aloysius sent sentries out in search of prey.

But that man would not find the victim he sought.

Chapter Fifteen

IRDFINNAN WAS MORE IMPOSING THAN JACQUELINE expected. The walls rose higher and the river was both wider and more agitated than had been visible at a distance. It churned as it passed, murky and heavy.

The sentries barred the bridge with their swords and she reined Lucifer to a halt. They were fully armed, a surprising detail in this apparently peaceful corner of the realm.

Perhaps their guardian took the trusteeship of the King of the Isles most seriously.

Or perhaps he defended Airdfinnan for another reason. Jacqueline wished she had pressed Angus for more of the tale.

One sentry pushed up his visor to consider her, his eyes narrowed in suspicion. "What happened to the knight who owns this steed?" he demanded by way of greeting.

Jacqueline's heart sank. Angus had been here, and, worse, she did not know what had transpired. Curse her impatience to see matters righted!

She had best disguise the truth until she was before the priest himself, when she could plea his case.

"I stole his steed and fled," she declared, which was not entirely untrue. "I seek sanctuary here, and would request an audience with Father Aloysius."

"How do you know our lord's name?"

Jacqueline feigned a laugh. "All have heard the repute of Father Aloysius at Airdfinnan, as well as the justice of his administration."

The men exchanged a glance, then lowered their blades. One took the reins of Lucifer and led the beast across the bridge. Though the bridge was sturdy enough, the surface of the swollen river was treacherously close. Indeed, at one point the water swelled between the chinks of wood.

Lucifer shied when the wood was not fully visible, fighting the bit. The sentry cursed the steed and made to force him onward, but Lucifer was more stubborn. He planted his hooves and refused to move farther. As the sentry cursed and tugged, Lucifer showed his teeth and snorted. When the sentry raised his hand to strike the horse with the ends of the reins, Jacqueline cried out.

"Let me," she insisted. She slipped from the saddle, waving the man away. He went but two paces and the destrier eyed him balefully. "Leave us," Jacqueline suggested. "He will not move whilst you are here."

"He would move if given a sound whipping."

Jacqueline stroked Lucifer's nose. "Nay, he probably would not," she said quietly. The beast exhaled and a shiver rolled over his flesh. She spoke to him quietly as Angus had done, slowly easing away from him. He stretched his neck after her, seeking the reassurance of her touch.

And when she moved beyond his reach, he stepped after her, so intent upon pursuit that he did not note the water swirling around his hooves. Jacqueline whispered and coaxed, rubbing his nose then retreating, until the length of the bridge was behind them. Her own shoes were sodden, as was the hem of her kirtle, but they had made the crossing.

Lucifer snorted and pranced a little when he was on the solid footing beneath the portcullis. Jacqueline smiled and gave his ears a congratulatory scratch, nigh jumping from her skin when a throat cleared behind her.

"And who might you be?"

She spun to find an elderly man standing in the shadows. He was garbed in dark robes that fell to the ground and his head was tonsured, what remained of his hair as white as snow. His eyes were a merry blue, his gaze sharp but kindly.

"Father Aloysius?"

"Aye, though I have not the pleasure of your name, child."

"I am Jacqueline and I seek an audience with you."

"Indeed." His gaze flicked over the stallion. "When last I saw this steed, it was ridden by a man claiming to be a knight."

His choice of words gave Jacqueline pause. "Aye, 'tis a knight's steed and I confess that I stole the beast, so great was my desire to flee."

Again, a half truth. The priest watched her carefully. "The roads are thick with brigands in these times."

"Aye, 'tis true enough."

"But 'tis uncommon for a woman to travel alone. What brings you so near our gates?"

"I was traveling to the convent of Inveresbeinn, where I am to become a novitiate. I was kidnapped by the man who rode this steed."

"And you escaped him when?"

"Just this very day."

Her host pivoted and immediately dispatched a trio of men-at-arms with a command too low for her to overhear. The men mounted their horses and galloped through the gates. He then smiled at her, summoned another man to tend to Lucifer, and gestured through the portal. "Come in, my child."

Jacqueline looked after the men uncertainly. "Where are they going?"

"It matters not. You must be weary. Come in."

"But—"

"But naught." The elderly priest shook his head. "Why trouble yourself with the vagaries of the world of men?" His voice was soft and soothing, and he moved slowly, the darkness of his robes making him look frailer than he probably was.

He led her past the heavy wall that encompassed the gates and into the enclosed space. The ground was hard trodden within what of the courtyard she could see, the square building that had seemed so small from a distance looming up before her.

She looked for the garden that she knew must be here, but could not glimpse it. Perhaps 'twas behind the hall. Perhaps 'twas gone. The prospect saddened Jacqueline.

Perhaps Angus spoke aright and Edana truly knew naught of what she spoke.

The shadows of the hall embraced them as they crossed the threshold. This building was only a single story in height, a board set simply in its midst. There was a screen that no doubt hid the living quarters of the priest, and a fire smoked in a brazier. Lanterns flickered, for the windowless hall was dark even in the afternoon. The decor was so plain as to be monastic, with the exception of the large embroidered tapestries adorning the walls.

"Welcome, welcome to Airdfinnan." Father Aloysius gestured. "If it pleases you, I would have you join me at the board. I would much like to hear of your ordeal and your escape."

Jacqueline glanced over her shoulder, her head still spinning at how rapidly she had been ushered into the hall and Lucifer led away. "I did not know that monasteries kept men-at-arms."

Father Aloysius chuckled. "Traditionally they did not, of course. But times change and we are forced to adapt. 'Tis a burden thrust upon us in holding Airdfinnan in trust."

"But what of the destrier? I should ensure he is settled . . ."

"Child! 'Tis not fitting labor for a demoiselle. Indeed, you must be sorely troubled after what you have endured at the hands of a lawless rogue."

He clapped his hands and gave instructions tersely, smiling upon Jacqueline when he was done. "Though 'tis not our custom to entertain women, I shall surrender my corner of the hall to you. I beg of you to consider this as your own home and refresh yourself accordingly."

Though the bath supplied was only a bucket, Jacqueline delighted in it. Behind the screen, she shed her garments, reassured by the silence that followed the retreat of the men, and gave herself a hearty scrub. The washing cloth supplied was rough, though most effective in scouring away the dirt that covered her.

Even having to dress again in her travel-stained garments did not trouble her, for she felt much better. She rebraided her hair, then stepped out behind the screen once more.

Father Aloysius spoke to one of his charges on the far side of the room, laying a hand upon the man's head, then turned to Jacqueline when the man retreated. The priest smiled paternally and crossed the hall.

"I thank you for that courtesy," she said politely. " 'Twas most welcome."

"And I apologize for the simplicity of what we have to offer." He poured red wine into a waiting silver chalice, then turned and offered it to Jacqueline. "A restorative," he said with a smile. "I confess 'tis my weakness, wrought of years living in Rome."

Jacqueline accepted the chalice, surprised by the weight of

the silver. 'Twould have been expensive to make, despite its simplicity, and she wished that her brother-in-law Iain, who labored in fine metals, could have the chance to see it.

Though that only made her miss Ceinn-beithe with unexpected vigor.

Another chalice was brought, its lines as simple as the first. Father Aloysius poured himself a draught, then raised his cup to Jacqueline. "To the prevailing of goodness throughout all of Christendom."

"As God wills it," Jacqueline replied, then sipped of the wine. 'Twas rich on her tongue and unfamiliar. She had a vague recollection of wine drunk at celebrations at Crevy-sur-Seine, but she had been six years at Ceinn-beithe and was more familiar with their own ale.

Wine was a luxury that must be imported from more southern climes and cursedly expensive here where few trading ships came. Indeed, Eglantine and Ceinn-beithe's priest had long past decided that water would serve for communion. 'Twould be changed to the blood of Christ regardless.

Jacqueline took another sip, marveling at the memories the taste provoked and at how very far away France and Crevy seemed. Yet even distant Crevy was not a quarter the distance that Angus had traveled.

In spite of the silver chalice and wine, Father Aloysius seemed to keep to an austerity typical of the Cistercian order. Jacqueline glanced up to find the priest watching her with a benevolent smile.

"There, you look more at ease."

"Are you of the Cistercian order?" she asked.

"I beg your pardon?"

"I had thought that you were the abbot and priest of a monastery hereabouts and the simplicity of the hall puts me in mind of the Cistercians who shun worldly riches. To what order is the monastery a daughter house?"

" 'Tis not a daughter house any longer," he said firmly. "I cede to the authority of none."

Jacqueline hid her surprise at this. She fingered the chalice and considered those three vows of which Angus seemed determined to remind her.

What of poverty?

"Save Rome itself," she could not help but chide.

He smiled. "Of course. Do not misinterpret me—I simply do not believe that the will of God is well served by tiers of authority. The tithes then rise proportionately to support administration, instead of being spent upon the sick and the needy, as must be truly God's will." He waved a hand at the interior of the hall. "Similarly, there is no merit in lavish spending upon plate and ornament when there is labor of substance to be done in the world."

"Is Airdfinnan a monastery now?"

"Nay."

Jacqueline frowned. "But how then does a priest come to hold sway over such a key fortification? Surely the concerns of the secular world are not your own?"

Father Aloysius shook his head. "If only they were not. I hold Airdfinnan in trust, and 'tis a fearsome burden to be sure."

"In trust for whom?"

"In trust for a man who in all likelihood is dead." Father Aloysius sighed with the weight of his burden. "The second son of Fergus MacGillivray, that illustrious chieftain who put his trust in me, is named Angus. He departed on crusade some fifteen summers past and there has been no word of him. Only God knows if he has gone to his reward or if he someday will return." The priest smiled. "We can only remain vigilant and protect his inheritance in the hope of his return."

Servants brought bread and cheese as well as cold sliced

meat. Jacqueline was ravenous and needed no encouragement to eat, even as her thoughts whirled.

Father Aloysius ate little himself. "You have endured much, I would wager," he murmured. "How long has been your ordeal?"

Jacqueline frowned. "I am not certain. Four days perhaps."

"You must have been terrified at what such a man might do to you."

"Aye, at first I was."

His white brows rose. "Only at first?"

Jacqueline held his inquisitive gaze. "I quickly realized that he was not only a knight but a man of honor. He is Angus MacGillivray, but then you must know the truth of it, for you all recognize his steed."

The priest shook his head and leaned forward. "Oh, my child, you are indeed too trusting. 'Tis true enough that a man came here, upon the steed you now ride, and also true that he made his claim of being Angus MacGillivray. He is not that man. He is naught but an imposter, a thief who would steal what is not his to claim." He leaned over to pat her hand. "He has a certain confidence in his lies. I am not surprised that an innocent maiden like yourself was so readily deceived."

"But how do you know that he is not who he claims to be?"

"I *knew* Angus MacGillivray." The priest's gaze hardened. "I sewed the crusader's cross upon his tunic with my own hands. And I do not know this man. He lies, 'tis as simple as that."

He spoke with heat, then drained his cup, setting it down with a thump as if challenging Jacqueline to disagree. A boy hastened forward to refill the cup.

Jacqueline stared at the remnants of her meal and wondered if she had erred. Could Angus have deceived her? Was it possible that he was not who he claimed to be? He could have lied to Rodney, who was not of these parts.

But he knew the land as one raised here, and she could not imagine that he lied when he finally told her his tales. Surely if he sought to fool others, he would be quick to confess his concocted tales and seek to convince all within earshot?

And how would Edana have recognized him on sight and called him by his name if he were not the man he claimed to be?

She glanced around herself once more and decided that Airdfinnan was not so small a prize. Edana had to pay no price for acknowledging Angus, but Father Aloysius would have to cede Airdfinnan. How many monasteries in Scotland could afford to indulge the priest's taste for wine?

A lump rose in Jacqueline's throat for she realized the tenuousness of her situation somewhat too late to repair it. 'Twas not reassuring to realize that Angus had tried to warn her.

She glanced up to find the priest's gaze bright upon her and forced a smile as if naught troubled her. "I did not realize there was a monastery in these parts," she said, her tone light. "Where is your foundation?"

" 'Twas nestled in the woods on the far side of the valley, but we moved within these walls at the request of Fergus himself when he knew himself to be leaving this life." Father Aloysius crossed himself at the mention of his deceased benefactor. "And shortly thereafter, much of the foundation burned to the ground, a tragic incident but perhaps a sign of God's intent that we should remain protected by these walls in such times of turbulence. There are still a few monks who choose to live there."

The armed guards thus kept not only that turbulence at bay but ensured that none could recapture Airdfinnan.

"What will happen to Airdfinnan if Angus never returns?"

Father Aloysius smiled. "That remains to be seen. The King of the Isles would have Airdfinnan held by hands he can trust, though I believe we have shown our trustworthiness these fifteen years. And King William of Scotland would make it his own to grant to one of his allies, if he had the choice. Perhaps 'tis better for all to have such a key holding in the hands of the just authority of the church."

So 'twas not only Angus who chafed for possession of Airdfinnan.

" 'Tis fortunate indeed that you were still here, that you might recognize an imposter for what he was."

Father Aloysius's smile was cold. "He was not the first and he will not be the last. 'Tis my sacred duty to protect Airdfinnan from all who would seize it for their own greed alone."

Their conversation was interrupted by hoofbeats on the wooden bridge. The sound echoed so loudly that it could not be missed.

Father Aloysius rose, his gaze bright. "And? What has been discovered? Bring the men here to me immediately!"

In short order, the three men he had dispatched made haste to the board. All three fell to one knee in homage to the man acting as their liege lord. Jacqueline wondered what pledge of fealty Father Aloysius had demanded of them. She then frowned as the one farthest from her flicked back his cloak.

'Twas of deepest crimson, and she knew the price of red dye well enough. Nay, this man could not have afforded this cloak.

And indeed, he had not worn it when he left. She would have remembered as much. Her mouth went dry, for she feared she knew precisely where he had found it.

Though the man who had worn it this morn would not have surrendered it easily. Jacqueline gripped the board, fearing the news they brought.

"He is dead, my lord. Cut down in the road and left to the picking of beggars." The middle one then offered a sword and a familiar though bloodstained tabard.

Jacqueline leapt to her feet. "You killed him!" she cried in outrage. "You killed him so he could not press his claim to Airdfinnan! You are no priest—you are a murderer!"

The accusation was out before she considered the wisdom of uttering it. Jacqueline clapped her hand over her mouth in horror and stared at Father Aloysius.

That man waited, then responded with surprising calm. "You must forgive our guest for her outburst. She has survived a most fearsome ordeal." Father Aloysius shook his head. "And indeed, 'tis not uncommon to hear that captives become sympathetic to the aims of their captors."

Jacqueline did not believe her trust of Angus was displaced, but she held her errant tongue.

The priest took the tunic that had once been white and shook it out. Jacqueline knew the color drained from her face when she saw the fullness of the stain, for none could have survived any wound that would make the blood pour with such vigor.

The priest accepted the broadsword, with a satisfied smile.

Surely Angus was not dead? But 'twas unmistakably the sword of Fergus MacGillivray. What had happened to its bearer? Jacqueline swallowed and prayed for Angus with such fervor as she had never shown in prayer before.

"You have brought his corpse?" the priest asked, his fingertip trailing over the distinctive hilt of the blade. He flicked a glance to Jacqueline and smiled coolly. " 'Tis our Christian duty to see that even this criminal might be buried with some grace."

"Nay, my lord, we never saw it."

Father Aloysius's eyes flashed even as Jacqueline caught her breath with new hope. "What nonsense is this?"

"We found the tunic and the blade."

"Found? *Found*?" He crumpled the tunic in his fist and cast it on to the board. "How does a dying man shed his belongings, without leaving his corpse?"

The men looked between each other. " 'Twas an old beggar, a leper, who found him, in truth. He was dragging his plunder all away, intent on having compensation for his find from the Templar house some ways east of here. We relieved him of his booty."

"And you let him go?"

At their sheepish nods, Father Aloysius roared. "But what of the corpse?"

"His directions were so garbled, my lord, that we could not retrace his steps, and, indeed, night was beginning to fall."

"We desired only to bring you the news you awaited with all haste."

Father Aloysius was not pleased by this, though Jacqueline was delighted. At least there was not proof that Angus had died—which meant she could hope anew for his survival. "Why did you not bring the man here? How else are we to be *certain* he speaks the truth?"

The men grimaced, and only one had the courage to speak in a hushed whisper. "But he was a leper, my lord."

"We could not bring him here, lest he infect all."

"Edmund was the only one to touch him, and look how he scratches at his hand already."

The man who must be Edmund, the one who wore Angus's red cloak, scratched his wrist furtively. "Would you bless me, my lord?"

"And why should I bless you when you have failed in such a simple task?" the older man snapped. "You have no evidence that a man is dead unless you see his body with your own eyes."

The men stared at the priest in silence, until Father Aloysius heaved a sigh and rubbed his brow. "I apologize for my anger. I am most vexed that we are tormented by this criminal and would merely have assurance that he will plague us no longer."

"Aye, my lord."

Father Aloysius placed a hand upon Edmund's brow and muttered a blessing, which seemed to relieve the man. Then the priest spoke firmly. "You will return to the site where you found this leper. You will bring me the body of the man who wore this tunic, or you will bring me the leper, or you will not return to this hall. Do you understand?"

"But, my lord—"

"But naught! I must have proof that this brigand who feigns to be the heir of Airdfinnan is truly dead. Already he abducted this novitiate and deceived her. Truly, there is no telling what other wicked deeds he has performed. I must know that he draws breath no longer if I am to sleep at night."

"Aye, my lord." They bowed and backed out of the hall, Edmund pausing to scratch his hand.

Jacqueline knew she had not heard the last of her outburst, though she understood that Father Aloysius would say naught of it before others. She took a step back when he turned to face her, his expression so ominous that she feared her own fate.

"Rest assured, Jacqueline," he said smoothly, "that I shall not let you depart from this keep until I am certain of your safety."

"But I thought to go immediately to Inveresbeinn."

" 'Twould be most treacherous." The boy refilled the wine goblets and Jacqueline understood that this show of concern was for his benefit. "As your host, I cannot allow you to risk your own life so foolishly. Let us see this matter resolved fully first."

Father Aloysius smiled, but his expression no longer seemed so kindly. "I am certain the abbess will understand. In the meantime, I will pray that you are released from the wicked delusions this man has obviously fostered within you."

Jacqueline realized that she would not be suffered to leave without Father Aloysius's approval and that he would not give it. She was a prisoner here, and at his dictate.

Oh, she should have listened to Angus's warnings!

Indeed, she wondered how much the old priest guessed of her regard for Angus. She realized with dawning horror that she was being kept captive here not only to keep her silent concerning Angus's claim but to bait the trap.

The priest believed her presence would draw Angus back to Airdfinnan. She could not be the cause of his demise!

Father Aloysius reached across and patted her hand once more, his tone sympathetic. "You are fortunate indeed to have escaped a man who scorns the law of men and God. You will see this in time, my child." He glanced over the board. "Perhaps a sweet to end your meal?"

'Twas appalling that he could think of such social niceties at such a moment. Either Angus was dead or the departed men would see to it shortly. She hoped against hope that he had outwitted them and would do so again, but she feared for him.

They were three and he was one, after all.

Even worse, she knew 'twas her fault that he was hunted. If not for her, Angus would have been leagues away.

Before Jacqueline could reply, the priest had summoned a boy. "Go, Gillemichel, and fetch the box of figs for our guest, the one upon the high shelf in the kitchen."

The boy flicked her a look that would have meant naught to Jacqueline, had she not heard Angus's tale. As 'twas, her heart quickened in dread.

Figs! It seemed that Angus was not to be the only one who never returned from Airdfinnan.

Father Aloysius smiled at her as the boy disappeared. "We are honored to have received such a rich gift from a visiting priest. You must partake of this luxury."

"I am afraid I have no taste for figs," Jacqueline lied, "although your generosity is indeed gracious."

The priest's smile faded. "Nonsense! You are merely polite in declining extravagance. No doubt your mother raised you well."

"Aye, she did, but 'tis true enough that I cannot bear to swallow figs."

His eyes narrowed. " 'Tis unusual to have such a distaste of a foreign luxury. Most would welcome the chance to indulge."

"True." Jacqueline managed a thin smile. "And 'tis foolish of me, perhaps. But I once heard a tale of a man killed by poison hidden in figs and since then I cannot force them down my throat. I would not waste your treasure, though your generosity in offering them is most appreciated."

They stared at each other unsmilingly, each understanding the position of the other with painful clarity. The boy slipped the box onto the table, glanced between them, then retreated.

Neither touched the box.

"You should have one," Jacqueline suggested, the devil having claimed her tongue. "Do not desist on my account, I beg of you. I should feel terrible if my whimsy tainted your delight in such a precious gift."

His lips tightened. "In truth, I have eaten too much this day. Perhaps another time."

Or perhaps not. Jacqueline was glad she had eaten well before Father Aloysius guessed her support of Angus. She might not dare to eat again within these walls.

How long would she be here? None knew of her presence

here, so none would be inclined to rescue her. Save Angus, who was in no position to aid her. And if he came for her, they both would disappear. Despair swept over Jacqueline and she blinked back tears. The priest left her there, evidently confident that there was nowhere she might flee. The two guards hovering at the door watched her warily.

Jacqueline looked at the stained tunic upon the board and felt sickened by its portent. She folded her arms about herself and shivered. She had thought to do right but had disregarded Angus's counsel and her plans had gone sadly awry.

But 'twas Angus who undoubtedly would pay the ultimate price. Aware of the watchful gazes of the guards but uncaring, Jacqueline bowed her head and wept for what she had wrought.

❊

Angus had forgotten the grille.

Oh, he had a vague recollection of his father's long-ago threat to put a metal grille over the drainage hole from inside the fortress. But on that day, some twenty years before this one, he and Ewen had been so impressed with their own cleverness in breaking into the keep that they had not paid much attention to their father's bluster. Fergus MacGillivray had always taken such pride in his claim that Airdfinnan was secure beyond belief that they had expected him to roar when proven wrong.

Roar he had, but it seemed that Fergus had done more once his roaring had been complete. Now Angus regretted that they had never tried to repeat the deed, but there had been other challenges to face.

On this day Angus was put much in mind of his brother and their boyish pranks, for he had faced a goodly share of challenges. He had persuaded the guards that he was a leper when they had considered arresting him, and then he had circled around Airdfinnan without being spotted. Ewen would have delighted in this game.

But after all of that, Angus had not been able to see the drainage hole when he reached the far side of the keep. He had feared it had been blocked up.

There was no other way into the keep if it had, so he had dared to check. He found it, just where he recalled, though submerged some two feet below the river's swirling surface.

Yet his father had ensured that an iron grille was locked over its mouth. Angus lingered low in the water and considered his choices as he reviewed the stationing of the guards.

They were everywhere that he would have placed them himself. 'Twas as if Aloysius expected a confrontation, and not one from a single man. Angus eyed the walls and knew he could not scale them unseen, not even on this side and not even with a grappling hook. There was not so much as a shadow to hide a man. He could not pass through the gates, and this was the only breach in the walls.

Indeed, he had not even been certain he could squeeze through it. He was no longer a boy of ten summers—but then, 'twas not of import if the way was barred. He took a deep breath and ducked beneath the surface, forcing his eye open. 'Twas a lattice of cursed complexity, as one might have expected from a man so concerned with defense as his father.

Angus swore silently, fearing what fate befell Jacqueline, for she had been within the keep for hours. In frustration, he grasped the grille and twisted it hard. His father would be sorely vexed to know the result of his planning!

The grille moved.

Desperate for breath, Angus broke the surface, inhaled greedily, and dove down again. He grabbed the grille again and wrenched it, vastly encouraged when it shifted again.

Another breath and he tried again, the metalwork coming free suddenly in his hands. He broke the surface, then leaned back against the wall and breathed heavily, lifting the metal just slightly from the water that he might examine it.

And Angus smiled when he saw the rust. If the water rose this high with any frequency, it would have been only a matter of time before the grille drifted free upon its own.

Father Aloysius was apparently less concerned with worldly matters than Fergus had been, for Angus knew his father would have checked this potential weakness each year when the waters receded.

Providence was again upon Angus's side. He closed his eye, recalling how the drain had inclined slightly from the opening, perhaps for half a dozen paces, then turned sharply vertical. Once there had been only a wooden trap over that opening, so that none would step into the hole, but he and Ewen had easily pushed it up into the courtyard from the underside.

He would hope that 'twas still thus, and he would hope that he could hold his breath long enough to reach that far. If the water was high enough that he could not take a breath at that grille, or if 'twas sealed, he would be hard pressed to return this far to take that second breath.

He would not think of the practical uses of this drain. Indeed, 'twas the least of his worries. He would not consider his own terror of being trapped below the earth in a space of men's devising, a space cold and wet and dark where a man might easily breath his last. Nay, he would think of the light shining through the grille at the other end and ignore the shadows betwixt here and there.

He would think of Jacqueline.

Angus's heart pounded with only the anticipation of what he would do, he told himself, not with terror. The demons gnawed at his thoughts, gleeful that they might soon be able to seize his wits, but he struggled to ignore them.

The fact that he might fail did not change what he had to do. Angus took a trio of deep breaths, remembered his brother's optimism and spirit, then dived beneath the murky surface once more.

Chapter Sixteen

OR THE SAKE OF HER CURIOSITY, JACQUELINE SOUGHT the wondrous garden of Edana's tale. She could not bear to think that tale had not had some foundation in truth.

She was delighted when she found it at the rear of the keep, though 'twas secured behind its own high walls. There was one gate in those walls, one wrought of fancifully turned iron bars and locked against intruders. Jacqueline hung on to the bars and peered inside as best she could.

It looked as most gardens did in the spring, half of the plants appearing dead and the rest clearly uncertain whether they desired to live. Someone had tended it recently, for 'twas not unkempt, but there was naught in bloom.

She craned her neck and peered through the bars, then squeaked in surprise when a man cleared his throat behind her.

'Twas another priest. He nodded and drew a key from his cassock. "Good day to you. You must be the guest of whom Father Aloysius spoke."

"Aye, I suppose I must be that *guest*."

He gave her an odd look, then unlocked the gate and stepped through it, excusing himself as he passed her. He pulled the gate resolutely behind himself, shrugging apologetically.

"May I see the garden?"

He hesitated, then shook his head. "I think it would not be for the best."

"Whyever not?"

His gaze flicked to the hall, then he smiled for her. "I should not like to displease Father Aloysius. He prefers that the garden not be visited overmuch, and truly I am here on his sufferance."

"What does that mean?"

"I have a fascination for plants and herbs, though Father Aloysius has no obligation to indulge me. I heard of Airdfinnan's gardens years ago and when I was sent to this area last year, I wrote and asked to see them." The priest smiled. "They were much neglected and there are many here that I cannot name, but I have persuaded Father Aloysius to let me tend them in the hopes that much can be learned."

"They do not use the herbs in the kitchen?"

"It appears none has the skill."

"Then why do you not have an apprentice?"

He looked at her, then shook his head, bemused. "I have wondered much the same, though 'tis not my place to question the decisions of those above me."

"Even if they err?"

He studied her. "You are a most uncommonly forthright guest."

"One might say that I am not a guest."

The priest shook his head with a frown. " 'Tis not my place to know of it, or I would have been told." He made to turn away, but Jacqueline called after him. 'Twas clear that he was not about to risk his own desires.

"To how much would you turn a blind eye, if doing so ensured your access to this garden?"

He paused, glancing back to survey her in a silence that stretched so long that she feared he would say naught more.

" 'Tis of great import to me to study these plants," he said finally. " 'Twas most difficult to convince those who hold sway here to let me come."

"Aye, I can imagine as much."

At her vehemence, he shrugged. "I would hesitate to suggest that I have not been made welcome here—"

"Though you have not been."

He chuckled at a bluntness he clearly found unexpected. Jacqueline instinctively liked him, despite his caution. Perhaps 'twas a useful trait within these walls. He was not unlike Ceinn-beithe's priest, who spoke carefully and seldom criticized his fellows.

"I am Father Michael," he said, returning to the gate, though still he did not open it for her.

"I am Jacqueline."

" 'Tis a delight to meet you, Jacqueline." He inclined his head. "Perhaps we shall see each other again." He walked into the garden, pausing to touch a leaf here and a bud there.

Jacqueline gripped the iron once more and called after him. "Why is the garden gated?"

"I understand it has always been thus."

"Why?"

" 'Twas said that the chieftain of Airdfinnan feared for the health of his sons."

"I do not understand."

"There is much that is toxic in a garden of medicinal herbs and evidently there once were bees here, for there is a skep. No doubt he did not wish his sons to frolic here unaccompanied, lest they taste something or trouble something they should not." The priest smiled. " 'Tis not an unfitting impulse for a father."

"Nay. 'Tis not." Jacqueline took a deep breath, concluding that she had naught to lose by seeking this priest's aid. Father Aloysius already knew that she favored Angus's suit for

Airdfinnan, and 'twas possible that this man did not fully agree with Father Aloysius.

Sooner or later she would have to eat, and she wagered that whatever she had the chance to consume would be poisoned. She had not much time.

This priest might be her sole chance to see Angus avenged and herself freed. Father Michael might well be deceiving her, but her situation could hardly be made worse.

"Just as 'tis not an unfitting impulse for a father to bequeath his own holdings to his son."

Father Michael eyed her anew. "Of course 'tis not."

"Yet Airdfinnan is held by no blood of the chieftain Fergus MacGillivray, despite that man's own desire."

" 'Tis held in trust, for the return of his son Angus from crusade." Father Michael shook his head. "Though I have heard that he is gone these fifteen years and it seems unlikely he will ever return."

"Especially if Father Aloysius would ensure his demise when he does."

"What is this?" The priest closed the distance between them with quick steps.

"Angus MacGillivray is returned. He has been here and I have been in his company. But Father Aloysius commanded Angus be killed rather than surrender Airdfinnan."

"That cannot be so. 'Twould be a travesty of justice!" But Father Michael was not so convinced of even his own claim. His gaze roved over Jacqueline's features, as he clearly sought some hint that she lied.

" 'Twould be wicked indeed, but 'tis no less than what he has done." Jacqueline leaned closer. "I am here because I foolishly believed a priest would do what was right, though Angus warned me otherwise. Now I am imprisoned here, as a 'guest,' though perhaps I was only admitted at first in the hope that my presence would draw Angus to his death."

She shook her head, unable to halt her tears. "But Father Aloysius has dispatched sentries to see Angus dead, and I, as the only witness of this injustice, am undoubtedly intended to never leave this keep alive." She held the gaze of the intent priest. "Is the study of your herbs worth leaving this wickedness unpunished?"

They stared at each other, she willing him to believe, he clearly fighting his warring convictions.

" 'Tis a fable you tell, no more than that," he said finally. He inclined his head then turned hastily away, returning to his inspection and dismissing her.

Jacqueline's heart sank as she watched him go. When he did not so much as look her way, she turned away. 'Twas not right! She turned and surveyed the courtyard, guessing that none who had pledged fealty to Father Aloysius would aid her or Angus.

That meant she could not afford to die within the circle of these walls. She had to escape.

Jacqueline had to see Angus avenged. She owed him no less for her role in his predicament. She might not be able to save him from those sentries, but she could do all she could to see his name cleared of Father Aloysius's lies.

It seemed a paltry exchange, though she knew Angus would want no less. First, of course, she had to see herself freed.

Angus had insisted that Airdfinnan could not be assailed from the outside, but she was inside its walls. Keeps, after all, were designed to be defended against attack, while prisons were intended to keep prisoners within. She surveyed the high walls of Airdfinnan and decided that it worked effectively as both.

There had to be some way to escape. The greater good had to prevail!

Glumly she trod around the perimeter, seeking some

weakness. There were at least three ladders wrought of wood lashed together, no doubt the means by which the men scampered to the summit of the walls. All lay on the ground, and when she tried to lift one, Jacqueline found 'twas too heavy for her.

She muttered a curse worthy of Angus's vocabulary and continued on. She found Lucifer in a stable. The stallion was not pleased with his situation and showed his mood by stamping repeatedly, snapping his reins, and snorting the feed granted to him all over the floor. He trod in it and shat in it and bared his teeth at the stable boy who tried to approach him.

Jacqueline spoke to him and scratched his ears, and he deigned to be soothed, though he kept a watchful eye on that stable boy and flicked his tail in dissatisfaction. She lingered with him long, wishing she could explain Angus's fate to him and wondering if his mood was due to his sensing some dire portent. Her mother maintained that horses knew more than people imagined they did.

Jacqueline stroked Lucifer's nose and wondered what would become of a knight's destrier in a place where there were no knights. He nibbled at her hair, tugging the braid playfully, as if he too had need of encouragement.

Perhaps someone would eat Lucifer. One heard of such vulgarities. Or perhaps he would be sold to a king or a prince visiting from afar. Unless, of course, Rodney returned in a timely fashion and claimed his knight's belongings.

What had happened to Rodney? And how had her parents taken the revelation of her capture? Jacqueline was mortified to realize that she had nigh forgotten about them. Perhaps Father Aloysius could be persuaded to send word to them of her safety.

But then, perhaps not.

'Twas up to her to ensure the survival of herself and

Lucifer, up to her to ensure that Angus's name was not left sullied, and up to her to calculate how that deed might be done. Jacqueline smiled at the stable boy, who eased closer to the calmed stallion. Lucifer brayed at him and stamped ferociously, snorting with satisfaction when the boy fled.

"Perhaps there is a bit of the devil in you," she commented, and gave his rump a farewell pat. The destrier snorted and nosed through his feedbin once again, no doubt waiting for the stable boy to feel bold again.

Jacqueline strolled, knowing she was not unobserved but seeking to look only mildly curious about her surroundings. In truth, she was thinking furiously, increasingly frustrated by the fact that the only apparent exit was the guarded gate.

She paced the perimeter and ducked through every lean-to, finding the smithy, the butcher, the buttery, and the henhouse. She avoided the chapel, for all knew that the sacraments offered by wicked priests were wicked in themselves. She would take no mass or offer no confession in this place, even if it meant she died unshriven.

She found women doing the wash, though they refused to return her greeting or even acknowledge her presence. They scrubbed unceasingly, mute but fairly exuding resentment all the same. She wondered at this, then recalled Father Michael's caution.

The sun was sinking as the sound of pots echoed from the hall. Father Michael departed, locking the gate to the garden securely. Jacqueline watched him, but he did not so much as glance her way. He ducked into the hall and her heart sank with the surety that her charges were soon to be repeated.

She had best decide what she intended to do and decide it quickly. The guards changed with no interruption in their vigilance, no moment when the ladders were unattended. The sentries paced along the top of the wall, spaced with disquieting regularity, watchful as hawks on the hunt.

The women wrung out the last of their washing and flung what looked like men's chemises over a makeshift line. They dumped their cauldrons of water and Jacqueline jumped back, certain the area would be flooded. But the water barely spread across the ground at all.

'Twas then Jacqueline heard the gurgle of water flowing down a drain. She trotted after the women, her heart pounding as she spied the wood lattice nailed over what was obviously an outlet to the river outside.

Here was her salvation!

She feigned indifference and strolled past the hole, noting that 'twas wide enough for her, but acting as if she had not even seen it. 'Twas nailed down securely, the lattice so tightly fashioned that a rat would have had difficulties slipping through it.

Somehow she had to remove that wooden lattice. Feigning the bored demoiselle though her heart raced madly, she visited Lucifer again.

"I will return for you," she whispered, rubbing his ear. "Somehow I shall do it. Or I will buy you from him. Fear not!"

The steed looked unlikely to fear anything. She took his brush, as if she had all the time in the world, and worried about those large nails in the lattice even as she brushed him down.

'Twas when she brushed his flank that she spied the awl. It had fallen in the straw underfoot, perhaps dropped by a frightened stable boy when Lucifer objected to his presence. No doubt the boy had not the audacity to return for it.

It mattered naught—the tool was there. And in the twinkling of an eye, 'twas hooked through Jacqueline's belt and hidden in the folds of her kirtle. Her mouth was dry, her heart hammering, her gaze quickly flying over the courtyard as she sought her moment.

She knew 'twas time when the stable hands retired to the

kitchens. Jacqueline ducked into the shadows. She needed a distraction and knew where to find it. She slipped into the henhouse, unlatched the door, and shooed the chickens out of their nests. They clucked and bickered and complained in a most promising fashion as they made their way out in the courtyard.

But then they pecked the earth and hovered close to the henhouse, causing no ruckus at all.

Nay! This could not be! Where were the dogs when she had need of them? Jacqueline glanced around the courtyard, knew she had no time to trouble herself with chickens, and continued her quest. Keeping a careful eye on the guards, she crept from shadow to shadow, hugging the walls wherever she could, gradually coming closer to that wooden lattice.

She had not much time. The women lingered at the portal, exchanging boisterous comments with the guards as they passed through the gates. The yard was momentarily silent, the chickens having disappeared. Wretched birds. They were always making noise at Ceinn-beithe, but these seemed of a different, more tranquil breed. Fortune would seem to be against her.

All the same, she had to try. Jacqueline dashed across an open space, her breathing labored as she flattened herself against the wall just a few steps away from the lattice.

So close 'twas and yet so far. The sunlight glistened upon the wet wood and gleamed upon the enormous nails. There were six of them.

Six! She knew she could not crouch beside the opening and work the lattice free without being seen. And she doubted she could work those doughty nails free that quickly. She chewed her bottom lip in vexation, unable to fight the sense that this would be her only opportunity to seek freedom.

As if he sensed her dilemma, Lucifer suddenly seemed

possessed by demons. He snorted and neighed and kicked when the stable boy came near. Jacqueline saw the chickens flutter from beneath his feet, feathers flying, and knew that Fortune again smiled upon her. The other horses took up his attitude, the chickens scurried and squawked and evaded capture in a most noisy fashion.

Jacqueline did not hesitate. She lunged for the grate, dug her awl beneath the edge, and tugged. The wood splintered, but the nails were long and did not give. She swore through gritted teeth, sparing another glance toward the ruckus in the stables. Every eye seemed trained upon the balking steeds and the stable hands and now the ostler who tried to quiet him.

At least for the moment. Jacqueline gave a mighty wrench and cursed as only the corner of the lattice gave way. She dug the awl more deeply beneath the wood and jumped in fear when 'twas snatched from her hands by pale clammy fingers.

She had not a moment to stand, let alone to flee before a man shoved the lattice open. His teeth were gritted, his flesh of the pallor of a corpse, his eye wild. She screamed, then clapped her hand over her mouth when she realized what she had done.

'Twas Angus who glared up at her, dripping and out of breath, his fingers clenching and unclenching the awl.

He was not dead, nor even wounded! Jacqueline might have flung herself upon him in relief, if he had not looked so furious.

For the guards had looked their way when she screamed, and even now a shout rose from the walls.

In a heartbeat they were surrounded. Angus was divested of the awl and his hands were roughly bound behind his back. He fought but had no chance.

Indeed, Jacqueline felt ill for the second time that day, but not because her hands were bound. Nay, Angus had come to rescue her but through her own inability to be silent, now they both would die.

❋

Father Michael was troubled by this Jacqueline's assertion.

'Twas true that he had long suspected that matters were not as they should be at Airdfinnan, but 'twas not in his nature to meddle. And he knew that Father Aloysius would see him banished from this marvel of a garden without a second thought; though he had been concerned by the other priest's insistent questions about herbal poisons, particularly those that were difficult to detect. 'Twas no accident that Father Michael kept much of his knowledge to himself, and he told himself often that 'twas to the greater good to pretend his ignorance was more extensive than it was.

And he found it worrisome that he had arrived to find the burnt rubble left of the monastery entrusted to their order but Father Aloysius claiming himself answerable to none. Pride was the most troublesome of the great sins, in Father Michael's opinion, and Father Aloysius seemed to have struck a great lode of it when Airdfinnan fell to his trust.

The younger priest had been taught to be wary of the beguiling words of women. 'Twas perhaps timely to recall that Eve had been the one to tempt Adam so fatefully and that she had accomplished the matter by persuasive argument alone.

Still, in his own family, there were women in whom he placed every faith. And the demoiselle had seemed so sincere that he could not simply leave the matter be, even though he knew he should do precisely that.

He entered the hall, intending to ask Father Aloysius about his outspoken guest. 'Twas always worth discovering the other half of a tale before making one's own conclusions. But the hall was nigh empty, the rumble of men's voices carrying from the kitchens. From behind the screen that separated the quarters of Father Aloysius from the common hall, he heard a muttered voice.

"And to the abbess of Inveresbeinn, I extend my good wishes for her continued good health." Father Aloysius spoke slowly and in Latin, his words evidently being inscribed in a missive. "I also send news of a novitiate pledged to Inveresbeinn who has come to my gates in distress. She is named Jacqueline, and it appears she has been abused by a brigand. Because her health is precarious as yet, I would assure myself of her well-being and her safety before dispatching her to your care, as she was originally destined."

Father Michael straightened, knowing full well that there was naught amiss with the well-being of the Jacqueline he had met.

"Read that again to me, if you will."

While the servant did so, Father Michael crept closer and halted beside the board. The table had been abandoned after a meal and not cleaned fastidiously—even as he lingered there, a dog dared to take a bone from the edge of the table. There was a box of figs, and being somewhat hungered himself, Father Michael helped himself to one.

An odd scent, one that would be noted only by an herbalist with a sharp nose, halted his gesture when the fruit was but an increment from his lips.

He sniffed it again, knew 'twas aconite he smelled, then replaced the fruit in the box, newly wary.

There was a bundle of cloth left upon the board as well, so wrapped around itself that he thought at first 'twas no more than a rag.

But proximity revealed the red stain upon it. Father Michael cast a furtive glance about, then unfurled the garment. 'Twas a tunic of the fashion worn by knights and one heavily stained with what could only be blood. He fingered the cloth thoughtfully, noting the red crusader's cross stitched upon its front.

He bent and smelled the cloth, his keen nose identifying foreign spice and smoke beneath the overriding scents of man and iron. This garment had recently been on foreign shores, unless he was mistaken.

Indeed, the inside of the tunic bore marks that could have been wrought only by chain mail. He recalled the dark destrier in the stables, a remarkable beast, so much more remarkable for the rarity of its kind in these parts. He guessed that the wearer of the tunic had also been the rider of the steed.

Jacqueline insisted that a knight was being hunted for declaring himself to be Angus MacGillivray, the same man who was known to have departed on crusade. He knew it should not have mattered to him to have learned that she was pledged to be a novitiate, but it did. He was more inclined to trust the conclusion of one who chose a path so similar to his own.

A man posing as a knight would need considerable wealth to feign his station so completely as this. Father Michael had learned long ago that the truth is often the most evident explanation—'twas a lie that required a network of falsehoods to support it.

Yet he was a cautious man by nature. He would be certain before he made a bold accusation. There was one place that would know of any crusaders returned to this land. King William had endowed a Templar monastery not ten miles from Father Michael's own foundation. He would ask the Templars what they knew of this matter.

He bundled the tunic hurriedly beneath his cossack, then, on impulse, seized the figs as well. 'Twas thievery to take them, but he could not have borne the burden of his conscience if he returned to find that earnest maiden poisoned in his absence.

Jacqueline might be right, or she might be naught but a pawn in the game of men; either way, she did not deserve to die.

He thought of it as protecting God's own novitiate.

As he hustled through the gates, acting as if naught was amiss, Father Michael had an encouraging thought. The Templars wore such a cross as this upon their tabards, and, were this man of their own ranks, they would see his death avenged, regardless of his name.

"I suppose you are angered with me."

Angus leaned his brow against the cold wall of Airdfinnan's dungeon and shook his head. "Why should I be angered with you?" he said with a calm he was far from feeling. "When a man has spent a year incarcerated, what is another night or two?"

"You *are* angry with me."

Angus sighed, his flesh creeping to find himself in such painfully familiar circumstances. 'Twas his darkest fear to be imprisoned again, and he fought against the tide of terror rising within him.

" 'Tis more reasonable than being pleased, would you not say?"

Jacqueline said naught to that, but then his tone had not been as courteous as he might have hoped. The silence between them did naught to aid him. He was aware of the precise dimensions of this chamber despite the darkness that enveloped them.

He heard the drip of water on stone, felt the chill of the stone walls press against his flesh. He closed his eye and felt the sweat run down his back. He was trapped. Again. Entombed in darkness, in a cold dank prison below the surface of the earth, again by men who would prefer he died quietly and with a minimum of trouble.

His father had built but a single cell beneath Airdfinnan's hall. 'Twas hewn from the rock of the isle itself and blessed with no such convenience as a drain. He supposed they should be grateful that such design offered no opportunity for rats to enter.

Steep stone steps hugged one wall, leading down to the pit that was not even square. The chamber itself was about half a dozen of Angus's paces in diameter. The single door was a trapdoor that had no edges from beneath and was bolted twice with heavy iron bolts from above.

Fergus had made the dungeon cursedly effective, though it had seldom been used in Angus's recollection. He and Ewen had locked each other here in fun and always been soundly chastised for their actions, but those games had occurred before Angus had learned terror in a similar cell.

He took a shuddering breath and trained his gaze on the thin line of light that crept around the trapdoor. Already he wanted to scream.

"I thought you were dead," Jacqueline admitted.

"It seems the news was premature."

"He offered me figs already," she said sourly, and Angus peered through the darkness, straining for a glimpse of her features. Had she been fool enough to eat them? "I did not accept one, but it seems we are ill-fated together, Angus."

She came to his side and leaned against the wall beside him, the sweet scent rising from her uncommonly reassuring.

Of course, there would be a price for her companionship. He could fairly feel her gaze boring into him, and he knew 'twould not be long before she asked something of him.

"How long were you there, beneath the grate?"

"An eternity."

"They should never have attacked you from your blinded side," she said with startling heat.

Angus blinked. Jacqueline was not slow of wit, so he could not conceive of what she meant. "You do understand that they meant to arrest me as an intruder."

"Of course I understand that!" She paced the width of the cell and back. "But 'twas so, *so discourteous*!"

"Discourteous," Angus echoed in astonishment.

"After all, there was never any doubt of the outcome—for the love of God, there were *eight* of them! They could have shown you a measure of courtesy, at least."

Jacqueline laid a hand upon his arm suddenly. "I am sorry, Angus. I am vexed because I know I am doubly responsible for our plight."

He shook his head. "You only tried to aid me."

"But I should have listened to you first. And I should not have screamed like a fool. 'Twas a deed more typical of my sister Alienor." She made a low sound not unlike a growl of a discontented cat. "And God in heaven, but I have no desire to be compared to her! 'Tis most galling."

He smiled despite himself, recalling how he and Ewen had loathed being compared each to the other, and they had been close.

Jacqueline suddenly leaned closer. "But I was not expecting there to be anyone in the drain and you looked like a corpse." Her fingers moved over his flesh gently, as if she sought to reassure herself that he was truly alive. "I feared you were dead or soon would be. They brought your tunic and 'twas heavy with blood—"

"A ruse, Jacqueline. I knew Aloysius would seek me out after your arrival here. I but granted him what he sought, in the hope 'twould pacify him."

"You were right and I was wrong. Again. I should have

listened to you, instead of racing to these gates." She sighed and he could imagine that her fair brows drew together in a frown. "I never thought that a priest would act unfairly."

Angus shook his head. " 'Tis no crime to believe good of those around you. Indeed, had I my choice, I would never have you learn how deceitful men can be."

"But you have never deceived me," she said softly. " 'Tis what Father Aloysius insisted, though I know he lied. He said you had lied about your identity, but I knew 'twas not true. He said he did not recognize you, but 'twas another lie, for if you were not who you claim to be, how would Edana have known you? And how would you know these lands if you had not been raised here?"

Her faith in him warmed his heart, but Angus said naught. He reminded himself that hers was an infatuation, that she was destined for the convent by her own choice, that he had naught to offer her and that he had already taken more from her than was his right.

For all their volume, his arguments were less persuasive than he might have hoped.

Aye, he was glad to have her here with him, though 'twas selfish and he knew that well. Jacqueline's bright presence made the darkness easier to bear.

"What would you have done if I had not appeared?" Jacqueline asked.

"Returned to the river, though I hoped the women might drop something of use to me."

"While instead they dumped washing water upon you." There was a welcome tinge of laughter in Jacqueline's tone. "You smell of soapwort."

" 'Tis better than what I smelled of before."

She laughed then, the merry sound echoing in the small space. "At least they used much of the herb, otherwise you might have smelled of the sweat of monks. My mother oft said that many of their kind were unconcerned with worldly cleanliness."

Not wanting her to fall silent, Angus seized upon her comment. "You speak of your mother with great fondness. Tell me of your family."

"Truly?"

"Truly. I should like to know."

Chapter Seventeen

ACQUELINE EVIDENTLY NEEDED NO MORE ENCOUR-
agement than that.

She told Angus of her family, of her mother and her mother's marriages, and more of this Duncan whom she seemed to regard as her own father though they shared no blood. She told of her elder half-sister, speaking with affection despite that woman's obvious selfishness.

Jacqueline spoke of the charm of her younger sister, Esmeraude, and the sweetness of Mhairi, the youngest sister of them all. She sprinkled her descriptions with anecdotes and memories, pranks the girls had played upon each other and adventures they had had.

She told him more of leaving France, of her fears for the future at that time, of her delight with the beauty of Ceinn-beithe and its wildness. She expressed frustration with the social expectations and rigid rules in France, then laughed as she acknowledged that she was aware of few beyond her obligation to wed "the old toad."

She spoke wistfully of two young nephews at Crevy-sur-Seine, whom she had yet to see, having left for Scotland when her aunt was pregnant with the child who had become the heir. She told of weddings and birthings and games the girls had played upon each other as children. She informed him that Duncan was a fine storyteller and regaled him with a favored tale.

Angus was content merely to listen. The sparkle of Jacqueline's voice filled the chill of the dungeon, her tales prompted him to smile secretly in the darkness. With her voice alone, she pushed his demons back into the distant shadows where they belonged.

When she spoke of those two young nephews at Crevy, he was struck with a recollection of his brother, then with the stark realization that he had no family left to his name. Unlike Jacqueline, who gloried in the telling of her family's foibles and endearing traits, there was no one of whom he might tell her.

No one who still drew breath, at least.

He wondered what his father would think of that and knew 'twould have been a fearsome disappointment to the man who believed he founded a dynasty here at Airdfinnan.

"How can you leave them all?" he asked abruptly, interrupting Jacqueline's tale.

"What do you mean?"

"You are surrounded by a family and 'tis clear you regard them with affection. How can you surrender that to become a novitiate?"

"How did you leave your family?"

"I believed I had to, to save them, but you have no such reason. You know that they will not be permitted to visit you nor you to visit them. You will have no tales of them, you will not even know if they bear children, if they wed, when they die."

"You echo my mother." She sounded stubborn. "I made the best choice for me with all I knew at the time."

"And now?"

"What person of merit retreats from their word?"

"A person who has learned to appreciate what they might lose."

"I told you that a woman could choose only between the convent and the altar." Her voice was resonant with challenge. "I cannot see that there is any other alternative for me. My choice is made and I embrace it fully."

He suspected then what she wanted of him, what under other circumstances he might have readily granted. But Jacqueline would not have an alternative presented from him, for he had naught to offer her. Angus knew she deserved a man who could make her happy, who could ensure her safety and well-being.

While association with him had only brought her to a dungeon from which she would probably not escape. It seemed he had already done sufficient damage without promising her what he could not grant.

He did not take what was not his to take, and he did not guarantee what was not his to give. 'Twas as simple as that.

Angus felt Jacqueline watching him, until finally she heaved a sigh. He heard her climb the stone steps to the trap-door and push against it impatiently. Angus did not tell her that 'twould not open—she knew the truth of it. She knocked and shouted, but there was no response.

"You would think that he would at least address us," she said irritably. "He could sentence us, or order our death. 'Tis most vexing to be ignored."

"He will not suffer there to be an opportunity for his men to be swayed by the truth."

"You cannot mean that we will be left here simply to starve!"

"It may be thirst that claims us first." Angus shivered despite himself for his garments were still wet. Perhaps he would take an ague and die first.

That gave him a thin hope. "If I die first, you must be certain to tell them so."

" 'Tis hardly likely that you will die first. You are larger than I am and more robust."

"And I am wet and chilled to the bone. Nay, Jacqueline, 'twill be me, and I will have your pledge that you will tell them of it. When you do, you will do your utmost to persuade them that you do not believe I was Angus MacGillivray. Do you understand?"

He should have known better than to expect easy compliance. She strode down the stairs, made her way unerringly to him, and poked him hard in the chest. "You will not die! I shall not permit it."

Angus chuckled. "I had no idea you had such influence."

"Do not mock me in this!" She struck his shoulder and the wet cloth smacked against her hand. "You are wet."

"Aye. This is what comes of lurking in a drain for hours on end."

"And you would stand here, like a fool, waiting for illness to descend upon you."

"It would seem to make little difference."

"It makes every difference. Now, shed your garb and shed it now."

"I will do no such thing."

"You will not be shy in complete darkness, not after what we have done together and not when your very life is at stake."

"You will not dictate what I shall do."

"I will, if you are fool enough not to follow sense yourself."

And he had been witless enough to think her faint of heart. Had that been only days ago?

"It matters not," Angus began to argue, but she seized his

chemise in her hands and tore it from his chest. 'Twas already halfshredded by his own actions, but still her action startled him.

"Stubborn wretch of a man," she muttered.

Angus protested but her hands were on his wet chausses and he chuckled at her determination as he caught her hands in his own. 'Twas not all bad to have someone care for his welfare again. "I see that you will not be swayed. Perhaps you might leave me some garb."

"Only if you discard it."

"Ah, vixen, it has been long since a woman tore my garments from my back in her lust to have me naked."

She gasped in outrage and Angus wished he could have seen her blush.

"You will not shock me into retreating on this," she whispered with heat. "I would see you well, Angus, and there is no argument you can make to dissuade me."

There was naught a reasonable man might say to that. He shed his chausses and wrung them out, the water dripping coldly on the stone floor even as he stood nude in the darkness. He heard Jacqueline doing something but could not guess what, until she laid her palm in the middle of his chest.

"You are too cold, so turn and brace your hands upon the wall."

He did so, and she began to rub him down, as if he were a war-horse who needed to be rid of his sweat. The cloth she used itched as wool did and launched heat over his flesh in a most pleasurable way. Indeed, she warmed him truly. When her breasts brushed against his arm with only a whisper of linen between them, he knew she used her own kirtle.

"Where did you learn to do this?"

"My mother insists upon doing thus with those unfortunates who inadvertently fall into the sea. She believes that invigorating the skin coaxes the body to recover from the shock."

"A most practical woman."

"What works for horses, as my mother says, will work for men."

"Your mother is fond of horses?"

"As am I. She hunts often, with a peregrine as they do in France, but I have no taste for the hunt. I prefer simply to ride."

"And you tend your own steed."

"Of course! The grooming builds a bond betwixt rider and steed."

"According to your mother?"

"Aye."

"She has taught you well, and must have learned of horses from men who are accustomed to relying upon their steeds."

"Her family are nobly born. My uncle is a knight and a lord, both my father and first stepfather were knights as well. I had never quite believed her tales of destriers and their size until I saw Lucifer."

"He is a fine beast."

Her hands stilled. "Where is he truly from?"

"Damascus. He was bred in Damascus."

She leaned so close that he felt the fan of her breath. "Why did you call it hell?"

"Because 'twas my hell."

"How so?"

"Do you always ask so many questions?"

"If I waited for you to tell me of things, I should never learn anything at all," she accused, amusement underlying her words. "Indeed, I might die of curiosity."

"I had no idea it could be a fatal affliction."

She laughed and leaned against him. "Which reminds me—how did that sentry obtain your cloak?"

"He stole it from me."

"And you pretended to be a leper."

"I am not such a fine sight that 'twas difficult to persuade him of it."

She chuckled again, tapping her fingers on his shoulder. "I must tell you that you sorely troubled him. He was scratching himself in the hall as if he were truly afflicted. I would not be surprised if his own fears forced sores to rise on his flesh."

"And you are much amused."

"He stole your cloak and I feared he had killed you for it." She spoke fiercely. "He deserves to suffer for his crimes." And she returned to rubbing his back with such vigor that Angus feared she would scrape the hide from his bones.

But he had neither the will nor the heart to stop her. He was inclined to do anything that might encourage her to continue her chatter.

"So, why was Damascus your hell?" she asked pertly, and nigh dismissed his good intent with but a few words.

"Because I was imprisoned there. Cease your rubbing, I am quite dry enough." He turned but she retreated, keeping the wool from his grasp.

"Why?"

"I will not tell you of it."

"For how long?"

Angus propped his hands upon his hips. "You are a cursedly stubborn woman, wherever you are."

"I seek only the truth."

"And you will not have it. I will not speak of that place." He was resolute and she must have heard the truth of it in his tone.

"Then tell me of Lucifer. How did you come by him?"

"There is no wager here. I do not have to tell you one thing or the other. Indeed, I do not have to tell you anything."

"Then we shall sit in silence and wait to die. Aye, that is a far finer plan," she retorted more sharply than he might have expected. "Let us feel the hours drag by with agonizing slowness and brood upon naught but our own misfortune. Perhaps we will perish sooner for such a resolute refusal to aid ourselves, even if it does feel to be a much longer time."

Angus said naught to that. 'Twas undoubtedly better that she was vexed with him. He was far too aware of her presence, of her fragility, of the threat he could pose to her when his terrors assaulted him.

He knew they would find him here.

'Twas only a matter of time.

Angus looked and discovered that the thin line of light had gone. He swallowed, all too aware that darkness fell. He would stay awake as long as he could, for 'twas in sleep that the greatest fears attacked.

He must keep Jacqueline as far from his side as possible. He knew not what he would do when the demons of memory claimed him.

Jacqueline sighed and spoke more tentatively than was her wont. She was always prepared to put sharp words behind them, and 'twas a trait he much admired. "I would thank you for coming to my aid, however I have compromised your intent. 'Twas noble of you to try to save me."

"I did not come for you," Angus lied, deliberately keeping his tone harsh. "As you undoubtedly recall, I had already released you from my own captivity. 'Tis not my responsibility to ensure your safety for all time."

"I see." Her tone turned irritable. "Then why are you here?"

"I came to retrieve Lucifer, of course. The beast was wickedly expensive, and I can ill afford to lose him." He sighed as if troubled by lesser matters than he was. "Though it seems again that he is aptly named. This folly may well cost my soul."

Her silence was eloquent.

Indeed, Angus nearly winced from it.

"I had no idea," she huffed finally. He heard a rustling, as if she drew her kirtle over her head once more. Angus had no doubt that she faced him, with her chin thrust in the air. "I will say good night, then, and wish you pleasant dreams."

'Twas better this way, Angus reminded himself, though that did naught to ease his certainty that he was a lowly cur. He donned his damp clothes and braced his back against the wall, seating himself upon the stairs that he might watch for the first glimmer of dawn.

And in his weakness, when the lady's breathing slowed and the darkness pressed upon him, he collected her and gathered her close. 'Twas only to ensure that she was warm, he assured himself, knowing even as the thought was formed 'twas a lie. Angus wrapped his arms around her, compelled himself to remain awake, and waited impatiently for the dawn.

⚙

Jacqueline awakened, cossetted by unfamiliar warmth. It took her a moment to recall her circumstance and another to realize that Angus cradled her against his chest. She sat up with a start and his arms fell away from her. There was a faint bit of light in the chamber this morning, perhaps due to the angle of the sun, and she eyed him warily.

His expression was guarded, a perfect reflection of her own uncertainty. There was a good measure of stubble upon his chin, and shadows beneath his eyes. He looked dangerous and disreputable.

" 'Twas warmer for both of us," he said simply, then set her aside and began to pace the width of the smail room.

"You did not sleep."

"What difference to you?"

"Did you?"

He sighed, granting her a censorious glance. "Nay."

"Whyever not? Did you fear we would be assaulted by night?"

He almost smiled. "Nay, I am not so noble as that. I simply had no need to sleep."

"Liar. You look to be exhausted."

"It matters not."

"Of course it matters!" Jacqueline bounded to her feet and strode after him, matching his pace though he ignored her. "You have need of your sleep if we are to take advantage of opportunity and escape. 'Twill avail naught if you are exhausted, for I cannot carry you."

"Ah, yes, the prospect of escape." He halted and spared a pointed glance to the trapdoor. "And how would that be managed?"

"I do not know! Not yet, at any rate."

"I do." He spoke firmly. " 'Twill *not* be managed. We shall be left here to die like dogs, forgotten in the shadows."

He resumed his pacing, but Jacqueline would not leave the matter be. "We will not die here. We *cannot* die here."

"There is precious little we might do about it."

"Well, we must at least have the conviction that all will come right."

He slanted her a glance. "Must we?"

"Of course we must! For 'twill."

"You cannot bend all to your will, Jacqueline," he murmured, and she wondered fleetingly whether he meant that she had bent him to that will. He looked so forbidding that she did not ask.

She did not want to hear his denial.

"If we are to make the most of whatever opportunity is presented," she reiterated firmly, "then we must have our wits about us and hope in our hearts."

Angus paused his pacing. "I think it unwise to deceive

ourselves in this. You are a woman of sense, so use that sense. There is no merit in believing matters to be other than they are."

"I understand how dire our circumstances are, but I know that despair will assist us less than hope. God grants aid to those who aid themselves first, and I will not admit that I am defeated until I truly am."

He regarded her for a long moment, then inclined his head. "I stand corrected. Your counsel is most wise."

"Then you will sleep?"

Angus gave a breathless laugh, then glanced around the chamber. "Not willingly. Not here."

"Does this place remind you of Damascus?"

He stiffened, a sure clue that she had found a truth. "Why should it do as much?"

" 'Tis a dungeon, and if you were imprisoned in Damascus, I should think 'twas in a dungeon—"

"Do not think, Jacqueline." Angus left her on the step as he began to pace the cell restlessly.

"Why should I not think?"

"Because 'twill make you curious," he said with more savagery than she thought the matter deserved. "And there are matters about which you should not be curious."

His countenance was so grim that another woman would have abandoned him to his mood. But his warning came too late—Jacqueline was already curious, and she meant to do something about it.

"We must do something to keep our wits about ourselves." Now she paced alongside him, though there was scarcely room. "I have told you tales, 'tis your turn to tell me one."

He watched her grimly. "I have no tales to tell."

"You have a thousand tales but you choose not to tell them."

That ghost of a smile touched his lips. "Is it not the same?"

"Nay!" Jacqueline stopped and glared up at him. He looked bemused, not angered, which she knew considerably increased her chance of winning some confession.

As long as she did not ask for too rich a prize.

"Tell me of Lucifer," she cajoled. "How did you come by him?"

Angus chuckled and shoved a hand through his hair. "Vexing wench. If I tell you of Lucifer, will that sate your lust for tales?"

"Probably not." Jacqueline grinned, unrepentant. "But 'twill do, as a beginning."

He sighed heavily but she was not fooled. "I suppose I owe you something for your insistence upon seeing to my welfare."

She laughed. "I suppose you do."

"You will be cold," he suggested with apparent idleness. "Sit beside me that we might share our warmth."

Jacqueline could not deny him that. 'Twas not all bad to be close to Angus MacGillivray.

She sat beside him on the steps and curled under the welcome weight of his arm. He smelled of soapwort, 'twas true, and of his own flesh, and she tingled where they touched.

When he urged her closer, she nestled trustingly against him. "Now," she demanded, tapping a finger upon his knee, "you have no further excuses, Angus MacGillivray. Tell me of that destrier and how you came to ride him."

He took his time finding the beginning, but Jacqueline was content to wait. Aye, prompting him would only feed his natural reticence. "I was in Damascus," he said finally.

"Before or after your imprisonment?"

"I was in Damascus," Angus repeated firmly. "And without a *denier* to my name."

"After your release, then," she concluded, and he gave her a stern look.

"Who tells this tale?"

Jacqueline smiled and held a finger to her own lips. "Not me." Then she could not hold her tongue. "But why were you even imprisoned?"

Angus chuckled beneath his breath. "I should let you be consumed with curiosity for the tale."

"But you will not." She heard the change in his own tone. "You mean to tell me!"

"I shall tell you what I am prepared to tell you and not a word more." He smiled crookedly. "You have found me in a weak moment."

"Hardly that. I doubt you have any such moments. You have simply chosen to tell me now. Why?"

"Perhaps I would savor silence in my final days."

His expression was so mischievous that Jacqueline could not have been insulted. She laughed and leaned back against him. "Tell me, then, tell me as much as you dare."

"I suppose there is naught to be done but begin at the beginning," Angus mused. "I arrived in Jerusalem after a year's journey and many unexpected adventures. The last of which was the attack of thieves on the Jaffa road, which left my comrade dead and me relieved of my purse."

Characteristically, he did not dwell on this misfortune, nor did his tone waver, though Jacqueline was appalled. "Fortunately, I managed to save my comrade's body and flee to the gates of the Holy City.

" 'Twas there I met Rodney, for he was standing sentry there. No doubt he was pleased to meet another from his homeland, even in such poor circumstance, and he was quick to offer his aid. He took me to the Templars, insisting that any father would want his son in such august company. He served them as a sergeant in those days, and so then did I.

"But the master of the order saw promise in me, for some reason, and he had me trained as a knight. I welcomed the opportunity and earned my spurs beneath the order's care. And I joined the order, laboring as a knight, praying, fasting, fighting."

"Which is why you know so much of poverty, chastity, and obedience."

"They are more challenging vows than many at first believe."

"But you kept your vows."

"Aye, I did. And in the years after my arrival, it seemed that my aid was needed most in Outremer. There were many earthquakes, which caused not only devastation but the fear that they were a portent of worse to come. Around the same time, a most able warrior by the name of Saladin had come to lead the Saracens. He was bold and valiant and much skilled in strategy.

"Many in the Latin Kingdoms of Outremer feared his influence, and, worse, his plans for Jerusalem. The King of Jerusalem himself had pledged not to build a fortress in the valley of the upper Jordan River, though 'twas a strategic site. 'Twas at the ford where Jacob wrestled the angel that the Templars then began to build their fortress of Chastelet."

"In defiance of the treaty?"

"The master of the order reminded all that the treaty was made with the king, not with the Templars."

"Surely a convenience."

"The defense was needed for the protection of Jerusalem—perhaps that was why the King of Jerusalem provided his own troops to encircle and protect its construction. Saladin too saw its import, for he offered tremendous ransom to have the construction stopped. Naught halted the rise of those walls. Chastelet was completed in six months, and garrisoned with fifteen hundred mercenaries and sixty Templar knights."

"Including you."

"The king's troops withdrew once the fortress was complete, and many of the elite of the Templars returned to Jerusalem in his escort. Saladin attacked the new fortress but was repulsed—then he surprised the retreating party by surrounding them at Marj Ayun. The king of Jerusalem and Raymond of Tripoli escaped."

"What of the others?"

"The grand master of the Temple, Odo de St. Amand, was captured and most of the remaining Christian troops were slaughtered. 'Twas a horrific loss."

"What of the other knights?"

"There is a practice in the East of ransoming a nobleman or a military leader to his own side for as much coin as possible. The knights who did not die were captured and taken to Damascus to be imprisoned until they might be ransomed. It is, however, contrary to the rule of the Temple for a knight of the order to be ransomed for more than his belt and his sword. The grand master refused to be ransomed, as did the knights of the order captured with him."

Angus frowned at the floor of the dungeon. " 'Twas interpreted by the Muslims as treachery. Since the Templars had so recently defied a treaty made with the King of Jerusalem, the order was held to be faithless. 'Twas determined that the knights were spies and should be compelled to confess to their true intentions."

Jacqueline lifted her hand to his face.

Angus met her gaze. "What better way to deter a spy than to relieve him of the tools of his trade?"

"They only took one eye."

"I never knew when they intended to collect the other." He smiled wryly. "Perhaps that dread was part of their intent."

"But you were released."

"We were all released. The grand master died in that Damascus prison a year after capture. By then matters had changed—Saladin had, after all, razed Chastelet to the ground in the interim and felt no threat from it or perhaps from us any longer. 'Twas evidently felt that a gesture of goodwill was seemly. What knights of the order survived were permitted to escort the grand master's body back to Jerusalem for burial. They even returned what weapons were obviously of sentimental value."

"Such as your father's sword."

"Odin's Scythe." Angus shook his head in recollection. "I shall never forget the first touch of sunlight upon my flesh, nor the sight of Rodney, holding Lucifer as he awaited me there. I was weak and sickened but he tended me without complaint and he never would hear a word of compensation for the acquisition of that steed."

"Was he not at Chastelet?"

"Nay, he had been ordered to remain in Jerusalem. There was a time when he regretted it, but later he came to appreciate his fortune. I was commended upon my return to Jerusalem for my service to the order and asked my one desire."

"You wished to come home," Jacqueline guessed.

"Who would not?" Angus looked around the dungeon, and she thought she saw a suspicious glimmer in his eye. She ached anew for him, knowing what he had found, but his voice echoed softly in the chamber. "Indeed, after that, who would not?"

❋

Angus said naught more that day. Jacqueline could see his exhaustion, though he paced restlessly and kept his gaze fixed upon the sliver of light visible to them. His shoulders sagged when the light disappeared, and she could sense that he mustered his strength.

Angus seemed to fight his need to sleep, though she had no such success. She curled up on the step, disappointed when he declined her invitation to join him. All too soon she fell asleep to the sound of his regular footfalls as he paced the cell.

She was awakened by a blood-curdling yell.

The cell was as dark as pitch, though she smelled fear within it. Angus thrashed against the walls and shouted gibberish. Jacqueline sat up, stunned when he swore with diligence, and knew he needed aid of some kind.

She eased closer to his side, guessing his position by the sound. He flung out a hand, bellowing incoherently, and barely missed her.

His fist struck the wall with alarming force, and she realized that he was still asleep. She backed away from him in fear. He muttered angrily, raged against unseen enemies, and struck out at atrocities that only he could see. She could smell the sweat that ran from his flesh and fairly taste his terror. She knew that he was snared in dark dreams of recollection.

Dreams perhaps prompted by him finally surrendering his tale to her, and that by her request. She was responsible yet again for his misfortunes.

Her own heart hammering with trepidation, Jacqueline approached Angus. He roared in anguish just as she drew near, then flung out his hands as if to defend himself. She ducked beneath his arms and wrapped her arms around his waist.

" 'Tis Jacqueline," she whispered, but he grasped her shoulders in his hands as if he would fling her away.

"Nay, nay, nay."

"Aye, 'tis me. Angus! You are but dreaming. You must awaken!"

He denied her vigorously, struggling against her grip once more. She felt the fury building within him again and recalled how he had been reassured in the cavern. She unfastened the tie in her hair, with agitated fingers, and shook out her braid, casting her hair over his flesh.

He trembled as she gripped him in fear, but then suddenly he stilled. For some reason, the touch of her hair made Angus pause.

Jacqueline whispered soothingly to him, insisting he dreamed and reminding him of her name. She lifted a lock of hair as he had done once and ran it across his face.

Angus shuddered and his breath left him raggedly.

"Jacqueline," he whispered hoarsely. His grip upon her changed, no less urgent than before but now he held her closer instead of trying to cast her away. He buried his face in her neck and inhaled deeply.

When he kissed the hollow of her throat sweetly, the tears rose to Jacqueline's eyes, so great was her relief.

When his lips found hers, Jacqueline could deny him naught. He kissed her with a hunger unexpected, as if he could not ever sate his desire for her. Angus cradled her against his chest and rained kisses across her face, her neck, her shoulder, murmuring her name like a litany. There was a desperation in his touch, a need that she could not deny.

The heat rose immediately between them, their very flesh seemingly kindled to the flame. They tasted each other and touched each other and demanded of each other with a new-found urgency. Jacqueline found herself bold in the darkness and enflamed by his ardor. She kissed him with hunger, letting her tongue duel with his, delighted that she could make his desire rage.

He was within her in no time at all and she welcomed his heat. They moved together, tormenting and pleasing each other, summoning a tide so great and one that deluged them so quickly that they were both left gasping.

And then they loved again, more slowly, each caress

punctuated with endearments. The pleasure was no less for
their leisure, and, indeed, Jacqueline was amazed to learn
that Angus could coax her response yet a third time in succession.

'Twas then she slept, curled against him, her feet in his lap
and his fingers enfolded in her hair.

✦

As Angus held Jacqueline close in the darkness, he struggled
to understand how she had dismissed the clutch of his nightmares. She was fearless, he realized, uncaring for her own
safety when she could lend aid to another.

And for her assistance, he was grateful.

He had no doubt that Jacqueline would ask him again of
what he feared in the night, of what had happened in that
prison, just as he knew he would never tell her of it. She had
no understanding of the wickedness men could inflict upon
each other in the name of whatever goal. She might be
destined to learn of it, but Angus would not be the one to
teach her.

He loved her, just as she was, this contradiction of innocence and defiance. Angus loved her optimism that justice
would prevail and her determination to do whatever was necessary to ensure that it did. He loved the way she laughed
and the keenness of her intellect, he loved how she did not
admit defeat readily and defended those for whom she cared.

He loved how fearless she could be, how she argued with
him when she believed him mistaken and how she questioned all she did not understand. She was a beauty to the
bone, his Jacqueline. She was a marvel to him, appearing so
soft and sweet, yet hiding a core as resolute as steel. He, who
had never expected to love again, had been healed by this
one woman in more ways than one.

And because Angus loved Jacqueline, because she had
given him so many gifts, he would give her the sole thing she

desired. He would ensure that she did become a novitiate at Inveresbeinn, for her own choice was all this lady wanted.

She had told him so a dozen times, after all. 'Twas her choice and he would ensure that she had it.

'Twas the least he owed her.

Now, all he had need of was a scheme to see them free of this place, and that with all haste. The beauty curled against his heat was too full of life to perish like this.

Chapter Eighteen

E UTTERLY STILL," JACQUELINE COUNSELED IN AN UN-
dertone when Angus was yet on the verge of wak-
ing. Indeed, he was astounded that he had managed
to sleep at all. He reached for her but she was gone, on her feet
and out of his reach.

And before he could pursue her, she began to scream so
loud he thought his ears would be rent.

"Zounds!" he muttered, and she dug her toe none too gently into his ribs.

"God in heaven!" she cried. "He is dead! I am trapped here
with a dead man. Aid me, someone!" She screamed and
screamed and screamed, apparently so overcome by fear that
she could do naught else.

"You are too overwrought," Angus advised in an undertone. "They will think you mad."

"When I wish your advice, I shall ask for it," she replied at
equally low volume.

She bellowed anew, entreating those above for assistance.
"Aid me, I beg of you! May God have mercy upon your
souls. He is dead, dead in the night. 'Twas bad enough you
trapped me with a leper in this place, but now he is dead, and
I know not if there are"—her voice echoed with horror—
"*bits* of him loose down there."

" 'Tis a myth," Angus felt obliged to observe.

He earned another dig in his ribs for his counsel. "I am distraught," Jacqueline hissed. "And overcome with terror. If you would be so kind as to let me continue."

Without awaiting his reply, she screamed with new vigor.

Had their circumstance not been so dire, Angus might have been amused by the lengths to which Jacqueline was prepared to go. She murmured prayers, she gasped in horror, she made more noise than he could have ever imagined a single woman might make. But their situation was most serious—and of more import, her idea was not all bad.

So he dismissed his smile and lay as still as a corpse, hoping that her ploy would work. There was finally the sound of running footsteps and the murmuring of men above. 'Twas most annoying that Angus could not hear their words, but then 'twould not have been advisable for Jacqueline to halt. More footsteps sounded as men fled and he feared she would be ignored.

But suddenly the trapdoor was opened, the fresh air itself a balm to the soul.

"What ails you, woman?"

"Edmund! You must aid me. He is dead! You cannot leave me imprisoned with a corpse."

Jacqueline did a credible job of being incoherent with fear after that. Angus heard her ascend the steps, begging the men for their compassion. She wept and he peeked through his lashes to find her cringing and clinging to the man. Indeed, 'twas so unlike her normal manner that she might have been another woman.

Which just made him appreciate the woman she was all the more.

"I cannot release you, for Father Aloysius says you are allied together."

"Oh, Father Aloysius spoke the truth. I was deceived, cruelly deceived by this man and used for his malicious ends.

He persuaded me that he was the true heir to Airdfinnan, and I"—her words faltered convincingly—"I thought I had stepped into an old troubadour's tale. I aided him, like a fool, but Father Aloysius saw the truth. If only"—she sobbed like a contrite penitent—"if only I might have his forgiveness."

The guard descended the steps, wariness in his movements. "How did he die?"

"He assaulted me last evening. What could I do but fight for my chastity? Perhaps you heard my struggle?"

'Twas a clever appropriation of the sounds of Angus's night terrors.

"Perhaps," Edmund conceded, and gave Angus a cautious nudge with his boot.

"I tried to climb the steps, he followed, I pushed him and he fell. I thought that he merely hit his head, but on this morn he does not move." Jacqueline's voice wavered. "He is dead, I know it, and I will not be trapped with the corpse of a brigand, no less a leper!"

Edmund leaned down, putting his ear close to Angus's chest. Angus held his breath, half certain the man would hear the pounding of his heart. But Edmund straightened and coughed. "I can tell naught in this darkness. I will have to get another to drag him to the light."

"Why do you not do it yourself?" Jacqueline challenged.

"I will not touch a leper!"

She scoffed. "Though you will steal his cloak readily enough. How is your hand?" she whispered wickedly. "Does it still itch?"

"Witch!" Edmund lunged for the stairs and Angus took the opportunity Jacqueline offered. He leapt after the man, assailing him from behind.

Edmund was startled. He stumbled, but by the time he reached for his blade, Angus had already claimed it.

Edmund's eyes rounded in horror but Angus cut him down, seized his cloak, and kicked the man's corpse down into the cell. Then he thought better of it and retrieved the man's boots. He was delighted to discover that Edmund had a dagger as well as his sword and claimed that smaller blade too.

Garbed like Edmund, he climbed to the top of the stairs and peered over the lip by Jacqueline's side. Like the sensible woman she was, she had kept out of sight. Angus was pleased to note that Edmund had been sent to quiet her complaints alone.

This folly might succeed. He drew the hood of his own cloak over his head and marched from the dungeon with the swagger of a guard. He dragged Jacqueline to the surface with him, then dropped the trapdoor closed and latched it securely.

Not that Edmund would know the difference.

"It seems you told no lie," he murmured to her as he assessed the defenses between them and the gate. "There is indeed a corpse in the dungeon."

"What shall we do?"

Angus assessed the distances, knowing that he had to see Jacqueline freed first. "I think Edmund might release the prisoner. He could not be immune to such considerable charm as your own."

"They will not permit it!"

"Hold your hands behind your back as if they are bound. None will be able to see the truth of it with me so close behind you."

Jacqueline gasped even as she did so. "Do you mean to walk boldly through the gates?"

Angus smiled at her, not nigh as confident as he would appear. " 'Tis worth a try."

There were two more treasures left in this keep that were

rightly his own, and Angus did not intend to leave without them. Jacqueline did not need to know that detail. First he would ensure her safety.

He whistled, a distinctively high-pitched sound, and smiled when a destrier neighed in reply. The beast began to kick, fighting the reins knotted to the wall of the stall. Stable boys ran toward the stallion, but the beast would have naught of them. Lucifer bucked and kicked and proved his strength, for the bolt to which his reins were knotted suddenly gave free.

The steed reared, scattering the stablehands, then raced directly for his master, who scooped up Jacqueline as Lucifer came near and Angus dumped her onto the destrier's back. Though Lucifer was unsaddled, Angus trusted that Jacqueline's skills would ensure that she was not thrown.

"Hurry!" She reached her hand down to aid him to mount.

Angus sobered, gripping his lady's hand. "You will not turn back, regardless of what transpires. Pledge it to me."

Jacqueline's lips set mutinously, but Angus had not expected anything else. He pressed Edmund's dagger into her grip. "Ensure the sight of it is a surprise," he whispered, then he slapped the destrier's rump and bellowed at the beast.

Lucifer needed no further encouragement. Jacqueline's inevitable protest was drowned by the sound of the destrier's pounding hooves. The pair passed the hall. Angus hoped desperately that the guards at the gate would fall back from the charging steed.

"Edmund!" another man cried from behind him. "What is this that you do?"

Angus ignored the call, trying to look as if he strolled casually toward the hall. He had one more treasure to retrieve. The other guard shouted from behind, the sense that something was amiss growing quickly inside the keep.

The two men at the gate drew their blades to bar the passage. Lucifer did not halt. The steed raced through the opening at full gallop, and the men fell back. The guard behind Angus shouted an alarm, and sentries appeared on the walls with sudden speed.

Angus cursed to see that they had crossbows. He offered a quick prayer for Jacqueline's safety, then ducked into the hall. As he had hoped, his father's blade was laid gleaming upon the board.

But before it stood Father Aloysius. That man smiled, clearly having anticipated Angus's arrival, and parted his robes to reveal a jeweled scabbard. He withdrew a fine blade with deliberate leisure, then lifted it. Its blade shone wickedly.

"I was so hoping you would truly be your father's son."

"Why? So that you might surrender Airdfinnan as my rightful due?"

Father Aloysius shook his head. "So that you would be fool enough to risk your life for sentimentality. 'Twas your father's fatal flaw."

"My father may have had flaws, but noble intent was his greatest asset," Angus declared, lifting Edmund's blade before him.

He might not leave this hall alive, but he would see his father and brother avenged if 'twas the last deed he did.

❂

Jacqueline could not abandon Angus.

Unfortunately, Lucifer had the bit in his teeth and would stop for naught. She tried to halt him, or at least slow his gallop, but the steed did not heed. He raced madly through the gates, the sight of him undoubtedly striking such fear into the guards' hearts that they did not even try to lower the portcullis.

But then, 'twould not have descended in time, for Lucifer ran like the wind. No sooner were they through the gates than a cry echoed from within.

"Forget the woman!" a man cried far behind her. "Our lord is besieged."

The gate guards spun to face the courtyard and Jacqueline leapt from Lucifer's back. She landed badly, but flattened herself against the keep's walls, her grip tight on the dagger hilt as she considered what to do.

Lucifer thundered on across the causeway, his reins flying. Evidently he was too troubled by the bridge to be concerned with the loss of his rider. That suited her well enough.

Jacqueline closed her eyes at the sound of steel meeting steel and wagered a guess as to Angus's location. She could not blame him for seeking vengeance. But she had seen the liability of his blinded side, and he was already at sore disadvantage by dint of numbers alone.

She knew that Father Aloysius would like naught better than to see Angus dead and forgotten. Jacqueline could not stand aside and let that happen.

She peeked and found that the guards had fled to aid their master. Jacqueline ducked through the gates and hugged the shadows, grateful that all were occupied elsewhere. By the time she reached the courtyard, 'twas empty.

Jacqueline slipped into the hall unobserved, her dread rising when she saw Angus and Father Aloysius battling back and forth across the floor. A dozen men stood around the perimeter, their gazes fixed upon the battle. Angus fought well, she noted, and evidently was more skilled than the priest, but still—she counted quickly—he had to conquer thirteen men to leave this hall alive.

And he was not at his best, having been deprived of both sleep and food of late. Jacqueline considered the room from her vantage point in the shadows, seeking some aid she might give. She had to eliminate some of these men. One stood just to the right of the door, and she sidled up behind him.

"Good morning," she whispered.

As he turned in astonishment, she drove Edmund's dagger into his unprotected throat. He gurgled more loudly than she had anticipated and made a dreadful amount of noise in dying. Indeed, he struggled with her; Jacqueline had expected he would just fall dead at her feet. She twisted the knife, appalled by the need to do so, but he would kill her himself if given the chance.

He fell finally, but not before the man next to him turned at the sound. Jacqueline knew with sudden certainty that she had erred. Oh, she knew naught of warfare, that was the truth of it.

She dove for a sconce upon the wall, seized the torch, and touched it to the enormous tapestry that lined the wall. The wool immediately burned, the man charged her, and Jacqueline shoved the torch into his face.

He fell with much greater speed than the first, but Jacqueline grimaced. Angus spoke aright—burning flesh made a sickening smell, one she would not soon forget.

She had eliminated only two men and already a cry of alarm echoed through the hall. Jacqueline swung her torch and jabbed with her dagger, doing her best to light another tapestry afire. A man grabbed her from behind and she hit him with the burning torch.

Three. The count was what mattered. Three men bent upon killing Angus were dead or near enough to it to pose no further threat.

She thought she heard Angus swear when she faced the fourth man, but she focused upon her prey. He was heavily armed, save for his face.

She would aim for his eyes.

His gaze suddenly flicked over her shoulder in a most

telling fashion. Jacqueline pivoted and drove her dagger into the eye of a man who had crept up behind her. He screamed and fell away, her blade still planted.

She spun and swung the blazing torch wildly. She succeeded in setting the armored man's tabard aflame but not before he had cut her cheek. He screeched and danced backward, but Jacqueline lent chase, jabbing the torch into his face until he dropped his own blade.

'Twas frightening that she learned this gruesome labor as quickly as she did.

Jacqueline claimed the man's blade but dropped the torch as it burned low. She turned her back against the wall and silently reminded herself that she had wounded five. She was shaking with what she had wrought and her heart pounded in fear, but 'twas her own survival she would ensure as well as that of the man she loved. She had raised one hand to her stinging cheek when Angus raged toward her.

She caught a glimpse of a retreating Father Aloysius and noted that Angus swung a gleaming blade, before he cut down the man between them and confronted her. He was furiously angry and his chest heaved with his labors—indeed, he fairly seethed—though he spoke with uncommon temperance.

"I bade you flee. Indeed, I asked you to pledge it to me."

"But I did not." Jacqueline lifted her chin undaunted. "Who would guard your blinded side, Angus, if not me?"

His gaze softened, and he whispered her name as if he knew not what to do with her. He frowned as he eyed the gash upon her cheek, and his touch was gentle as he eased the blood away with his thumb.

"Where else?" he demanded tersely.

" 'Tis all."

He shook his head in amazement. "Perhaps you truly are marked by the favor of God."

"Angus!" she cried as a man rose abruptly behind him. Angus spun, the hilt of his blade in both hands as he swung it at his attacker. The man fell and Jacqueline averted her gaze. "Odin's Scythe rings true," he whispered, gripping the hilt of his father's blade anew.

Angus seized her hand and made his way toward the door. Few men approached him, those who still stood either easing back against the walls or tending to the fire before it spread further. Jacqueline guarded Angus from behind, a small dagger he had poached for her held high.

In but a moment they were in the courtyard, fleeing for the gates. Too late, Jacqueline saw that the portcullis had been lowered and four men stood awaiting them there, blades drawn. The armed men smiled in anticipation of a fight.

"They tricked us!" she cried, realizing why they had been allowed to leave the hall. She looked back and saw the black smoke rising from the wooden roof of that building. Men were running with buckets of water, and already the flames smoldered.

"We are not dead yet," Angus replied. He hastened her toward the far wall and lifted a ladder into place with a grunt while she guarded him with her dagger. Guards watched them but made no effort to intervene.

If Angus was troubled by this, he gave no sign of it. "Climb," he bade her. "And for once in all your days, be biddable."

Jacqueline assumed he had a plan. It must be a good one, for there were a number of sentries on the wall itself. They hastened closer as she watched. Several of the guards attacked from below once she and Angus had started to climb, and the ladder swayed as the men tried to tip it.

Angus descended anew and fought them, then scrambled back and hastened Jacqueline onward. She raced up the ladder, knowing he was fast behind her, but froze at the top.

A man's booted foot was planted on the top rung. She swallowed and looked up. A large man and formidable opponent, he smiled coldly at her and brandished his blade. His smile widened as he pushed the ladder out from the wall with his foot.

Jacqueline glanced back to find that one man from below had pursued them up the ladder. Angus fought, but retreated rung by rung, until he was standing on the rung below her. Jacqueline cringed and hung on.

"Duck," Angus muttered, the word so low as to be barely audible. "Now."

Jacqueline hunched low immediately and Angus swung hard, slashing at the knees of the man on the wall above. The man shouted in surprise, danced backward, and lost his footing. He fell screaming, his cry ending with a splash.

Angus had already turned, though, slashing at his other opponent on the ladder below. That man faltered and retreated. Angus stamped on his hands on the rung below and the man flinched, then began to cry out in pain. Angus ground the boot heel into the man's fingers and the man let go with a howl.

Jacqueline hastened from ladder to wall, Angus directly behind her, neither looking back. Angus paused at the summit, waited for their persistent attacker to crest the wall, then kicked the ladder away. It fell backward in a graceful arc and Jacqueline did not watch the man's fate.

She had no chance. Sentries flooded toward them from the left and the right. Angus looked one way, then the other, apparently unable to decide his course.

"What shall we do?" she whispered.

But his indecisiveness was all a ploy. When the men moved to capture him, Angus caught Jacqueline around the waist and leapt off the wall.

The men collided with each other behind him.

Jacqueline screamed in shock and clung to Angus, only glimpsing his smile before he kissed her to silence.

Then the waters of the river closed over them and her heart nigh stopped at the cold. They sank low, her skirts billowing, Angus's grip secure.

He kicked and brought them to the surface, only to duck beneath the churning waters anew when the guard who had fallen from above lunged for them. They came up sputtering and Angus stabbed at their opponent.

Angus seized her and dove beneath the waters as arrows rained down around them. Jacqueline kicked with all her might, and Angus forced them out into the swirling current.

Jacqueline was no swimmer but Angus was competent enough for both of them. She gripped his shoulders and glanced back at the keep, to see two men raise crossbows.

"Arrows!" she cried, then grabbed a fistful of Angus's hair and shoved his head beneath the surface. He sputtered but did not fight her.

Fortunately, Angus seemed capable of swimming like a fish. He shoved his sword into his belt and guided her to hang on to his waist from behind. He swam with graceful strokes, so long underwater that she feared she might faint. They broke the surface finally.

"Deep breath," he counseled, taking one himself before he dove deep again. The next time they came up for air, Airdfinnan was far behind them, and its arrows out of range.

Jacqueline laughed with delight and flung her arms around Angus's neck. "You did it! You truly did escape."

He allowed himself a smile. "I would not have managed it without such a stalwart companion," he insisted, a gleam in his eye. "I may have assessed you wrongly, Jacqueline of Ceinn-beithe, for you did find obedience in a most timely fashion."

"I knew you had a plan and that I had best not thwart it

again. Indeed, 'twas only due to me that you had need of one."

He smiled at her, holding her fast as the current carried them along. He could float, drifting on his back as if he were no more than a feather resting upon the water's surface. His dark hair was slicked back, making him look as sleek as an otter. "I had naught but the hope of success, which I had been given to understand might prove sufficient."

And from the look he bestowed upon her, Jacqueline was certain his feelings echoed her own. She did not press him for a sweet confession, knowing that Angus would only admit to such a thing when he and he alone deemed the timing to be right. But she was content indeed to be with him and certain that her future with him would soon be assured.

The stream grew shallow and slow once past the dams below Airdfinnan, and Angus soon helped her to shore. Her kirtle was heavy with water, so he bracketed her waist with his hands and carried her to dryer ground. The sun was high and burned with uncommon heat for so early in the year, a good portent for their health.

"We are near the pathway," Angus said when they had wrung the water from their clothes.

Jacqueline glanced around but was unable to identify this patch of forest as different from another. "Where we rode to that vantage point?"

"Aye." Angus offered her his hand and strode to the edge of the forest, plunging into its shadows with the confidence of one who knew his surroundings well. Jacqueline did her best to keep up with his pace, assuming that he meant to look down upon Airdfinnan again.

But he did not. When they reached the summit, he dug in the undergrowth, exclaiming with delight as he withdrew his boots and his armor. In a twinkling, he was dressed as a knight again, and slid his blade into its own scabbard with satisfaction. He had no tunic, of course, and his helmet was lost with his steed, but he was obviously pleased to have retrieved his belongings.

"And now we return to wrest Airdfinnan from Father Aloysius?"

Angus granted her a resolute glance. "And now we deliver you to Inveresbeinn."

"But this is not the end of the tale!"

" 'Tis all you will know of it, at least from your own experience." He began to march back to the pathway, evidently confident that she would follow.

Jacqueline did. "That is not fair! I have a right to know what comes of this."

"You have no rights here and you know it."

"But I am curious!"

"Then I shall write you a missive when all is said and done, and if you are a very good novitiate, the abbess will read it to you."

"You need not sound so skeptical that I will have that chance," she grumbled as she matched his pace.

"Poverty, chastity, and obedience," he murmured, that undertone of humor in his voice. " 'Tis all I have to say of that, vixen."

They reached the edge of the forest, but he stayed her with a gesture. Jacqueline listened and heard the echo of hoofbeats.

"A horse!"

"Or more than one," Angus agreed. He whistled distinctively, the shrill sound enough to curdle Jacqueline's blood.

But there came an answering whinny and the thunder of hoofbeats increased. Jacqueline glanced to Angus, but he was studying the road intently.

A black beast that could only have been Lucifer galloped into sight, his reins flying wildly behind him. 'Twas not long before hoofbeats echoed again and a gray horse appeared on the road. Though that steed's rider could not be clearly seen, his voice was readily identifiable.

"You faithless piece of horseflesh! 'Twas for naught that I saw you saved and that is the truth of it. I should have left you in Outremer where you would have been cut down years ago!"

Rodney roared and urged his horse to greater speed, but Lucifer paid him no heed. " 'Tis bad enough that you cannot tell me what has befallen the boy, but you might linger long enough to be caught! I should see you sold for sausage meat, for you are a cursed amount of trouble."

Lucifer stopped so suddenly that Rodney's horse sailed right past him. The stallion stood his ground calmly, quivering from his exertions but flicking his ears.

Rodney swore with a vengeance. He turned his steed, and cantered back, opened his mouth to tell the stallion what he truly thought, then fell silent as Angus stepped from the woods. Lucifer grazed with indifference, as if to assure his pursuer that he had known Angus's, location all the while.

"So you are not dead, after all," Rodney finally said.

"Not nearly."

"But not for lack of an effort, by the look of you!" Rodney dismounted, his relief evident despite his bluster and hastened to shake Angus's hand. "What madness seized you, boy, that you did not remain with the witch as we had arranged?"

"I thought it unsafe, as I recall."

It seemed so long ago that they had been sheltered in Edana's glade and Jacqueline marveled anew at all the adventures they had shared.

"And this one"—Rodney pointed at Jacqueline—"I can well expect that she has brought you naught but trouble, as women are so wont to do. I told you from the first, boy, that this scheme was ill-advised—"

"On the contrary," Angus interjected smoothly. "Jacqueline has saved my sorry hide and that more than once."

That confession silenced Rodney. He looked between the two of them and frowned, then was spared the need to answer—or to admit that he had erred—by the noisy approach of a larger party.

Angus stepped past Rodney to speak to his faithful steed. He checked the destrier from head to hoof even while the beast seemed to survey him similarly.

Then the party drew near enough to be distinguished each from the other, and Jacqueline gave a cry of delight when she spied Duncan, his brow as black as thunder, riding one of her mother's palfreys. He dismounted and cast off the reins, heading directly for Rodney.

"What madness seized you to flee us like that?" he bellowed. "How dare you attempt to deceive us after all we have done? We have tried to fulfill your expectations and have acted in good faith—"

"I had to chase the steed!"

"A likely tale and one I am disinclined to believe." Duncan shook his finger beneath the mercenary's nose. "If my daughter Jacqueline has so much as a bruise upon her finger, I shall see that you live to regret your part in this for all your days and nights."

"Good day, Duncan," Jacqueline said quietly.

Her stepfather had been so focused on the man responsible for his anger that he had not looked about himself, as was oft his way. He started at the sound of her voice, regarded her in shock and delight, then abandoned his argument to catch her in a tight hug.

"Jacqueline!" Duncan swung her high, kissed her cheeks,

then drew back to study her, his hands framing her face. "Are you well? Have you been injured?" Concern lit his eyes. "In any way?"

Jacqueline smiled and kissed his cheeks in turn. "I am most well and have not been abused. You need fear for naught."

His anxiety eased and he smiled. "Praise be," he whispered, hugging her again and kissing her brow. "Your mother would have had my hide otherwise." Jacqueline laughed, welcoming Duncan's attempt to lighten the mood.

Duncan stepped back then and eyed Angus, who considered their reunion watchfully. "You must be Angus MacGillivray, the man who would claim Airdfinnan."

"Aye."

"I cannot grant it to you, for 'tis not in my hands."

"I know that now." Angus bowed his head and offered his hand. "I apologize for seeking restitution from you in error. And indeed, I owe you compensation for wrongfully seizing your daughter."

"Her manner says much to your credit," Duncan said gruffly, and shook the man's hand. "What of Airdfinnan?"

While Angus told Duncan what they knew, the rest of the party from Ceinn-beithe surrounded them. Iain, Jacqueline's stepsister's spouse and Duncan's foster brother, had ridden to her defense, as had many of the Gaels committed to Duncan's hand.

They were rustic men, grim and reticent or garrulous with their rough charm, and their hearts were good. Jacqueline felt as if a dozen fathers or elder brothers expressed their relief that she was well. They engulfed her with their hugs and warm wishes, making her feel that she had returned to Ceinn-beithe itself.

A stab of loneliness pricked her heart, for she would never see Ceinn-beithe again once she joined the convent.

If she joined the convent. Jacqueline eyed Angus, willing a sweet confession from his lips.

She heard how the group had traveled with Rodney, intent on helping him win what they had not the right to grant, and how fearful they had been when she had not been with Edana, as Rodney so clearly expected.

'Twas then that Edana herself stepped forth and reminded them that she had insisted they ride to Airdfinnan. Jacqueline was surprised that the older woman had made the journey.

"You had no way of knowing they were here," Rodney protested. "One cannot object to a man balking at such advice."

"It has long been said that Edana has the Sight," Angus said, greeting the old woman with reverence. "And 'tis true enough that we were here."

" 'Twas not the Sight, Angus MacGillivray, that told me you would ride here," Edana corrected. " 'Twas the simple certainty that tales must end where they begin. This one began at Airdfinnan and so 'twill end here, one way or the other."

"Is that why you came?" Jacqueline asked. "For a storyteller must know the end of the tale?"

Edana cackled. "Perhaps. Or perhaps I just wanted to hear what tales fell from the silvered tongue of Duncan MacLaren. Even in my corner of the world, I have heard of his skill."

Duncan bowed in acknowledgment of the compliment, though Rodney regarded the old woman with skepticism. "So, tell us what will happen now, if you truly are a seer."

Edana chuckled, gesturing to Angus. "You have thanked a woman for her aid already once, but, before all is done, you will do so again."

"How can you see this?" Rodney scoffed. " 'Tis naught

but the whimsy of a woman who seeks to make other women of greater import than they are."

Edana appeared untroubled by this charge. "There are things one sees and things one knows. I speak of what I know, though I see that we shall not soon remain alone."

Edana lifted a hand. Jacqueline and the men followed her gesture as she pointed at the rising column of dust that approached the keep of Airdfinnan from the east.

Chapter Nineteen

T WAS THE TEMPLARS WHO ARRIVED, THE TWO PARTIES meeting on the road beyond Airdfinnan's sentries. Jacqueline was not privy to whatever was said between Angus and the leader, for she was left in the custody of the men from Ceinn-beithe, though Duncan was by Angus's side. The men conferred, then dismounted, retiring to the quickly pitched tent of the Templar master.

The men were efficient in setting their camp and beginning to prepare a meal, but not so busy that they did not watch Jacqueline. Each time she tried to draw near the council, a Templar abandoned his task and politely turned her away, even to the point of escorting her back to Edana.

"They have no place for women," the old woman muttered.

"Whyever not?"

Edana smiled. "Because they are caught betwixt one world and the next, these warrior monks. They pray like cloistered monks, then they wage war like men of the world. I oft have thought they must have some confusion as to the will of God."

"They seem to show no such uncertainty."

"Nay. But men oft can deceive themselves of what passes for the truth." Edana seemed to find this a merry jest, though Jacqueline did not share her laughter.

"But why spurn women? I too have been within Airdfinnan's walls and noted much of it."

"But you are young and beauteous, lass."

"That has naught to do with my wits!"

"Nay, but it has much to do with how troubled these monks are in your presence. They may be chaste, but they are yet men beneath their robes."

Jacqueline glared at the tent. "I would still like to know what they are saying."

"If desires were steeds, we should have a fortune in horse-flesh, lass." The older woman smiled, ruefully. "Come, let us bathe in the Finnan. I have been long without a good soak and 'twill ease the worries of both of us."

Jacqueline could not imagine what worries Edana might have, but she went with her. They found a pool where the water flowed more slowly and the rocks hid them from view. They bathed and laughed together, their companionship surprising Jacqueline. She quite liked Edana's tart commentary.

But she was shocked when the older woman rose from the water and let her hair hang wet down her back. 'Twas true that the tresses were whiter than white, as shining as fresh snow, and long, but that was not the source of Jacqueline's surprise. 'Twas that the woman herself was less crooked than she recalled. Edana cast her a smile and dried herself quickly, then hastily enfolded herself in her tattered garb once more.

"Do not look so startled, lass. It has long been maintained that the fount of youth itself is none other than the mighty Finnan. And indeed, I have heard tell that the pool of the lady's own well in my glade is fed by an underground fork of the Finnan, one that slips through the land of Faerie."

Once the older woman stepped out of the river, her vigor seemed to falter, as if proving the merit of her words.

Jacqueline offered her hand in assistance and Edana settled upon a rock, sighing with satisfaction.

"Even if 'tis a lie, a woman can savor the fleeting sense of youth once more, no less the conviction that all is possible."

Edana looked sharply at Jacqueline and Jacqueline studied her features, amazed what a difference the removal of dirt made. Edana must have been quite beauteous in her own time.

"Remember, lass, that each day is a blessing, though each night we all age a little more."

"Who could forget such a truth?"

"People forget it all the time," Edana retorted. " 'Tis a feat indeed to appreciate what one has for one's own, to reach for what one desires, yet never to be consumed by lust for what can never be."

Jacqueline found her gaze straying to the distant tent once more, wondering which of those categories addressed her love for Angus MacGillivray.

❊

On the following morning, the runner returned from Airdfinnan and confirmed that Father Aloysius would accept the impartial opinion of the Templar master in this matter.

'Twas understood by all that the archbishop would have the final say, as Airdfinnan had fallen beneath his jurisdiction, but none underestimated the influence the Templar master could wield. Pledged to neither the King of Scotland nor the King of the Isles, and independent of the archbishop himself, the master was answerable only to the pope.

Indeed, no one who chose to be perceived as just could ignore his counsel.

The horses were saddled, the five knights from the Templar foundation dazzling in their white tabards marked with red crosses. They wore red cloaks similar to Angus's own though theirs had seen fewer adventures. Their mail gleamed, their horses stamped, their caparisons fluttered in the breeze.

Angus was similarly garbed, though he had no tunic any longer. His mail shone dully beneath his stained cloak, though he sat upon Lucifer as regally as a prince. He watched the master and did not glance to Jacqueline.

The master of their foundation was garbed all in white, with the exception of the blood red cross upon his chest. His destrier was the only other of the same ilk as Lucifer. That stallion was dappled gray, though no less proud a beast. The other knights rode stallions, larger than the palfreys Jacqueline knew, but not so fearsome as these two destriers.

The Templar sergeants and squires were armed and mounted as well. When the pennant bearer lifted their standard before the master himself, Jacqueline felt that a foreign pageant came to life before her eyes.

The men silently formed a procession, the pennant bearer first, followed by two Templar knights. Then followed the master, then Angus and Rodney, then Duncan as a local dignitary and some of his men. Jacqueline and Edana rode together, the squires and sergeants and remaining knights behind.

Sentries were left at their camp and at intervals along their approach. It seemed the master was not entirely trusting of his host.

The wooden bridge groaned beneath the weight of the horses, and the Templars paced their approach accordingly, leaving no more than three upon the causeway at once. Again a sentry was posted on the shore along with one of the knights, another pair of sergeants taking up positions on either side of the gate. This master did not intend to be cornered inside Airdfinnan, Jacqueline guessed, which hinted at Angus's counsel.

Father Aloysius was waiting for them, garbed in robes so simple that he might have been a pilgrim seeking favor. He seemed bowed beneath the weight of his responsibilities and more humble than Jacqueline recalled.

"I welcome you to Airdfinnan," he said to the master. "We are graced by your presence." Father Aloysius folded his hands together and shook his head. "I would invite you to the hall, but as you can see, it has been ravaged by needless violence." He sighed. "We have yet to even bury our noble dead."

"You are not alone in your grievances, Father," the Templar master said curtly. " 'Tis why we are here, after all." And he strode to the sole chair that had been brought into the courtyard, claiming it for himself.

Father Aloysius's lips tightened, then he sat upon one of the benches to the master's side. The monks and sentries pledged to him gathered around. "I believe we should start with the crimes wrought against my holding."

"With respect, Father, we shall begin where I decree we shall begin," the master retorted. "And I believe we should begin at the root of the matter, in the identity of this man. If he is Angus MacGillivray, son of Fergus MacGillivray and legal heir of Airdfinnan, then his attempts to regain this holding were justified. And truly, he has destroyed only his own property in that case, which is his responsibility to repair."

Father Aloysius opened his mouth but the master held up a hand. "On the other hand, if he is not Angus MacGillivray, then he had no right to attempt to seize this holding and owes restitution, either to its rightful heir or to that heir's trustee."

The master shed his gloves and accepted a dossier from one of his squires, unrolling several pieces of vellum from within. "There are other issues, of course, and other matters requiring discussion, but let us begin at the beginning." He looked at Angus. "Who are you, and how can you prove it?"

Angus stepped forward and his voice carried over the company with confidence. "I am Angus MacGillivray, born to Annelise and Fergus MacGillivray, here at Airdfinnan, some thirty-one summers past."

"Who can vouch that you are who you say you are?"

"I can." Rodney stepped forward. "I have served him for fourteen years."

"And how did you meet?"

"I was serving as a sentry on the Jaffa Gates of Jerusalem. He came, having been beset by thieves upon that treacherous road, bearing the body of the man who had been assigned by his father to protect him in his journey to the East."

The master looked up. "And you chose to serve him why?"

"Because he was so young, no more than a boy; because he had lost the only person that he knew in that distant land; because he was valiant enough to ensure that his companion was buried as befits a man; because he spoke with the lilt of one from my own homeland." Rodney looked at Angus. "There were so many reasons, and I regret not a moment of what has ensued from that choice."

"Yet you did not know him before that day?"

"Nay."

"So you had no means of being certain that the name he gave you was truly his own?"

Rodney frowned. "Why would a man lie of such a thing?"

"That is precisely what we seek to determine on this day."

"Then, nay, I had no way of knowing that Angus was not who he claimed to be." Rodney clearly had not had his say. "But 'twould be beyond credible for him to have lied to me on that day, some fourteen years past, in order to make a claim on this holding on this day, after all that we have seen and done."

" 'Twould indeed have been remarkable," the master conceded, "though all those years in Outremer should have persuaded you that many incredible things are possible." He smiled primly. "Is there any other?"

"Iain?" Duncan prompted. "Can you speak for him?"

"Who is this?" the master demanded, and Iain stepped forward.

"I am Iain, son of Cormac MacQuarrie, who was the chieftain of Clan MacQuarrie and a sworn enemy of Fergus MacGillivray." He frowned. "And for this reason, I cannot say whether this truly is Angus or not. I knew Angus, but we were mere boys when our fathers quarreled. I have not seen him in over twenty years, and 'tis impossible for me to say with any certainty whether this is he or not."

"I see." The master looked over the assembly.

"Can the order itself not vouch for the man?" Rodney asked indignantly.

"Though 'tis true you two were hosted at our board but a month past, I have no evidence that either of you are who you claim to be."

"But there must be records!" Rodney protested.

The Templar master frowned in thought. "There are records of Angus MacGillivray serving the order with distinction; however, they do not carry a description of the man in question. And none of us harkens from Outremer. The same argument applies, for even one of us had been there some fourteen years past, there is no guarantee that his word was of merit then."

"There is one guarantee," Father Aloysius declared as he rose to his feet. "I was here at Airdfinnan and have been here almost forty years. I knew Angus MacGillivray and I sewed the crusader's cross upon his tabard." He pointed a finger at Angus. "And I know that this man is not Angus, for I do not recognize him."

"Ah." The master sat back and templed his fingers together as he looked between the two men. "So 'tis one man's word against another."

"Not quite." Edana spoke with sudden clarity. Indeed, she straightened beside Jacqueline and stepped forward with surety. She cast back her hood and her hair shone white in the sunlight. The years seemed to have slipped from her shoulders, and Angus stared at her in astonishment.

Father Aloysius paled. "Annelise!" he hissed. "But, but—"

Edana smiled, turning to survey the assembly. "I thank you, Father Aloysius. I did so fear that since you did not recall my son, you also would not recall me."

Jacqueline and most of the company gasped in surprise.

"But Annelise is dead." Father Aloysius shook himself. "I simply mistook you for her. She is long dead and buried in the village."

The woman shook her head. "One old woman is so much like another, is she not?" she mused. "I fled to Edana, for I had no where else to go. But she was dead when I arrived, an ancient crone cold in her hut in the woods. I waited and then I sent her body to you, claiming 'twas me." She smiled. "I was so afraid you would be curious enough to look within that sack and that my plan would fail."

" 'Twas putrid and stinking! I could not look within it."

Edana, who was truly Annelise, laughed. "I so hoped you would not be a man of the same ilk as my Fergus. Fergus would have looked," she said, looking suddenly as grim as her son could look. "He might have lost a meal, but he would have been certain."

She offered her hand to Angus, who still shook his head in astonishment. "Mother! I never guessed," he murmured.

"You never truly looked," she chided. "You assumed you knew what you would see, so can it be any surprise that you found what you expected?"

"I am sorry, Mother."

"I am not. In truth, I have dreamed long of this moment." She gripped his hand tightly and looked back at the Templar master. "This is my son. This is Angus MacGillivray, fruit of my womb, wrought of Fergus MacGillivray's seed. I shall swear it before you upon any relic you so choose."

"She lies!" Father Aloysius cried. "She has admitted that she bears a grudge against me. She has joined with a brigand to see her vengeance fulfilled."

"For what reason would she seek vengeance against you?" the master asked mildly. "I understood that Annelise went mad after the untimely death of her spouse."

"Because my father and my brother did not die without this man's aid," Angus declared, his grip fast upon his mother's hand.

"All men have need of a priest afore they die!" Father Aloysius declared.

"Not all men die because of another man's intervention," Angus retorted. "I learned much of poison in Outremer, and I know now that the figs you claimed to have been delivered by the favor of Cormac MacQuarrie were poisoned by your own hand."

"Why? Why would I do such a foul deed?" Father Aloysius appealed to the master. "This is madness!"

"What proof is there of these charges?" the master demanded.

Silence reigned. "There is none," Angus admitted. "Save the evidence of our own eyes, we who watched two vigorous men wither and fade to naught without warning."

"So there is no certainty of poison?"

"We were too innocent in those days to have discerned such wickedness."

The master frowned; Father Aloysius looked triumphant. Then Father Michael cleared his throat and stepped forward from the company. Jacqueline had not realized he was there, and she wondered which side he had chosen in this dispute.

She did not have to wonder long.

"With respect, I must add my commentary in this. 'Tis true that I was not here in those days and witnessed naught, but I have some skill with herbs." He heaved a sigh. "It may mean naught, but Father Aloysius has oft asked me about the poisons that can be derived from the plants in the garden I tend."

"I seek only to ensure that none are inadvertently wounded."

"Perhaps, but I must confess that I find your persistence in seeking such details to be troubling."

"Then you are lacking in caution," the older priest maintained crisply. "Any to fall ill within these walls would be my burden to heal. It only makes sense that I know the risks that surround us and the symptoms of their appearance."

"Perhaps. But then how would one explain this?" Father Michael removed a box from his sleeve, one so familiar that Jacqueline caught her breath.

" 'Tis the one from the kitchen!" a boy cried. "The one kept always on the top shelf."

Father Aloysius turned on the boy. "I told you to guard it with your life!"

"I thought someone else had put it away." The boy retreated red-faced from Father Aloysius's glare.

"You are concerned with this box," the master commented.

Father Aloysius smiled. " 'Tis rare indeed to have such a rich gift sent to us. I would not see it wasted."

"From whom was it sent?"

"I do not recall."

The cook cleared his throat. " 'Twas not a gift, my lord.

You requested we send for figs when next we ordered wine from the shipyards in London."

"Ah. Of course." Father Aloysius smiled. "I had forgotten. All the more reason to savor a treat acquired with one's own coin."

Father Michael shook his head. "I would not suggest that any partake of this fruit. It has been poisoned, just as this knight suggests was done before."

He offered the box to the master, who took one fig and sniffed it. "You are certain?"

Father Michael nodded.

The master looked unpersuaded.

Father Aloysius smiled. " 'Tis whimsy."

"Perhaps you would care for a fig, then," the master offered solicitously, and none missed the way the priest shrank back from the box.

" 'Tis not my taste."

"I thought it might not be." The master surveyed the documents before himself, then nodded. "There is another item of which we must speak. You should know, Father Aloysius, that I have received some correspondence from the archbishop himself."

"How pleasant."

"Perhaps not. He expresses concern with the lack of tithes delivered from your holding to the coffers of the diocese. It seems that many promises have been made but no coin has been forthcoming. He asked me to visit you—though, indeed, these matters have hastened my arrival—in order to determine the root of the problem."

Father Aloysius licked his lips then glanced from one knight of the order to the next. 'Twas clear that the archbishop believed some persuasion was necessary to encourage the delivery of those tithes.

"We have had a number of poor years here at Airdfinnan. Tithes are not what they were."

The master's gaze never swerved from Father Aloysius. "Cook, when did you last order wine from London?"

"In March."

"Is this customary?"

"At least twice a year, sometimes thrice."

"And how much did you order?"

The cook named a quantity that made the brows of more than one man rise.

"Does the entire household drink of this wine?"

"Nay. Not regularly."

"How much did you spend?"

The cook answered dutifully.

The master sat back and Father Aloysius looked somewhat less confident than he had before. "How remarkable that there would be such a sum available for wine, when the land was so impoverished."

"Revenue from previous years." Father Aloysius smiled. "Skillfully managed."

"Yet not so skillfully managed that a single *denier* has made its way to the archbishop in five years. I suspect he will be skeptical of the skill of your management." The master snapped his fingers, pointed to four of his men, and flicked his hand toward the hall. "Fetch the contents of the treasury."

"Nay!" Father Aloysius sprang to his feet, his dismay evident.

"I would suggest you be seated, Father Aloysius. They are most clever men and undoubtedly do not need your aid in this matter." He smiled coolly. "Especially as there is so little wealth here in Airdfinnan, according to your own claim."

Jacqueline would have wagered the opposite, by the priest's agitated manner. His fingers worked incessantly, his composure considerably less than it had been. He straightened when two of the men reappeared, settling back when he saw that they carried only a small chest between them.

'Twas laid at the master's feet and opened. The master reached in and metal gleamed in his palm. "Three silver pennies. 'Twould indeed seem that matters are most dire."

Father Aloysius smiled but had no chance to speak before Angus turned and strode toward the hall. "Where is he going?"

Annelise smiled. "Angus MacGillivray knows this keep better than any other. There are none more inquisitive than young boys." She raised her brows and continued mildly. "Though, of course, as you are certain that he is an imposter, you have naught to fear."

Father Aloysius, on the contrary, looked most fearful. Angus called for help, and Jacqueline was not alone in watching the door. 'Twas long before the Templars reappeared, lugging heavy sacks, though uncertainty made the time seem longer than it likely was.

"I see that loose board has yet to be repaired," Angus murmured, and his mother chuckled. The men cast the sacks on the ground in a pile. The master untied the top one, reached in, and removed a gold coin. He bit it, nodded at its authenticity, then turned to Father Aloysius for an explanation.

"Nay!" Father Aloysius cried, and leapt to his feet. " 'Tis mine, all mine! 'Tis wealth I deserve and wealth I shall spend for the greater glory of God!"

He snatched at the top sack but the master grabbed it. Father Aloysius seized the one immediately below and fled through the courtyard. To Jacqueline's astonishment, the men parted ranks and let him go. She looked at Angus in consternation and he smiled slowly at her.

What did he know that she did not?

A shout carried from beyond the gates, followed by a

splash. The master rolled his documents again and refastened their ties, apparently unperturbed. "I make my decision in your favor, Angus MacGillivray. Though 'tis not binding. I would be pleased to add my appeal should you petition the archbishop for the release of your hereditary property."

The master looked up as Angus bowed. "The donation of the missing tithes would, of course, strengthen your chances of success considerably. And I have heard rumors, as well, that both kings are troubled by the possibility of Airdfinnan, a particularly key location, falling under the influence of their enemies. You would be well advised to make your allegiances soon to best clarify matters."

"I appreciate your news, your counsel, and your support." Angus bowed again and the master smiled.

"And I appreciate your earlier counsel and your return. Welcome home, Angus of Airdfinnan. Men of your ilk are welcome wheresoever they find themselves." He stood and they shook hands firmly. "I look forward to a neighbor upon whom we can rely."

"My lord master!" one of the men cried from the gate. "Father Aloysius has fallen into the river and disappeared!"

"Fallen?"

"He jumped, my lord, when he saw our sentries blocking the end of the bridge."

"But did he not swim?"

"He clutched a sack, sir, and would not release it. Indeed, we offered him aid, but he spurned us to cling to his prize. He sank and did not rise again, until his body was down river and devoid of life."

The assembly exchanged glances of horror, until Father Michael stepped forward. "A priest could not kill himself," he said sternly. "For then he would be denied burial in sacred ground."

"It must have been a slip then," the master conceded, even

as he held the young priest's gaze steadily. "Let us be charitable to those who have departed this earth, in the hope that others will judge us with equal charity."

"Amen," said Father Michael, and the assembly echoed his blessing.

"But what of the treasure?" Jacqueline asked in frustration, even more confused when Angus and the master began to smile. "Surely there is naught amusing in losing it to the river?"

Angus stepped forward and opened the sacks, spilling the small stones that filled them onto the ground. It seemed that only the one set directly beside the master, the small one to which he held fast, was topped with golden coins. "Some men are worth their weight in gold," he said.

"While others are not," the master concluded firmly. "One does not win the trust of kings in matters of finance by being careless with riches. Your scheme was most fitting, Angus of Airdfinnan."

"And your men were most adept at gathering suitable pebbles and switching the contents of the sacks."

Chatter broke out among the other men and the master began to converse with his aide.

Angus turned to Jacqueline, his expression inscrutable. "There then is the end of your tale, Jacqueline."

Jacqueline's mouth went dry; she was certain Angus would ask her a question of great import. After all, he had proven himself and she had already pledged her love. But he said naught, simply watched her.

Duncan came to stand beside her. "I will escort you to Inveresbeinn, if you so desire." He glanced between the two of them when neither moved, a curious expression lighting his features, then addressed Angus. "I must admit that when my wife heard a knight had captured her daughter, she made certain conclusions about your intent."

"Indeed?"

"Indeed. She is of French origin and assured me that 'tis not uncommon for knights there to seize a woman they would wed. She thought you might be seeking a bride."

"Then she thought wrongly," Angus said so flatly that Jacqueline could not misconstrue his meaning. "I seek naught but Airdfinnan."

"And if 'tis returned to you?"

"Then I shall administer it. Alone."

The two men stared at each other, each one's gaze as steady as the other's.

"Has he touched you, Jacqueline?" Duncan asked, his voice low. "For if he has, I will compel him to treat you with honor."

Jacqueline saw the resolve in Angus. She had offered all she had and he wanted naught of it. She realized in that moment that the only situation worse than being wed for her beauty would be that of being wed by a man who cared naught for her.

"Nay," she said quietly, biting out the words. "He has been a man of honor."

Angus, to his credit, flinched. 'Twas so subtle a move that Jacqueline doubted that any saw it beyond herself.

She gritted her teeth and made to turn away, furiously blinking back her tears. Duncan offered his arm, his expression grim.

"Jacqueline."

She halted but did not turn when Angus uttered her name. He came to her side and she did not look up, for she feared he would see the expectation in her eyes.

"My mother granted me this last eve, and it seems now 'twould be a fitting token for you." A lump rose in Jacqueline's throat, but Angus offered a small branch of some flower.

'Twas heather, she saw as she accepted it, though the blossoms were white. It had been dried carefully, perhaps the previous autumn. Jacqueline looked up to find Angus sober. "She told me then 'twas a symbol of hope conquering adversity." He smiled crookedly. "That seems indeed to be the gift you have brought to this endeavor. I thank you."

Jacqueline stared at him, her heart in her throat. When he said naught more, she dropped her gaze and made to turn away.

"I would have one token from you, before you leave."

Anything! Jacqueline's heart cried, but she forced her voice to remain calm. "Aye?" She studied him, unable to fathom his thoughts.

"Aye. A single strand of your hair, if 'tis not too bold to ask."

She glowered at him that he should ask for such a token. "Why?"

"Because 'tis unlike any I have ever seen. It seems wrought of spun sunlight and is a marvel finer than gold."

Because 'twas *beautiful*. Now Jacqueline was prepared to weep, but she would not do so before him. She separated a strand and wrenched it from her scalp, fairly tossing it at him in her annoyance.

Angus coiled it carefully in his palm, seemingly unaware of her frustration. Then he smiled at her, that slow smile that lit his features and made her heart pound. He captured her hand and pressed a kiss into her palm, folding her fingers over his embrace.

"Be well, vixen," he whispered for her ears alone, his voice uncommonly husky.

Then he was gone, striding back to the men, tucking his treasure into his glove. Jacqueline's eyes stung with tears but she took a deep breath and squared her shoulders. Perhaps, for all his faults, Father Aloysius had been right in this.

Perhaps one could not truly know the heart of another in so short a time as she and Angus had spent together. Jacqueline found Duncan regarding her, sympathy and understanding in his eyes. He lifted one brow in silent query.

"To Inveresbeinn," Jacqueline said firmly, stuffing the piece of heather into her belt. "And with haste. I have dallied too long with the doings of those who do not concern me."

Chapter Twenty

HE LADY OF AIRDFINNAN FOUND THE NEW ABBOT OF the monastery, whom her husband had endowed, on his knees in her garden.

Annelise halted, not particularly wanting to talk to the priest and definitely not wanting to share her first visit here. But Father Michael heard her and straightened, wiping the dirt from his hands onto his cassock and regarding the result ruefully.

Then he smiled at her. His smile was filled with the innocence of a cherub, though there was a twinkle of mischief in his eyes, and she had already heard the music of Ireland in his voice.

"It seems unfitting for me to welcome you to this place," he said, "when you undoubtedly know it better than I."

Annelise would not be swayed by his manner or his words. She straightened, unconsciously summoning the stance of the lady of the manor though it had been long since she had stood thus.

Her gaze trailed tellingly to a clump of marguerite daisies, and when he glanced in that direction, her heart skipped. She made an obvious survey of the garden and was surprised to find that it had not fared so badly.

"It has been tended." She looked to the priest and noted now the pride in his gaze. "By you."

"I could not bear to watch such a treasure fall into ruin."

"But you were not here when I left."

"Nay, I have been here but a year. These gardens were thick with weeds but I could see its beauty even when 'twas marred. 'Twas like the beauty of a woman, which changes as she ages, becoming both less and more than before."

"One does not commonly hear priests speak favorably of women."

His smile broadened. "I am not a common priest."

They watched each other, still wary.

He stepped back and gestured in welcome. "Will you not enter the garden that you created?"

Annelise looked at the daisies again. Though they were not yet in bloom, the clump was even more sizable than it had been when she planted it. She hoped the flowers were yet as beautiful and abundant and dared only now to wonder what she might have done if she had found the plant dead.

She was standing before the daisies, assaulted by memories before she even knew that she had taken a step. As she touched one bud, nigh to bursting, her tears began to fall.

Conscious of the priest beside her, she snapped off the bud, crushed it in her fingers, and turned away, holding it to her nose. Its sharp familiar smell was like a blade through her heart, and she closed her eyes, thinking of where this plant's roots had found their strength.

"Oh, Fergus," Annelise whispered.

The cursed priest was too young to be deaf and he missed naught. "Fergus? Was that not the name of your lord?"

She spun to face him, wanting only that he be gone. "And what of it?" she demanded.

"But why . . . ?" The priest's gaze flicked to the small cemetery in the village, then back to the daisy, to the ground and to the bud in her hand. His eyes narrowed and she knew before he spoke that he was too clever by far.

"He is buried here? Why? Why is he not laid to rest in hallowed ground?"

"Ask your church!" she cried, and made to flee.

He caught her arm, the solemnity in his eyes keeping her from shaking off his grip. "I know naught of this. Tell me."

"Your predecessor forbade it. Your predecessor declared he would bury no unshriven pagan in hallowed ground. 'Tis that simple." Annelise took a deep steadying breath. "So I had him buried in his favored corner of the garden. There was little else I might have done."

The priest was not waylaid so readily as that. "But why? Was Fergus not baptized?"

"Of course he was baptized!" she retorted, as vigorous in her defense of her beloved as always. "My parents would have never permitted the match otherwise. They insisted upon it, but *that* man swore that Fergus had never converted in his heart and that he thus had no right to sleep with the blessed."

Father Michael studied her silently, undoubtedly seeing too much, though she could not look away. "You loved him."

"I still love him," she said fiercely. "He was the blood of my heart and the father of my sons. He sheltered me and loved me and protected me and was all a man should be to his wife. And more. And yet more."

Annelise took a shaking breath, fury driving her to say more than she should. "And yet the church in its infinite wisdom has seen fit to separate us. Those who were once joined for all eternity before her doors have been parted for all eternity by her doctrine." Her tone turned bitter. "Forgive me, Father, if I do not see God's grace in this."

She marched across the garden, hating that the priest had destroyed her moment with Fergus and hating more that she had revealed so much of herself. Mostly she hated that she owed him for the welfare of the daisy that marked Fergus's grave.

" 'Twas said by a mentor of mine that we can only hate that which we once have loved," the priest said quietly behind her. Annelise halted, old manners keeping her from being so rude as to walk away while he spoke to her, but she refused to turn to face him. "You were raised in the embrace of the church, were you not?"

"Aye." She could not help but glance halfway over her shoulder, wondering what ploy this priest used against her.

"And you loved all her ritual and ceremony, all her hymns and readings, all her tales and faith."

She heaved a sigh, unable to lie about this. "Aye. Once I was fool enough to believe such nonsense."

"You still believe it." The priest touched her shoulder, having drawn close without her noting it. She saw only understanding in his gaze. "You feel betrayed, and this is the root of your anger."

"And who would not feel betrayed by this injustice?"

He smiled sadly and shrugged. "None. You are right to be angry."

"Do not dare to tell me that this is part of God's plan."

He sobered then. "I am but a priest. I cannot speak for God, much less explain his plan. I know only that he is a great and loving God and sees far beyond what we might see." She opened her mouth to argue, but he lifted a finger. "His greatest weakness is his reliance upon men, who are fallible and weak and oft short of vision."

"A fine consolation 'tis to Fergus," Annelise argued. "And what of me? When the rapture comes and I am joined with my parents, what am I to tell them has happened to the fine man they chose for me? Am I to tell them that Fergus has been consigned to hell because of the error of a fallible priest?"

"Nay. With your permission, I shall write to the bishop of this diocese and request his approval that Fergus be buried anew, with all the ceremony of a Christian, in the cemetery beside the chapel. It cannot be argued that my predecessor had an entirely clear vision with regard to your spouse's soul."

"You would do this?"

"I would do whatsoever I could to restore the faith of a woman so cheated as you."

Now her tears rose with a vengeance.

"Who lies in the cemetery? I had thought it to be Fergus."

" 'Tis my firstborn son, Ewen. He alone lies there." The priest stepped closer, but 'twas she who raised her hand this time. " 'Tis time I tell the rest of it. Your predecessor"—how Annelise liked to not call him by name—"has a greater sin upon his shoulders. When Fergus lay dying, he went to him, to hear his last confession. After all that had been, Fergus refused him, for he did not want this man to know anything else that might be turned in his own favor."

She took a deep breath. "And there, while my husband lay dying in our own bed, that so-called priest told him how we would be parted for all time. He told Fergus that he had shamed me and tainted me by not truly embracing the faith. Fergus said naught but I knew that he feared he had betrayed my father's trust. He concerned himself with such things, with trust and pledges and vows."

"But not with faith?"

"Nay. He called it sophistry." Annelise shook her head, the tears scattering when she did. " 'Twas the most learned word he knew, and I never was convinced he knew the meaning of it." She smiled through her tears and the priest chuckled sympathetically. He was cursedly easy to talk with. "But Fergus was a good man and a good husband. He was as good a Christian as he knew how to be."

" 'Tis all that can be asked of any of us."

"One would think so. But his last words to me were an

apology and a plea for forgiveness." The bitterness rose again within her. "Fergus had naught for which to apologize and naught that man might have had the capacity to forgive. Is this the charity offered by the church? Is this the nature of forgiveness and compassion? Is this grace, to steal the dignity of a man while he lies dying? If so, I want none of it!"

Annelise glared at Father Michael, furious anew, but he did not flinch from her gaze.

"I cannot answer for the deeds of another." The priest spoke softly, then pressed her hand. "But I offer a chance to make this right. You have only to ask, my lady, and I will send my request this very day."

She exhaled shakily and turned away. "Then I beg of you to do this thing, for the sake of his memory if naught else."

" 'Tis as good as done. And the bishop is a compassionate man. I have high hopes of convincing him to take our side in this."

She looked at the priest, not daring to hope. "Do you believe me?" Suddenly it seemed very important to know. "Do you do this only to placate me, or because you believe my husband was wronged?"

"I believe you. Not only because the record shows Fergus's deeds, but because a good Christian woman such as yourself has no capacity to lie with such conviction."

"I am no longer Christian," Annelise said, her protest sounding as tired as she felt.

"Are you not?" He tilted his head to watch her, though she pretended not to notice. "I cannot imagine why anyone else would be concerned with all eternity, much less the rapture."

She scowled at him, disliking that he was so perceptive. "You are cursedly clever."

He chuckled then. " 'Twas why they sent me to the church. My mother used to say that I would drive them mad with all my questions, my father used to say that I would never finish a decent day's labor by the time I pondered every possibility."

His grin flashed, making him look younger and very engaging. He was indeed a most uncommon priest. She watched him, curious to hear of his life before he took his rows.

"There was naught for me but the priesthood, so I resolved to be as good a priest as I might be."

He seemed so honest, this priest, so straightforward in his speech. He certainly drew her secrets forth with ease. Annelise imagined that she might be able to trust such a man, despite what she had witnessed in his predecessor.

And she liked this one's explanation—that the weakness of God lay in the mortal men charged with his work. It made tremendous sense to her, for men, as she had seen, were both weak and fallible. She no longer believed that the church had all the answers, but she was somewhat startled to discover that she still believed that God did. 'Twas reassuring to open her heart to that conviction again.

"If I may be so bold, my lady, the feast day of Queen Margaret of Scotland is nigh upon us. I thought we might have a special mass in her honor. I should be delighted if you were to attend."

"I cannot take communion," Annelise snapped. "I have not had confession in some years." Even as she spoke, a yearning awakened in her, for she remembered distantly the awe she had felt in the mass and its miracle.

He folded his hands behind his back, not so readily dissuaded as that. "There is usually a priest in the chapel at vespers, if you had need of his services on any day."

She straightened and granted him her most quelling look. "The promise of a letter does not erase years of sorrowing."

"But one must clean a wound so that it heals."

She regarded him imperiously and he looked steadily back. "You are impertinent."

He smiled. "Perhaps. Will you not come?"

"I can well imagine that your family desired to be rid of you and your questions. Fergus would have called you a sophist."

"I should hope you would not agree," Father Michael said mildly. "For the charge of sophistry implies that the reasoning is misguided. I do not believe that you find my argument so flawed."

The man saw too much indeed. Annelise dropped her gaze.

The priest took no offense that she did not reply. Perhaps he was content with incremental progress. "May I escort you to the hall, my lady? 'Tis nigh time for the meal."

"Nay." Her gaze was drawn again to the daisies. "I came here to speak to another and would do so now."

"Of course. I apologize for my interruption." He inclined his head and strode toward the gate.

"I thank you, Father Michael," she called just before he stepped out of sight. He paused and glanced back. "For tending the garden in my absence, and in advance, for your letter."

" 'Tis an honor to help another soul return to the faith."

Annelise frowned at the crushed bud in her hand. Truth be told, the ache in her heart was lighter than it had been in some years. The priest spoke aright—she was too relieved by his intervention on behalf of Fergus to not be Christian in her heart still.

She shook her head, feeling the grief well up within her, knowing that she had felt abandoned by more than her spouse these past years. Aye, she had lost her faith and those two losses together had made the world a cold and lonely place.

She looked up but the priest was gone. She hastened to the gate, spied his retreating figure, and called after him. "If I were to come to the chapel at vespers on the morrow, would a priest be there?"

He halted as if he did not believe his ears, then turned back. "I shall ensure it, my lady," he said firmly, his approval of that more than clear.

She smiled at him. He looked so boyish and optimistic that she was reminded of what 'twas to be young. "And would that priest be both well rested and well fed? It has been long since my last confession indeed, and I would not have him faint or fall asleep."

He grinned. "I shall ensure that I am both rested and fed, my lady."

So, *he* would hear her confession. Annelise thought that he might make a good father confessor, this young man with his wise words. "On the morrow, then, Father Michael."

"On the morrow, my lady. I shall look forward to it."

Again he was gone. She turned once again and walked slowly back to that daisy. She had not wept all those years ago; she had not dared to show any weakness before the man so determined to destroy them all.

Aye, he would have twisted it to his purposes and declared that she wept for Fergus's immortal soul. He would have tried to even further diminish the respect that people had for her spouse. She had seen Fergus laid to rest in the middle of the night, left his grave unmarked but for a daisy, so fearful had she been that his rest would be disturbed and his body violated.

And all those years alone in the glade, she had been too angry to cry. Too bitter to concede any weakness. Perhaps she had feared that once she began to weep, she would not have been able to cease.

But now Annelise stood where she and Fergus had laughed

together so many times, the sun warming her back, the flowers unfurling beneath its touch. And all was finally setting to rights. Angus was back. She had not lost him. She was certain that Airdfinnan would soon be his, as it should have been all along.

She was reunited with Fergus not only for now but for all time. The priest would see matters resolved, even if she died this very day.

And that stole the heat of anger out of her heart. Annelise dropped to her knees before her husband's grave and laid her hands upon the sun-warmed soil, feeling his presence.

'Twas almost as if the heat of him rose to her touch. At that thought, the floodgates of memory opened wide, deluging her in the sight and sound and smell of him. Annelise wept, as she had not yet wept for the loss of her husband, lover, and partner.

She did not know how much time passed before the bells of the chapel made her raise her head. The sun had begun to sink behind Airdfinnan's walls, the shadows were drawing long in the garden.

And one of those fat buds had unfurled itself while she sobbed, a single white daisy catching the last ray of sunlight. As she stared, marveling at its beauty, a bee landed upon it, crawled across the golden center, and took flight again, its legs encrusted with pollen.

'Twas a sign. Fergus had always believed in signs and portents, and though Annelise had scoffed in those days, now she could take it as naught else. She had learned much in Edana's skin, though she had not expected to do so. She plucked the daisy and wove it into her braid as she rose to join the household at the evening meal.

She entered the hall with her chin held high and a new vigor in her step, for she knew that Fergus was well pleased with what she had wrought. 'Twas the closest she had felt to him in fifteen years, and she intended never to let him slip away again.

Aye, 'twould not be long before they two were together once more.

Chapter Twenty-one

B Y THE TIME SHE REACHED INVERESBEINN, JACQUELINE was certain that Angus would come for her. She secreted the tuft of heather in her barren chamber and knew she had but to wait.

She did not doubt that Angus was overwhelmed by the change in his fortunes, and she was not so innocent of the world that she imagined everything would be set to rights so readily as that. He needed time to see to the details.

And perhaps he needed time to miss her.

But the days passed and the nights passed and no knight arrived at the convent gates.

Jacqueline decided that if she had conceived his child, she would seek permission to depart, and if 'twas not granted, she would steal away. She would somehow contrive to reach Airdfinnan and tell Angus that he was to be a father. She was certain he would wed her then, for he was much concerned with honor.

But her courses came with perfect regularity, as if even her own body would defy her desire to have Angus by her side. Perhaps 'twas better, she reassured herself, for a match would be happier if she were certain that Angus wed her for herself than out of a sense of duty.

A month came and went, and then another, and Jacqueline

had to admit that 'twas possible the man did not miss her. It might well be that he did not love her—indeed, he had never pledged as much. She had thought he might, but then, how much did she know of men?

Precious little, it would seem.

Still, she could not bring herself to surrender that dried cluster of white blossomed heather.

Contrary to her own expectation, Jacqueline found no solace in the tranquility of the convent. 'Twas more than clear that she had no calling. She was restless within its walls, always pacing, always fidgeting, always glancing toward the gates.

And she could not explain it. There were no loose ends to the tale she had witnessed, so 'twas not curiosity clamoring for more news. The words in the Bible were as they had always been, and though they still held an allure, her thoughts oft drifted away from her studies.

Jacqueline found the days astoundingly long, the lessons overly tedious, and the *opus dei* hopelessly dull.

Angus clearly did not come. And if he had not come by now, he would not come at all. Perhaps he had granted her the heather not because he had to overcome adversity to ask for her but because he believed she had to overcome the adversity of her own character to be happy within these walls.

There was a sobering prospect.

Though 'twas disappointing beyond all, Jacqueline knew she had chosen her own fate. She resolved to make the best of it—for truly, if she could not have Angus MacGillivray, then she wanted no other man. The sole appeal of the secular world was that one knight; without him, she would be just as happy here.

Perhaps happier, for here her bridegroom was not physically demanding. Jacqueline studied with renewed diligence and labored with renewed vigor. She volunteered for every possible task, she gave her all to Inveresbeinn. She was exhausted when she fell into bed each night, though not tired enough that she was spared of dreams.

When she managed to sleep. Oftentimes Jacqueline lay awake long into the night and indulged her weakness for Angus. She recalled his caress—a deed best done while the keen eye of the abbess was occupied in sleep—his crooked smile, his wry retorts. She remembered all too well the warmth of him curled around her, the heat of him within her, and the security she had known in his presence. She thought of how his hard-won confessions delighted her, how his strength of character thrilled her, how his honorable intent made her heart swell fit to burst.

Aye, she loved him, with all there was within her.

And there was naught that could be done about the matter. Angus did not desire her, and she desired none but him. So, she would have none, though 'twas a poor exchange.

✹

Six long months after her arrival, when the bite of winter first tinged the air, she was summoned to the abbess. 'Twas the eve of Jacqueline's first vows as a novitiate, beyond her initial pledge to obey the abbess and pursue her studies with diligence.

Had word come from Angus in this moment of moments? Jacqueline fled down the corridor, without regard for proper decorum, and told herself she would surrender hope fully on the morrow.

Perhaps the white heather as well. 'Twas forbidden to have personal tokens, after all.

The abbess greeted her with eyes narrowed in disapproval. "You have much to learn before you take your vows on the morrow."

"Aye, Mother." Jacqueline bobbed her head, doubting that her impatience was hidden. If Angus came for her, she would be gone in a heartbeat. She hoped and hoped and fairly tapped her toes in her impatience to know the truth.

"Praise God that I forget what 'tis to be young." The abbess shook her head wearily, then continued sternly. "Your guests await you in the chapel. I do not approve of visitors, Jacqueline, and you had best impress that fact upon them. I make one exception for each novitiate, for the change to the cloistered life is not always readily made. This would be your sole exception and I bid you recall it well."

"Aye, Mother."

"You will return here and report fully to me what has transpired when your interview is done. As you know, we have no secrets at Inveresbeinn." The abbess eyed her sternly, and Jacqueline imagined that she knew full well about the heather and every other secret any novitiate might have.

"Aye, Mother." Jacqueline turned to race toward the chapel, wanting naught but to see Angus again.

"Comportment!" the abbess roared in a voice that nigh shook the walls.

Jacqueline obeyed with only the greatest of difficulty.

That made her smile in memory of Angus's conviction that she had not the mettle to pledge poverty, chastity, and obedience. Indeed, she would rather pledge her heart to him.

If only she had the chance.

She pulled open the heavy wooden door of the chapel, summoned a smile, and stepped into the interior. Her smile faded as her mother and Duncan turned to greet her.

She had thought that "visitors" meant Angus and whoever rode with him, perhaps Rodney. 'Twas ungracious of her to be disappointed, for her parents had traveled far for a brief visit. Jacqueline smiled anew with genuine warmth, though her heart was aching.

He did not come. He would not come. This was the choice she had made, and she had best accept the truth of it.

"Welcome, *Maman*, Duncan. 'Twas beyond good of you to ride so far when the abbess permits such short visits."

Her mother's gaze saw too much as always, though that woman came forward to seize her hands with a warm smile. "You were not expecting us," she chided, then kissed Jacqueline's cheeks. She surveyed Jacqueline shrewdly, too close to miss any flicker of emotion. "But who else would visit you before your vows, child?"

"No one," Jacqueline whispered, for 'twas true. She kissed Duncan in turn and squeezed both of their hands. "How is everyone at Ceinn-beithe?"

"Well enough. And you?"

"Well enough, *Maman*."

"You were right in this, Duncan," Eglantine commented, giving Jacqueline's cheek an affectionate pat. "I should never have objected to Jacqueline's decision. Look how demure she has become—surely this life suits you well, child."

"Well enough."

"Truly?" Duncan asked, his gaze searching.

"Truly. The choice is made and 'twas made by me." She spoke firmly if somewhat dutifully. "You have invested hard-won coin to see my desire fulfilled, and I shall do my best to honor your endowment."

Her parents exchanged a glance. "But are you *happy*, Jacqueline?" her mother asked.

"Does it matter?"

"Of course!" Eglantine framed Jacqueline's face in her hands. "You know I desire only to see you happy and naught else," she whispered with conviction. "Tell me what you truly desire, child. Tell me now, afore 'tis too late."

But 'twas not within the realm of her parents' influence to change her fate. Jacqueline smiled. "I merely wonder whether I might have been as happy if I had followed your advice. That is all. I miss you all in this place."

"Just us?"

"Aye." Jacqueline nodded, dropping her gaze that they might not see her lie. Naught more was said, though she knew they wondered.

Her mother stepped back and dug within her purse. " 'Tis true that we are not permitted to speak with you overlong," she said crisply. "But here is a letter that you might read at your leisure in which I tell you all the news of Ceinn-beithe."

She pressed the missive into Jacqueline's hands. "And here is another from Esmeraude, no doubt telling you how she has no one to torment these days." Duncan chuckled beneath his breath. "And Mhairi sends greetings as well, though even I would be hard-pressed to make sense of her scribble."

"And even Alienor sends some word," Eglantine continued briskly. "She wished to send you one of the brooches wrought by Iain, but I told her 'twould be taken for the greater glory of the convent. She insisted the abbess would wear no gift intended for you and had Iain draw it for you instead."

Jacqueline could well imagine her half-sister saying as much. She opened the missive and peeked at the drawing, which was lovely enough to make her breath catch.

Jacqueline—

I am not permitting Iain to sell this until you take your final vows in case you see sense afore 'tis too late. Think of this, sister mine. Only a witless fool would live with women when she could have a man in her bed instead.

Alienor

Jacqueline choked back a laugh and looked to her mother, whose eyes sparkled. Clearly she had read the missive or been told of its contents.

"I should wish another babe upon her," Jacqueline jested.

"Iain has seen to that. The midwife says Alienor will deliver in midwinter."

"She will be busy, if naught else."

"She has yet to learn to curb her tongue, our Alienor," Eglantine said mildly, then caught Jacqueline unawares with an incisive glance. "Do you agree with her?"

Jacqueline looked down at the missive. "I do not think I have this choice," she said carefully. " 'Tis the convent for me."

Her mother exhaled in exasperation, but Duncan laid a hand upon his wife's arm. "You know that our concern is solely for your happiness, Jacqueline," he reminded her.

"Aye, I know it." She hugged them both and stepped back, doubting that she would be allowed ever to see them again. Aye, she was effectively dead and gone from this world, just as her mother had tried to tell her all those months ago.

Her vision was blurred by sudden tears and she clasped her letters tightly against her heart. They were so precious and would undoubtedly become more so as her loneliness increased.

But how could she ask them to grant another rich gift to the convent to see her freed of this place? Indeed, her choices had already cost her family too dear.

"I love you both so very much," Jacqueline declared, her tears slipping down her cheeks. "I thank you for all the sacrifices you have made on my behalf."

"Ah, Jacqueline, you know I would do any deed for you." Her mother caught her close, hugging her so tightly that Jacqueline could not draw a breath. She did not want to, but returned her mother's embrace with equal ardor.

They parted finally, both trembling, then kissed each other's cheeks. Jacqueline could not help but think it might be for the very last time. Duncan embraced her as well and she sank to the bench as they departed. She lifted her tear-filled gaze to the crucifix above the altar and thought of sacrifices made.

She recalled her mother's sacrifice, in leaving all she knew so that her daughters might wed for love, as she had not. She thought of her mother's determination that there not be harsh words between they two, as there had been between Jacqueline's mother and grandmother over her mother's arranged marriage.

'Twould change naught, but she owed her mother the truth.

"*Maman*!" she called, and heard their footsteps halt at the rear of the chapel. She did not turn but bowed her head. "I would have you know that you called matters aright in this."

"I do not understand."

"You insisted that I pledged to join the convent out of fear, fear of men, fear fostered by Reynaud. You said that the right man, a man of honor, could dismiss my fear and show me the happiness to be found in love."

"Aye, I remember."

"And you were right, *Maman*." She swallowed, then attempted to lighten the silence behind her. "I wanted you to know, because I know how you do love to be proven aright."

She felt her mother's hand fall suddenly on her shoulder but did not look up. "Then why are you here, child?"

"My regard is not returned."

"But had you not told this man of your desire to take these vows?"

"Aye, but he did not protest my choice! He clearly had no desire to change my thinking."

"Perhaps he did not wish to test your vow."

Jacqueline met her mother's steady gaze. "Or perhaps, *Maman*, he did not desire me."

"Then he is a fool." To Jacqueline's surprise, her mother smiled at her, her eyes filled with warmth. "Or he is of a rare

breed of man who respects the choices of women sufficiently
that he does not challenge them. Such esteem does not mean
that his heart is empty; indeed, it oft signals the opposite."

And she turned to gesture to the back of the chapel.

Jacqueline turned, her heart nigh stopping when she saw
Angus standing beside Duncan. He watched her avidly, and
she had no doubt that he had heard her confession. Her
cheeks burned but he did not so much as blink.

"Do you stand fast in your choice," he asked quietly, "now
that you know what 'tis you face here at Inveresbeinn?"

Jacqueline straightened. "It seems I must."

"You could leave."

"I have no means to replace the endowment, and I would
not ask my parents to do this for me."

He folded his arms across his chest. "You might persuade
another to make the payment."

"I will not be bought and sold like so much chattel."

Angus smiled slightly then. "But brides are bought with
endowments all the time. Would you not accept a donation
made to this establishment in your name in lieu of that
dowry?"

" 'Twould depend upon the groom," she whispered.

He began to walk toward her. He was taller than she recalled, and his presence was as commanding as ever. He was
dressed in blue of so dark a hue it might have been black. His
tabard was edged in purple, the crusader's cross abandoned
for a purple thistle. His familiar red cloak was cast over one
shoulder, and he still wore that patch over his eye.

Airdfinnan suited Angus well, she saw, though there were
still shadows in the depths of his eye.

"Aye?" he asked, when they nearly stood toe to toe. "You
are particular then?"

"Very particular." Jacqueline held his gaze. "Indeed, there

is only one man who will do, and then only if he makes the pledge I yearn to hear."

"Is that the truth of it?" He shed his glove and touched her chin with his fingertips, coaxing her to look at him fully.

Jacqueline felt that familiar tremble dance over her flesh. "Aye, 'tis."

His gaze dropped to her lips. "The odds against any one man would seem most formidable."

"The man I would wed has a will wrought of the finest steel."

"He sounds most fearsome. Why would you wed such a man?"

She eyed him boldly. "I told him the truth of it already. 'Tis time he made a similar confession to me."

Angus's gaze searched hers as his thumb moved leisurely across her chin. He seemed to be choosing his words, but Jacqueline was too impatient to wait.

"Why did you come, after all this time?"

"There is something of yours that I would return."

"I left naught of import with you."

Save her heart, but she would not tell him that so readily again.

Angus's lips quirked. "So you might believe," he murmured, and she was certain that he knew the truth. But he reached into his purse and withdrew something so small that it nigh disappeared on his broad palm.

She leaned forward to look, startled to discover 'twas that single golden hair which she had granted to him. "You still have it?"

Angus stared at the hair, avoiding her gaze. "A lady's favor should not be discarded so casually as that. And truly it has become as a talisman to me."

"Of what?"

"Of beauty."

Jacqueline turned away, disgusted that he pursued her for her looks alone.

Angus halted her with one fingertip upon her elbow. "Are you not sufficiently curious to hear all of the tale?"

"Not if it involves golden tresses and a visage of unrivaled beauty. I have prayers to recite."

He smiled at her. "It involves but one golden hair, and though the hair is indeed beauteous, 'tis what it recalled to me that granted it such power."

"What power?"

His smile faded. "The power to banish memories best forgotten, the power to bring sunshine into darkness and healing where there was naught but pain."

She looked at the hair, then eyed him skeptically. "Because it is the hue of sunlight?"

He held it up between them, his gaze compelling her to believe him. "Because it reminds me of the lady who shed it, however angrily, and the brightness of her spirit. She is a woman whose heart is filled with hope, a woman of rare determination and of a character more generous and beauteous than any woman's face could be."

Angus watched Jacqueline so intently that she felt pinned to the spot.

"But I have discovered that the reminder will not suffice," he continued. "This hair, however beauteous, cannot laugh. It cannot find the good within the wicked, it cannot jest, it cannot even be curious."

Angus placed the hair deliberately within her hand and closed her fingers over it. "But all the same, for being a reminder of a lady who oft does all of those things, it has been a talisman for me. I thank you for the gift, for this and this alone has helped me banish the shadows that tormented me."

Jacqueline regarded him in surprise, trying to ignore the way her mouth went dry. "You have no more nightmares?"

Angus shook his head. "Not a one. Thanks to you."

Jacqueline fingered the hair. Gratitude was more than she had expected from him and yet so much less than she desired. "So you came to give your thanks to me?"

"Nay, I came because I have missed you," he said softly. "I miss both your laughter and your certainty that all will come aright. Be assured, Jacqueline, that I began for this convent a hundred times, but I had vowed to give you your choice as other men did not." He smiled ruefully. "I am weak, though, for I could not resist the opportunity to ask you to reconsider your choice afore 'tis too late."

She parted her lips but he set his thumb across them, silencing her.

"When we parted, I had no right to seek a bride. I did not dare to anticipate Airdfinnan would be ceded to me again, though the archbishop has done that very thing. The crops were good this year and will be better next, primarily due to the aid of those at Ceinn-beithe. That feud is long behind us. Though Father Aloysius had hoarded coin, 'twas not his to hold. The tithes were long overdue and treaties had to be confirmed with such gifts that my treasury is nigh bare."

He took a breath, again not permitting her to interrupt. "Though my circumstances are humble, I could ensure your comfort. Know that I would defend you with my own life and that I have taken care to have the coin to appease the abbess. Though I have Duncan's permission to seek your hand and your mother's blessing, the most important agreement is yet lacking."

Jacqueline did not dare to interrupt this inventory. She watched Angus, knowing she had never seen him show the least uncertainty before.

But he was uncertain of *her*.

"If you say nay, I shall not trouble you again. If this is your choice, 'twill be unchallenged by me." His gaze burned into her own as if he would will the truth from her lips. "You told me once that you would willingly share my bed. Does that mean that you would willingly wear my ring, that you would be my lady?"

"That depends upon why you ask," she said, her voice husky.

"There is only one reason to ask such a thing," he declared. "Because I love you."

Jacqueline blinked back her tears of joy. "All I ever wanted of you was your love, Angus."

"And in the end, 'tis the only offering which I can guarantee." He smiled and caught her shoulders in his hands, flexing his fingers around her as if he needed reassurance that she truly stood before him. Jacqueline smiled up at him, knowing she looked like a besotted fool and not caring a whit. She heard her mother sniffle happily.

Then Angus conjured a silver ring, richly encircled with a knotted design. He held it an increment before her left hand. " 'Tis the ring with which my parents pledged their troth. My mother entrusted it to me for good fortune in this quest."

"You had no need of such fortune," Jacqueline whispered, lifting her hand.

Angus frowned slightly as he slid the ring over her knuckle. "She said the token of a Celt might fill the deficit of your lineage as it did her own, though I cannot guess her meaning. She refused to say more."

Jacqueline laughed. "It matters not." When the ring was securely upon her finger, she looked up at him, certain all the love within her shone in her eyes. "You knew I would accept you," she whispered.

"I hoped, my Jacqueline." He caught her close and smiled

down at her. "I had naught but hope, though 'twas you who taught me that hope could oft be enough."

He bent and kissed her soundly, ignoring the consternation of the arriving abbess and priest.

❀

In due time, the joyous party left both chapel and convent, but not before Jacqueline retrieved her hidden token of heather. Angus noted it with a smile and tucked it into his purse with nary a word between them.

Indeed, they shared a smile so warm that the abbess clucked her tongue.

Jacqueline was not surprised to see Lucifer grazing beyond the walls, nor two palfreys from Ceinn-beithe and two other smaller steeds. A pair of squires tended the steeds, purple thistles embroidered on their tabards.

A dainty mare stood beside Lucifer, so lovely that Jacqueline caught her breath. She seemed fragile in her grace, for her ankles were uncommonly slender and her gait elegant. The horse was of the hue of deepest chestnut. Her mane and tail were darker still and hung long and silky.

"From Persia," Angus supplied. "Sent as a gift to the Templar master, who offered her to me when I expressed my admiration. I have always thought the Saracen horses most beauteous." The mare nickered at him as if she appreciated the compliment. "This one is cursedly quick of wit and fleet of foot. She escaped four squires and an ostler on her first day at Airdfinnan and granted them a merry chase."

He turned a smile upon Jacqueline. "I thought my intended bride might have need of a mount of her own, especially one that she might so readily understand."

Jacqueline laughed, thanked him, then stepped closer. The mare tugged at her reins, straining in inquisitiveness, her nose working as she sought to come closer to Jacqueline.

"I thought to name her Vixen, if you approve," Angus

suggested with an innocence of manner that made Jacqueline laugh again.

"She is beautiful and I think the name most fitting." Jacqueline greeted the creature, scratched her ears, and made a conquest in short order. Angus beckoned to the boys, but she waved them off. "I would not ride her this day, Angus."

"Whyever not?"

"After all these days apart and on our nuptial day, I would ride only with you, husband of mine."

Angus laughed, a rich and merry sound all the more precious for its rarity. He lifted her into his saddle, then swung up behind her, clamping one arm around her waist to draw her close.

Jacqueline waved farewell to her parents, then turned to look up at him. "Be warned, Angus MacGillivray, that I am not destined to be so dutiful a wife as one might hope."

He looked skeptical, though there was a warning twinkle in his eye. "Indeed?"

"Indeed. You told me the truth of it yourself." Jacqueline counted her shortcomings on her fingers. "I am not obedient."

Angus chuckled. "Nay, you are not."

"I fear 'tis a talent I will never conquer." Jacqueline sighed in mock consternation. "And Airdfinnan, I suspect, is not impoverished." She glanced up and, when Angus shook his head, she grimaced. "So I shall not manage a vow of poverty." She frowned as if much troubled by this.

"And?" Angus prompted mischievously.

Jacqueline knew he was well aware of the last of the trio of pledges made by a bride of Christ.

"Perhaps I shall endeavor to be chaste," she said solemnly, not in the least surprised when he tightened his grip upon her.

"Then I shall endeavor to keep you from succeeding," he said with equal solemnity.

"Is that a pledge, my lord?"

Angus grinned wickedly. "Aye, my lady. It most certainly is. Indeed, you have my word upon it."

He kissed her once again with vigor, oblivious to the chattering squires, and Jacqueline returned his embrace in kind.

She had the word and the love of a man of honor, and, indeed, Jacqueline could have chosen naught better than that.

About the Author

A confessed romantic dreamer, *USA Today* bestselling author Claire Delacroix always wove stories in her mind. Since selling her first in 1992, Claire has written more than twenty romances. Winner of the Colorado Romance Writers' Award of Excellence and nominee for *Romantic Times* Career Achievement in Medieval Romance, Claire has over two million books in print. She writes medieval romances for Bantam/Dell, as well as contemporary romances as Claire Cross for Berkley/Jove.

Claire lives in Canada with her husband.

Write to Claire at:

> Claire Cross/Delacroix
> P.O. Box 699, Station A
> Toronto, Ontario
> CANADA M5W 1G2

Or visit:

> Château Delacroix
> http://www.delacroix.net

If you're looking for romance, adventure, excitement and suspense, be sure to read these outstanding romances from Dell

Jill Gregory

☐	COLD NIGHT, WARM STRANGER	22440-3	$6.50/$9.99
☐	NEVER LOVE A COWBOY	22439-X	$5.99/$7.99
☐	CHERISHED	20620-0	$5.99/$7.99
☐	DAISIES IN THE WIND	21618-4	$5.99/$7.99
☐	FOREVER AFTER	21512-9	$5.99/$7.99
☐	WHEN THE HEART BECKONS	21857-8	$5.99/$7.99
☐	ALWAYS YOU	22183-8	$5.99/$7.99
☐	JUST THIS ONCE	22235-4	$5.99/$7.99
☐	ROUGH WRANGLER TENDER KISSES		
		23548-0	$6.50/$9.99

Claire Delacroix

☐	BRIDE QUEST #1 THE PRINCESS	22603-1	$6.50/$9.99
☐	BRIDE QUEST #2 THE DAMSEL	22588-4	$6.50/$9.99
☐	BRIDE QUEST #3 THE HEIRESS	22589-2	$6.50/$9.99
☐	BRIDE QUEST #4 THE COUNTESS	23634-7	$6.50/$9.99

✷

The
Temptress

coming soon from Dell

✷

Chapter One

Ceinn-beithe, Scotland
April 1194

THINK 'TIS A TERRIBLE IDEA," ESMERAUDE COM-
plained, watching carefully to ensure that Célie
heeded her. The woman who had been Esmeraude's nursemaid and later her maid grimaced though she
said naught more.

Esmeraude grinned, knowing she had the older woman's attention. " 'Tis terrible and you know it well!" she insisted.
"Why, for the love of God, should I choose a spouse in this
way?"

"Because you will love it," Célie said tartly.

They two were in Esmeraude's chamber, making the bed
ready for the night. Esmeraude helped, as was her way when
she wanted to win Célie to her side in some matter. She knew
the maid was not fooled as to her intent. Indeed, the older
woman watched her with mingled indulgence and suspicion.

Now Célie smiled and shook her head with affection. "Indeed, I can scarce imagine what you would enjoy more than to
have several dozen men competing for the favor of your
hand."

"They compete now and I do not enjoy it." Esmeraude
plumped a pillow, challenging the other woman to convince
her otherwise.

"They bring you gifts."

Esmeraude shrugged. "Fripperies that they would take to

any woman they wooed. 'Tis my face and the promise of my womb they court, no more than that. Do you not see, Célie? If I am to wed a man, I wish to love him with all my heart."

" 'Tis what your parents desire for you."

"Aye, but these men who come are too much one way or the other. They are men of extremes, too concerned with wealth, for example, or too indifferent to it. They show no moderation, indeed, they show no spark."

"Spark?"

"Aye! I would have a man who was neither too much of one thing or of its opposite, a man who is changeable, a man with a heart, a man who feels great passion for his beliefs yet will listen to other views. I would wed a man keen of wit but trusting of heart, neither too tall nor too short, nor too rich nor too poor, nor too amusing nor too dour." She smiled with confidence. "A man exactly perfect for me."

Célie laughed right from her toes. Truly she laughed so hard that she had to wipe away a tear.

Esmeraude did not share her amusement. "And what makes you laugh in that?"

"I suppose your man must be handsome, and well wrought too."

"Of course!"

"And where would you find this man?"

"I do not know, but I would seek him out." Esmeraude smiled. "It would seem only fitting."